"WOULD  ER RUINI

James shook ... he'd misheard.

Celine wrench... away and stood with her back to him. "Forget what I said. I knew you would refuse. You're too much of a gentleman and now you will consider me quite beyond the pale."

"Celine," James said, deliberately keeping his voice level and soft, "did you just ask me to compromise you?" No young female asked such a thing of a man . . . even a man who already intended to do exactly what she'd asked him to do.

"Yes. But don't give it another thought. You must think me very foolish."

"I don't," he said quietly. He thought her marvelous; an answer to his prayers. . . .

If You've Enjoyed This Book,
Be Sure to Read These Other
AVON ROMANTIC TREASURES

FORTUNE'S MISTRESS *by Judith E. French*
THE MASTER'S BRIDE *by Suzannah Davis*
MIDNIGHT AND MAGNOLIAS *by Rebecca Paisley*
MY WILD ROSE *by Deborah Camp*
A ROSE AT MIDNIGHT *by Anne Stuart*

Coming Soon

COMANCHE WIND *by Genell Dellin*

HIS MAGIC TOUCH

STELLA CAMERON

An Avon Romantic Treasure

AVON BOOKS ◆ NEW YORK

HIS MAGIC TOUCH is an original publication of Avon Books. This work has never before appeared in book form. This work is a novel. Any similarity to actual persons or events is purely coincidental.

AVON BOOKS
A division of
The Hearst Corporation
1350 Avenue of the Americas
New York, New York 10019

First Avon Books Printing: April 1993

AVON TRADEMARK REG. U.S. PAT. OFF. AND IN OTHER COUNTRIES, MARCA REGISTRADA, HECHO EN U.S.A.

Printed in the U.S.A.

RA 10 9 8 7 6 5 4 3 2 1

For our son, Matthew Cameron

Chapter 1

"S in, my friend, like beauty, is in the eye of the beholder." James St. Giles, Earl of Eagleton, looked not at his companion but at the raucous, glittering crowd that jammed Covent Garden's Theater Royal for the evening's presentation of *Romeo and Juliet*.

As always, the big, swarthy man who was rarely far from James's shoulder took his time to answer, and when he did, his soft voice held its customary hint of menace. "No doubt you'll tell me the author of your wisdom?" Won Tel stood in the shadow of the box's red velvet curtains, the lines of his broad, high-cheekboned face gleaming faintly in the dim light of a nearby lamp.

James tapped his lower lip with a long finger. "I was told this wisdom by the man whose opinion I trust most. Myself."

Won Tel's hoarse laugh would have chilled most who heard it. He tugged at his luxuriant black beard. "If that is true, and I'll not doubt it is, then the world's as sorry a place as I thought and I am saddened."

"You, my friend, are a liar." James spared his servant a thin smile. "You thrive on sin. And this"—he flipped a hand to indicate the restless audience that

1

crammed the five tiers of boxes and galleries—"this should feed your conviction that English society is essentially contemptible. Perhaps more so under the influence of our precious Regent. I, for one, regard myself fortunate to have managed to remain at a distance—a great distance—for so long."

The audience seemed barely aware of the impassioned performance on stage. Rather, they gawked about and gestured among themselves, each apparently determined to outdo the other in outrageous antics or fabulous dress. James pretended not to notice that his own person was attracting considerable fluttering of fans, female giggling, and distinctly dangerous leaning from flanking boxes.

"We could always abandon this scheme of yours and return to Paipan, my lord," Won Tel said.

"*Not* until I get what I came to London for!" Swiveling, James turned the full force of his gray-eyed stare on the other man. "This *scheme* of mine, as you call it, is all I will live for until it is *finished*—until *they* are finished! And remember that unless I tell you otherwise, I am simply James Eagleton, shipping magnate. My Uncle Augustus is finally persuaded to accept that I will acknowledge the title, but only when I'm convinced it will be useful. Remember, I have taken great pains to assure no word of my father's death, or my relationship to him, becomes known in England. It would be a pity if some chance remark of yours warned my enemies of my presence. Forget the name of St. Giles and forget the earldom—until I decide to use it like an axe on the necks of Darius and Mary Godwin."

Won Tel's expression didn't change. He bowed, presenting the top of a dark blue skullcap of the same heavy silk fabric as the unadorned, high-collared tunic he wore over full black pantaloons gathered into tall, glistening boots without heels. The boots were specially designed to allow their wearer to move swiftly and silently ... a fact known only to James and his enemies. Unfortunately for the latter, the discovery invariably accompanied punishment that robbed the victim of either the will or the means to comment.

The man straightened and said tonelessly, "My duty is done, then. Before your father died I promised him I would always remind you that there is never only one choice in dealing with dangerous matters."

James made fists on his thighs. His muscles felt coiled, had felt so in the months since the death of Francis St. Giles from injuries suffered beneath carriage wheels. "Here there is only one choice. The Godwins will be reduced to nothing. And I *will* have what is mine—what was rightfully my father's before me." He shifted restlessly on the foolish little blue velvet and gilt chair clearly not intended for so tall a man. "I will have my retribution." That his dying father's last wish had been for James to wreak vengeance in both their names would remain a secret pact between the one living and the one dead.

"Very well. The third box from the left is the one you seek, Mr. Eagleton. On this level. It is immediately opposite."

Narrowing his eyes, James swung back toward the theater and snatched up his opera glass. "You should have told me the instant you knew."

"I did, Mr. Eagleton," Won Tel said in his still voice.

James knew better than to ask how the signal had been received. "I don't ... Third from the left? This tier?"

"Correct."

"There are only two females in the box. Where is Godwin?"

Won Tel raised an opera glass to his own eyes. "The girl must be the daughter. The woman—"

"The woman is of no concern to me. She is obviously some sort of companion." James trained his sight on the girl. "That cannot be the Godwin daughter. And the other is too young to be her mother. Damnation! Your informant has failed you . . . and me."

"Mr. Eagleton—"

James waved Won Tel to silence. "I had counted on this opportunity to make contact. This business *will* be quickly accomplished. The Godwins have cost me more—cost my *family* more than their two miserable lives are worth."

"Yet you intend to leave them that much."

"Oh, yes," James said softly. "I intend to leave them their lives, not that they are likely to be particularly grateful, I think. Leave me and find out what's amiss. I have no reason to remain at this circus if Darius and Mary Godwin are not here."

Wordlessly, Won Tell slipped through the drapes at the back of the box.

James spared a moment's notice for the hapless players on the stage, then busied himself sweeping his opera glass past the opposite boxes again, trying to match faces with the descriptions his father had given him.

Pointless. Francis St. Giles had been remembering the Godwins as they had been twenty years ago, not as they would look today.

Through the glass, James stared again at the two women who were useless to him. They were both notable in that they concentrated intently on the production. The older, dark-haired female might be thirty or a little more; a slender, serious-faced creature some might find appealing. Her austere black gown, of exceedingly simple cut, marked her as some sort of elevated servant to the other.

And the other . . .

"We are confounded, Mr. Eagleton." Won Tel glided back behind James. "The Godwins are not yet in London."

"What?"

"The Godwins are—"

"I heard you, dammit. What in God's name are you talking about? Our information stated that they would be in Town by the beginning of April. It is now the tenth."

"They changed their minds. But take heart. Word has it that they may arrive any day. And the girl *is* Celine Godwin, the daughter."

Very slowly, James raised the glass once more.

"The Godwins have launched her on a Season," said Won Tel. "That is the primary reason for their being in London."

"You just told me they *aren't* in London."

"They will be. The girl and her companion were sent on ahead."

Either his glass lied or the chit was considerably more pleasing to the eye than he had been led to believe.

Won Tel settled a hand on James's shoulder. This gesture was the only sign of familiarity that ever passed between the two. The first time Won Tel used the calming signal, James had been a boy of not more than twelve and Won Tel barely nineteen. In the almost twenty years since that day there had been many occasions tense enough to warrant a restraining hand upon James.

"Word also has it that the Godwins may be in need of funds."

James stiffened. He did not waver in his scrutiny of the tall, golden-haired creature whose sea-green silk gown—if his eyes didn't deceive him—was completely lacking in any ornament and somewhat ill-fitting.

"I'm told they hope to use Miss Celine's marriage to deepen their shrinking pockets. Oddly, there seems to have already been an offer for her from a very wealthy man. Wouldn't you say that should make the expense of a Season unnecessary?"

"I would say so, yes." James smiled grimly. "Doubtless you will soon find out what is behind all this." Won Tel's mysterious facility for extracting excellent intelligence was equaled in usefulness by his insight, a fact well known only to James and to beautiful Liam, the one other human he trusted implicitly. Since the death of Francis St. Giles, Won Tel had spoken scarcely more than a few words to anyone but James and the Chinese girl.

The first act of the play was drawing to a close amid a crescendo of animallike hoots and screams of laughter. James sat back in his chair and trailed an arm over its back. "So, the girl is to become the means of keeping the Godwins in a manner to which they never had any right."

"Quite possibly."

"Would you say that might make her their most prized possession?"

"There would appear to be no doubt that the girl holds much value for the parents."

Hooking a thumb beneath a lapel on his perfectly tailored black coat, James expanded his chest. "Quite. Much value indeed. Come. The evening may yet prove to my advantage." Magnificent chandeliers suspended from the circular domed ceiling burst to their full brilliance, signaling an intermission, and James swiftly left the box with Won Tel at his heels. "It is time for the first move toward my goal. We both know that I intend to ensure that Mr. and Mrs.

Darius Godwin are left with nothing they value. *Nothing.*"

Celine clapped until the stage was bare of all but the lovely temple drop scene dedicated, so appropriately, to Mr. Shakespeare.

"What a pity Mama and Papa can't be here to see something so wonderful," Celine told dear Lettie Fisher. "I must be certain to tell them how grateful I am for everything they're doing for me."

"You must indeed."

Celine knew, without checking Lettie's face, that her companion would be hiding a knowing smile. "You probably think me very bad, don't you, Lettie?"

"I think you are delightful. You have always been delightful and I thank God they haven't managed . . . I thank God your spirit has remained unbroken." Lettie's Dorset brogue flattened the vowels in her speech.

Lowering her lashes, Celine affected a demure expression. "Is that not another way of saying I am an accomplished actress and manipulator?" She and Lettie had a pact: during conversations touching on the more bizarre elements of her upbringing, they never mentioned Celine's parents by name.

"You are a survivor, my child. Praise be for that."

Lettie had been Celine's nanny, her sole champion throughout childhood, before Mama and Papa appointed her companion and maid to Celine when she turned fourteen.

Celine returned to watching the antics of the dandies parading before the orchestra pit. "Why would it be desirable to appear so foolish?"

"The dandies?" Lettie leaned to see more clearly.

"Yes. See how they pose. It's a wonder the height and stiffness of their ridiculous neckcloths don't cause them to choke." She sighed. "Are there no worthy men in London who are as yet unmarried?"

Lettie chuckled. "I'm inclined to doubt that a man exists who'll live up to your lofty standards."

"Is it so lofty to want to marry a truly good and kind man, and to marry him for love?" Celine flipped open the fan of stiffened green lace which she'd been fortunate to gain with the purchase of her dress and for no extra expense. "Oh, Lettie, if only that odious Bertram Letchwith would decide the obvious."

"And what would the obvious be?"

"Why, that I'm too tall, too ugly, and too dull. Then he would change his mind and cry off."

"If trying to make the man believe such rubbish is the only way out of this match, then you'll undoubtedly be Mrs. Letchwith within the year."

Lettie sounded as desperately unhappy as Celine felt at the prospect of her marriage to the fat, middle-aged merchant her parents were determined to welcome as a son-in-law. Why, Letchwith was at least as old as Papa and had an unmarried son many years older than Celine. Percival, who was even less well-favored than Bertram Letchwith himself, continued to live with his father and appeared to accompany him everywhere.

"There *has* to be a way out," Celine murmured. "There *has* to be. David has told me how it should feel when one is confronted with someone with whom one can hope to build a relationship based on the deepest affection."

"David Talbot is a good man," Lettie said of the young clergyman assigned to Little Puddle, the village close to Knighthead, the Godwins' Dorset home. "Just as he was good when he was a boy." David was the son of Little Puddle's previous vicar and had grown up in the village.

"You don't agree with David's opinions on the subject of love?"

"I think he is as much of a dreamer as you are and, despite his habit of meddling in nasty matters that don't concern him, I still think it's too bad the pair of you don't—"

"Hush, Lettie! I've told you before that David and I are the dearest of friends—nothing more. I shall know the man I want to marry, if and when I meet him. Now, do not spoil a perfectly lovely evening with this depressing prattle."

"You began what you call this depressing prattle. You always do—at least a dozen times a day. I really would like to know what kind of man we're looking for, Celine. How shall I know him?"

"Fie!" Crossly, Celine raised her shoulders, remembered how any such movement drew the bodice of her dress perilously tight across her breasts, and immediately rearranged herself. "*I* shall know and that is enough. Yes. I shall know the man."

"Miss Godwin?"

Celine jumped, swung around in her chair, and blushed wildly. A tall man—a very, very tall man— stood inside the box, only feet from her. He must have entered most quietly ... quietly enough for him to have been there while she'd talked to Lettie about ... Botheration, surely he had not overheard.

The man bowed. His hair was black and slightly curly in a way Celine found quite irresistible. And his shoulders were remarkably broad inside a beautifully tailored black jacket that showed off his snowy, understatedly elegant neckcloth and the whiteness of his shirtfront and cuffs.

He straightened again. His face was clever, with a high-bridged nose, distinct cheekbones, and a wide, firm mouth. He smiled, very slightly, showing strong teeth. At that smile, Celine noted his eyes and drew in a quick breath. A chill passed up her spine. She had never seen eyes quite like them; irises of steely gray, flecked and ringed with black, and with an unblinking quality that made them appear to see into her very mind.

"Have I shocked you, Miss Godwin?"

"I . . . no, oh, dear me, no." She sounded exactly like the silly twitterpated pusses present in such irritating numbers at every London gathering she'd attended. "It's just that you surprised me, sir."

"Are you acquainted with Miss Godwin?" Lettie exhibited no sign of being overly impressed with their visitor. "I am Lettie Fisher, Miss Godwin's companion. I don't believe I remember you."

He smiled, really smiled this time, driving deep, dimpled grooves into his cheeks. "No, madam, and I really must apologize for my impulsive decision to approach you both." Now his attention centered on Lettie, and Celine studied the entire man, from his exceedingly handsome, tanned face to his broad shoulders and chest—no buckram padding needed there—to a flat stomach, lean hips, and impressively powerful legs that filled tight-fitting pantaloons and silk stockings so smoothly that Celine was loath to look away. How the pigeon-bellied, chicken-legged Bertram Letchwiths of the world must detest such magnificent specimens.

When Celine did draw her gaze upward it was to meet once more that disturbing, steely-silver stare. She did not allow herself to blush again, or to lower her eyes in the expected falsely demure fashion. "Why *did* you decide to approach us?" she asked him in a cold voice she hardly recognized as her own. She did recognize the shifting sensation in her breast and the warmth flooding other parts of her. These must be the sensations David had warned her against, the sensations responsible for the downfall of previously respectable women.

"May I, Miss Godwin?"

Celine listened to his deep, resonant tones, then started as she realized he had offered her a large, bronzed hand. She hesitated before placing her own fingers lightly on his—and pressed her other hand to her throat as he bent to brush his lips across her very sensitive skin. Celine glanced at Lettie, who merely smiled. He lingered altogether too long over what should have been the merest of touches.

Celine withdrew her hand sharply. "Do I know you, sir?"

"Forgive me," he said. "I had not expected you to be so . . . That is to say . . . Please forgive my gaucheness." He bowed again and appeared at a loss for words.

He had not expected her to be so—what? Celine settled her mouth severely. Wait until David heard of her admirable reaction in the most difficult of circumstances.

"Oh, I am entirely remiss," the man said abruptly. "I am James Eagleton, most recently of Paipan, a small island in the South China Sea. I am barely returned to England from those parts and I fear I am still adjusting to the ways of—shall we say the *civilized* world?"

His smile quite disarmed Celine, and she allowed her own lips to soften—but only slightly. "Were you in the Orient long?" She shouldn't ask questions of a stranger, of course, but he did make her so very curious, and just the mention of such foreign and exotic places sent a thrill of excitement through her. His being mostly a foreigner explained his rather unusual manner, and probably the tanned appearance of his skin.

"I've lived abroad since I was a small boy, except

for the periods I spent at school in England, of course. But you must wonder why I have taken the liberty of approaching you."

Hadn't she been saying as much ever since he arrived?

"My box is opposite." He gestured vaguely. "Someone who stopped to introduce himself noticed you and mentioned your name."

Celine glanced across the theater. "I'm surprised either of you could see me. I suppose you have one of those opera glasses I've heard about."

For an instant she thought his look became speculative. "Exactly. But that is of no importance. I understand that you live in Dorset."

"I do." Why would so evidently successful and handsome a man bother with her?

"Capital. I've just bought property there myself."

She suppressed a retort that Dorset was not a small county and that many people lived there.

"Imagine my surprise when I learned that you are, in fact, residing at Knighthead!"

Celine became quite still. "You know my home?"

"I know of it. It is somewhat north, but close to the village of Little Puddle."

"Yes." Beneath his severely cut white silk waistcoat, Mr. Eagleton's chest was indeed remarkably solid-looking. "Yes, close to Little Puddle."

"A delightful Jacobean house of moderate but pleasing proportion. Some of the most enviably beautiful stained-glass windows in any private house . . . so I'm told. And the gardens are . . . I'm told the gardens are charming, the result of much effort expended by . . ." A muscle twitched in his cheek, but then he smiled, a little stiffly, Celine thought. "Perhaps I'm muddled, but I thought it was said that a lady who used to live there was responsible for the rose garden and the general design of the rest of the grounds. She liked sweeping expanses of lawn and employed a most unusually informal manner of random massing of rhododendrons and the like. Am I right?"

Celine frowned. The man disconcerted her. "You describe the grounds well, sir. As for the design, well, there I fear you are wrong. My own mother has often told me what an arduous task it was to turn the estate into its present form. Evidently it was much in need of work when my father bought it."

Mr. Eagleton raised his angular jaw and stared over Celine's head as if seeing something new— something that made him angry? She remained silent. Beside her, Lettie had faced the theater also and was busily reading the performance program.

Celine found she could not look away from this still man, this man so visibly powerful that his presence seemed too large for the confines of the box. The panicky little waves that rode into her stomach were unfamiliar, but they were not totally unpleasant. In fact, what she felt bore the closest resemblance to that emotion David had mentioned as being important to avoid at all costs: Pleasure! Pleasure that was purely physical with only the most tenuous attachment to any involvement of the mind. This sort of Pleasure, David had warned her, could lead to an insidious fleshly thrill that was almost impossible to contain before it precipitated . . . Passion.

A shudder racked Celine. She knew, only too well, the fate of women who gave in to Passion. Enough of this foolishness. "Thank you for paying us a visit, Mr. Eagleton. I do hope you'll enjoy Dorset."

It was with difficulty that James calmed himself enough to look once more upon the girl who sat before him. Not that she was less than delightful to the eye. "I'm sure I shall enjoy it very much," he told her, careful to keep from his voice the wild rage that throbbed in his brain. The Godwin woman had dared to take credit for his own gentle mother's creations in the treasured gardens she'd been forced to leave. And Darius Godwin had lied to his daughter. After so long, the lie had doubtless become accepted as fact by everyone. By everyone but Augustus St. Giles, Third Marquess of Casterbridge—and James. James was the marquess's nephew and sole heir. Upon James's recent arrival in England, the childless marquess had joyously welcomed the only son of his dead younger brother, Francis, to the family's magnificent estate, Morsham Hall on the Dorset coast. James was, in the old man's own words, "the answer to a fervent prayer. The promise of a future for an ancient family threatened with extinction."

The second act of the play commenced, but Celine Godwin continued to face James, and he felt sealed to the spot by the yawning evils of old treachery and by the potential tool this luscious girl could become.

"When do you return to Knighthead?" he heard himself ask.

The instant upward arch of a fine brow let him know she was aware of the impertinence of his question.

"Forgive me if my curiosity offends you. I have been too long away from society and I still forget that propriety is more rigid here." He lied, but she was unlikely ever to know as much. "Blackburn Manor is . . . is the first English home I have owned. I am like a child with a new plaything." The fleeting thought came that he was long overdue for a plaything of quite another kind. James had always easily conquered women, but he found himself bored by the thought of another such conquest. The female before him might be anything but boring . . . exactly, in fact, what he needed.

"Blackburn Manor?" She leaned closer, and James

noted, with a tightening between his legs, that the fullness of her high breasts caused the apparent poor fit of an otherwise flattering dress. "If it is the Blackburn Manor I know, the house that belonged to old Squire Loder before he died, then it is scarce three miles from Knighthead."

James's mouth dried. "The very place," he told her. By God, she was a succulent piece. The small, filmy sleeves supposedly holding the gown in place at her milky, gently rounded shoulders were inadequate and presently in the process of sliding further down her arms with every unconscious move. "I take it you've been to Blackburn."

"Not actually inside. The squire was quite a hermit, or so I'm told. But I ride a great deal because . . ." She hesitated. "Riding is a great boon to me and I ride past the manor several times a week." She averted her face and drew in a deep breath. The movement all but freed a thrusting, pale pink nipple.

James swallowed and pressed his teeth hard into his bottom lip. The swell of her breasts made him long to touch skin that resembled ivory satin, to pull the bodice down until he could fill his hands with her, to push her onto sweet-smelling grass, or soft sheets, or this very floor, and taste her full lips, her throat, that enticing nipple that would become a hard bud between his teeth. And when she whimpered and writhed beneath him, begging for all he would take such pleasure in teaching her, then he would take his time with the rest . . .

He tensed his thighs and gave thanks that the lights had lowered enough to conceal the bodily evidence of the pictures his mind so vividly painted.

"I wish you joy with your plaything," Celine said suddenly.

The impression that she saw his thoughts almost made him gasp. But she referred to the manor. "Yes.

Thank you." Ah, yes, there was potential for joy here—or, more likely, intense gratification while he extracted from certain others a dear recompense for their greed.

"Is something wrong, Mr. Eagleton?"

"Nothing." She must see some hint of his turmoil—and his excitement. "I do hope you will permit me to call upon you." He hadn't forgotten quite everything about the rituals of polite society.

She looked directly up at him, and he clenched his hands together behind him. This was a golden girl, a girl drawn in tones of honey and cream with light in her rich, heavy hair. How well he visualized that hair released from its bonds and tumbling about her shoulders, slipping through his fingers and across those magnificent breasts.

"May I call, Miss Godwin?" Surely she heard the thickness in his voice.

"You are most kind. But I shall not return to Dorset until after the Season. Otherwise I should be happy to receive you."

Not so quickly, my soft little prize. And I will make you my prize. Yes, you shall become my plaything. "I had meant that I'd like to call upon you wherever you're staying in London."

"Oh." For an instant her apparent coolness wavered. "We are in Curzon Street. But I'm not sure . . ."

He smiled reassuringly. "Thank you. Until we meet again, then?"

"Until we meet again." Her lashes fluttered down, and James withdrew.

Letting the curtains fall into place at the back of the box, James joined Won Tel, who waited at the end of the corridor.

"You have the appearance of a man who has been

in battle," Won Tel remarked. "One who has fought and won and enjoyed every moment."

"As usual, your powers of deduction are remarkable. I have fought and won—at least for the moment." Striding on, he reached steps leading down and took them two at a time. "That battle was a very small one, my friend. Ahead lies the war, but I find I am beginning to contemplate it with a great deal more pleasure than I had expected."

"Will you—"

"Explain myself?" James gave a short laugh. They reached a lower hall and he strode on. "Yes, I will explain. I just met a beautiful girl with a magnificent body. She has great tawny eyes that belie her frozen manner. A young female like a wild animal, skittish yet curious, sleek and supple, untried yet ripe. Gad, but how ripe she is."

Won Tel laughed. "Are we speaking of Miss Godwin?"

"We are indeed." They gained the street, and James gestured to his coachman, who lounged with others of his station who had settled in to idly gossip away the hours until the end of the performance. "Won Tel, this night has produced even more than I had dreamed of. I have just made the acquaintance of a woman who will help me get exactly what I came to England for."

"I'm pleased for you."

The clatter of hooves approached, and James spared Won Tel a satisfied smile before the coach drew to a halt. "You should be pleased for me. If my instincts serve me well, even as she serves my purpose for wanting her, my innocent helpmate will learn a great deal . . . and I shall enjoy guiding her through every lesson."

Chapter 2

Darius Godwin shifted to allow the woman easier access to the fastenings on his breeches.

"Good, good." She crooned over him in the same soft, encouraging voice she'd used on the one previous occasion when the Letchwiths had brought her to Dorset.

"Lie back." Her voice was hypnotic. "I want to do everything for you, my warrior. You've earned a prize and you shall have it."

Allowing her to push him to lounge on silken cushions heaped on the floor of his secret little temple in the woods, Darius watched her move over him. She was plump, the way he liked his women, and brazenly artful, not like the falsely innocent pieces Bertram and Percival preferred.

Even now he could hear wails of anguish and loud moans coming from the far side of the windowless building's only room. Tonight the Letchwiths were enjoying their favorite sport with lusty zeal.

"You're troubled, love," the woman beside him said. "Relax and only think about the lovely things Summer Peach is going to do for you."

Summer Peach. Yes, now he remembered the name she used, just as he was beginning to remember each subtle little way she touched him.

"Oooh, so strong." Summer, still completely dressed herself, had worked his breeches down until his cock sprang free. Immediately she bent to take him into her mouth and smooth her lips back and forth over the length of him. "Lovely," she murmured, and crawled up to lick circles around his mouth.

A shriek came from the girl the Letchwiths shared. Darius had watched their perverse rituals before and would watch again before the night was out. The thought brought a fresh pumping in his rod, and he breached the pattern of his own seduction by reaching for Summer's full breasts.

"Ah, ah." She pushed his hand away. "Naughty, naughty. And you know you'd be sorry if you spoiled our game."

Darius nodded, but he was especially eager tonight. The result would be both an exquisite added stimulation to the sweet agony of waiting and the promise of repeated enjoyment of Summer Peach's luscious body.

Slowly, she unbuttoned his shirt and laid it open. "Such a hard man." She chuckled and reached, without looking, to stroke his shaft again. "So hard. The hardest man in the land."

Darius writhed up to meet her. She was right. He was hard and he was also glad he hadn't allowed himself to become the mountain of blubber that was Bertram Letchwith, or flabby like the soft and scrawny Percival, who more often than not sweated for hours to gain release between the legs of his "virgins."

"We need a little drink," Summer told Darius. Leaning over him, trailing her luxurious red hair across his skin, she grabbed an open brandy bottle by its neck, raised his head, and tipped some of the golden fire down his throat. When he would have wiped at the trickle on his chin, she stayed his hand and licked the drops away. Then she dipped first one, then another and another finger into the bottle, wetting them, before snaking her hand between his legs to hold the bulging sack of his manhood.

Summer moved fluidly, setting down the bottle, swinging around until she was astride him, her face in his crotch, her legs spread so that her skirts rode up to reveal a bush as red as her hair and the swollen, gleaming pink folds between.

It was not by accident that Summer's shins clamped his upper arms, stopping him from touching her while she lapped up the traces of brandy so strategically placed.

"Hurry," Darius moaned, watching her grow moister, creamier, more ready for him.

"Shush," Summer admonished, but her voice grew higher and Darius smiled his satisfaction. There wasn't a woman alive who could remain aloof from his prowess. This one's body was weeping its need upon him.

Darius bared his teeth. "Closer," he urged. "Come closer and I will please you."

As he'd known would be the case, she could not resist. She sank until his tongue could find and goad the nubbin fattened by her arousal. While stimulation jolted his own loins, Darius incited her to shrieking frenzy. But even in that frenzy the practiced voluptuary knew the limit of her own will. She jerked beyond his reach.

Panting, Summer Peach changed position swiftly and sat atop his naked belly. Looking down upon him, she ran her tongue over her lips and wriggled to let him feel her dampness. Pushing down, she teased the tip of his cock with the opening to her alley and this time she cried out with him, drawing her mouth back from her teeth and arching her back.

"Summer," Darius moaned. "Let me inside you, my gentle one."

She flung the back of a hand across her brow in mock distress. "What if we are discovered? I shall be ruined."

"That," he told her, as he knew was expected, "is the chance we take. At any moment we may be found, but we shall enjoy each second until that time."

In truth, from the outside, his temple, placed deep in the most forested reaches of Knighthead's lands, appeared to be a simple storage building of weathered timbers and wattling. There might be those who knew of the building, but, apart from the select group of men Darius had chosen to share his nights of enjoyment, none would guess what passed inside its walls.

Summer shifted, sinking just enough to let him begin to enter her. But then she rose again, smiling. Watching his face, she pulled her skirts up to her waist and sat with his shaft thrust up between her thighs. For seconds she fluttered her fingertips over his tip until he cried out.

"What do you want? Tell Summer."

"Show yourself to me."

"Show myself?" She opened her brown eyes wide. "I don't understand what you can mean. Show what?"

"Your tits. I want your tits." The darkness was gathering in his brain, the heat. Soon, if she waited too long, the game would change. He didn't want that to happen, not until later. Later he would become the violent aggressor, and he knew from the last time how she loved that. But first he wanted it this way.

As if she felt the slipping away of his tenuous control, the whore flung back her hair. Slowly, her white fingers went to the satin ribbon that laced her bodice together between large breasts.

"Yes," he murmured. He deserved this for all he'd suffered in the damnably long, frustrating years of his imprisonment at Knighthead. His imprisonment with the cold woman who was his wife and who found her own forms of pleasure . . . quite different forms from his.

The satin ribbon slipped from its bow and Summer began to unthread it entirely, pulling it from the eyelets until shimmering, wine-colored satin began to part, revealing, inch by inch, her pale and swelling flesh.

"Yes." Darius thrust his hips. "Yes." This time her knees held down his arms. That bitch of a wife was cold with him. But he knew how hot she was with the unlicked cubs she took to bed, or anywhere else she could get them. He knew because she had told him, with great detail. But soon he would have his revenge. Bertram Letchwith would give him the blunt he needed to tide him over in the last months at Knighthead. He was near his goal. He could feel it. Bertram and his weak seed could have Celine, and Mary could have Knighthead—or what was left of it. Darius would finally gain the prize he'd spent twenty years of his life finding, and he'd be free.

Free. His head swam.

"Now, my strong one."

Darius passed his tongue over his lips.

With a final tug, Summer pulled away the ribbon and cast it aside. Slipping her hands inside the sagging bodice, she jerked it below the great white globes of her breasts and swung forward, offering them to him. And at the same instant, she freed his arms.

Whimpering, Darius plucked at her, kneaded, strained upward until he could suckle a distended, darkly rosy nipple while he pinched and rolled the other between his fingers.

Summer Peach cried out, screamed out her pleasure and her lust. He would have her again and again before this night was out.

"Now!" The word tore from her arched throat, and in that instant she impaled herself on him, drove down, bucked, and drove again. Her breasts shuddered above him and he caught at them, reaching up to fasten his mouth again even as their bodies jarred together and he began to spill into her.

Falling onto him, the whore ground and ground, shouting triumph at the waves of fulfillment he felt pass through her and clench around him while he emptied.

With a great final writhing, she threw herself aside and fell, panting, on the cushions beside him.

Darius, his energy sapped, allowed himself to float. Just a little while and they would be ready again. His brain was drunk with the thought. Blindly, he stretched out an arm until he found her breast and squeezed. "Soon?" he mumbled, certain in the knowledge that she understood.

"Oh, very soon," she said and pulled him until he rolled to rest his head on her shoulder. A small adjustment and he was able to rest with her nipple in his mouth.

"A pretty sight."

Darius heard Bertram Letchwith's sneering tones but didn't bother to open his eyes.

"Perhaps I could be persuaded to enjoy some of what you seem to prefer," Bertram said. "Percival is exceeding slow about his business this evening."

Darius took his mouth from Summer Peach's breast and turned onto his back. Bertram stood over them, his corpulent, naked body showing signs that he had not been slow about *his* business and that he was, even now, more than interested in what Darius *preferred*. "Join us." Darius waved graciously at the cushions on the other side of Summer.

"Generous of you," Letchwith said, sinking down awkwardly and propping his square head on a plump fist. "But I shall probably await my next turn with sweet Lily." Idly, he played with one of Summer's breasts, weighing and pushing it up.

Irritated, Darius managed with difficulty to stop himself from warning the man off. Perhaps the time was right to broach a certain other matter. "Are you sure it wouldn't suit you to call off the business of Celine's Season? After all, it would seem you could go ahead without the conventions and have her to yourself the sooner without all this fuss."

Letchwith raised oddly innocent blue eyes to Darius and gave a cherubic smile. "The thought appeals, certainly. But I'm afraid you'll have to keep your side of the bargain. I want the girl to be seen. Every young buck of the *ton* shall dream of rutting the beautiful Celine, only to watch her taken by a better man. At last I'll be recognized for the force I am."

Darius knew a moment's discomfort for Celine, but only a moment. It was fit that a girl learn to be a submissive woman at the hands of her husband. His pleasures should be hers to fulfill. Darius's own failures in the marriage bed were the result of not subduing his wife early enough.

"You like this, don't you," Letchwith said, leaning until he could push Summer's breasts together. The woman watched him passively as he bent to fasten his moist, red little mouth over the very nipple where Darius had so recently sucked.

"When will you return to Town?" Darius asked, increasingly anxious to be rid of the Letchwiths.

"Early on the morrow," Bertram said, almost disinterestedly. He sat up, a large, white Buddha of a man with thinning, colorless hair arranged in waxed curls about his moonlike face. "It is time for me to become better acquainted with my bride-to-be."

Slowly, Bertram trailed stubby, dimpled fingers over Summer's belly and into the triangle of red hair between her thighs. His shining lips parted and he held his tongue between his teeth. Watching his hand, he paused, then delved, made rapid little tweaking motions until Summer squealed and writhed toward him.

Bertram met Darius's eyes and, even as the whore clutched at his cock, he smiled his glee and pushed her away. "Don't agitate yourself, Darius. My tastes are too subtle for this slut."

Darius held his tongue. Later his "slut" would be the one to pay for that insult.

"Percival!" Letchwith shifted restlessly. "Damn the boy. Let us hope he will somehow find more spirit after the wedding."

"After the wedding?" Darius rose and began pulling on his clothes. "Why should the wedding affect Percival one way or the other? Dress, woman. We must not waste the night." He enjoyed the ritual of undressing almost as much as the act of rutting itself.

"After the wedding," Bertram said and chuckled at the sight of his bleary-eyed son, wearing only a shirt, stumbling toward them with an arm around the shoulders of a disheveled female whose white muslin gown hung in revealing shreds from her lush body. "After the wedding I shall be as willing to share as always. But I may await Percival's satisfaction with a great deal less patience."

Chapter 3

There should be absolutely no impediment to his plan. None. No, without doubt, there should be none. Resting his elbows on the mahogany desk in the library of the handsome house he'd secured in Grosvenor Square, James tried to concentrate on the pages before him. Every morning brought fresh dispatches from Paipan on the state of the shipping and trading empire he'd inherited from his father. The business was thriving and would continue to thrive. With his very capable fingers on the pulse of world events and his ties to the East India Company mutually beneficial, the steady growth of his fortune was ensured.

All was well in Paipan, and he knew exactly what must be done here in England.

"Bloody hell!" He threw the papers down and jammed his pen into the standish. "There is no impediment, dammit!" Except for the amazingly unresponsive Miss Godwin herself. That delightful face and form—and those wary golden eyes—had plagued his concentration throughout the two days since their meeting at the Theatre Royal. Why *hadn't* she responded to him? He could have sworn she was tempted, but something held her back. That something, whatever it was, must be carefully but quickly disposed of.

26

Miss Celine Godwin had become the missing piece in his attack plan, the piece that would make up for all that he did not know by giving him two invaluable weapons: time and opportunity.

He drew his cigar box from the back of his desk and curled his fingers over the lid. "I will have you, Celine," he murmured through clenched teeth.

Discover the power of the eye.

James thought, as he thought a thousand times a day, of the scant clues passed on by his father mere hours before he died, the clues that had sent James on a mission he would accomplish or die attempting.

Francis St. Giles, lucid to the end despite his injuries, had said, "*My mother told me I would have to discover the power of the eye. She said the answer would lead me to the Sainsbury gems. They're hidden in a cellar vault beneath the library floor. They'd been in her family for generations. Always passed down through the females. In the absence of a daughter, she wanted to give them to me—her younger son—because I would not inherit my father's fortune. She promised that at the right time she would reveal the rest of what I would need to know to open the vault. Unfortunately she died before whatever would have been her 'right time.' I should have gone back and searched for what was mine. I always intended to do so. Soon the Sainsbury gems will be yours by right. Take possession of them, James. Discover how Darius Godwin betrayed and usurped me, and destroy him—for our honor. Destroy him and take back Knighthead. Knighthead is your home now, as it should have been mine. The gems await you beneath the library floor at Knighthead. You are a man of enormous wealth. Valuable as they are, you have no need of the gems, except as the means to punish the Godwins. I know they somehow learned of their existence. And I know they cannot have found them. Do this for us, James. Use what they covet most to destroy Darius and Mary.*"

Francis St. Giles, his wife, and their young son, James, had been summarily banished by Francis's father for reasons Francis told James he did not know. And Darius Godwin, trusted friend, had become the man who, with his visibly triumphant wife, had serenely walked in to take possession of Francis St. Giles's beloved Knighthead on the very day Francis set out to remove his family from England.

"Godwin shall pay," James had vowed to his father. "And I'll recover everything that is ours."

"The power of the eye," James said aloud. Alone it meant nothing, but with what details his father had been able to give and with what lay in the false lid of the insignificant marquetry cigar box beneath James's hand, he would fulfill his promise to Francis St. Giles.

He opened the box, felt beneath the lid for the hidden spring, and caught the two items that fell out. The first was a woman's delicate gold chain and locket, the second a man's heavy gold ring with a deeply engraved insignia that had no meaning to James. His father's instructions, passed on from his mother, then the Countess of Casterbridge, had been that he should guard the pieces well, that the ring would lead the way to the treasure, and that without the locket, possession of that treasure would spell death.

No more.

But James would make it enough. With Celine Godwin's help.

He replaced the jewelry, snapped shut the lid, and pushed the box from him. "And you *will* help!"

The door flew open and Liam marched into the room. "You are shouting at yourself," she announced, neatly slipping her hands inside the long sleeves of a high-necked, flame-colored gown. "We should return home."

Regaining his composure, James regarded her impassively. "We will not be returning to Paipan soon, as you well know considering how many times we've had this discussion." Even in his irritation with the girl for harping on the subject, James could not help thinking that if he could have chosen a sister, he would have wished her to have Liam's spirit.

She stood in the shaft of early afternoon sunlight that streamed through a narrow sash window, a glowing jewel of a creature whose rich brocade gown was, in fact, cut as a simple, straight shift with a small collar and satin buttons from neck to hem. When she walked, slits at the sides revealed slim black silk trousers worn underneath. Drawing herself to her full almost five feet, Liam said, "This London is unsettling to you, Master James. You need—"

"Liam," James said, with only the gentlest of warnings in his tone. "Enough. We will remain in England until I have completed my business here." Any mention of the true nature of that business would be exceedingly unwise. This small and perfect woman regarded him as hers to protect. In the nine years since she had come into the St. Giles household, she had found many ways to prove her fierce loyalty, ways that could cause grave discomfort to any object of her negative attentions. In the matter of Darius Godwin and his wife, Mary, James intended to dispense justice on his own behalf.

"There is something you are not telling me," Liam said. She approached smoothly, a deceptively sweet smile on her soft lips. "What is troubling you? Tell me. You know I will help you in any way I can."

"You will help me by curbing your curiosity." But the sight of her kind concern and quiet countenance brought its customary calming effect.

Her smile widened. "Ah, so I do have something to be curious about." She came to stand on his side of the desk, bringing her own elusive scent of wild lilies. "Tell me." She wore brocade slippers that matched her gown, and these she placed precisely together.

James shook his head. He pushed back his chair and swung his booted feet onto the desk. "How are you progressing with the household staff?"

She tossed her head, displaying to advantage an intricate arrangement of braids threaded through with the narrowest of scarlet satin cords.

"Liam?"

"They show promise," she said at last. "The cook, Mrs. Uphill—a strange name—she bangs things most ferociously and orders all the others around, but—when she thinks I am not looking, of course—then, as I have instructed, she takes most of the water from the vegetable pots. I think she is pleased because you are pleased with what she makes. But these English—how they boil with *so* much water." Liam rarely remembered that James was a member of the race she had disparaged since setting foot on their soil.

"I see." James locked his fingers behind his neck. "Tedious for you, I'm sure." Liam could always make him laugh. Her animation inevitably touched anyone she favored.

"The servants are still reluctant to exercise as I have instructed them, but I shall persevere."

James gave a bark of laughter. "Exercise? Do you mean you are taking the poor devils through their paces as if they were members of our household on the island?"

She set her mouth primly. "It is only right—and good for them. In time they will thank me." Suddenly frowning, Liam leaned to loosen James's neckcloth, remove it, and undo several buttons on his loose white linen shirt. "You are adopting the ways of these stuffed peacocks in London. There, now you will be more comfortable." From an invisible pocket, she produced a flat, enameled pot and raised its hinged lid. "And more comfortable yet."

Deftly, Liam tilted up his chin and smoothed light oil down the corded muscles in his neck. James closed his eyes and breathed in the subtle scent of sandalwood.

He sighed and caught her little hands between his. "Thank you." He would be more comfortable when his mission here was completed. "Play for me. I confess I am tense."

"As you wish." Slipping quickly over rich silken carpet in shades of deep red and black, she lighted incense in three golden bowls supported in the mouths of ebony dragons. Then she went to kneel before the fireplace and pulled her highly polished wooden *Ch'in* across her lap. Her dark head bowed over the instrument of such ancient origin. Instantly, her slender fingers drew haunting notes from the seven long strings.

Liam had come into his household at the age of ten, a tiny, perfectly beautiful black-haired child with the palest olive-toned skin and eyes that spoke of an unbreakable spirit. On that never-to-be-forgotten day, in a chaotic marketplace on the Chinese mainland, James had watched with seething fury as the small girl was placed on a platform to be viewed for purchase by several overfed, bejeweled men garbed in rich fabrics. Won Tel had whispered to James that these were princes who had traveled from distant desert provinces to secure fresh blood for their harems.

Won Tel's firm hand had restrained James until, in response to a gesture from one princely bidder, the auctioneer had begun to strip away the child's clothing. The impatient buyer, trembling with excitement and accompanied by a chorus of lewd shouts, lumbered to the platform and began probing and squeezing.

Even now, after so long, James shut his eyes against the memory.

What had ensued would undoubtedly live forever in the minds of that cursed auctioneer and the fat lecher who had given the order. At the girl's cries and her futile attempts to pummel her captors with fragile fists, James had moved like a madman, using to advantage the slim and deadly stiletto Won Tel had given him as a gift. Afterward, the auctioneer had been left to look at life through only one eye. His Highness the prince had screamed mindlessly and clutched his tattered, blood-soaked robes to his crotch. In the future he would have little use for females.

"Won Tel is behaving like a mountain bear with a thorn in his paw."

James inhaled, drawing in the elusive, heady aroma of Liam's precious island incense. He hadn't noticed that she had ceased to play. "If you pester him as you do me, I am not surprised."

The door opened again, this time to admit the subject of conversation. Won Tel crossed to where Liam knelt and offered her a hand. "Your talents are required in the kitchens." He laughed, throwing back his head to show fine, strong teeth. "The cook has apparently found live 'beasties' in her scullery. She insists they be removed immediately. Otherwise she intends to leave forthwith."

Liam grabbed his big hand and leaped to her feet. "These people will not learn that food should be fresh. The beasties, as she calls them, are merely two small pigs I purchased from a farmer traveling through that market the other day. He delivered them to the tradesmen's entrance as I required, and the animals are suitably caged. They will remain so until they are slaughtered for cooking."

James turned away and struggled to disguise a grin. Turning back, he said, "Evidently you still have work to do in establishing yourself as housekeeper, Liam. Do go and calm Mrs. Uphill."

Muttering in her native dialect, Liam sped away. As soon as the sound of her voice faded and the door was shut, James and Won Tel laughed together.

"I fear our exotic little female warrior will give these people an education they will never forget," James said at last. "I believe I made the right choice in giving her a task to keep her busy. It wouldn't do to allow her to become involved in the other matter."

Won Tel was immediately serious. "We're to have a visitor shortly. Your uncle, the marquess, sent word that he intends to call."

"Damn." James swung his feet to the floor. "Don't refer to the man as my uncle again. What does he think he's doing following me here? I told him he'd hear from me soon enough." Upon arriving in England, James had traveled directly to Dorset and set up the terms of his agreement to accept his inheritance. The marquess had eventually approved those terms, including James's insistence that they not see each other until he gave the nod.

"Calm yourself, Mr. Eagleton." Won Tel's hint of a smile held satisfaction. He was always best pleased when the scent of action was fresh. "Your ... the gentleman needs you and will continue to need you. He will be easily persuaded to whatever course you set for him."

"I do not have time to waste on devising sops for my ... for Casterbridge."

"No." Won Tel sank onto a divan strewn with dark green silk cushions. "It's been two days since you made the acquaintance of the Godwin girl. I'd thought that by now you'd—"

"I don't need your opinion of what I should have accomplished by now." Damn, but Won Tel had an irritating way of voicing James's own concerns just when he was trying to deal with them. "I will move on her in my own good time. There's no hurry."

"Really?"

James got up and turned to stare morosely out at the lawns and stunningly pretty plantings behind the house. Swallows dipped and soared across a crystal-blue spring sky, skimmed the tops of tender-leafed trees. "Hell and damnation. There is a hurry with the girl, but I'm determined to approach her in just the right way. There was something about her, Won Tel. Something different. She's an innocent, I'm certain of that. But there was a wariness in her that I wouldn't expect in one so young and inexperienced. What have you discovered about this man who's made his suit known?"

"A good deal. None of it pleasant."

James swung around. "Tell me."

"Perhaps we should wait until the marquess has paid his little call. I've a suspicion that when you've heard me out you'll want to make immediate plans for a visit to Miss Godwin."

"Has she formed a *tendre* for him?" James asked sharply. "Is that the reason for the urgency? Is there some danger that she may do something impetuous?"

"Like elope with the fellow?" Won Tel shook his head. "I doubt it. My concerns are of an entirely different nature. Please, be patient."

"Patient?" James said through gritted teeth. He began to pace. "I've been patient for too long and my father was patient for too long before me."

"Your hot blood will be your undoing," Won Tel

said. "Only a few months ago you were unaware of Knighthead . . . and the treasure."

James stopped pacing. The two men's eyes met and they regarded each other quietly. On the day of Francis St. Giles's death, James had shared the essentials of his father's last wishes with Won Tel. No pledge of silence had passed between them, but since that moment, the fabulous treasure that was even more the object of James's quest than regaining possession of Knighthead, had never been mentioned . . . until today.

"I am aware of the treasure now," James said slowly. "A few months. A lifetime. It is of no consequence how long I have known of its existence. My father was certain that his father disowned him because of some plot devised by Darius and Mary Godwin. And I believe he was correct. I believe, as my father did, that Godwin somehow learned that the treasure was hidden at Knighthead and became determined to find a way to make it his. For that he needed his old boyhood friend—my father—to be put out of his own home."

"You do not have proof."

"I will. My parents and I lived at Knighthead until I was almost eleven. Then, for no reason that my grandfather chose to explain, he banished my father. He told his own son that he was a disgrace and that he would be better off out of England. My grandfather refused ever to explain my father's supposed crime against what he called family honor."

"It was all a long time ago."

James slammed a fist into the desk and leaned his weight on its surface. "And you think I should forgive and forget?"

"You know that I am merely doing what I have always done. I am trying to ensure that you consider well before taking steps that may be irreversible and

not necessarily completely to your advantage." Won
Tel transferred his attention to the black lacquer chest
at one end of the divan and traced an ivory dragon
set into its lid. "Are you still certain that Godwin has
not already discovered the treasure?"

"More so. Had he done so, he would long ago
have left Dorset. Remember that he remains at
Knighthead not as its owner, but by some sort of arrangement made by my grandfather—an arrangement I dare not, as yet, even discuss with my uncle.
If there were some way to remove himself from such
a position, I don't doubt Godwin would grasp it.
And if he'd taken possession of my grandmother's
secret bounty, he would be very unlikely to need his
daughter's marriage as a fresh source of blunt. I suspect that even now, while Mary Godwin is supposedly not well enough to travel, the two of them are
searching for the Sainsbury jewels."

"James, for almost twenty years the Godwins have
been in possession of Knighthead. Your father told
you the jewels are hidden there. He also told you he
thought Godwin overheard your grandmother talking about their history—how they came to be hers to
dispose of—and where they were. Why would he
still not have found them?"

"Because, like me, he still does not have all the
pieces of the puzzle."

"Do you intend to spend twenty years of your life
searching for trinkets, too?"

"No," James said, pushing himself upright. "No,
because I do have certain advantages Godwin
doesn't have." Of the ring, the locket, and the location of the vault, Darius Godwin supposedly knew
nothing—and neither did Won Tel. For his own sake,
it might be as well if James's trusted servant did not
know quite everything.

"Very well." Won Tel spread his hands. "I stand

ready to do whatever you ask of me. But I hope the gaining of a pile of stones and some pretty baubles is worth the risks you may have to take. James, as you will discover, these are dangerous people. It is possible they are quite mad people."

Dangerous people. Mad people. Almost an echo of his father's final warning. Even as Francis St. Giles had sent his son to finish old business, he had warned him of the dangers of dealing with people who had spent twenty years of their lives in a futile search.

James's gaze flickered over the cigar box. "Won Tel, I always consider what you say, but never mistake my true motives in this venture. My father and mother left behind what they loved most. My mother died many years before her time because she lived in a climate to which she was totally unsuited. She did not complain to my father because his business ventures thrived and gave him satisfaction. She would not risk causing him to abandon what had become a substitute for his home. After my mother died, my father discovered how long she had suffered. His bitterness destroyed his heart and soul. He planned to come here himself and do to the Godwins what I am now doing. The accident stopped him. It is for them, my parents, that I seek retribution."

Won Tel pulled repeatedly on his beard and mustache. His eyes, beneath shaggy, veiling brows, glittered darkly. "Again, *Mr. Eagleton*, I am your right hand in this—and your left if necessary."

James nodded briefly. "As we discussed previously, it would be as well if Liam never finds out—"

"Say no more." Won Tel gave a wide grin. "Our little hellcat has very long claws and they are always at the ready to defend her Master James."

"Quite. So, enough discussion. Tell me what you've learned about the Godwins and the suit for the daughter."

"I think we . . . ah." Won Tel raised a finger. "It's possible the Marquess of Casterbridge is arriving, Mr. Eagleton."

James trusted Won Tel's extraordinary hearing implicitly. "Then greet him, man. And I do believe you will now remember my current name without repeating it *quite* so often."

Showing no hint of amusement, Won Tel swept from the room. It had been decided that, in the interests of security, no butler would be engaged. To date, those who had called appeared fascinated by the mysterious Mr. Eagleton's peculiar household. Later these callers spoke to others about an odd man, presumably of indeterminate Eastern Origin, who served as butler, and an exotically beautiful girl—in a Chinese way—who held a position as housekeeper. To the latter explanation had quickly been added a variety of other suggested duties for Liam, handmaiden to Mr. Eagleton being the kindest version.

"Yes, yes, yes. As you say. I'll find me own way."

At the sound of Uncle Augustus's booming voice, James looked at the ceiling and prayed for guidance. He must not allow his enthusiastic relative to interfere with what must be done. No doubt the old man intended to make a fresh appeal for James to publicly acknowledge his identity and take his position as heir to the Casterbridge titles and estates.

James thought, too late, that he should have greeted his uncle in the blue salon, a room not yet made over in the Asian fashions he favored. But, since his uncle was already approaching the library, the flamboyant furnishings here would have to suit.

"Ah, there you are, m'boy." Augustus, Third Marquess of Casterbridge, entered . . . with a stunning, red-haired young beauty on one arm and a ravishing brunette of somewhat greater maturity on the other. "M'dears, allow me to introduce James *Eagle-*

ton, the son of me oldest and dearest departed friend, er, Alfonse Eagleton. Of the Northumberland Eagletons, of course. James is recently returned from the East. Paipan. His own island. Fr— Alfonse bought the place. Shippin', y'know. Disgustingly successful, too, I might add. More blunt than he knows what to do with, or so I'm told."

James realized his mouth was open and snapped it shut—and caught sight of Won Tel pressing his lips firmly together.

"These lovely ladies are kind enough to spare a little of their time for a decrepit and ailing old man." Resplendent in a claret-colored coat, yellow pantaloons, a starched muslin neckcloth in Oriental Tie and a pearl-gray silk waistcoat embroidered with sprigs of pink roses, Casterbridge's patrician face glowed healthily, and his straight back and sprightly gait suggested anything but failing health.

"This"—he inclined his head toward the brunette—"is Sibyl, Countess Lafoget. She is the widow of my dear old friend Comte Lafoget. He came here during the inconvenience in France."

The countess slowly withdrew her clearly fascinated gaze from the smoking incense, inclined her head at James, and offered a delicate hand. "Madam," he said, touching his lips briefly to smooth, white skin. Either Lafoget had come from "the inconvenience" in France at an exceedingly early age, or he'd married a woman young enough to be his granddaughter.

"And this," Casterbridge said, looking not at the redhead but at James and with minute intensity, "this is Lady Anastasie Blenkinsop, the daughter of the Earl of Wheaton."

James repeated the required greeting ritual. This time the soft hand placed in his lingered—at the lady's pleasure. Lady Anastasie wore yellow muslin, dampened—as was the fashion among faster females—to reveal more of a voluptuous body than it shielded. She raised large, worldly green eyes to James's and achieved a coquettish smile that was, at the same time, a pout of invitation.

"I am delighted to meet you, Mr. Eagleton." With her hand still pressed into his, Lady Anastasie leaned forward, no doubt to give him an even better vantage point on her undeniable assets. "The marquess assured me that you and I might have much in common."

James held his bottom lip in his teeth and raised a brow. What, he wondered, might that be?

"I had the misfortune to lose my fiance on the Peninsula some months ago," Lady Anastasie continued. She sighed hugely, expanding already quite remarkable breasts. "So I was persuaded to endure another Season. To divert me from my sorrow, of course."

"Of course." And Casterbridge had, no doubt, decided that James might be just the one to help in that diversion. The marquess was undoubtedly already on the hunt for potential female breeding stock to assist in filling the too-long-empty Casterbridge nursery. Evidently the man had the wisdom to sense when enough possessions—and certain other possibilities—might overcome even the supposed lack of a title. If James was not mistaken, such was the case with Lady Anastasie.

She sighed again, and James noted the countess's bored little yawn.

"My lord." Collecting himself fully, James carefully extricated his hand and offered it to his uncle. "It is very good of you to call, but I certainly cannot keep you—"

"Not at all. Not at all." The marquess beamed and managed to shake James's hand without disentan-

gling his arm from Lady Anastasie's clinging grip.
"Least I can do for Alfonse's boy. I remember a time
when Alfonse and I were explorin' in, er, China.
There was this killer tiger that had wiped out whole
villages full of savages and . . . well, we were in this
killer tiger's, er, domain, and I happened to turn me
back at an inopportune moment and . . . well, if it
hadn't been for Alfonse . . ."

James dared a glance into Won Tel's eyes and
promptly succumbed to a gale of coughing.

"Then there was the time—"

"Please." James, unable to postpone the amenities
further, indicated one of the three divans. "My father
was a very private man—do sit down—and he de-
tested personal praise."

"Just so." The marquess's eyes shone with knowing enjoyment. "Anyway, we must get on. Promised
my two lovely butterflies that I'll take them for a
turn in the Park. New open carriage, y'know.
Canary-yellow. All the rage."

"I'm sure." James longed to get the marquess alone
and restate the terms of their relationship. "Didn't I
hear that you'd decided to remain in Dorset during
the Season this year, my lord?"

Casterbridge puffed up his cheeks. "You might
have. I'll probably not stay in Town much beyond a
week or two . . . perhaps three. Month at the outside."

James fixed the man with a warning stare.

"Tell Mr. Eagleton why we're here," Lady
Anastasie said in her whispery, honeyed voice. "I just
know he'll be pleased."

"Yes," said the marquess. "Almost forgot. Having a
little fete at Casterbridge House a week from next
Saturday, m'boy. The invitation will be along, but
Lady Anastasie here was anxious for an excuse to see
you in person."

Lady Anastasie coyly lowered thick, blacked lashes, but made no attempt to deny her interest in James. "The marquess tells me you do not know anyone in London. I shall look forward to making sure you are not lonely at the fete." The lashes fluttered up from those enticing, too-old green eyes.

"Augustus," Lady Sibyl said, gazing up at the marquess, "I think we have imposed upon your friend's son long enough. And besides, we do not wish to miss all the sunshine and the company in the Park. Come Anastasie . . . before your gown quite dries out."

James had barely an instant to enjoy Lady Anastasie's venomous glare at the countess before an approaching flash of red warned of Liam's imminent arrival.

Slipping silently across the thick Persian carpet, she reached Won Tel's side. James saw his companion give Liam a frown of warning she never saw. Liam's own fine, straight brows drew together as she regarded the backs of their visitors.

"Liam!" James waved her toward him. "Come. You're just in time. Please meet an old friend of my father's, the Marquess of Casterbridge."

She glided to his side and faced the marquess and his companions. Bowing, she said, "I'm happy to meet the marquess," in her clear, high voice.

Predictably, Casterbridge's face registered fascinated delight. "Not nearly as happy as I am to meet you, m'dear."

Lady Sibyl also smiled charmingly.

Lady Anastasie did not smile. "How clever of you, Mr. Eagleton. We must forever be seeking ways to be original. Your little Oriental curiosity is quite a coup."

"Liam is—"

"Most gratified by the person's compliment," Liam

said quickly, slipping her hands around James's arm to hold it as the other women held on to Casterbridge. She leaned against James and smiled adoringly up at him.

"Your charm and graciousness are an example to us all, my dear," James said, enjoying the moment. He touched a smooth cheek before looking again at his visitors.

Pure glee painted a wicked grin on the marquess's ruddy face. "I really would rather stay, but . . ." He shrugged eloquently. "My countess and my *person* are anxious to be gone. I'll look forward to seeing you at the fête, my boy."

James inclined his head. He would pray, for her own sake, that Lady Anastasie would not make the mistake of further baiting Liam. The result could be disastrous, and not for Liam.

With James and Liam following, Casterbridge swept his entourage past a bowing Won Tel into the foyer. Won Tel moved forward to hand the marquess his top hat and ivory-handled cane.

At the door, the marquess turned back. "This promises to be an interesting Season, wouldn't you say, James?" His glance moved from James to Lady Anastasie, who was favoring James with another gaze filled with suggestive promises.

"Interesting, indeed," James agreed. Far more interesting than his overzealous uncle could possibly foresee. "Enjoy your drive."

Lady Anastasie curved her supple body, displaying yet again an expanse of softly swelling pale breast . . . and the enticing flare of hip beneath almost diaphanous muslin, and looked at James over a rounded shoulder. "A week from Saturday, then?" Her attention flickered in the region of Liam. "Be certain you are well rested, Mr. Eagleton. These affairs can be *quite* stimulating. And, *naturellement*, I'll be glad to help you in any way I can."

With that, the threesome left.

"I'll be glad to help you in *any* way I can," Liam repeated with a long, breathy sigh.

"Now, now." James suppressed his laughter. "The lady—Lady Anastasie, by the way—she was simply being polite and welcoming to a stranger."

Liam stood in front of him and crossed her arms. She tilted up her chin. "As I thought. You are quite unprepared to deal with these wily English women. I, on the other hand, am very prepared."

"You will not interfere in my affairs." Damnation, but Casterbridge should have kept his distance. "Lady Anastasie is a gentle innocent with an unfortunately provocative turn of phrase." May he be forgiven for being a liar!

"Hah." Liam poked his chest with a sharp forefinger. "Gentle innocent?"

"Yes—"

"She desires your *body!*"

Chapter 4

"**P**lease, Celine." Lettie blocked the path to the stairs. "Don't do this."

"I know what I'm about," Celine said, but she hugged Lettie quickly. "You worry too much."

"*You* don't worry near enough. If your mama finds out what you've been up to, she'll—"

"She won't find out," Celine said deliberately. "She and Papa were impressed that I wished to make do with an allowance. I told them I would attend to my own expenses and not overspend or ask for more money."

"Oh, Celine!" Lettie's voice rose to a wail. "You didn't tell them you planned some scheme to save money from your allowance for other purposes."

"I'm not saving it for myself. And I'm being very sensible. My idea is thrifty. A way to reuse things other people have already used means they are twice as useful and, best of all, they cost a fraction of what they would cost new."

"It's such a risk." Lettie ground her hands together. "Eventually it's bound to get about that you buy your gowns from ... Well, you know how spiteful these lofty people in London are. What will we do if they begin to notice that your gowns have already been worn by other young ladies?"

"Lettie, those other young ladies have their own reasons for selling their finery to me. They have much greater appetites for such things than I do, and that's why they're so anxious to sell to me. They'll be most careful not to let our arrangements slip. It's all perfect, and I'm determined to continue to make it work for David's sake—and Ruby Rose's and the other women we'll be helping to start a new life away from their degrading existences in London. David is providing sanctuary and a living for Ruby Rose at the moment. He couldn't afford to pay a cook as well as a housekeeper, yet he chose to make the sacrifice. You know he needs all the help possible with his mission."

"His mission!" Lettie slapped the skirts of her gray morning dress. "You know how fond I am of David, but his wild schemes with these fallen women will surely cause him woe. Worse yet, he may pull you into mischief, my lamb. His mission should be the guiding of the villagers' souls in Little Puddle."

"All souls need to be guided." Celine paused, guiltily aware of a certain personal tendency to obstinate rebellion against piety. "Don't you think Ruby Rose's soul is every bit as important as that nasty Mrs. Strickland's?" That pinch-puss was David's housekeeper and a very intimidating woman indeed who was vociferous in her displeasure at being called upon to train Ruby Rose.

"Mrs. Strickland has her own problems, I'm sure," Lettie said severely. "Being David Talbot's housekeeper might be enough to turn any good woman into a shrew. And shame on you, miss, for your sharp tongue."

"And my *wayward ways*? Papa and Mama always talk about those."

"I'll not allow you to be changing the subject, Celine. This scheme of yours will be your downfall—

and the end of me, I shouldn't wonder. You're worrying me into an early grave."

"Nonsense. The saving of Ruby Rose's soul is the best possible motive I could have for sending money to David. And I'm really not doing anything dishonest."

Lettie's dark eyes shone with wrath. "There's dishonesty and then there's dishonesty. Finding ways to supposedly be thrifty, then not telling your parents that you're giving their money away, is definitely dishonesty."

"Aha!" Celine laughed and twirled around, filling the soft skirts of her high-waisted lavender muslin dress until they ballooned, then twisted about her body. "Aha, aha. But, dearest Lettie, *which* of those dishonesties is it? I contend that it is dishonesty in a good cause, which makes it the very best of deceptions if, indeed, it is deception at all."

"Honey-tongued flibbertigibbet," Lettie exclaimed, but her indulgent smile drove dimples into her cheeks. "Master David Talbot had no right to drag you into this rattlebrained scheme of his."

Celine planted her lavender satin slippers and grasped Lettie's shoulders. "Ruby Rose and all the other women we intend to help are *not* a rattlebrained scheme. They are women who, through no fault of their own rather than inadequate guidance ... They are good women who, because they were not warned of the potential dangers ... Well"—she raised her palms—"they *fell*."

"They fell? Fallen women are what you're talking about. Master David has no business talking to an innocent young girl about *fallen women*. And the next time I see him I shall tell him so."

"You'll do no such thing," Celine said, frowning. "He's shy enough as it is. Don't you think it's hard for a quiet man like David to come to London and go to the unpleasant places where these women live and work?"

Lettie's mouth fell open. "He told you about those places?" she whispered, stepping closer to Celine.

"Certainly. And they work very hard just to make enough money for all those dreadful, gaudy fripperies they wear in the streets to . . . to attract the attention of men!"

"What?" Lettie's voice rose to a squeak. "Wait till I see that young man."

"I don't understand you. David considers social awareness most essential. It is important to try to help those less fortunate than ourselves. The fallen women crave the attention of men. For that they feel they must dress outrageously to be noticed. It's all part of a kind of sickness."

"It is not right for David to talk to you about such things."

"Such things? Why not? Ruby Rose is a dear, gentle woman who, through no fault of her own, succumbed to . . . to certain sensations. She was . . . intoxicated by those sensations and quite unable to free herself without help. Even working for someone quite dreadful seemed acceptable just to experience this, this . . ."

"Well!" Lettie crossed her arms. "I pray you do not really understand a word of what you're saying." Her pretty mouth was set in a prim line.

"I most certainly do. The poor things—all of those like Ruby Rose—have to live in small rooms in houses overseen by older females with the most avaricious appetites for money."

"David Talbot told you this, too?"

"Yes. Of course he did. He has to go to these . . . Do you know these greedy females often bear the title of abbess? I think that's what offends David most deeply. They pretend to an almost holy cause. By al-

lowing the dear, fallen ones to live in these ... Do
you know they call their homes nunneries?"

Lettie shuddered.

"Exactly!" Celine took a deep breath. "Horrible,
isn't it? I'm so glad you finally understand the wor-
thiness of our cause. Those wicked *abbesses* charge
our unfortunates outrageous sums for their miserable
rooms and work them so hard—very often all
through the night, I understand. Usually there are
some sorts of agreements made that force young
women like Ruby Rose to remain there. And that's
what David needs the money for. To pay off these
frightful opportunists so that they'll allow their ten-
ants to leave. And to stretch his very meager stipend,
of course. What he's paid barely covers existing expenses at the vicarage."

"Poor Mrs. Strickland," Lettie muttered.

"What does Mrs. Strickland have to do with this?"

Lettie peered over the banister to the entry hall below.

"Lettie?"

"Oh, nothing, nothing. How is Ruby Rose doing
with her cooking lessons? Isn't that what you told me
David decided she should learn? Cooking?"

"Exactly!" It really was most gratifying to Celine
when Lettie decided to be enthusiastic about things.
"Eventually Ruby Rose will be able to earn an honest
living in a respectable household and support herself. In the meanwhile it must be a great help to Mrs.
Strickland. Before she started teaching Ruby Rose to
cook, she had to do everything at the vicarage."

"Mm. Teaching Ruby Rose must be very helpful."

"Exactly! It certainly is. Why, I heard Mrs. Strickland say Ruby Rose must be a reward for something
in the past. Wasn't that nice?"

Lettie slowly shook her head. "Very nice. I don't
wish to talk about this any more and, if you have a

mite of sense, you'll be very careful not to speak of it, either. Mr. and Mrs. Godwin would—"

"I *know* that." Immediately, Celine regretted snapping. "I mean that I'm always very careful what I say in front of my parents."

"Yes."

Lettie looked directly into Celine's eyes. There were those things that need never be said aloud. Lettie and Celine avoided discussing the difficult times they'd shared during her parents' black moods—*wild turns,* as Lettie called them. Locked in their rooms, sometimes for several days at a time, Celine and Lettie had grown accustomed to the sounds of dragging and banging and the raging voices of the Godwins. Secretly Celine believed the large number of bottles of hock and other strong drink her parents consumed to be responsible for the bouts of near madness. She knew she must never give them cause to be angry with her. The scars of childhood beatings were not visible on her body, but existed in areas of her memory usually kept closed. Life was too full of changes and joys to leave time for dwelling on ugliness.

Celine smiled. Perhaps it was time to break the old silence. "Think, Lettie. Why should it be anything but good to realize that there are those who have a harder life than I do? Perhaps contemplating these poor fallen women will help me the next time we go through one of the wretched wild turns!" She pressed her fingers to her lips. Never, never had they spoken in detail of Mama and Papa's rages.

"I suppose it might," Lettie said softly, turning aside her face. "My poor lamb. But I must suggest that you do not, under any circumstances, let slip a mention of any of this to your parents—not about the wild turns, or this business with David Talbot."

"I promise I won't," Celine sang out. "Now, *please,*

Lettie, let us go down. Miss Isabel Prentergast is already overdue for her call."

Sighing, Lettie tweaked the lace at Celine's neck and smoothed her cheek. She stood aside, then fell in behind Celine to descend the stairs. "Perhaps Miss Prentergast has changed her mind." There was definite hope in Lettie's voice.

"I assure you she hasn't." Celine paused and laughed up at Lettie. "Miss Prentergast needs money. My sources tell me she has a quite insatiable appetite for whist."

"No!" Lettie's hand went to her throat. "What would her papa—"

"And mama say?" Celine finished the sentence. Giggling, she almost skipped down to the entrance hall, where a shabby Indian carpet in faded muddy shades covered not quite enough of highly polished but worn oak floors.

In the parlor Celine halted and frowned. "I know I shouldn't complain, but don't you think this room is exceedingly stuffy, Lettie?"

"I'll open a window."

"No, no," Celine said, irritated. "The windows *are* open. I meant all these stiff, boring old furnishings. Who would choose so many dull browns and lifeless greens? And all the gold braiding is in shreds. And the draperies are so ... brown and *tired*."

"You complain too much," Lettie said, but without reproof in her voice.

"I know." Celine sat on a lumpy chaise and arranged her skirts. "I should forever keep the plight of the poor fallen women before me and be grateful."

Lettie only sighed.

"You dislike London," Celine said, deliberately changing the subject. She patted the seat beside her.

Lettie sat down and looked at her hands. "Not London, exactly."

"But what goes on here? The Season? All the coming and going and doing?"

"Partly."

Celine's stomach felt suddenly funny. "You're worried about this matter of Bertram Letchwith," she said gently, determined not to show her own horror at the prospect of a match with the man.

"No! No, of course not." But Lettie's lower lip trembled.

"We are worrying about nothing," Celine announced firmly. "You'll see. There will be no firm offer from him and no match."

"Oh, my poor, dear little girl, how can you think as much after all that's been said?"

"I can think it because it makes absolute sense. Surely, if Mr. Letchwith were truly set on me, he wouldn't be pleased about this Season. My theory is that he *isn't* at all set. He intends to use this Season to look around more. And he probably assumes, correctly, that seeing me with other single young ladies will show me unfavorably. He'll settle on someone else. And Papa and Mama know this and are anxious for me to find an alternative myself." Celine caught Lettie's hand. "There! You see? We have nothing to worry about."

Lettie sighed again and made a dismal attempt at a smile.

She herself, Celine decided, must find ways not to think about Mr. Letchwith at all. "There hasn't been ... I don't suppose anyone has called while I was out. Yesterday, perhaps? And Baity forgot to mention it?" She avoided looking at Lettie.

"Who exactly were you expecting to call?"

Instantly, Celine envisioned eyes like a winter morning's gray sky.

"Celine?"

So tall, so strongly made, with such well-muscled legs ...

"*Celine?*"

"Exactly! That's exactly ... What did you say, Lettie?"

"Featherbrained miss. Exactly this. Exactly that. And there's exactly nothing in that pretty head of yours. You said something about expecting someone to call, and I asked who that might be."

Celine plucked at a loose thread trailing from a particularly unpleasant-looking puce-colored rose on the chaise. "No one. Not a soul. I simply thought it possible that a friend might have left his card."

"*His* card? As I thought, young lady. You're moping after that rake in gentleman's clothing who had the audacity to approach you at the theater."

Celine scowled. "I am not. And he was no rake. Mr. Eagleton was a gentleman."

"Don't frown. You'll get wrinkles. You aren't an authority on rakes and gentlemen, Celine. Mark my words, he's a rake and he saw a lovely girl and decided he'd try to sweep her off her feet with his worldly ways."

Mr. Eagleton certainly *had* seemed somewhat worldly—in the nicest, most intriguing of ways. Celine straightened her back. No doubt poor Ruby Rose had entertained the same such thoughts about a gentleman she met, and look where it led *her*.

"Miss Prentergast is very late."

But Ruby Rose probably had a quite marvelous time with her thoughts and the sensations they caused before she actually ... *fell*. What exactly, one wondered, *did* happen when a woman actually fell?

"Celine, you're dreamy this morning. What is the matter with you?"

Celine heard the bell at the front door and turned a brilliant smile on Lettie. "Miss Prentergast, at last."

Or it could be that Mr. Eagleton had decided to call after all.

Baity, short, stout, shiny bald, and perfunctory, entered. "A Miss Isabel Prentergast."

Blond and bouncy Isabel Prentergast popped around Baity and trotted into the room. In her wake, virtually obscured behind the sheet-draped bundle she carried, came another woman.

"Thank you, er . . ." Miss Prentergast waved a dismissing hand at Baity, who promptly left.

"Good morning—"

"We must hurry," the girl interrupted Celine and shooed the overburdened servant toward a chair. "Put them there, Millie."

"Is everything all right?" Celine asked. "You haven't encountered some, er, difficulty?"

Miss Prentergast made a warning face. "You may wait in the hall while I discuss my fitting, Millie." As soon as the servant withdrew, the girl glanced significantly at Lettie, then at Celine. "I do think we should keep this between ourselves, don't you?"

"Lettie is my companion," Celine said promptly. "And my friend."

"How very unconventional. I find one can't be too careful with servants. Such wagging-tongued creatures. I led Millie to believe you were a modiste."

Celine ignored the outraged sound Lettie made. "How clever of you, Miss Prentergast. Perhaps we should deal with our business quickly."

"Do call me Isabel. And I shall call you Celine." A smile made an unremarkable face almost pretty before Isabel hurried to unveil her offerings.

At Celine's first social venture, a small salon given by the wife of a politician who evidently knew Celine's father, she had listened disinterestedly to girlish chatter—until someone mentioned the enormous cost of gowns. It seemed that some young ladies felt it mightily unfair that they could not indulge in all the titilating pastimes enjoyed by their more wealthy peers. Most families were already stretched beyond their financial limits to afford a Season at all, and the largest expense was for the wardrobe, particularly gowns that were often worn only once.

The perfect solution had occurred to Celine. She would buy some of these now useless creations, change them as much as possible, and use what she saved by not buying new clothing to help David. So far, her discreet inquiries had produced several very willing sellers.

"Well?"

Celine had not realized that Isabel was waiting for a reaction. "Mm?"

"You don't like them?" Isabel pouted defensively and tweaked the bodice of a lovely pale pink satin. "My mama paid a fortune for this, but it's far too noticeable. I shall not wear it again lest gentlemen think I am *completely* portionless." She cast her round blue eyes dramatically heavenward.

Celine advanced and poked at a delightful edging of silver roses along the neck. "Pink doesn't become me." She wrinkled her nose. "And I really don't care for such gaudy fripperies."

"Gaudy *fripperies*!" The offense Isabel exhibited was obviously genuine. "The silver at the neck and hem are most singular. Everyone said as much."

"Ah." Celine sighed hugely. "That is another point, of course. Even if I did like the silver"—oh, how she did indeed love it, she thought with regret—"it would make the gown too easily recognized. So . . ."

"It could be removed," Isabel said quickly. "That would be the merest of inconveniences."

"To a modiste," Lettie put in with a wry note.

Isabel ignored her. "Really. A few little snips and it would be gone."

"Mm."

"Naturally," Isabel rushed on. "Naturally, the price would be adjusted accordingly."

"Mm. How much did you—"

"Oh, no. We must not speak aloud of such matters." She produced a notebook and a gold pencil from the charming little flower-decorated straw reticule she carried over a wrist. "We will write down our negotiations. Talking of money is really *too* vulgar. Mama always says as much."

In small, neat strokes, Isabel wrote a figure and showed it to Celine.

"Oh, dear. You must be exceedingly rich to afford such extravagance. I'm afraid—"

"It is a beautiful gown," Isabel protested. "A copy of a French design. It was much admired."

"Mm."

Puffing, Isabel wrote another figure in the book. "There."

"Mm."

"Oh, really!" Again Isabel wrote.

This time Celine took the notebook and studied what was written there with fierce concentration. "May I?" She used Isabel's pen to write figures of her own. "This reflects an allowance for the removal of the ornamentation."

Isabel peered around Celine's arm. "So little? But I need—" She stopped and would have been chagrined had she seen Celine's satisfied little grin.

"Oh, I almost forgot." Celine wrote again. "You are a good two inches shorter than I. That means that I am buying two inches less dress than I require. This total reflects the necessary adjustment."

Isabel made a strangled noise.

"Of course," Celine said sweetly, "if your pockets are really so shallow that you need much more, then I'll understand if you try to find another buyer."

"My mama and papa are very nicely fixed, thank you kindly. The figure you mention will be quite adequate." Isabel raised her nose disdainfully.

A further half-hour disposed of the purchase of the second creation. An elegant leaf design, embroidered in twisted black and gold satin thread, covered the primrose-yellow muslin's low-cut bodice. Since Isabel was decidedly slimmer at the chest than Celine, there might be some difficulty in making the bodice fit, but Celine decided they would find a way.

"And so it is done," Isabel said happily when the transactions were completed. She showed no squeamishness about tucking away the money Celine gave her. "I really can't imagine how you bear the idea of wearing castoffs, you poor thing."

Celine smiled. "It is indeed a hardship. But, since we both have interests to protect, I don't suppose our arrangements will be mentioned, will they?"

"No." Isabel's blue eyes turned a trifle hard. "I don't suppose they will be. Anyway, we're unlikely to be in too many of the same places."

Celine eyed her sharply, but made no comment. Isabel was referring to the fact that her rank in society was considerably higher than Celine's and that, therefore, Isabel would be invited to many affairs from which Celine would be excluded.

"I may have another gown to . . . well, you know . . . after the end of next week. If I do, I'll bring it and tell you all about the marvelous fete I've been invited to. It's expected to be quite the most lavish affair of the Season to date—perhaps of the entire Season."

"Really?" Celine contrived to appear bored.

"Oh, yes. The Marquess of Casterbridge is opening up Casterbridge House in Park Lane for the first time in *years*. And I am *invited*! Mama says *everyone* will be there. Every pink of the *ton*. Every member of the *haut ton* who *is* anyone. Oh, I can hardly wait." Isabel produced a fan of painted blue parchment the same shade as her carriage dress and flicked it open. She eyed Celine assessingly over the top. "It's such a pity you won't be there."

Celine noted, not without irritation, that the other girl automatically assumed herself the favored one . . . and she was right. "No, I don't suppose I shall." Letting her eyes sweep past Lettie, she added. "I already have a previous engagement."

Before Isabel could respond, the parlor door opened once more to admit Baity. He offered Celine a card on a silver tray. One corner of the card was turned down, indicating that the caller awaited a response.

Celine read, and her hand went to her heart. "James Eagleton" was engraved in bold print on heavy, creamy stock. The name stood alone.

"Um, show the gentleman in," Celine told Baity. She turned to Isabel. "I do so appreciate your visit, and I'll hope to see you again soon. Perhaps after the fete?"

While Isabel smoothed on white gloves, she kept an expectant eye on the door. "Yes," she said, distracted. "After the fete."

Without looking, Celine felt Lettie stand up abruptly at the sound of the door opening once again. The man who entered captured the immediate and total attention of the three women in the room.

Mr. James Eagleton strode forward, going directly to Lettie and taking her hand in his. "How delightful to see you again, madam."

"Miss Fisher," Lettie said. But her voice was faint, and Celine noted an unusual brush of color in Lettie's cheeks.

"And Miss Godwin." Mr. Eagleton turned to Celine. He stood quite still and looked intently down into her face. "You are even lovelier than I recalled."

"Oh." Celine's legs felt wobbly and her heart beat faster. Remembering herself, she said, "Good morning, Mr. Eagleton. How nice of you to call."

"Mr. Eagleton?" Isabel Prentergast spoke in a breathy voice quite unlike her own. "*The* Mr. James Eagleton?"

A strange annoyance snapped apart the soft cloud of trembling warmth that had settled over Celine. Isabel was making spoony eyes at Mr. Eagleton. Quite disgusting.

"I am James Eagleton." He laughed, showing his strong, very white teeth and curving his firm mouth in that ... in that *way* he had of curving his mouth.

"The James Eagleton who *owns* an entire *island*?"

"Paipan is quite a small island, but yes."

Isabel tottered closer. "And you have ships? And, um, a trading empire?"

Mr. Eagleton inclined his head modestly. "I fear it is all quite true."

"It's marvelously exciting," Isabel said hoarsely, offering her hand without being given the slightest encouragement.

Celine clamped her mouth shut.

"And you are?" James asked politely.

"Isabel." She drew out each syllable of the word in the way one heard of opera dancers speaking. "Isabel Prentergast." Then Isabel positively thrust her hand at Mr. Eagleton, quite forgetting that about its wrist swung her not-quite-fastened reticule. Even as the contents scattered, Isabel was gazing up at Mr. Eagleton.

"Oh, dear," he said, and Celine took pleasure in noting his amusement. He bent to gather the notebook and pencil, the lace-edged handkerchief and hartshorn ... and a pot of rouge!

"I'll do it!" Isabel said, bending in a most ungainly fashion to scoop together her possessions.

Really, to be caught carrying rouge! How frightfully embarrassing.

At last Isabel was recovered if slightly mussed. "Lady Anastasie Blenkinsop is a friend of my family, Mr. Eagleton," she said, pushing at an escaped curl.

He hooked his hands together beneath the tails of his perfectly tailored black coat. "Really?"

"Oh, yes. She told us all about your stra— your interesting household."

Mr. Eagleton showed an odd agitation. "No doubt. Could I summon your carriage for you, Miss Prentergast?"

"I . . . well, I suppose so. Is it true that you have a Chinese—"

"Quite true," Mr. Eagleton interrupted. "Come, I'll help you."

"Lady Anastasie said you would be at the Casterbridge fete. Doesn't it sound *divine*? Can you bear to wait for the day?"

Mr. Eagleton's hand closed on Isabel's elbow. "It should be a most stimulating event."

"Poor Celine," Isabel said, straining to look over her shoulder. "She isn't invited, of course. But I've promised to come and tell her all about it."

"Is that so." He ushered the girl, virtually on her toes to keep up with him, into the hall and was heard to ask Baity to call the carriage.

Moments later he returned looking as smoothly collected and handsome as when he'd arrived. Again it was to Lettie that he first gave attention. "Miss Fisher, I do hope you don't consider my visit precipitate. I had some small difficulty ascertaining the exact number of this house. Since I was then in the neighborhood, I decided to presume upon your patience. If you would prefer that I leave . . ." He bowed.

Lettie seemed to consider.

Celine waited, willing her companion to be agreeable.

Glancing at Celine, Lettie said, "We have no urgent

matters to attend, Mr. Eagleton. I believe Celine would enjoy a little company. She is too much alone.

"Celine, I'll be taking these gowns to your chamber and starting the work that needs to be done on them. It's a wonderful afternoon. Why not show Mr. Eagleton the gardens? I'm particularly fond of the roses, sir. I like to think my efforts have made them come along a bit even in the short time we've been here."

Amazed, Celine watched Lettie leave the room. What could possibly have come over her cautious companion? Usually the presence of any male meant that Lettie remained in attendance, like an anxious mother swan with her only surviving cygnet.

"Miss Godwin." Mr. Eagleton touched her arm, and Celine jumped.

He smiled and she saw again the black flecks in the gray of his eyes, the black rings around those burnished steel irises. Where his impeccably white neckcloth met his skin there was an arresting contrast with his tan and with the black hair that curled there. The corners of his mouth turned up even more, and vertical lines formed beneath his high cheekbones. There was, she noted for the first time, a slight cleft in his sharply defined jaw.

"May I escort you to the gardens?" he asked.

Slowly, she raised her hand. He took it gently and rested it on his forearm, and then his fingers folded over hers. Oh, dear. Oh, dear. This breathlessness, this thumping in her breast . . . It was the beginning of the other . . . the sensation she should avoid. Celine knew it.

"Shall we go?"

"I . . . yes."

Definitely, this was the beginning. And Celine found she had absolutely no will . . . and no desire to stop.

Chapter 5

James mulled over the odd behavior of Celine's companion . . . entirely remiss behavior. To leave a young, inexperienced girl in the dubious protection of a man—a stranger—should be unthinkable. Ignorance? he wondered, or some sly design? No matter. Either motive would serve his needs as well.

He still felt it, that wary hesitancy. But, even stronger, he felt the fire in Celine, the promise of passion. James strolled with her through the dismal house, aware, as he had been at the theater, of her honey-gold hair, her soft, creamy cheek with the faintest blush of color, the full swell of smoothly feminine flesh above the square neckline of her filmy dress.

A golden creature like a ray of polished sunshine passing through drab surroundings that seemed to fade before her and in her wake.

"As Miss Fisher said, Miss Godwin, this is indeed a beautiful day." He had never yet lost his head over a woman and he would make damn certain he didn't do so now—most especially now. Unfinished business was his only interest here.

"Lettie loves the sunshine and the spring flowers." Her soft voice was slightly husky—and compelling. "I love them, too," she added, allowing a small, upward glance in his direction.

They left the house by a door on the far side of a surprisingly lushly stocked conservatory. James felt the pressure of her fingers increase on his arm and instinctively stroked the back of her hand. A gentle little thing, this Celine Godwin, if he weren't much mistaken.

A picture of that foul creature Letchwith sprang to mind. James clamped his teeth together. Won Tel had gathered his intelligence well, and there was now a thick compilation of facts on many aspects of the life of Darius Godwin. His business dealings, his gambling excesses, his sexually perverse practices—and those of Bertram Letchwith and his son, Percival—all were documented in detail. Other names had come to the surface, like grimy scum on heated dirty water. All of these men were known to belong to a certain League of Sporting Gentleman. The interests of the Sports were known only to themselves—and to the women they employed—and now to James.

James also knew the plans Letchwith had for Celine Godwin. He breathed deeply of the clean spring air and reminded himself of his mission—his only mission: to finish the Godwins and claim the Sainsbury gems.

"I do believe it's warmer than I'd expected," Celine said.

James realized he had omitted to suggest a parasol. "We can move into the shade of the arbor," he told her, indicating arches laden with early-blooming climbing yellow roses. "We'll be cooler there." And hidden from the house.

"Those roses are Tillie's Charmers," Celine said. She stepped a little away from him to avoid a broken stone in the path, and her grace made him catch his breath. The girl swayed like a young tree in the breeze.

"Tillie's Charmers," James repeated, never taking

his eyes from her thick, downcast lashes. "I doubt there's a rose as charming as you, Miss Godwin—even a Tillie's Charmer."

The faint blush on her cheek became a furious glow, but a pleased one, he thought. Unless he was much mistaken, this blossoming girl was unaccustomed to compliments.

He must concentrate. And he must calculate very carefully every move he made. His concentration belonged entirely to the purpose he had set himself here today: to begin the steady, and rapid, seduction of Miss Celine Godwin. And the calculation would lie in the area of gauging how far and how fast he could move toward that seduction without frightening her off.

"Ah," she said, withdrawing her hand from his arm. "Here we are. See how thickly the roses grow? One can hardly see an inch of sky between them."

Convenient, James thought. "Yes, indeed." One could also not see the house at all, and anyone inside the house would, in turn, be unable to see into the arbor.

In an unconscious gesture, Celine Godwin brushed the cascade of ringlets upward from her neck. She walked a little in front of James, both elbows stretched up while she held her heavy hair. And as she walked, light before her shone through the flimsy lavender dress, painting the outline of her body as clearly as if she were naked. He drew in a breath. Her hips were rounded, flaring from a very small waist, and with each step they swayed gently, provocatively. The instant jolt he felt was strong—not unexpected, but very, very strong. He tensed his belly, willing the evidence of his erection not to show—unlikely though it was that such a one as Celine Godwin would closely examine *that* region of his body.

"The roses have a heavenly scent," he said. The only heavenly scent he desired was that of her satiny skin—preferably nude and presented for his pleasure in a place of his choosing. For a mad instant he visualized her so in this garden, perhaps on the grass beyond the roses, with the shadows of the nodding blooms dappling her face, her breasts, her belly and legs—and the softly secret place between her thighs.

"There are wood hyacinths here," she said, stopping and stooping to touch delicate sheaths of pink, blue, and white blossoms. "I think I like their scent best of all."

James went down on one knee beside her and bent to inhale the scent she spoke of. Sweet. But it filled the barest part of his senses. Every nerve strained toward the golden girl so close at his side.

"Your island is in the South China Sea?" she said, surprising him.

He raised his face and found her very close. "Yes."

She touched the blossoms he held with one finger. "Paipan. It sounds . . . far away and mysterious." As she leaned over him, the arch of her neck was so near, a few inches or so and he could start a slow brushing with his lips. And a few inches downward would take that brushing to even more enticing areas.

"Is it mysterious?"

He ran his tongue over the dry roof of his mouth. "I suppose it might seem so to a stranger. To me it is home. It has been my home since I was a boy."

"I suppose you will return there soon, Mr. Eagleton. You sound as if you miss it." She dropped to kneel, then sat on her heels with her hands relaxed in her lap. At this proximity, her tawny eyes were the color of fine, warmed brandy.

"James," he said.

"I beg your pardon?"

"Forgive me. I can be abrupt, I'm told." Smiling took effort. "I would be honored if you called me James."

She bowed her head and said, very softly, "James. It's a good name. Strong. It suits you."

Damnation. Damn it to hell. She could have some strange, brain-numbing effect on him if he weren't careful. "Might I presume to call you . . . Celine?"

Peeping at him once more, she smiled. "If you would like."

"Oh, I would like. I'd like it very much. Such a beautiful name. So appropriate."

"Nobody ever said such things to me before." She clapped a hand over her mouth and turned her head away.

Very slowly, very carefully, James slipped a finger and thumb beneath her chin and pulled her face toward him again. "Don't be shy, my golden girl. Many men must have longed to tell you how absolutely lovely you are. You simply aren't the teasing coquette most of them expect and so they are bewildered and, finally, confounded." He made himself laugh lightly. "For that I am grateful because now I can quite overwhelm you with my sweet accolades."

"You make fun of me," she whispered.

"Do I?" Inch by inch, watching her mouth, he brought his own down until his breath mixed with hers. "Do I make fun, golden girl?"

"Y-yes."

"Why do you think so?" With care that cost him dearly, James touched his lips to Celine's in a feather caress that stung his skin exquisitely. She made a small, whimpering sound and her eyes flickered shut.

James drew back and studied her heartbreakingly lovely face. The lines were drawn tense, her lips moist and slightly parted. Tendrils of her hair moved softly, whipped by a tender breeze.

There was no room for the heart in this. "Tell me why you doubt your own beauty."

A sigh raised her breasts, and James clenched his hands on his thighs. Each move must be calculated.

"I am too tall, too plain, and I have wayward ways."

Now he really laughed, tossed back his head and laughed aloud. When he caught his breath, he blinked and saw her wounded expression. "Tall, plain, and wayward, hmm? I think I should dispel these myths forthwith."

"My mama and papa always say I have wayward ways."

God in heaven, how he hated the Godwins. "They do? Why would that be?"

"Because I have a very strong mind and often do things they would not approve of."

He thought for a moment. "Things they would not approve of? Does that mean they don't know what you do?"

She looked abashed. "Sometimes."

"Then how do they know you are wayward?"

"They just do and I just am." Her pointed chin came up.

"Well, you are not too tall and you are most certainly not plain."

"But I am," she insisted, edging closer in her fierce attempt to present her evidence. "And I assure you I'm most terribly tall."

"You reach approximately an inch above my shoulder. I consider that a perfect height for a woman." Particularly for a woman whose length he burned to hold against his own. "And as for your face . . . Well, let me see."

James framed her face with his hands and studied

it seriously. "Finely arched brows. Yes, I like those. And a slightly tilted nose. Mmm. Eyes like those of a wild doe gazing at a pretty scene. Delightful. And your mouth ... Celine, you have an absolutely perfect mouth. May I kiss you? Really kiss you?"

She looked startled, but just as quickly, her attention centered on his own mouth and she leaned ever so slightly even closer.

"Is that yes, Celine?"

She nodded almost imperceptibly, and he took her at her word. Careful not to part his lips, he pressed them to hers, spreading one hand over the nape of her neck, urging up her face and deepening the kiss just a little. Tentatively, her arms went over his shoulders, and he felt the tenor of the contact change. She began kissing him back.

Her ineptness, the hesitancy of the movement of her mouth on his, inflamed James until he longed to tear away her clothes, and his. He longed, most of all, to rip open his breeches and relieve the springing, pulsing ache between his legs.

"Ah, yes," he murmured against her lips. "Exactly like that, gentle one."

She came to her knees against him, innocently pressing more and more insistently. James shifted his hands to her neck and stroked her there, touched his fingertips to the sensitive hollows behind her collarbones, found the delicate spots beneath her ears. Her breathing became faster. He bent to kiss the places his hands had been and saw the rapid rise and fall of her breasts.

Smoothly, he slipped his hands over her shoulders, pushing down the tiny gathered sleeves, then, steeling himself to wait, he surrounded and held her tightly, pressing his hand to the small of her back and the place where her hips began to flare. She was incredibly pliable and supple, shifting beneath his touch as she would shift beneath his body when he drove into her . . .

James felt sweat break out on his brow.

He knew what he would do, what he must do. He would work his way into this girl's life until she thought only of him. He would become the center of everything for her, and then he would ask for her hand in marriage. The Godwins would be easily dazzled by his fortune, and they need not find out who he really was until he was supposedly ready to marry Celine. By that time, he would find a way to convince them he knew nothing of the old crimes against his parents. Then would come the crying off. The Godwins would be left with a ruined daughter who would never provide them, through an advantageous marriage, with the handsome settlement they planned to use as their salvation. And then the final revenge . . . utter destruction of everything the Godwins had worked to accomplish and acquire, and the virtual loss of the one good thing they had produced—their child.

Celine moaned softly against his throat, and he realized that, following his example, she was tentatively kissing his neck. Her hands had found a way beneath his jacket and waistcoat, and she kneaded his chest with feverish intensity.

Unlike Bertram Letchwith and his disgusting son, James had never relished the deflowering of innocents. However, with the offspring of his hated enemies, where it would serve as a weapon against them—even as he enjoyed Celine's admittedly tantalizing charms—the steps would be justified. The trick would be to get her to the point where she could not turn back from him before her parents learned of the danger that approached them.

Raising her chin, he kissed her fully, passionately, holding nothing back this time. He opened her mouth with his lips and felt her shudder. This was a woman only waiting to be awakened. Barely a second passed before she responded, imitating the thrusts of his tongue with hot little forays of her own.

"You are so sweet," he said against her cheek. "So absolutely perfect."

"James" was all she said, and her voice broke on the word.

"Yes, yes, my sweet one." He kissed her again, and as he did so, he used his palms to push the fragile sleeves that were scarcely more than straps from her shoulders and gradually down her arms.

When he could restrain himself no more, he lifted his face from hers and looked down—in time to see her breasts leap free above the sliding bodice. He sucked in a breath. "So beautiful," he whispered, unable to look away from the firm, milk-white mounds tipped by urgent pink buds that tilted up as if begging for his attentions.

"Oh!" Celine let out a cry and tried to cover herself.

James gently held her arms to her sides and continued to feast his eyes upon her. "Too beautiful to be hidden from a man—from the right man—any longer," he told her. Shifting, he cradled her in one arm, urged her back into an arch that offered the perfection of her breasts as a gift to be taken.

He looked into her eyes once more, then bowed to lick a nipple. Her small scream brought his smile and he returned to her mouth for an instant, silencing her. But very soon he touched the tip of his tongue to the nipple again, flicked it back and forth until she wriggled and managed to grab his hair. With more strength than she could have known she possessed, Celine forced his mouth hard against her breast, and he obliged by sucking her nipple deep into his mouth, by biting very gently that turgid bud.

"James," she gasped. "Oh, James."

Smiling yet again, he moved to the other breast and worked diligently, producing soft little shrieks of pleasure even as he used his fingers on the nipple he had abandoned.

"I feel . . . I feel so hot inside," she panted. "I ache, James. There is such . . . such sensation. Burning, and—" She became suddenly rigid.

He lifted his mouth a fraction but could not bring himself to leave the voluptuous flesh that caused his cock to bruise itself as it surged and surged against the confines of his clothes.

When she remained silent he asked, "You burn, my golden one? A good burning?"

"I am . . . Oh, dear, I am . . . I can't be."

"Tell me," he coaxed her.

"I think I am wet. How can that be? And there is the oddest of . . . sensations in a . . . certain part of me." Her voice rose and weakened with every word.

James smiled again and returned to suckling her. While she pushed herself helplessly against him, he slipped a hand beneath her skirt and ran his palm up her leg, over a silk stocking, until he reached incredibly soft skin above.

She became still. "James! What are you doing?"

He must be careful here. "Just a small thing to relieve the burning, my sweet one," he told her and deftly tucked his hand around the springy bush of hair at the apex of her thighs.

"Oh, oh, no, James. Oh!"

He delved into the wetness that had so amazed her. Delved and parted the fattened, completely feminine folds that shielded that tiny woman's bulb that could bring her to a place she had never dreamed of.

"Oh! Oh, James!"

He raised his head and listened, but heard no approaching footsteps. Watching her heaving breasts, her pink tongue darting over moist lips, James rubbed that awakened nub until Celine ground against him of her own volition. She jarred down on his hand, gritting her teeth, mindlessly tossing her head.

And his own lips parted, drew back with the exultation of watching what he wrought in her. Wanting to see that other part of her aroused body reach its release, he pushed up her skirt until it bunched around her pale, utterly perfectly shaped hips. Her thighs jerked and her wetness slicked his fingers. She was lost, carried away on the sea of wanting he had created. The tops of the embroidered lavender silk stockings had worked down to rest almost at her knees.

James bent over her, biting at her nipples once more, licking the fullness of her breasts, before driving her, with a last strong stroke, to her shuddering climax.

"Oh" was all she whispered before sagging in his arms.

James gathered her close, held her while her eyes remained closed, while his own breathing calmed . . . but not the jabbing need in his crotch. From here on he must tread like a man in a house made of spun glass. He had her where he wanted her. But one wrong move and his carefully constructed trap could shatter.

"Come, my dear," he said into her ear. "Your companion may come looking for you, and we wouldn't want her to find you like this, would we?"

Her eyes flew open and gradually focused, "Oh, dear."

"Oh, dear, indeed." Gently, he pulled up her stockings and eased down her skirts. "We have found something very special, but there are those who would take that from us. Do you understand me, Celine?"

Her eyes were wide—and horrified. "Yes. I understand."

Something in her disquieted him. "I hope you do, because if you want us to share these wonderful moments again, you must do as I tell you."

Then she almost scrambled away. He caught her as she would have run, her breasts still exposed, back toward the path. Instead, James pulled her down beside him once more and smiled. He kissed her mouth lightly while allowing his thumbs to pass, very delicately back and forth over her nipples. "Hush, golden girl," he told her. "Hush. You have had a shock in this new and wonderful experience. You will become accustomed to it."

Celine didn't answer. She held very still while he covered her with the bodice once more and put the sleeves back where they belonged.

"Men are not susceptible to it, are they?" she asked abruptly.

James frowned, perplexed. "Susceptible?" He stood, drawing her up with him.

"To the sensations that would cause them to ... fall?"

"To fall." He shook his head. Then her meaning became clear and he smiled. "The sensations. Of course. I understand what you mean. We do have them but not in quite the same way, I think."

"You are able to remain in control."

She sounded so forlorn that he tried to gather her against him.

Celine stepped firmly away. "David will be so disappointed in me."

James gaped. "*David?* Who is David?"

Her eyes filled with tears. "He is an old friend of

mine. He is also a clergyman. He will be disappointed that I have fallen. But perhaps it isn't too late for me to be saved."

The impact of what she was saying hit James forcefully. "Now, see here—"

"No. No, I must go and send a message to David. And then I'll return to Dorset. Otherwise the only alternative will be a nunnery."

"A nunnery? Bloody hell." James didn't bother to apologize for his language. "Nunnery, my foot. You'll stay right here and you'll not mention a word of what has passed between us, do you understand?"

She stared at him. "I must go into the house."

"You must answer me."

"Why? You will soon tire of my demands upon you. Oh, dear." She passed the back of a hand over her brow. "I had no idea exactly how powerful the sensations were. No wonder they are so hard to cure."

"They aren't going to be cured, dammit!" James yanked her against his chest and glared down into her eyes. Celine stared back and he saw dull resignation in her face. There was only one thing for it; he must take a wild but necessary step, and take it now.

"Celine."

"Yes."

"I'm going to tell you something and I want you to promise you won't share it with anyone else until I tell you the time is right."

"I promise," she said lifelessly.

"Very well." He swallowed. "What I have discovered with you is entirely new. I'm not sure what it means but it is very important."

Slowly, the darkness in her eyes faded. "It is?"

"Yes. What just happened, happened between you and a man who has never known such passion before. I believe I am somehow deeply in need of you and there is to be no more talk of nunneries."

"But—"

He held up a hand to silence her. "No more questions. We must wait and see what happens. Meanwhile, not a soul is to learn of what has transpired between us. Can you promise me that, too?"

"The falling doesn't matter?"

"Absolutely normal sensation, my dear. Absolutely. You enjoyed it, didn't you?"

She nodded, her eyes downcast yet again.

"And you promise you won't tell anyone?"

"Yes, James."

"Good. Then I want you to stop worrying about it. Just leave all this in my hands." He winced. God give him patience.

"Very well," she said, entirely too primly.

"My word!" Inspiration didn't arrive a moment too soon. "I almost forgot the message I was asked to give you."

She waited, her arms crossed tightly beneath her breasts, and achieved a quite different effect from the one she undoubtedly now desired.

James willed his body to be still and his brain to function lucidly. "On my way way here I happened to run into the Marquess of Casterbridge."

She frowned.

"You remember. The Casterbridge that . . . Miss Prentergast mentioned him."

"Oh, yes. The one having the marvelous fete."

"I expect you'd like to go."

She inclined her head, and a spark of animation returned to her face. "I'm not nearly important enough to be invited."

"Oh, I assure you, Celine, that you have far too low an opinion of yourself. Why, the reason the marquess stopped me was because I'd mentioned my intention to seek you out. He asked if I'd tell you your invitation to the fete had become mixed up with other papers on his secretary's desk. It'll be out shortly—by tomorrow, I'm certain." Yes, he was very certain, he'd see to it personally. "Meanwhile, Casterbridge begged me to invite you in person."

"He did?"

"He most certainly did."

The pieces of his plan were beginning to fall nicely into place.

Chapter 6

O h, but there really was *too* much to do! Patience,
Celine told herself, she must have patience.

Freda, a maid who had been part of the Godwin
household for as long as Celine remembered, knelt
beside her. "Turn a bit," the maid mumbled around
the pins held between her lips.

Obediently, Celine shuffled a step to the right.
"How does the ruffle look?" A gathered length of
Belgian lace removed from another dress was being
added to the hem of Isabel Prentergast's pink gown.

"Other way." Freda thudded awkwardly on hands
and knees. Plump as a younger woman, she had become overly bulky in middle years.

"How does it look?" Celine repeated. She must finish here and hasten to Bond Street to attempt some
transactions she had in mind.

Freda made a senseless noise. Red-faced and puffing, wisps of her wiry gray hair springing free of its
pins, she waved Celine to turn more.

This bedchamber would depress a less determined
spirit than Celine. Plum-colored bed curtains, plum-
colored quilt, worn plum-colored upholstery on
chairs near the soot-blackened fireplace, and horrible
plum-colored carpet on the wooden floor. Dispiriting
indeed. Why, oh why, were Mama and Papa so . . .

Why did they neglect everything so? Celine fastened her attention on sunshine streaming between faded plum-colored velvet draperies—on the dust motes floating in that sunshine—and willed her mind to be quiet.

Her spirit was exceedingly determined. Everything about her was exceedingly determined, and she must be gone. Now! "How much longer, Freda?" Another note had arrived from David Talbot, and in his gentle way, he'd conveyed his concern over shortage of funds.

"I reckon as how you should've made that fancy modiste put her own mistakes right," Freda grumbled from the floor, evidently finally relieved of the pins. "Then you wouldn't be rushing a poor old body the way you are."

Celine almost squealed with frustration. "If I hadn't known you could do a better job, I most certainly would have insisted she did." Celine pursed her lips. Surely she could be forgiven a few minor fabrications since they were in so good a cause. David would have the money he needed. Celine would see to it, but not if she couldn't get out of this dismal room, into that clear sunlight outside and to the bustle of Bond Street.

"Hmm." Freda sounded slightly mollified. "Never heard the like. Making a beautiful gown like this too short. Other way."

Celine revolved in the opposite direction and heard the door open. In the dressing table mirror she saw Lettie come into the room. Their eyes met and Celine raised her brows in question. Every day she expected to hear that her parents' arrival in London was imminent. Lettie shook her head, put a linen-draped bundle on the bed, and stood with her hands behind her back.

"How are we doing, Freda?" Lettie asked.

"I was telling Miss Celine as how she ought to dismiss this fancy modiste she's so fond of," Freda said without preamble. "Can you imagine? She makes a gown three inches too short, but she's so high-flown and impressed with herself that she's got our Miss Celine afraid to complain."

Lettie shook her head. "That's the way it is in London at this time of year." She glowered at Celine, who smiled angelically.

"This isn't my first time in London, Lettie. I've been coming with the dragon . . . sorry, I'm sure . . . with Mrs. Godwin since she was still Miss Mary Detterling. I know a fair amount about London, I can tell you."

"Of course," Lettie said, sounding suitably chastised.

Celine had been reminded, many times, that the Curzon Street house had been the dowry Mama brought into her marriage with Papa.

"If I was you I'd ask for a reduction on my account," Freda said, her voice rising with her umbrage. "That green dress she made for the theater is a shameful thing."

"It's pretty," Celine said defensively, catching Lettie's eye again and looking immediately at the bundle on the bed.

"Pretty on a body shaped like a pole," Freda said, bending to her task once more. "If we didn't know better, I'd have said the foolish biddy thought she was making it for someone else."

Celine sent another desperate stare in Lettie's direction. Lettie gave one of her small I-told-you-this-was-a-mistake smiles.

"That dress weren't never made for a young lady with your fine curves, I can tell you," Freda continued. "Some parts of a woman's body were given her by God to be admired. God intended you to be admired a great deal, Miss Celine."

Celine flushed and looked down at the bodice of the pink satin. She and Lettie had already, very carefully, removed the silver roses from the neckline. Now it looked a trifle plain and revealed far too much of what Freda alluded to.

"Perhaps . . ." Lettie said, swaying, her head tilted thoughtfully. "Perhaps the merest hint of a lace edge would . . . *add* something to the neck?"

Freda made an impatient noise. "Can't think why. She'll be the toast of this fancy fete she's going to. There's many a girl would give her eyes to look the way Miss Celine does in this dress."

"I agree," Lettie said, smiling and looking quickly away. "But it could be that there's a trifle too much to look *at*, d'you think Freda?"

Celine felt warmer. Unwillingly, she recalled some of the things Mr. Eagleton had said—and done—to her in the garden. *So beautiful.* And she'd been entirely exposed to his eyes . . . his hands . . . *Too beautiful to be hidden from a man—from the right man—any longer.* The almost painful aching she'd felt then swept over her again, as it had too many times since that afternoon. Yesterday morning a single yellow rose had been delivered. This morning there had been two. No card had arrived with either token. Baity had informed Celine that the bearer of the roses had been an oddly foreign-looking—fierce-looking, in fact—gentleman in strange garb. When Celine asked if this person might be Eastern, Baity confided that he "wouldn't be at all surprised," and Celine concluded that this must be some member of Mr. Eagleton's reportedly unusual household.

"I wouldn't do a thing to the neck if I was you, Miss Celine," Freda said. "Like I've said, there's plenty—"

"We'll add lace at the neck," Celine said, more abruptly than she intended.

Freda sniffed. "Whatever you say. It'll not be of this piece though, miss. There's not enough."

"I'll find ... I'll speak to the modiste about purchasing something," Celine said, keeping her gaze averted from Lettie's. "I must be quick, Freda. It will be necessary for me to speak with her at once in case the perfect thing is not readily available."

"We can't hurry these things," Freda said, sounding huffy. "If only we had just the right ornaments, we could catch up the satin here and there at the hem—over the lace. Of course, it would make the dress look different, and you probably wouldn't—"

"Exactly!" Celine clapped her hands. "Freda, you're a wonder! What do you think we should use?" She ignored the small noise Lettie made.

"Well, miss, I'm sure I don't know."

"Don't give it another thought. Make the necessary allowances and I'll, er, I'll make a stop at the appropriate establishment and purchase something just exactly right."

Freda puffed up visibly. "Something a little glittery, perhaps." She sat back on her heels and pushed at the springy hair around her face. "We could use the same at the neck ... if you think you'd like it, of course."

"Exactly! A wonderful idea," Celine agreed, genuinely pleased with the notion. "And now, if you've done everything you—"

"Not quite." Freda bent to her task once more and began gathering the hem into loops above the broad lace pinned beneath.

Celine turned up her palms and looked desperately at Lettie, who hadn't moved from her station near the bed. "I'm sure it would be better to await the final adjustments until we have all the necessary materials."

Lettie raised her shoulders and stared steadily ahead. No help there.

"Freda, please help me out of this thing." She closed her mouth. She needed to get to Bond Street in time to keep an appointment with a modiste who, after buying some discarded trimmings and other articles Celine had offered the day before, had expressed condescending interest in acquiring further "superior" items. The woman had made certain it was understood that she wouldn't pay a penny more than the goods were worth and that she didn't expect them to be worth very much. Celine hadn't failed to see the calculating light in the woman's eyes and was ready to be a more forceful bargainer today. "Freda, please. I need to get to the shops in time for . . ."

"In time for what, Miss?" Freda asked.

Celine's temper was almost entirely exhausted. "In time to select the things you say you want, of course." She hoped Freda wouldn't notice the scrap of green silk escaping from the draped heap on the bed and recognize it as part of the dress Celine had worn to the theater—and ask why the gown was there.

"I'll go for you," Freda said expansively. "I'd be happy to talk to that modiste—"

"No! No, thank you, Freda." This deception was too tiring. "You're very sweet, but I do think I should choose what I want myself. Freda, dear, could we please finish this later?"

"Later you're off to that rout—in that yellow dress. And, by the way, that was too short, too, remember? I never, it does tempt a body to say nasty things."

"Yes." Celine shot Lettie a furious glance. "Well, we dealt very nicely with the yellow muslin—or rather *you* dealt nicely with it. I did think the slip trimmed at the bottom with gold pleating a splendid idea. Such

a lovely complement to the decoration on the bodice."
She only hoped the addition would be enough to disguise Miss Prentergast's rather distinctive gown.

"Seemed a natural thing to me," Freda said, but her pleasure at the positive attention showed clearly.

"You are truly clever with these problems, Freda." Please, let there be a way to ensure that the maid didn't say too much about all this to Mama when she finally arrived in London. "And now I must go—or I won't be back from Bond Street in time to prepare for the rout."

At last Freda clambered laboriously to her feet and loosened the tapes on the pink satin. With infuriatingly slow care, she eased the garment over Celine's head and spread it on the bed. Straightening, she looked down at the linen-draped dress beside the pink.

Clutching the folds of her chemise, Celine leaped between Freda and the bed. "Thank you, dear Freda," she said and dropped a kiss on a round, red cheek. "You must be tired. Have a cup of tea and a nice rest."

"Rest?" Freda appeared puzzled. "I've got my duties to attend to."

"Yes, yes. Of course you do. But I think there are times when you deserve extra recognition for your, er, *talents*. And your loyal service." Celine turned to Lettie. "Don't you agree?"

"Oh, *exactly*." Lettie's thinned lips and raised chin conveyed her disapproval. "I'll attend Miss Celine now, Freda," she said.

"You don't want me to help you dress, miss?"

"Thank you, Freda. Lettie will help me. I'll let you know when the other goods we need for the dress are delivered."

Holding her breath, Celine kept a pleasant smile in place until Freda, darting curious glances over her shoulder, left the room.

"You'll march yourself into a pretty muddle if you

aren't careful, young lady," Lettie said. "Deception always leads to downfall, mark my words."

"You sound like David," Celine said before she could stop herself. "I mean you sound ... Oooh, I don't know what I mean. I absolutely must get dressed and go shopping."

"Shopping? Is that what you call it?"

"I will not argue with you, Lettie. I am quite set on what I intend to do. I should wear something that won't draw attention to my person."

Lettie made a muffled sound.

"And what does *that* mean?" Celine asked.

"Nothing. It doesn't mean a thing. Have you thought more about who may have sent the roses?"

Lettie could be infuriatingly persistent. "No. I told you I think it's probably someone playing a trick on me." She had steadfastly insisted that she had no idea who her admirer might be.

He'd said he might be deeply in need of her.

Celine shivered. How could he be? He didn't know her and certainly would not even like her if he discovered what a duplicitous person she was.

"Are you cold?" Lettie asked, sounding solicitous.

"No."

"You shivered."

"No matter."

Lettie did not appear convinced. "Very well. But I worry about you." Concern softened her dark eyes. "Isn't it wonderful that you're to attend the Casterbridge fete?"

"Yes. Wonderful." In fact it was so exciting that every time she thought of the event she could scarcely breathe. But at the moment there were other affairs to attend to. "I'll put on my lavender dress. No one will notice me in that."

"We should be very grateful for all these invitations that have started to arrive."

"Why—" The lavender muslin. Soft grass and wood hyacinth . . . and Mr. James Eagleton . . . No, not the lavender muslin.

"We need plenty of opportunities to bring you to the attention of eligible men. We must concentrate on finding agreeable suitors, Celine—suitors who will make your parents forget that nasty Letchwith man."

"Yes." James Eagleton had seemed so sincere in his declaration, but, as David had warned, the wrong kind of man invariably pressured a young female into behavior that suited him, yet was potentially dangerous to her—to her honor. And such men frequently used pretty words to muddle a girl's sense of decorum. David did know so many useful things.

"What did Mr. Eagleton think of our flowers?"

Celine jumped. "Flowers?"

"In the garden? When you took your walk the other afternoon. You did talk about the flowers, didn't you? I hope you took the trouble to point out some of our more beautiful species."

"I really don't remember. But Mr. Eagleton was most congenial." Celine smoothed her hair. "I think I'll wear my blue walking dress. The dark blue."

"You really are in a hurry, aren't you?"

"Yes, I am," Celine said crossly. "I'll get the dress myself, since all you seem to want to do is stand with your hands behind your back asking ridiculous questions."

"I'll get the dress," Lettie said, and swept an arm forward. In her hand she held three yellow roses. "Another gift from your mystery admirer. I wonder who he can be."

Celine's heart made a mighty leap and she spread a hand over her breast.

"Baity was given a message by the person who delivered these."

"He was?" Celine said faintly. Her legs felt quite weak.

"Yes. The message was . . ." Lettie frowned. "Now, let me make sure I remember this exactly."

Celine would not show how desperately she wanted the message remembered . . . *exactly*. She fussed with the cover over the green dress.

"Yes, I think I have it. 'Charmers indeed'—at least, that seems the way it began."

"Oh, do hurry, Lettie," Celine snapped.

Lettie smiled. "Yes, I've got it right. 'Charmers, indeed.' That's what the man told Baity to tell you. 'But such charmers pale beside the beauty you showed me.' That was the whole message," Lettie finished.

"Oh!" Celine dropped abruptly to sit on the stool near her dressing table. Her legs, her whole body, trembled. He was ungentlemanly enough to remind her of the most embarrassing moment . . . the most fascinating, but still the most embarrassing moment of her life.

"What could this person have meant by his message?"

Celine looked slowly into Lettie's shrewd eyes and knew that her secret was least partially guessed.

"You're blushing, Celine. Is there something you'd like to talk to me about?"

"Nothing. We'll send Baity for a cab. It'll be better not to take our own carriage."

"You're right." Smiling, Lettie handed Celine the roses. "Tillie's Charmers. Just like the roses in the arbor. Isn't that a coincidence?"

"Yes." Celine bent her head and pretended to inhale the sweet fragrance. "Truly, it is a coincidence."

"Oh, and I almost forgot. The man said one more thing. He said you should not forget the most important thing he told you."

Chapter 7

"**D**ammit, man, we've lost them."

"Not so, Mr. Eagleton," Won Tel said, his face close to the coach window. "There is a degree of caution necessary in these matters and it is being observed. Nothing more."

James scanned the throng swarming about them. "This damnable horde is blocking us in." He could no longer be certain that the cab they'd followed from Curzon Street, the one carrying Celine Godwin and her companion, was still in front.

"Be calm, my friend." Won Tel sat, upright and alert, on the edge of his seat. You are not adjusting well to this different life."

James glowered. "Sometimes you are too ready with your opinions. I am merely anxious to complete this business. I want to retrieve what is mine and get out of this hellhole."

"There are those who consider London the most civilized place in the world."

Crossing his arms, James stared morosely through the window at the hustling mass of humanity. Even spring sunshine failed to lessen the pallid appearance of the faces. "No doubt those who call this place civilized have never been elsewhere. Are you certain this intrigue of yours with the girl is not a work of your imagination?"

Won Tel only smiled.

"Why would she behave so strangely? And what—"

"It has been on your instruction that I've followed the young lady everywhere, you'll remember. I've merely told you what I saw in Bond Street yesterday. And now, since we are clearly headed for Bond Street again, you may make your own deductions."

The coach swayed and jarred, its wheels grinding slowly over uneven cobbled streets. A sharp turn rocked James, and he scowled afresh. "Bond Street it is," he said darkly, seeing the sign. "Tell the coachman we'll go on foot the moment it seems prudent."

"He already knows."

James bowed his head. "Of course he does." Won Tel invariably was two steps ahead. "Does he also know how to appear in the middle of this madness at the exact moment we require him again?"

"Leave these matters in my hands," Won Tel said with a small smile. He was dressed as usual—if such dress could ever be usual—in his blue tunic, black pantaloons, and gleaming boots, with his skullcap in place. He gave another enigmatic smile. "Take heart, my friend. I'm certain this trip will prove a valuable annoyance. It has been my experience that the knowledge of another's secrets may be very useful in binding that person to oneself. I believe Miss Godwin has a secret or two she'd prefer to keep hidden."

James chuckled. "How glad I am that you are my friend rather than my foe. Is there fresh news of the Godwins?"

"They continue to be closeted in Knighthead. Evidently the man Letchwith and his son visited but left again and are even now expected back in Town. I'm led to believe the Godwins cannot be too far behind."

"Then there is no time to waste." James shifted forward in his seat. "I have much to accomplish before they arrive." He had already accomplished a most satisfactory start with Celine. His thighs tensed, and other parts of him. Most satisfactory, and a definite inducement to pursue his somewhat altered strategy as quickly as possible.

Won Tel's voice intruded on his musings. "Do you plan to marry this girl?"

James regarded his companion narrowly. "Why would you think I had such a plan?"

"It would appear a natural deduction."

"Why?"

Won Tel looked steadily back at James. "You are a man of honor. Hard, yes, but ... honorable. Since you pursue this female with a single-mindedness that suggests you intend to entirely possess her, the assumption that you intend to ask for her hand is—"

"*Don't* guess at my intentions." The man was right, damn his eyes. Deflowering innocent girls had never been a pastime in which James indulged. His tastes leaned in the direction of worldly women who understood the needs of hot-blooded and passionate men. "I merely intend to use Miss Godwin as a means to gain entrance to Knighthead. If she and her parents come to view me as a potential suitor, they will welcome my presence in their home—particularly since we will be neighbors."

"The Season is far from over," Won Tel said. "Your patience is already thin. How will you contain yourself until summer?"

How indeed. "Don't concern yourself with my self-control."

"Darius Godwin and his wife have made an arrangement with Letchwith. With Letchwith's arrival, you will soon have competition for the fair Celine's company."

"She *is* very fair," he murmured to himself. "You say this man is not ... He is perhaps unlikely to appeal to a young female?"

"He is close to sixty. He is short, quite grossly obese, and exceedingly plain. I believe devilish ugly with a small, wet mouth over which he constantly passes his tongue was how he was described to me. Also there was mention that he and his son—in their capacity as members of this club of theirs—are constantly on the hunt for fresh young virgins whose absence will not be mourned by any family. James ..." Won Tel leaned forward, an intensely serious set to his features. "I believe the Letchwiths intend to make Miss Godwin a part of their unholy practices."

James crossed his arms over his chest. "That cannot be my concern." She was beautiful. Innocent. "Surely it must be time to get on with this charade." Innocent, but so ready for the careful guidance of a man who could make her what she was intended to be—his able partner in the fleshly delights.

"It is also rumored that the removal of the Letchwiths would be an economic catastrophe among the more imaginative doxies in London."

James tried not to think about Celine's wide eyes. "All levels of society must be maintained—even the lowest. When in God's name are we going to get on with this matter?"

"The coachman will knock when the ladies leave their cab."

He needed a woman, James decided. He needed to spill the pent-up juices that threatened to muddle his thoughts with someone who would make him forget Celine Godwin's pale and perfect body. The Lady Anastasie had a certain appeal. Willing and anything but innocent. He'd lay odds she knew a thousand little tricks designed to draw a man to ecstatic release. He shifted in his seat. It wasn't Lady Anastasie's practiced ministrations he wanted. Celine Godwin's legs above the lace stockings had been so smooth, so soft, so untouched. He'd been the first man to touch her, of that he had no doubt. And, as her thighs had fallen helplessly apart, he'd been the first man to touch those plump, moist women's parts and find that swelling little spot that had responded to his probing fingers.

His cock leaped.

He'd played her breasts, her hardened nipples, like instruments intended only for his use. And she'd keened her pleasure even as she'd succumbed with languid greed to his ministrations.

She was obsessing him, possessing his mind when it needed to be clear.

"Liam may become hard to control," Won Tel said suddenly.

James looked at him sharply. "Liam always follows my wishes."

"She saw me with the roses."

"But you didn't tell her their purpose."

"You underestimate our little Chinese dragon. She asked to accompany me to deliver the gift 'to your love,' as she put it."

James cursed loudly. "And you told her I have no love? You told her to keep her attentions on the kitchens and the pigs, or whatever her latest mischief is?" Liam must be protected, for his sake and for her own. "You did make it plain that she has no part in our business here?"

"I made it plain. But I have not seen her since early this morning and I cannot be sure where she is."

"And you wait until now to tell me?" James roared. "What are you telling me? What do you think she may be about?"

Won Tel appeared unusually discomforted. "It seems possible that she guesses your interest in a particular woman. You must admit, gifts like the roses are not something she's seen you employ before in such situations. She asked if the woman was worthy of you."

"Saints preserve us." James pounded a fist against his thigh. "Did you tell her this is none of her affair?"

"Yes. But she persisted. And when I refused to give her an answer, she said my silence was answer enough. She also said that no colorless English miss would have the luxury of tormenting a man too good for any woman."

"Fustian!" James rolled his eyes. "There must be no question of Liam involving herself in this."

Won Tel became intent on the scene beyond the window.

"She didn't know where we were going today?"

"I didn't tell her."

"And no one else did?"

"I assume not. Unfortunately, Liam has a way of getting the information she requires."

James grunted. "She would not be able to get this information. I'll speak to her later."

A sharp rap came at the peephole behind the coachman's box. The coach ground to a halt.

"At last." James reached for the door handle, only to feel Won Tel's restraining hand on his wrist. "Come on, man. They must be alighting."

"Patience."

The peephole slid open and the coachman's ruddy face appeared. "The parties are leaving their cab, Mr. Eagleton. You'd best be quick now."

Shaking off Won Tel's hand, James leaped from the coach and searched in all directions.

"All of London must have descended upon this street today," he said to Won Tel, who already stood beside him. "Where . . . There! There they are."

Celine Godwin wore a chip bonnet decorated with

blue flowers and tied at one ear with blue ribbons. The honey-gold curls at her nape bounced as she walked. And she walked very quickly, as did Miss Fisher, who was again dressed in black taffeta. Celine's dress was of deep blue material that molded to her legs as she hurried along. Each woman carried several parcels.

James let out an exasperated sigh. "They are shopping, my dear friend. Nothing more."

Won Tel pulled him close to the buildings. "Watch and wait. And be ready to move quickly."

All about them swirled the motley collection that was London as the Season swung into session. Servants on errands for their masters and mistresses scurried about their missions with single-minded determination. The smell of hot eel and mutton pies drifted, savory but unappealing to James. He heard the pieman's cry of " 'Ere they are! 'Ot pies! Penny apiece!" The next scent was more subtle and the man who carried a keg by a leather strap called, "Peppermint water! Halfpenny a glass!"

"Damn, Won Tel," James said through his teeth. "This is madness. Keep your eye on those women."

"Fear not," Won Tel responded.

James waved aside a crone who thrust a bunch of dried lavender in his face and whispered hoarsely, "For good luck, your lordship. Never turn away a gypsy's good luck."

James spared a glance for the woman's seamed, brown face beneath a grimy kerchief, for her dark, crafty eyes, and hooked a coin from his pocket. This he thrust into her hand even as he ducked away in pursuit of the flying blue skirts of his quarry.

He no longer felt Won Tel at his shoulder and glanced back, searching for his cohort. There was no sign of him and James pressed on, to be confronted by a band of young dandies, arm in arm, laughing raucously and intent on knocking all in their path into the gutter.

Exasperated, James paused near a window, keeping an eye on those flashes of blue.

The dandies, strutting, their corsets producing unnaturally pinched waists and puffed-pigeon chests, their necks stretched by impossibly high, starched neckcloths, peered down through monocles at passing females and tossed insulting comments: "One wonders that a fella isn't moved to run screamin' from that cow face." "A pity its mother—if it had a mother—failed to drown it with the rest of the litter."

James made fists. This was not his affair. Young bloods considered such nonsense part of their passage to manhood—not that they would do that state much justice when they arrived there.

"Oh!" A servant girl of not more than fifteen shrieked, and James saw that the lanky fop nearest to him had speared the little female's petticoat with his walking stick. While his companions hooted and slapped backs, the man pranced about, pretending difficulty in undoing his mischief.

James felt an old and well-known calm slipping around his mind. With one deft move, he slid his right hand beneath his left sleeve and removed the stiletto he'd carried since the day Won Tel had presented him with the gift. In the whirl of noise and the crush of coming and going, no one saw a flash of sunlight on a sliver of polished steel. But many saw the sudden outpouring of sawdust from a gash in the humiliated dandy's padded calf.

Smiling, James whisked his knife back into its sheath and swung his shoulders to sidestep the gathering crowd of laughing spectators. Even the girl, now free of her tormentor, giggled into her cupped hands.

Won Tel appeared, gliding swiftly toward James.

Flared nostrils were the single sign that he was irritated. "Is your entertainment finished, Mr. Eagleton?"

James ignored the question. "Where is Miss Godwin?"

"You may be grateful that I, at least, am not easily diverted." Won Tel inclined his head. "The next alley. Keep out of sight and you'll see them soon enough. They should not see you. I will be close." With that he mingled with a cluster of people around a barrel organ. James saw him drop a coin into a tin cup held by a capering monkey before seeming to melt without trace into the melee.

Alley? James crossed the narrow, dark passageway and stepped into a shop doorway where he could watch the entrance to the alley Won Tel had indicated. Why would two very respectable and defenseless women risk leaving the comparative safety of a busy street and enter a place where danger could very well lurk?

He had just decided to ignore his servant's warning to remain out of sight if he felt the ladies were in any peril at all, when the women appeared and out of instinct, he flattened himself against a window.

They came in his direction.

". . . very foolish," Celine was saying as she drew level with the doorway. "She needn't think I'll give her another chance. There are plenty who'll be delighted to get their hands on what I'm offering."

The Fisher woman said something James couldn't hear. Celine scowled and said: "They aren't going to catch me. I'll keep my dealings well disguised . . ." She walked beyond his hearing.

"Catch?" James muttered. "Dealings?" Bloody hell, was the girl of the same evil cloth as her scheming parents? What manner of wrongdoing could she be about?

He waited another second before leaving the safety of the doorway ... and immediately stepped back again. Celine and her companion stood only feet away, apparently arguing fiercely.

James tilted his top hat lower over his eyes and waited—and became aware of a glimpse of strikingly brilliant emerald-green—and the shimmer of gold embroidery—and a matching golden glitter in shiny black hair.

Liam!

He left the doorway once more. Better to risk being seen by Celine and remove Liam from the scene than to contemplate endless meddling in his affairs.

Won Tel appeared at his elbow once more. "You saw her?"

"Liam? Yes. Damn her." He saw with relief that Celine and Miss Fisher had moved on. "Where is she now?" Ever fleet of foot, Liam had slipped from sight.

"Not far away," Won Tel said with grim conviction. "Let us hurry about our business and return to Grosvenor Square. Perhaps I should not have bothered you with this matter."

"You should most definitely have informed me," James assured him. "The girl may be about to show me an unexpected boon."

"How so?" Won Tel remained a pace behind, and soon the women turned rapidly to enter another dim alleyway.

"If—as I suspect—she is up to some mischief, I shall discover it and use it as a further weapon against her parents. Most eligible men—even, perhaps, Letchwith—would cut a girl of questionable character." He smiled at Won Tel. "However, an understanding man like myself might be persuaded to overlook a little indiscretion and step in to rescue the poor chit before she was consigned to the shelf—at least until she's served my purpose."

"Admirable," Won Tel murmured and added, in an even lower voice, "Liam is on the other side of the alley."

James looked sharply ahead, in time to see Liam, head bowed, drift behind a strolling couple. He went to follow, but pulled back. Celine and Miss Fisher were once again in sight. James made no attempt to hide. The two women were talking and laughing together and so intent on some shared delight that they noticed no one.

"Ah," James said quietly, watching the two continue along Bond Street. "I think I begin to see what caught your interest, Won Tel."

"I knew you would. Odd, don't you agree?"

"Odd, indeed. Our innocent little miss is up to no good. Back there she passed by close enough for me to overhear her speaking of not getting caught and of some sort of dealings. If I hadn't been so anxious to dispatch this afternoon's matter I would have found it unusual that two women should be burdened with packages *before* they went shopping."

"Quite so," Won Tel agreed. "Yesterday, I myself did not notice this fact immediately. As you see, they now have only one large bundle. There were several before their last stop."

James made up his mind. "Liam will do no more than watch our progress." He wished he completely believed what he said. "I intend to turn this little escapade to my advantage. The sooner we expedite matters, the better. Stay out of sight until I am finished."

With that, and ignoring occasional glimpses of Liam's distinctive tunic, James abandoned stealthy pursuit for his customary confident stride.

He hadn't far to go. Sunlight brightened the entrance to yet another alley, and the women, predictably, popped into the opening.

Sighting a small flower girl, James smiled a tight smile of satisfaction.

"Do buy a bunch, sir," the child said. "I'm a poor girl, sir. Buy a bunch."

She was, if he were to guess, not more than eight. He took a sixpence from his waistcoat pocket, selected a bunch of violets, and gave the young seller the coin. "There you are, little one."

"Oooh, a sixpence!" Wide-eyed, she stared from James to the money. "I ain't never 'ad a sixpence before. Thank you, sir. *Thank* you!"

He walked on, into the alley. In Paipan the only poor were those who chose, out of indolence, to be so. He preferred not to contemplate the numbers of London's homeless, particularly the children, who were helpless to escape their plight in this city.

Was Celine selling stolen goods? Did the despicable Godwins keep their own daughter so strapped for funds that she was forced to steal from them, perhaps, and then sell to whatever scurrilous fence she could find?

The only door in the wall to his right stood open and he peered cautiously into a gloomy interior. The clear sound of Celine's voice reached him: "No, it's not nearly enough and you know as much. You are trying to take advantage of me, mademoiselle, and it simply will not do. Three times what you offer is my selling price. I won't take a penny less."

"*Mon Dieu!*" came an unconvincing "French" voice. "*C'est impossible a faire.*"

"Nonsense," Celine responded promptly. "It most certainly *can* be done—if not by you, then by someone with more vision. Come along, Lettie."

James leaned against the wall and waited, twirling

the bunch of violets. His mission began to promise some entertaining diversions.

"All right, all right," a flat cockney voice said resignedly. " 'Alf as much again, then."

James smiled at the "Frenchwoman's" transformation.

"Not enough," Celine's voice rang out.

"You drive a 'ard bargain and no mistake. A guinea more and that's me last and final offer. Take it or leave it."

"Done!" Celine announced.

"I'm sure fair trade in goods will please you," the buyer said.

"Trade in goods will certainly *not* please me," Celine retorted. "I will take cash, if you please."

An audible sigh reached James. "Oh, very well, then. Come on through into the shop. It don't do to 'ave the likes of you seen comin' and goin' through the back door."

James swept off his hat and stuck his head inside the door in time to see Celine part with a pale green dress. He frowned. The same dress she'd worn on the night of their first meeting, if he was not much mistaken.

The dress was set carefully amid heaps of fabric on what appeared to be some sort of worktable, and a rotund woman in black bombazine trimmed with billowing flounces of white lace waved her visitors before her toward a door.

A modiste's workroom behind a ladies' fashion establishment, James decided, retreating. The girl had obviously been selling her own clothes. Most interesting. He set off at a brisk pace and stationed himself at a vantage point near the door to the shop. An element of surprise could be a great ally, and Miss Celine Godwin was about to be exceedingly surprised.

His wait was short. Within minutes, the door opened and Celine, a gleeful smile on her pretty lips, emerged with Miss Fisher at her elbow. Celine drew up her shoulders and closed her eyes for a moment, an expression of pure ecstasy bathing her face. Miss Fisher appeared anything but ecstatic. She took Celine's blue reticule and tugged the top wide. While Miss Fisher waited, Celine dropped coins inside and allowed the reticule to be replaced upon her wrist before walking on again . . . directly into James's path.

The element of surprise.

Chapter 8

"**M**iss Godwin!" Approaching directly, James swept off his hat and bowed low. "What a fortuitous surprise."

"Fortuitous?"

James straightened and looked down into alarmed, tawny eyes. "A stroke of pure luck." His blood pumped harder. Surely a man of his experience couldn't be turned into a moonling over a slip of a girl—albeit the most provocative, most enticing, most alluring girl whose acquaintance he ever remembered making.

She gazed up at him without a trace of guile. "How so, James—I mean, Mr. Eagleton? Why is this pure luck as you put it?"

"Simple." He gave Miss Fisher a conspiratorial smile that suggested he and she shared a worldly comprehension of matters that Celine had yet to understand. "It is pure luck because I had been planning to come to Curzon Street to see you."

"You had?"

"I had."

"I see."

"Do you, Celine?"

She hugged her reticule to her breast and looked desperately at her companion. Miss Fisher looked away.

"What is it that you see, Celine?" he continued, keeping his voice low and even but full of confidence.

"Well, Mr. Eagleton—"

"James."

"Um. . ." She looked again to Miss Fisher, who continued to study passersby. "Um, James. James, I don't think I see anything at all. I think you have . . . Perhaps you would explain this fortuitous set of circumstances."

"But of course." He smiled and abruptly reached for her hand.

"Oh." Still holding the reticule tightly, she extricated one hand and put it in his. A delightful rosy blush shot over her cheeks and tinted her neck—and the tops of her breasts, pushed upward from a low, square neckline by the pressure of her grip on the reticule.

James didn't fail to note that Miss Fisher moved a few steps away to study items in the shop window. If the idea were not preposterous, he might assume the girl's companion had determined to aid his quest. He bent to place a slow, lingering kiss on the back of Celine's hand. "Mm," he murmured, so softly that only she would hear. "You smell wonderful, Celine. Like those *charming* roses in your garden."

"You really shouldn't say such things," she said breathlessly.

"But I think I absolutely should."

"Not here."

"Here would not be my choice, but it will do until I can have you somewhere else."

"Mr. Eagleton!"

"James."

"Well . . . James."

He slowly raised his head and, at the same time, stepped closer and brought her hand higher until his knuckles brushed that luscious, softly swelling flesh above her bodice.

"Mr.—James," she whispered hoarsely, but without removing her hand, and thus the opportunity for his covert touch. "You really shouldn't."

"I believe I should."

"Why?"

"Because I want to."

"You do?"

"Yes. And so do you." Without appearing to move a muscle, he slipped a finger beneath her bodice, into deep, warm cleavage.

She opened her mouth but James sent her a silent shush. While he continued to gaze into her eyes and smile, he contrived to pass his finger over the naked, rounded curve of her breast to an already stiffly budded nipple. Celine gasped and she clutched his hand tightly. With a swift, curling motion he lightly pinched that peaked, eager flesh in his crooked finger and watched with satisfaction as her lips parted. The jolt that passed through her shot from her squeezing fingers into James's body. His rod leaped, turned hard and heavy.

Enough. Enough to reestablish what he already knew. This was a piece made for passion, and he must have her. Eventually he would mold her into a voluptuous temptress and—somehow—he would contrive to partake of her again and again.

James removed his artfully concealed finger and whispered, "There is so much more that you are meant to enjoy, my golden girl. Will you let me show you how?"

Her eyes held a dazed brilliance. "More?"

"Much, much more. I'd like to tell you about it."

"You . . . you must not." Her vision had begun to clear.

"Oh, but I think I must."

The next deep breath she took made James wish he could dispense with this propriety nonsense and carry her away. He glanced around and considered almost wildly the possibility of hustling her into his coach and telling the coachman to drive—anywhere—until James told him to stop. And in the coach he would teach Miss Godwin a great many things that would make a wonderful start on the education he had in mind.

"Why were you coming to Curzon Street?" Her soft, shaky voice snapped him back to the moment.

"I was coming . . ." Liam stood a few feet away, her chin boldly lifted, her hands threaded into her sleeves. Her eyes were cold obsidian and unflinching in their perusal of Celine.

"James? Why were—"

"Yes, yes." He returned his attention to Celine. "I was coming to Curzon Street to see you." Remembering the violets, he thrust them into the hand he'd held and stepped back a few inches. "A small, simple token of my esteem."

"They're beautiful. I love violets." She smiled a little, and his heart turned. "I love roses, too. Especially Tillie's Charmers."

He affected an innocent air. "Those were the roses in your garden."

Celine's smile broadened. "Do not play with me, James. Thank you for the roses you sent, but such gifts are inappropriate under the circumstances."

Liam had edged closer. She avoided James's eyes and only stood still again when she was near enough to hear every word spoken.

James cleared his throat. He would attend to Liam later. "If I had sent the roses, they would be perfectly appropriate. Beautiful flowers for a beautiful girl. What could be more fitting?"

The small, exasperated noise Liam made was,

thankfully, unnoticed by Celine. With supreme control, James managed not to look at his infuriating charge.

"I intended to call and ask if you would do me the honor of allowing me to drive you in the Park tomorrow afternoon. Say at four?"

"At four?"

"Yes." This was going to be remarkably easy.

"Tomorrow?"

"Yes." He had never been in favor of the upper-class English habit of keeping girls totally ignorant of life between men and women ... until now. "My man—who has an uncanny ability in foretelling such things—tells me the day will be pleasantly warm."

Another disgusted puff from Liam.

Muscles in James's jaw flexed. "You will have to wear something quite light. And do not forget a parasol so that you need not fear for your complexion." Although, were she more worldly, she should certainly fear for her virtue. "I'm certain your companion will gladly agree to act as chaperon." A complication he would deal with as necessary.

Celine half-turned away. Her face, James noted with mild concern, had paled a little, and she stared ahead as if saddened by something only she could see. "Fallen," she said, evidently to herself. "Oh, dear. Oh, dear me, no."

"I beg your pardon?"

She brought the violets to her nose and regarded him steadily. "That will not be possible."

"Good. I will arrange for refreshments ... I beg your pardon?"

Celine drew herself up as tall as she could and gave him a cool, almost angry stare. "I said that it will not be possible for me to accompany you tomorrow."

"But—"

"And now I must take my leave of you."

"*Why* can't you come to the Park?"

A fidgety motion forced him to glance at Liam. She took agitated little steps from one foot to the other and glared with fierce concentration at Celine's back. There was potential trouble there.

"I cannot come to the Park because ..." Celine's throat moved sharply. "I cannot come because ... because I am to attend a rout tonight and I will be too fatigued to do anything exerting tomorrow," she finished in a rush.

James seethed. *Bloody hell.* The little baggage was becoming wary of him after all. This had not entered into his calculations. "Surely you will be recovered by tomorrow afternoon. What rout could keep a girl from her bed so long that she could not arise in time for a little drive the next day?"

"The Arbuthnotts'." She looked around almost wildly. "Lettie, we must return home or I shall be late."

The Arbuthnotts. Reining in his annoyance, James bowed graciously. "I must not detain you. Let us hope the rout is pleasant. Good afternoon, Miss Fisher."

"Good afternoon, Mr. Eagleton." Miss Fisher returned to her mistress's side, her dark eyes assessing yet not unfriendly.

"Thank you for the violets," Celine said. She threaded her hand through her companion's elbow. "I trust you will have a delightful ... a delightful ..."

"Rest of the day?" James suggested, already formulating the next step in his plan.

"Exactly! A delightful rest of the day." She left him, almost dragging poor, patient Miss Fisher with her.

After a few seconds, James turned to Liam. He covered the space between them in one long stride and grabbed her hand, pulling her along beside him. "You, Liam, have made a grave mistake this afternoon."

"How so?" Her voice soared as she was forced to run to keep up.

"Spying. Following where you have no right to be. It will never happen again. Do you understand?"

"Ouch!" Her sudden loud shriek caught the attention of several passersby, and James dropped her hand.

"You try my patience," he told her in a deliberately menacing tone.

"And you try mine, James."

"I—"

Won Tel materialized at his side. "I could not stop her approach so I thought it prudent to hope she would not cause too great an inconvenience."

"Inconvenience? She caused inconvenience. We can be grateful Miss Godwin didn't notice her."

"Miss Godwin?" Liam raised her oval jaw and lowered her eyelids as if trying the name in her mind. "Miss Celine Godwin of Curzon Street. The house where Won Tel delivered the roses, no doubt."

If this were less important, James might have laughed at her audacity. "We are going home, and nothing like this will ever occur again. Won Tel. The coach."

"Is she what is known as a toad?"

Startled, James turned back to Liam. "A toad?"

"Miss Godwin. Is she supposed to be a toad? One of these insipid people's so-called incompetent beauties. A demon-of-the-first-water in the haughty *ton*."

Won Tel grinned. "I will summon the coach, Mr. Eagleton."

James addressed Liam. "Miss Godwin might be considered a *toast*, Liam. Perhaps even an *incompara-*

ble. Possibly a *diamond-of-the-first-water* by the *haut ton.*"

"I understand," Liam said, with no sign of chagrin. "I shall bear your instruction in mind. It is well she realized she is unworthy of your generous attention."

James crossed his arms and willed his coach to arrive. "You will not meddle in my business again. If you do, I'll—"

"It is well that the toad did not continue to press herself upon you."

"*Toast.* Celine did not press herself, Liam. Here's the coach."

"You will, of course, make no further attempts to be kind to this incompetent."

James eyed the heavens and sought guidance. "This discussion is over."

"That is as well," Liam said. She approached the curb where Won Tel waited with the coach door open. "That incompetent toad is so vain as to preen before you—to try to entice you with her obvious tricks—and then she does not accept an offer any woman would die to receive. You must not think of her again."

Won Tel lifted Liam into the coach and James climbed in behind her. Won Tel followed and closed the door.

"Yes," Liam said, sitting primly against the squabs. "I am pleased that Miss Celine Godwin will not trouble you further."

"I'm glad you're pleased," James said distractedly. It was he who would do the troubling, and much sooner than Celine would possibly expect.

"Why are you so pleased, Liam?" Won Tel asked.

James looked sharply at his companion.

"I am pleased," Liam said, "because I would rather concentrate on the duties James has asked me to perform in his household." There was no ring of truth in those words, James decided uncomfortably.

"What else would you be doing?" Won Tel asked coolly.

Liam gave a sudden, brilliant smile. "Nothing—probably nothing." She leaned forward, dismissing James and Won Tel by appearing fascinated by the scene outside the window. "No, I would definitely not be doing anything other than whatever James needs most."

James hauled a booted foot atop the opposite knee and drummed his fingers on glistening black leather. He wished he didn't mistrust Liam's innocent declaration. Undoubtedly he would have to keep a close watch on her as long as they remained in England.

He reached up to rap on the coachman's peephole. When it slid open then he said, "Grosvenor Square." And as the coach rolled on he settled back and thought, with anticipation, of that night's rout at the Arbuthnotts' . . . and of Celine Godwin . . . and of a fortune in gems awaiting him.

Chapter 9

B *itch!*
       Darius Godwin drew back and flattened himself against the wall beside the window in his beloved *wife's* private parlor. *Private?* Yes, private as far as he, her *husband*, was concerned—but not closed to a blushing blond stableboy who trembled, naked, before her avid eyes. Darius filled his lungs with night air that seethed with the promise of thunder.

Dearest Mary thought he was otherwise engaged. Remembering, he smiled. He *had* been otherwise engaged—with an enticing piece Bertram Letchwith had sent his way for the evening. But now he had more important matters in mind, and his wife's present dalliance was an inconvenient intrusion.

Curiosity overcame him, and he positioned himself to peer again through a gap between heavy draperies and into the dimly lighted room.

Darius recalled that the boy's name was Colin. He'd been at Knighthead only a few weeks . . . more than long enough for Mary to notice a beautiful male body hovering between the last awkwardness of adolescence and the first flowering of virile manhood.

The boy stood before her now, close before her, his hands crossed protectively over his crotch. While Darius watched, Mary, resplendent in yards of trail-

ing, diaphanous white wrapper, sank to her knees
and pulled the garment open until her breasts were
revealed. Supporting their weight, she smiled at the
boy and ran her tongue over her mouth. She was in
profile, and Darius saw her utter a few words.

Eyes on Mary's big, white breasts, the boy slowly
dropped his hands, and his member sprang thick
and full.

Even through the glass, Darius heard Mary's triumphant, laughing shout of anticipation. This was
her lifeblood, this seduction of untried boys. He
curled his lip but did not turn away. First he would
watch the bitch and her little male whore, then he
would let her know what he had seen. He would
threaten to expose her perversion. That would ensure
her assistance in what must be done—and soon.

His thighs locked. She had taken Colin's ballocks
in her squeezing fingers and urged him to her lips.

Darius's hand went to his own rod. He'd thought
himself spent on the ripe, black-haired doxy he'd had
three, nay, four times in his hidden sanctuary in the
woods. Not so. Even ungainly Mary, of the frowsy
blond hair that sprang in dull curls about her full,
mottled face, could arouse a magnificent male speci-
men such as Darius Godwin. He was a man among
men, a stallion ever ready to mount a willing—or
unwilling—piece of female flesh.

The stableboy's glistening rod slid easily in and
out of Mary's mouth while she kneaded his straining
boughs. A moment's fierce pumping and she withdrew, laughing at the helpless thrust of her victim's
hips. With a ludicrous attempt at grace, she rolled
onto her back, pulled her wrapper entirely open, and
spread her legs.

When she'd aided the boy between her thighs,
guided him to sink into her whore's alley, there was
a brief, awkward rocking that went at cross purposes

until the newly blooded "master" learned his rhythm. Darius drew his lips back from his teeth and studied the boy's face, raised unseeingly toward the window.

What was he thinking? Darius wondered. Behind those glazed blue eyes, what heated images eased the foul act he performed?

Celine, perhaps? Darius smiled grimly. Now those would be pictures to spur any man on to swift release. Yes, it could be that the lusty stableboy saw not the fat, aging woman who tossed and sweated and bucked about his thighs, but the soft, full-breasted body of the innocent girl who would soon become Bertram Letchwith's plaything.

Bored with the spectacle, Darius turned away and skirted the house to enter by the kitchens. He dallied in the pantry to tear a leg off a roasted chicken before sauntering slowly through stone passageways and up a flight of stairs from the basement to the ground floor. What he had to discuss would not wait much longer.

He arrived at the end of the corridor leading to Mary's sitting room and hovered in the shadows until—predictably—her door opened and Colin emerged. Mary was easily bored with any diversion and would be in a hurry to dispatch the boy once he'd served her purpose. His face was pale now and he looked left and right—without seeing Darius—before slipping rapidly away in the opposite direction.

Relishing what lay ahead, Darius rapidly approached the sitting room and threw open the door without knocking.

"What . . .?" Mary, her wrapper hanging open, stood before the fire. In her upraised hand she held a great goblet of red wine. "How dare you come in here without my summons."

Darius closed the door behind him and swaggered across the room with exaggerated steps until he stood in front of her. "It occurred to me that you might enjoy a taste of some mature, some practiced male prowess, my sweet one." With his teeth, he tore off a chunk of dark chicken meat and chewed, and while he chewed he brought the greasy, half-gnawed leg to rest on her right breast. "Doubtless a woman of your appetites has extensive needs no mere boy could meet."

She flushed a deep scarlet. "What are you suggesting?"

Tilting his head, he made a shiny trail to her nipple and sneered in satisfaction as the great, dark center puckered erect. "I'm suggesting that you do for me what you just did for my servant." Using the bone, he flipped the wrapper wider apart before continuing to draw a line all the way to the still damp bush between her legs. "Open my breeches, *wife*. Suck me, *wife*. Invite me onto the rug to rut with you, *wife*."

She raised her sagging chin. "Where were you? How do you know what happened here?"

"I know," he told her. "I need not explain myself to you. Open your legs."

Casting him an insolent glare, Mary tipped up her goblet and gulped wine until drips coursed from the corners of her mouth. She wiped them away with the back of her hand. "You've had your chances at me. Once I begged for your company in my bed. I no longer want you—have not wanted you many a year, and well you know it."

Grinning, with one hand on a hip, Darius affected a fencing stance. "*En garde*," he whispered, and slid the chicken leg into her woman's folds. Baring his teeth, he rubbed back and forth, anticipating her reviling shriek.

No shriek came. Instead, the shock in Mary

Godwin's eyes faded. Her lids drooped and her mouth fell slackly open. She parted her legs and arched her belly toward him, undulated, panted in mounting excitement.

Abruptly, Darius turned from her and tossed the chicken leg into the fire.

"Oh!" In a flurry of white lawn and pale, swaying flesh, she flew at him, clawing his neck. "Damn you! Damn you!" Dropping the goblet, she clutched at his breeches. "Satisfy me, damn you."

"No." With a forearm, he fended her off until she backed to fall onto a chaise. "Cover yourself before I cast up my accounts at the sight of you."

A small whimper rose, but she clutched her garments to her and cowered against the cushions.

"That's better." With his booted feet braced apart, he stood with his back to the fire. "We have business to attend to. Bertram is anxious that we assist him in as speedy a marriage as possible."

"But Celine is—"

"In London. Yes, of course she is. Damnable waste of money it is, too. He insists upon it still. The pinks of the *ton* are to see her beauty and then, when she is betrothed to him, recognize what a splendid fellow he is because she is besotted with him."

"But Celine is—"

"Not besotted with him. That is of no account. *His* perception is our only concern. The sooner he is satisfied and can be married off to the chit, the sooner we will get the blunt we *have* to have. And we do have to have it, wife, if we are to continue to support our style of living and this house. We *must* support them until we find the gems. Then we will be free and away from here. London with be ours. Society will be ours. At last we will be recognized and accepted as is our due."

"Twenty years," Mary muttered.

He glared at her. "Yes, twenty years of searching. But we *will* find the Sainsbury gems. It was for them that we duped Frances St. Giles and his foolish old father. We have risked much and we will gain much."

"I wish it did not depend upon Celine. What if Bertram cries off?"

"He will not cry off." He moved a foot closer to the fire and spread the tails of his coat to warm his backside. Thunder rolled a long way off and a chill seemed to enter the room. "When that boy was rutting with you he was probably imagining rutting with Celine. It was her flesh he drove into. Her breasts he fondled and sucked."

"What?" Mary screamed, rising from the chaise. "You did watch. You did see, you dung heap. It was not her he made love to. It was me! I'll kill you!"

Locking his elbow, he met her flailing, rushing body with a hand applied to her throat. Mary gurgled, grappled with his arm, and all but slipped to the floor. Darius waited until she regained her balance and dropped his arm. "You will obey me, madam. Sit."

Mumbling, she subsided once more onto the chaise. "She is a nothing. A stupid nothing fit only to be used to gain what we need. No true man would want her."

"Bertram and Percival want her very much," Darius said softly. "They intend first to share her virginal body, until she is well-seasoned in the art of pleasing Bertram, and clever in the matter of playing the innocent for Percival. Then it will be her duty to her husband to follow his wishes and perform for his friends in the manner they prefer at their gatherings. She will scream most piteously when they enter her *untouched* body, one after another according to the lots they draw. And if she is very wise, and very good, it will be at least a few years before they tire of her."

Mary sniffed and settled her wrapper more closely about her. "It's about time she paid us back for all we've done for her. Ungrateful little wretch. And then Lettie can go. I've looked upon her accusing eyes long enough."

"We shall have to be careful there," Darius reminded her. "The woman knows too much. We may have to consider certain steps."

"That will not be difficult to accomplish. You may leave that to me."

He spared her a smile. "Indeed. And I'm sure you will deal very well with the matter. You have always dealt well with such matters."

Mary smiled in return. "We have a talent for manipulation, my love, as Francis St. Giles and his dearest wife, Sophie, learned—to their horror."

Darius nodded. "It helped that the old fool of a marquess was so easily controlled."

"I still relish the perfection of our plan," Mary said in a hushed voice. "To have drugged Francis and left him in a whorehouse. To have stolen his ring and left him to awaken thinking he had poked a whore and fallen into a drunken stupor. And he believed it was the doxy who took his ring. Perfect!"

"Perfect according to our plan," Darius agreed. "He believed the whore took his ring and gave it to his father. Can you imagine the twisting of his bowels when the marquess offered him that ring? Francis took it!" Darius slapped his thigh gleefully. "He took it without question and sealed his fate. He thought the little whore had carried the ring to his father and the old man's disgust was because his son's loose morals offended his religious standards. Francis never argued his cause and his father banished him from this house. He never discovered that *you* gave the ring to the marquess, or that you told a much different story from the one he thought had damned him."

"And because Frances never offered a defense, the marquess believed my story." Mary wriggled with delight. "Oh, it is too long since we have spoken of this. It gives me such pleasure to know that neither of them ever had any idea what we had done. Your son defiled me, I told that old fool. He ruined me, and it if were not for poor, dear, Darius, I would be consigned to life as some tolerated, unmarried companion in another woman's house. And he *believed* me!"

"And to atone for his son's sin, he gave us what we wanted—this house—Francis's house." Darius felt again the deep satisfaction that triumph had brought.

"He did not give it to us," Mary said, her voice growing hard, her expression petulant. "He loaned it to us."

"For as long as we need it," Darius reminded her. "Praise God his heir honored his wishes."

"Augustus hates us."

"You have no proof of that."

"His silence proves it," Mary said. "As does his refusal to entertain us or to consider making Knighthead ours in the true sense of the word—as he should."

"He will not put us out. That is all that matters. We will get the blunt we need from Letchwith and we will find the gems. I know this. I *feel* this. And then we shall be free." *He* would be free—of her and of every leaden impediment to the life he deserved.

"Sometimes I fear Francis will return."

"He will never return," Darius said, convinced he was correct. "If there were to be a reconciliation with the new marquess after their father's death, it would have happened then—years ago. It did not and never will. It is almost certain that Augustus knows nothing of what occurred before Francis was banished. His father must have instructed that there be no further contact with his younger son."

"I watch the papers for word of his return," Mary said distractedly. "The possibility haunts me."

"It does not haunt me," Darius said, puffing up his chest. "He will forever believe what he believes and will never dare to return to England. There could never be question of his risking that Sophie might hear of his supposed fornications."

"Sophie loved this house." Mary gazed into the distance and smiled. "How perfect it would be to see her face if she learned that *I* was the reason for her misery, that because her husband seduced me and left me, she has had to suffer in obscurity all these years."

Darius looked at Mary from beneath lowered eyelids. "Let us remember the truth—at least between ourselves. Francis didn't seduce you. He didn't touch you. That was what made you such a perfect ally for me. You hated that he didn't want you, and nothing was too devious or disgusting as long as you had your revenge on him and on his family."

She tossed her head. "He was a fool. Wherever he is, I'm sure he thinks of me and of what we could have had together. I pray that he suffers greatly, that they both suffer greatly.

"I pray for their untimely deaths."

Chapter 10

Dear Knighthead. Dear ivy-covered yellow stone walls and graceful terraces. Dear stained-glass windows winking their brilliance in the morning sun. Dear soft green lawns and mounds of rhododendrons; pink, white, and purple. Dear gentle hills of Dorset stretching to the sea. Dear—

"Are you unwell?" Lettie broke into Celine's thoughts. "You look pinched."

"No." She tried to smile, but failed. "Yes . . . oh, dear, perhaps I am unwell. Perhaps we should write to Mama and Papa and ask them to arrange for me to go home at once." Celine sighed and looked at her hands, limply laced on the soft skirts of Isabel Prentergast's yellow muslin. Tonight her indomitable spirit felt a trifle bent.

The carriage bearing them to the Arbuthnott rout in Berkeley Square lurched onward a short distance and stopped again before Lettie said, "You weren't feeling ill before we met Mr. Eagleton this afternoon." She leaned to pat Celine's hand.

"What has Mr. Eagleton to do with this?" she asked snappishly, drawing away. "Really, Lettie, you do invent peculiar connections sometimes." Irritating connections that usually touched the heart of a situation.

119

"Do I?"

"Yes, you do. I *hate* all this." Celine's wave took in the line of coaches that stretched before and behind their own. "It is completely stupid!"

"Stupid?"

"Exactly!"

"I take it you mean that the considerable attention given to the accepted way of dealing with events such as this rout doesn't meet with your approval."

"Exactly!"

Lettie closed her eyes and settled her chin into the discreet width of dark fur trim at the neck of her brown pelisse.

"What is it?" Celine asked crossly. "Are you tired?"

"I'm not tired."

"What then?"

"I'm thinking," Lettie said.

Celine hated it when Lettie closed her out. Of all the people in the world, Lettie had always been the one Celine knew she could trust. "What are you thinking?"

"That I wish I had some magic that would make you happy."

Instantly contrite, Celine shifted forward in her seat and took Lettie's hand. "I am happy when I'm with you." If only she could explain to Lettie that she, Celine, was completely bemused and confused about the way she felt—about the way Mr. James Eagleton had made her feel ever since she first met him—about the way he'd been making her feel more and more of whatever it was that he made her feel with each fresh meeting . . .

"I wish we knew more about him," Lettie murmured.

Celine jumped, and her free hand flew to her throat. She didn't have to ask to whom Lettie referred.

Lettie's grip tightened, twining their fingers together. "There's something . . ." She shook her head.

"What?" Celine asked urgently.

"Nothing." Lettie shook her head again. "Please be careful. You're very young and very beautiful. He's a handsome man. There's no denying that. Handsome and charming and evidently very successful. A fine catch for some lucky girl. And I think he may be a good man. But there's something . . ."

"Oh, don't keep saying that!" Celine sat back in her seat and frowned into the darkness that gathered at the edges of the streetlights' polished yellow arcs. "There's no reason to worry about Mr. Eagleton one way or the other. And I do know it is he of whom you are speaking. My acquaintance with him is of the most casual nature, I assure you. He is simply being polite because . . . because . . ."

"Because?" Lettie prompted softly while she smoothed a curl away from Celine's cheek.

"Because he's a polite man," she said, tossing her head. "Look at this ridiculous fuss about nothing. Miles of coaches inching along to some affair where most people don't know one another. Such foolishness."

"And how do you know so much about routs, miss? This is your first one."

"Freda told me. She said all the lights in the Arbuthnotts' house—and, by the way, I do not know the Arbuthnotts and cannot imagine why they have invited me—but all the lights in their house will be on so that their precious rout may be admired from without. And people will move from room to room talking about nothing in particular to no one in particular." She paused for breath. "And the food—what there's likely to be of it—will be awful, and the sole point of the entire affair is merely to be *seen*. And the whole thing will be too *hot*." Folding her hands once more, she raised her chin, daring Lettie to argue some redeeming aspect of the night's proceedings.

"The dress looks lovely on you," Lettie said, her smile fond. "I only hope no one recognizes it."

"So do I," Celine said. "I also hope this shabby carriage isn't too noticeable in the dark."

"When you are at the rout no one will know what manner of carriage you arrived in," Lettie said, but she looked unhappy. "And I already told you that Mrs. Arbuthnott is someone your mother knew when she was growing up. Evidently Mrs. Godwin wrote to Mrs. Arbuthnott and told her you'd be in town for your Season this year but that she wouldn't be with you immediately. Mrs. Arbuthnott, you will remember, made a point of writing a very nice personal note on the invitation. She's looking forward to your company."

Celine touched the thin strand of black and gold braid Lettie and Freda had contrived to twine with the curls at her crown. "Do I *have* to stand with Mrs. Arbuthnott?"

"Yes," Lettie said simply. "At least for a while. Of course, it's perfectly appropriate for you to talk to anyone else you know."

"I don't know anyone."

"Perhaps you'll meet a fascinating man."

"I've already met a—"

"*Exactly*," Lettie said with a wry smile. "You've already met a man who fascinates you, haven't you?"

Celine was overcome by a desire to cry. She never cried—almost never cried. A huge, painful lump seemed to fill her throat, and she swallowed with difficulty.

"Oh, my pet." Steadying herself against the rocking of the carriage, Lettie crossed to sit beside Celine. "Is it true? Have you . . . Do you think you might be coming to care for Mr. Eagleton?"

Celine sniffed and gave Lettie a watery smile. "I really have so little experience in such matters." Her cheeks burned. What she meant was that other than her very considerable—much too considerable—experiences with James Eagleton, she knew absolutely nothing about what happened between men and women.

Lettie patted Celine's arm. "As your companion, and with your mama and papa not here, I could tell Mr. Eagleton that his interest isn't reciprocated and—"

"No! No, please don't do that, Lettie."

"You do care for him?"

"*Please*, don't press me in this. I'm mostly troubled by the thought of Mr. Letchwith." That much was true.

"Yes," Lettie agreed. "And I do believe Mr. Eagleton is very, very well fixed."

"What does that have to do with Mr. Letchwith?"

Lettie turned her face away. "I was just thinking aloud. I only meant that your parents would be more inclined to look favorably upon a suitor other than Mr. Letchwith if the other gentleman has a considerable fortune. Not that Mr. Eagleton is likely to be the only eligible man to notice you."

"I think you get ahead of yourself," Celine said. "Mr. Eagleton has been pleasant. That certainly doesn't mean he's about to offer for me." No, James Eagleton had said and done a great many . . . *intimate* things, but he hadn't so much as suggested any serious intention.

"No, he hasn't." Lettie sounded preoccupied. "At least, not yet. But that doesn't mean he won't."

"You're worried about Mr. Letchwith," Celine said. "So am I. But surely Mama and Papa wouldn't be paying for a Season if matters with Mr. Letchwith were already decided . . . Do you think so?"

"I don't know what to think. But I suppose you're right. Your parents never spend a penny on—" Lettie closed her mouth firmly.

"On anything or anyone except themselves if it can be avoided. Exactly," Celine said, with more than a little hope that she was right. "I should be obedient and loyal at all times. I know it's wrong to criticize them, but I think I can be forgiven for the moment. It seems perfectly obvious that Mama and Papa are still anxious to find a more suitable match for me."

"A match that'll bring them more blunt, you mean," Lettie muttered.

"Probably," Celine agreed. If only she could meet and at least find agreeable some man who would be just right and who would fill Mama and Papa's requirements. "It isn't *fair*!"

"What isn't fair, my lamb?"

"That girls have to be as good as auctioned off like ... like *horses*. Going, going gone—to the highest bidder. And no thought for whether or not they are in love with—"

"Being in love isn't considered particularly important, Celine."

"Not to some," she said truculently and thought of James Eagleton. Was she ... Was what she felt for him love? Or was it merely ... *lust*? She shuddered.

"Celine, I can't abide seeing you so sad. There has to be a way out of this. We'll find it. Trust me."

Celine smiled and kissed Lettie's cheek. "Don't worry, dear Lettie. Everything is bound to resolve itself nicely." Even if she had to run away, for she certainly would never, never marry the sickening Bertram Letchwith. "I do believe that I am simply overwhelmed by so many new things happening so quickly."

"Of course you are. And all this nonsense about

trying to get money for David Talbot is making it worse, I shouldn't wonder."

At that, Celine rallied. "It isn't nonsense, and I find being in the way of doing business quite exhilarating."

Lettie made a snorting sound. "The truth is that you like a bit of danger, my girl. What you're doing isn't suitable for a young lady, and I still think I ought to have a few words with David Talbot."

"Please don't. You know how shy he is. He'll be mortified."

"He *should* be mortified for talking to an innocent like you about such worldly matters."

"David is my friend. What he tells me is only for my own good, to ensure that I am as prepared as possible."

"Prepared for what?" Lettie asked sharply.

Celine made an airy gesture. "I'm not sure, but I suppose I'll know should the occasion arise." What would Lettie say if she knew that her charge was naturally worldly—that without David's warnings firmly in mind she would undoubtedly already have followed in Ruby Rose's footsteps and become completely *fallen*?

The coach stopped yet again, and this time the coachman jumped down from his box and opened the door. "A moment, ladies," he said, putting the steps in place. Duly, he marched up the front steps of a formidably grand gray stone house and rapped loudly on the door.

"Silliness," Celine hissed. "It's like Freda told me. Lights ablaze everywhere. Look in the windows. Such a crush. And they know people are coming. Why does everyone have to knock? It would be quicker if—"

"That's the way it's done," Lettie said, and Celine realized guiltily that her companion was also nervous. "It's time to go in."

Too quickly, Celine passed into an elegantly proportioned hall. Ornate carved white cornices caught the eye, but Celine winced at the oppressively dark red of the walls beneath—not that she was afforded more than glimpses of the decor through the dense, shifting throng of guests.

In an anteroom, Lettie took off her pelisse and fussed about Celine, tidying her hair, fluffing her skirts above the pleated gold hem of her slip. "You look absolutely lovely," she said, but her voice wobbled. "We're to go to the purple salon on the next floor."

Lettie led the way, almost officiously pushing a path to the stairs and scurrying up while darting glances back at Celine.

At the top of the first flight of stairs there were as many people as in the rooms below. "Pointless," Celine whispered into Lettie's ear. "We could leave and no one would know we had even been here."

"Hush. Mrs. Arbuthnott most especially asked that you go to her direct. If you don't, she's bound to contact your mama to ask what became of you."

"Oh," Celine wailed softly. "I *do* hate this. How shall we know Mrs. Arbuthnott anyway?"

Lettie stopped so abruptly that Celine walked into her.

"What do you mean, how shall we know her?"

"I mean exactly that. Do you intend to ask every lady in the room if she is Mrs. Arbuthnott?"

"Of course not!"

"Very well." Celine crossed her arms. "What then?"

"Celine Godwin!" A familiar female voice soared over the din. "What *are* you doing here?"

Bracing herself, Celine turned and looked down into Isabel Prentergast's bright blue eyes. "I'm attending a rout," she said through gritted teeth. "What are *you* doing here, Isabel?"

Isabel stared, then laughed and batted Celine's arm lightly with her fan, a white lace fan threaded with scarlet ribbon. "You are funny. Such a sense of humor." Those blue eyes swept over the dress Celine wore, and any amusement Isabel felt congealed into a false little smile. "And such a . . . striking dress."

"Thank you," Celine said demurely. "Yours is charming, too. The scarlet edging is quite daring and very dramatic."

"And it's what sets the dress apart, don't you think?" Isabel said, her eyes quite hard now.

"Indeed," Celine agreed. "In fact, without the trim it might be impossible to remember it as the same gown."

"Quite." Craftiness crept into Isabel's tone. She dropped her voice. "Perhaps we could, er . . ."

"Perhaps," Celine said loftily. "I'll be at home tomorrow should you wish to call." Isabel's appetite for gaming must be tiresome for her. It was fortuitous for Celine. *Fortuitous. What a fortuitous surprise,* James Eagleton had said. She let out an exasperated puff. If she could only forget the man. She might never see him again, anyway. He'd only been playing with a green girl, that much was obvious, and—

"I do believe you might have chosen a less dangerous event than this to wear that dress," Isabel's whispered comment curtailed Celine's errant thoughts.

Lettie, who had been standing on tiptoe to peer into what was obviously the purple salon, turned back to Celine. "We must go in. I think I know how to accomplish our mission."

"What does she mean?" Isabel asked rudely. "Why are you accompanied by a servant?"

Celine regarded Lettie's unflattering brown silk dress. "Lettie is my companion." She must find a way to secure one or two attractive gowns for Lettie, who had a nice figure and an arresting face and would look quite charming if suitably attired.

"Companions *are* servants," Isabel said offhandedly. "I must go. *Please* try not to be noticed too much in that gown. You would be mortified if others realized it's been made over for you."

"And you wouldn't be mortified if others realized it used to belong to you?"

Isabel flipped the blond curls that cascaded at the back of her head. "I should be forced to admit that you are a charity case who cannot afford new dresses."

"Really?" It was Celine's turn to fashion a cool expression. "And why would that story be believed more than one I might devise? Such as that you did not give the dress to me but sold it because you needed money."

"No one would believe you." Isabel laughed nervously. "But let's not argue. I'll call tomorrow, and I'm sure we'll have forgotten all about this little unpleasantness."

"I'm sure."

Celine watched Isabel depart in her quite sumptuous sprigged white muslin and imagined its bodice cleverly embroidered with seed pearls to match the pearl-studded white turban that would make the best of her own dark blond hair.

"You will *not* buy more dresses from her," Lettie said urgently. "Now. Come with me. We will listen— discreetly, of course—to conversations until we learn which lady is Mrs. Arbuthnott."

"A capital plan," Celine said. "And I *will* buy more dresses from nasty Isabel Prentergast."

"You won't," Lettie said, arching her neck to see as she began threading a path into the salon. "Pay attention to what people are saying. Listen for names."

Celine trotted obediently in Lettie's wake. The ladies' dresses were so marvelous. And the gentlemen's evening clothes looked quite dashing—except for those with the dandyish affectation that seemed to be employed by some rather senior and quite unsuitably shaped men, as well as by the haughty young bloods who posed and preened and appeared so bored with the proceedings that Celine wondered why they didn't leave. After all, *they* didn't have companions who were determined to put them through their paces whether they liked the exercise or not.

"Ah!" Lettie stopped, and for the second time Celine bumped into her heels. "There. The lady in purple. I'm certain that must be Mrs. Arbuthnott."

"The large lady?"

"Yes."

"Wearing the purple that's not quite the same shade as the walls?"

"Yes."

"With the silly purple lace cap covered with wax cherries?"

"Celine! *Yes*. And she is your hostess and a very kind person. Be so good as to remember your manners."

"I didn't intend to tell her how silly a lace cap with a crown that rises at least twelve inches above her head looks, particularly when its cherries bobble almost down to her eyes."

"Come with me, young lady," Lettie said, but a smile hovered about her mouth. "Excuse me, madam, but are you Mrs. Arbuthnott?"

The florid woman who confronted them raised a lorgnette and trained narrowed eyes upon Lettie. "Who wishes to know?"

Celine straighted her back. "Good evening Mrs. Arbuthnott." There was no doubt, from her manner and from the tittering group that surrounded her, that this pompous creature was their hostess. "I am Celine Godwin and this is my companion, Miss Letitia Fisher. My mother sends you her regards and thanks you for including me in this evening's festivities."

The woman frowned. "Godwin? Godwin?" She swiveled her head on its fat-ringed neck. Diamonds blazed upon her considerable bosom, at her ears, around her wrists, and on her plump fingers. "Do we know a Godwin?"

There were negative murmurs, and Celine felt herself grow pink. She drew herself up and, for once, was grateful for her height. "My mother was Mary Detterling. I understand the two of you were friends as girls."

"Good evening, Miss Godwin." A slightly built young man with a pleasant face, fine blond hair, and a charming smile bowed before Celine. "Roland Yeatbury at your service." He took the hand Celine finally remembered to proffer and kissed it as if hers was the most desirable hand he'd ever held.

"Roland, *Viscount* Yeatbury," Mrs. Arbuthnott's fruity voice intoned.

Celine bobbed. "How do you do, my lord?"

"At this moment I do very well," Yeatbury said, and his smile became mischievous. "How do *you* do?"

She liked him instinctively and said in a voice meant only for him, "Better, thanks to you, my lord."

His pale face turned slightly pink and Celine bit her lip. She'd brought him pleasure, this important man. Was there something about her that was too forward, too suggestive of wayward tendencies ready to be unleashed? She withdrew her hand.

"Mary Detterling, did you say your mother was?" Mrs. Arbuthnott said. Her small mouth was pinched almost to nothing as her eyes darted from Celine to the viscount. "Yes, I do believe I remember her. Married some sort of country squire's younger son, didn't she?"

"Mama." A young woman as tall as Celine, but much thinner, threaded an arm through Mrs. Arbuthnott's. "Won't you introduce me to your old friend's daughter?"

"Beatrice. There you are." Mrs. Arbuthnott swiveled her head from side to side again, in the manner of an anxious turtle. "Roland has been quite beside himself looking for you."

Beatrice was not only rather thin, but also remarkably plain, except for fine eyes the color of dark sapphires and exceedingly thick black hair that shimmered in an intricately plaited chignon. Celine noted that Viscount Yeatbury didn't appear to notice Beatrice's presence at all. Rather than being 'beside himself looking for her,' he continued to stare at Celine with puppylike appeal in his eyes.

"I'm Beatrice Arbuthnott," Beatrice said, smiling at Celine. "We're so glad you could come, aren't we, Mama?"

"Very glad." The woman's voice held no conviction.

Celine decided that she could come to like Beatrice. "Your home is very ... spectacular." In truth she'd rather live in her own rather threadbare house in Curzon Street than in this overdressed museum of a place.

"Celine. May I call you Celine?" The viscount was not to be distracted.

"Um, certainly."

"Thank you. And you must call me Roland."

"Steady on, old chap." Another, taller man of similar years, splendidly attired in military dress, separated from the crowd behind Mrs. Arbuthnott. "Have

a care with Roland here, Miss Godwin. Quite the ladies' man."

The viscount's smile wavered. "That's a blasted lie,
Teddy, and—" He shot a horrified look at Celine.
"Forgive a man his slack tongue. No intention of of-
fending, I assure you."

Celine giggled. She was beginning to enjoy herself.
"And no offense taken, my lord—Roland."

Conversation and pleasantries swelled around her.
Lettie, after touching her arm and indicating a corner
where other chaperons were seated, moved swiftly
away.

Mrs. Arbuthnott declared loudly that she had remembered Mary Detterling quite clearly now and
seemed disposed to be pleasant to a girl her daughter
evidently found engaging.

"I say, Celine," Viscount Yeatbury said as the heat
in the salon became intense. "Could I tempt you with
a glass of lemonade?"

"Why—"

"You can certainly tempt *me*, my lord." An extremely pretty red-haired girl presented herself beside Celine. "I simply cannot force my way to the
supper tables. I would surely faint."

A slight crook of one eyebrow was the viscount's
only sign of possible displeasure. "I'll do my best to
accommodate you, Miss . . . ?"

"Daphne DeClair." She pouted coyly and swayed
slightly in pale blue muslin that revealed an arresting
figure. "*Lady* Daphne DeClair. We've met. Or at least
I feel as if we have. My brother Benjamin has mentioned making your acquaintance at White's. Surely
he mentioned me to you."

Celine felt embarrassed for the prattling girl.

"I can't say that he has. Celine, I'll try not to be too
long."

"What an interesting dress." Lady Daphne turned

the full force of a calculating blue stare on Celine. Pure dislike shone there. "I do believe I may have seen another exactly like it."

"Really." Time to move on, but how? Celine searched for Lettie.

"Oh, yes. In fact, I seem to remember that the person who owned it told me that it had been made especially for her." Lady Daphne bent to see the hem of Celine's dress. "I don't recall the pleated gold, but, of course, an added slip, perhaps . . ." She allowed her voice to trail away.

A frantically bobbing head and a dash of scarlet brought Celine's attention to Isabel Prentergast. Isabel shook her head and pressed a warning finger to her lips.

"Oh!" Lady Daphne clapped her hands over her ears. "What a widgeon I am. Forgive me, Celine. Isabel will be so cross with me."

A pool of silent concentration formed within the group.

"I do believe I'd really like that lemonade, my lord," Celine said.

"Fustian! I have ruined your evening," Lady Daphne cried. "Please don't feel badly that you had to borrow a dress to come. We all know what a strain the Season can be on those of less ample means."

A glance at Isabel's horrified face brought Celine perilously close to laughter. "You are too kind, Lady Daphne," she said, clearing her throat. "But you are also not quite correct in your assumptions."

The girl's eyes sharpened once more and her pretty mouth took a malicious downward turn. "Pray explain."

"I'll be happy to, but not here where I would undoubtedly bore people. However . . ." She flipped her fan, silencing Lady Daphne's attempt to interrupt. "However, I will be delighted to share a very useful system I have devised that I'm sure you will find most advantageous."

"But—"

"No, no," Celine said, smiling her kindest, most understanding smile. "You deserve to hear about my discovery in its entirety. If you wish, we'll arrange a meeting. Roland, I believe I shall come with you to the supper tables after all."

"Delighted." The viscount offered an arm and Celine placed her hand upon his wrist. "Please excuse us," he said, guiding her past a bemused-looking Lady Daphne.

"Thank you," Celine said softly.

"Entirely my pleasure," he said. "Perhaps we should take a turn on the terrace. Escape the crush. A fella can't hear himself think in here."

Celine giggled. "I rather thought all this was exactly as it was supposed to be." No matter that she was revealing herself as new to the London scene. She truly liked Roland.

He laughed aloud. "You are wonderfully unspoiled, my dear. A delight indeed."

A gangly man stepped into their path. "Indeed," he mimicked. "Celine is *indeed* wonderfully unspoiled, aren't you, my dear?"

Celine's heart and stomach seemed to leap. She clutched Roland's arm. "Good evening, Mr. Letchwith."

The man pulled his lips back from his teeth, but no light entered his pale eyes. "Come, come, now. There doesn't have to be any formality between us. You know I'm Percival to you, sweet one."

"Who is this person?" Roland asked.

"I'd like some lemonade," Celine said desperately. "Could we get it now, please?" Several nearby guests made no pretense at not eavesdropping on the exchange.

Before she could protest again, Percival Letchwith covered her hand on the viscount's arm and pried it loose with thin, clammy fingers. He bowed to Roland. "I'll be glad to take Celine for refreshments. She's really very shy and knows nothing of the world . . . or of worldly behavior. Forgive her for giving you the impression that she is free to toss her attentions in any direction she pleases."

A woman with luxurious plumes attached to her head with glittering combs stared from Celine to Roland and on to Letchwith with open interest. Celine had either to allow this man she hated to keep his loathsome grip on her or make a scene for which her mama and papa would never forgive her.

The viscount raised a quizzical brow. "There is some formal connection between you and this man, Celine?"

"I am Percival Letchwith." Percival attempted an echo of Roland's raised brow and succeeded in drawing attention to blacking that had been poorly applied to straggling, colorless hairs. "I am acting for my father, who cannot be here this evening. Celine and I are to become related."

Now her heart felt perilously close to stopping completely. "That is not . . . It is not appropriate for you to make such statements, Mr. Letchwith."

"Oh, come, come now, dearest little Celine. Sir, as I said, she is enchantingly shy. She is also very modest and would not want to show how excited she is at the prospect of becoming my stepmother."

Chapter 11

"**S**hall we?" Percival Letchwith raised his beaked nose and thrust his sloping chin forward. "I think we won't take time for the lemonade, don't you, m'dear? Where is your chaperon? I'll dismiss her and escort you home myself."

"Never." Celine, smiling through gritted teeth, pretended to trip while she yanked her hand away. "Touch me again, sir, and I shall scream," she said beneath her breath. "And I assure you that my scream is legendary."

Viscount Yeatbury continued to stand at her other side, a troubled frown creasing his smooth brow. Celine tilted her head at him and said gaily, "Our lemonade seems ill-fated, Roland. Perhaps we should try once more to reach the supper tables."

Those guests who were closest, and who had paused to observe a possible source of a little new *on dit*, lost interest. The hubbub around Celine freshened.

Percival Letchwith was not to be so easily dispatched. "Need I remind you, Celine, that your parents are unlikely to be pleased if they hear of this rudeness? And neither is my father."

Celine feigned puzzlement, "Lewdness, Mr. Letchwith?" She searched around. "Where?"

"I said," Letchwith began very loudly, "I said your parents are . . . are . . ." Realizing that silence had again descended—on much of the salon this time—he closed his mouth and turned to see what had caused the rustling air of expectancy.

Murmurs rippled, bending elegantly coiffed heads and stirring the sea of richly textured and colored gowns.

A woman close to Celine stepped forward to gather a comment. Then she moved back, leaned toward the man at her side, and whispered gustily, "It *is* him. I didn't think he accepted invitations."

"Evidently he's accepted this one," came her companion's gruff response. "Can't imagine what all the fuss is about meself. After all, it isn't as if he *is* anyone."

"*That* kind of money always catches attention. Can the rumors be true, do you think? About the other matter?"

The man curled his lip. "Probably. Never did trust these foreigners."

"*Is* he foreign, Frederick? I mean, *really*?"

" 'Course he is. Wouldn't catch an Englishman dabbling in . . . Well, Dottie, y'know what I mean, that sort of thing just isn't *done*."

The lady giggled. "Not unless it can be kept under the sheets, mm?" Her mottled cheeks shone through heavy white powder. "But I imagine, if he's as rich as everyone says he is, that there'll be many a family prepared to look the other way. After all, even without a title, he'll be a brilliant catch for some chit."

Before Celine had further time to consider who the subject of this titillating exchange might be, a collective sense of a breath held, followed by a released sigh, preceded the drifting apart of guests in the vicinity of Mrs. Arbuthnott. A passage formed, and

Celine saw a tall man's black curly hair moving in her direction.

There was only one man whose presence she could feel in her flesh and bones ... and heart.

James Eagleton, a darkly arresting figure in black evening dress, strode, unsmiling, to stand before their hostess. "Mrs. Arbuthnott?"

The gold lorgnette flashed and that lady inspected her newly arrived guest with an appearance of avid interest. "I am Hedwiga Arbuthnott. You're the Eagleton fellow?"

Celine pressed a hand beneath her breasts. A sensation like the fluttering of a thousand birds' wings made her tremble.

"James Eagleton, madam. At your service."

Mrs. Arbuthnott smirked and flipped open a gold fan embellished with lacquered purple peacocks. "If certain people are to be believed, your service might be exceedingly entertaining."

A collective gasp dissolved into chuckles.

Celine could not imagine what was amusing but decided she did not care a fig for Mrs. Arbuthnott or her evident baiting of James Eagleton.

"What exactly are you doing here, Mr. Eagleton?"

At Mrs. Arbuthnott's bald question, another gasp burst from the onlookers.

James appeared not to notice. He'd chosen that moment to examine the faces of his audience ... at least until he found one that held his attention.

Celine's lips parted.

His glittering gray stare watched her mouth for an instant before settling, unwaveringly, on her eyes.

Celine's hand went to her throat.

He turned up the corners of his mouth, and now his gaze shifted down a fraction, and down a fraction more.

Celine took in a deep breath.

His broad chest expanded beneath a startlingly white shirt that was as notable for its austere simplicity, as were his immaculate neckcloth and the waistcoat that fit without a wrinkle over a flat midsection.

Celine spread her fingers above the low neck of her gown.

He shifted his stance, bracing his feet apart. Surely no other man's trousers fit every solid muscle, every taut line ... followed every curving shadow ...

Celine's face grew hot and she quickly looked upward again.

James Eagleton's lips parted in a smile that said, as well as any words, that he'd watched her watching him—and that he gained satisfaction from the thrall in which he could hold her.

Mrs. Arbuthnott tapped him so suddenly with her fan that several people jumped. "I asked you a question, Mr. Eagleton."

"Which was?"

"Why are you here?"

"You invited me."

"And you declined, sir."

"Did I?" His eyes never moved from Celine's. "How odd. Perhaps I did. I must have found a reason to change my mind."

Celine discovered she couldn't look away. He was telling her that he was here because of her, because she'd mentioned coming to the rout this evening.

James bowed faintly, and she lowered her lashes. Why could he make her heart gallop and her legs weak? Why had he only to look at her to produce this heavy, warm longing ... this longing for what? His touches were new, nothing she had ever experienced before. Why would he want to take time to make her feel the piercingly wonderful sensations she longed to feel again, even now? He gained nothing ... *did* he?

"How much of what is said about you is true, Mr. Eagleton?"

At that, he turned to his hostess. "What exactly *is* said about me, madam?"

"That you have an . . . *unusual* household."

"Some might consider it so."

"But you do not?"

"I consider myself the most fortunate of men." He contrived to catch Celine's eye once more. "I pursue only those alliances that serve me well . . . and bring me pleasure . . . inside and *outside* my household."

She brought *him* pleasure?

Percival Letchwith sniffed so explosively that several heads turned. "I do believe the bounder is looking at you, Celine," he muttered, not quietly enough. "We shall depart at once."

"I shall depart when I am ready to depart," she told him. "And *not* with you."

The drone of conversation and soaring bursts of laughter had resumed. Only those immediately in the vicinity of James continued to watch and whisper together. Lady Daphne closed on Viscount Yeatbury once more and proceeded to chatter in low tones while contriving to turn him away from Celine.

Percival Letchwith placed himself in front of her, deliberately blocking any view of James. "You appear hot, m'dear," he said, his light eyes lingering at the level of her chest. Dropping his voice, he added, "I suggest you do as you're told, girl. My father would not appreciate learning that you have been less than accommodating to his son."

Celine's stomach churned . . . and her temper boiled. "I owe no uncommon attention to your father, or to you. Kindly go away."

Before she guessed his intention, Percival's hand closed on her wrist and he pulled her closer until she was forced to stare either into his face or at the fussy cascade of lace that didn't quite disguise his concave chest. Celine chose the lace.

"Release me, sir."

"You will do as you are told, you little fool," Percival whispered hoarsely. "It isn't for you to state your desires. Your parents are right—you need a firm hand, and my father and I are just the men to see to it that you get that firm hand."

Celine felt a rushing sickness. Even as her blood seemed to drain downward, there was a dizzying heat in her head. She would not be consigned to these odious men. She would *not*.

"Good evening, Miss Godwin. How very pleasant to see you here."

She raised her eyes until she saw James Eagleton's handsome face. He stood behind Letchwith, looking down at her over the other man's stooped shoulder.

"G-good evening, Mr. Eagleton. The pleasure is mutual."

Percival tightened his grip and gave her a little shake. Slowly, still holding her wrist, he turned toward James and said, "I'm Percival Letchwith. This young lady is—"

"Mr. Letchwith's father is an acquaintance of my father," Celine said hurriedly. "Mr. Percival Letchwith, this is Mr. James Eagleton."

"I *know* who he is." Percival's high voice cracked. "I doubt there's anyone in the house who *doesn't* know who he is. Now, if you'll excuse us, sir?"

"I'll gladly excuse you." James's bared-teeth smile was ferocious. "This is uncommonly good fortune—for you."

Percival rocked onto the balls of his feet. "How so?"

"Because I hadn't thought to locate you so easily."

A suspicious glimmer hovered in Percival's eyes. He said nothing.

"There was a man asking for you. At the front door. Bit brash and mannerless."

Celine watched Percival's reaction with interest. He sucked in his thin lips and rolled them out again, then repeated the process. Protruding veins pulsed beneath white skin at his temples.

James laughed. "I can see you don't believe me. Can't think why, but no matter. He probably had the name wrong. Kept shouting something about a sporting club or some such foolishness."

Percival's fingers slowly uncurled from Celine's wrist. "Sporting club? Are you sure, man?"

James shrugged offhandedly. "Don't give it another thought. Anyone can see you aren't a sporting sort."

Celine smothered a laugh, but Percival showed no sign of having noted the insult. "Egad," he mumbled. "Egad." Leading with his nonexistent chin once more, he minced rapidly away without so much as another glance in Celine's direction. The last word she heard him utter was another strangled "*Egad.*"

"Egad," a different voice said, soft and deep, close to her ear. "You, my golden girl, are a vision. Shall I rescue you from this very unpleasant place?"

Slowly, she raised her face to James's and said, "You have been on my mind," without ever having intended to say such a thing.

"Good. And you have been on mine."

Lady Daphne, spinning away from Viscount Yeatbury, trotted to stand at James's elbow. She gazed at him with undisguised admiration. "You're the James Eagleton of shipping fame, aren't you?"

The smile on his face became fixed. "Yes."

"This is Lady Daphne—"

"Daphne is quite formal enough among friends." Lady Daphne interrupted Celine, then appeared freshly interested in her. "Is Celine an acquaintance of yours, Mr. Eagleton?"

"She is."

Lady Daphne sighed. "Oh, dear. Perhaps *you* can persuade her to forgive me for the addlepated faux pas I made earlier. Do tell Celine that I would rather cut out my tongue than upset someone so sweet and charming."

James's response was to raise one dark, arched brow.

"You will help, I can see that. Isabel is cross with me, too, so you see there's nothing a poor girl can do but try to make amends, is there?"

James inclined his head.

A flutter of scarlet and white materialized, and Isabel Prentergast rushed to thread an arm through Lady Daphne's. "Do leave well enough alone, Daphne," Isabel said. Her cheeks were deeply pink. "I'm sure Celine would prefer that we not draw any more attention to the situation, wouldn't you, Celine?"

Celine regarded Isabel's anxious face and felt sympathy.

Lady Daphne's eyes gleamed spitefully. "Isabel has such a gentle heart. She wants to save everyone, even though that simply isn't always possible. There are times when it's best for certain people to accept their position in life. Don't you agree, Celine? Now that you've realized the potential for disaster that lies in such . . . well, in presuming upon the tender sensibilities of people like Isabel?"

Celine took a deep breath. Viscount Yeatbury and his military friend hovered in attendance, together with several other men. Two more girls of similar age to Celine crowded in.

Lady Daphne rested her closed fan against her bottom lip. "I think Isabel deserves recognition for being so charitable, don't you, Celine?"

Isabel Prentergast's face was a dull shade of red.

There had to be a solution to this conundrum . . . *There was!* Of course, it was a terrible gamble, but . . .

"Doesn't Celine look wonderful in *Isabel's* dress?" Lady Daphne delivered her killing thrust with triumphant vigor.

There was no choice left. Celine smiled in all directions and swayed, stroking her yellow muslin skirts. "Our secret is out! And Isabel must take the credit for a wonderful idea. Perfectly marvelous, in fact."

"Oh, no." Isabel frowned and her throat jerked. "It was entirely Celine's idea. I merely decided that if I could help her implement it, I would."

Lady Daphne gave a gurgling laugh of glee. "Well done, Isabel. Place the credit squarely where it belongs. Honesty is the only thing, don't you know."

"What is all this?" James asked quietly.

Celine smiled up at him and summoned the courage to continue. "Isabel did agree that the idea was good. Simply put, it has seemed to me a shocking extravagance—in the face of so much need among such vast numbers of people—that many, many beautiful gowns are worn so few times. I decided the best solution to this dilemma was for those young females who felt similarly concerned to, er, effect exchanges. In this way, a true service could be done in the name of thrift and charity. After all, can it be said that this gown appears any the less . . . *interesting* for having been used by someone else before me?"

A lusty male denial sounded.

"Do you mean you *borrowed* that gown from Isabel?" Lady Daphne asked, sounding peeved. "She didn't *give* it to you?"

"Quite so," Celine announced loftily. "I have decided that this shall be my effort in the name of social awareness. After all, are we not all taught that young ladies should learn very early of the value of good works—and make them a part of their lives?"

"Here, here," Roland said solemnly, drawing forth a rumble of agreement.

Celine turned to Isabel. "Thank you for being brave enough to help me in this. Rest assured that the money I did not spend on a new gown is, even now, furthering the education of poor, honest, deserving women."

"Commendable," Roland said, smiling at Isabel.

"Amazing," James muttered.

Celine didn't look at him. Warmed by the positive reception of her announcement, she squared her shoulders and said, "My personal motto has become: Second is best. Never wear a oncer."

"Admirable," a male voice said.

"Truly, she is an *originale*," said another.

"Never wear a oncer," a pale girl in stark white repeated to herself.

The gamble had worked ... at least for now.

Chapter 12

"**M**ay I escort you to the supper tables, Celine?" James asked, offering her his arm. "You must be quite exhausted from your exertions and in need of that lemonade."

Returning Isabel's tremulous smile of gratitude, Celine allowed James to lead her away while Roland remained kindly at the other girl's side.

"I should tell Lettie where I'm going," she said, suddenly breathless.

"I'm certain Miss Fisher would quite approve of your being in my company. After all"—he bowed in response to a man's greeting—"we are hardly alone."

"I suppose not." She was, Celine decided, not breathless because of any supposed exertion but because James's large, warm hand rested atop hers on his steady arm, and with every step she took her hip brushed his hard thigh.

They left the salon and descended the stairs. Celine was startled to hear the word *oncer* whispered with almost reverent respect on more than a few occasions. *On dit* developed flying feet in such an assembly.

Rather than guiding her toward the rooms where refreshments were served, James made a sharp turn at the bottom of the stairs and walked rapidly toward the back of the house.

"Where are we going?" Celine asked, all but running to keep pace.

"How thirsty are you?"

"I . . . not very."

"Neither am I."

A door opened into a dimly lighted library which was, surprisingly, empty of guests.

"Oh, how lovely." Celine trotted happily at James's side. "Empty. There is actually fresh air in here."

"There is even more air outside." French doors stood open onto a terrace.

"You know this house? You must have been here before."

"Never." James walked with her to the low stone railing edging the terrace. "Houses have gardens. Houses of this variety have terraces leading to those gardens—at the back of those houses. Simple deduction, my dear. How many dresses have you *borrowed*?"

The abruptness of the question surprised Celine. "Um . . . several. Do you not consider my plan a fine one?"

"Possibly. When we met you were wearing green. Did you borrow that dress?"

She raised her chin, disliking his aggressive tone. "Yes, I did."

"The color suits you. I hope you'll wear it again."

Celine stared unseeingly into the garden. From behind a layer of clouds the moon shone, blue-gray, on shrubs and trees. "The dresses are only borrowed," she said, disliking the fabrication she felt forced to invent. "They are not mine to keep."

"So, you wear the dress once and return it."

"I . . . I don't keep the dresses." She would explain to David this tale she had spun. He would understand and tell her that the cause was just and that she should not concern herself about small, necessary untruths ... almost untruths.

"Explain your position with the man, Letchwith."

Celine bridled. "I do not have to explain anything to you, sir."

"No, you don't. My name is James. Will you answer my question?"

"I have no position with Percival Letchwith ... James."

"But it is possible that you are attached in some way to his father?"

She faced him. "How do you know that? I mean, no! No, it is not so."

"Gossip spreads rapidly, my dear. I heard there is talk of your betrothal to Mr. Bertram Letchwith, who is a wealthy merchant and a close friend of your father's."

He sounded—angry? "There is no betrothal," Celine said thoughtfully. Why angry?

"Perhaps it is your father's wish that you marry this man."

James loomed over her. At this moment he appeared overly large and more than a little menacing, and he stood extremely close.

"Let us walk in the gardens. Perhaps you will feel more free to speak where there is no danger of being overheard." His eyes glittered and the parting of his lips showed a flash of very white teeth.

He seemed more dangerous than any threat of being overheard. "I think not." But she wanted to go into the garden with him, wanted to feel again the thrill of their being alone—together.

"Are you afraid of me, Celine?"

It was as if he saw her very thoughts. "I am afraid of nothing," she announced firmly.

"Nothing?" He laughed, and the sound played

along her nerves. That laugh held a challenge—and it held the offer of Pleasure.

"Almost nothing," she said, more subdued.

"Then walk with me between the trees, golden girl. I need space and air—and I need you to help light my way."

Her heart turned. Surely he toyed with her.

"Celine, will you?" He took her hand between both of his. "A little way. I'll keep you safe."

His tone mesmerized her. "Yes. But I must return soon or Lettie will worry about me." She knew she should not go, that no young lady should risk compromising her honor, even if only through unfounded rumor.

"I'll return you soon enough."

Their progress down the wide stone steps was languid. James held Celine's right hand in his and rested his left lightly at her waist. A path wound between hedges that reached above Celine's head. Soon there was no hint of light from the house behind them and she felt cut off . . . and deeply excited . . . and afraid.

"I think this is far enough," she said at last and in a small voice. "The air is fresh here and there is plenty of it, don't you think?"

"Mm."

They stood beneath the swaying branches of a chestnut tree. The moon made of the leaves a shivering chiaroscuro over the grass at their feet.

"The scent of the flowers is lovely."

"Mm."

James eased Celine back against his chest and folded his arms around her waist.

"Sweet Williams, I think. And night-scented stocks." Her heart beat so fast and wild. Surely he heard it, felt it?

"Mm."

Gently, he rubbed his jaw against her hair. Gently back and forth. Gently. Gently.

"Country flowers are my favorites. Sweet. They remind me of home. Of Dorset."

He stopped rubbing for an instant.

"Sometimes—whenever I can—I ride Cleopatra toward the coast at night. The wind on my face smells of salt from the sea and of wildflowers. Cleopatra is my dear little gelding—"

"Gelding?"

"Oh, yes."

"Cleopatra?"

"Oh, yes. I've always loved the name. It sounds so brave."

"But . . . never mind. Is he a black?"

"A gray. He knows every word I say."

"A gray gelding called Cleopatra?"

"Exactly! You would love him if you saw him."

"I'm sure I shall," James said, and he kissed her temple softly. "I'm sure I could come to love anything that mattered to you, Celine."

He was an enigma; one minute hard and cold and fearsome, and the next so gentle he made her want to cry. Only she never cried.

Almost without her noticing, James slid his hands from her waist and spread them wide over her ribs, resting his thumbs on the soft and very sensitive undersides of her breasts.

He kissed her cheek, her jaw, her neck, her shoulder.

Celine felt James's breath, warm as silk, sliding over the swelling flesh above her bodice. He made a deep, satisfied sound.

He did gain pleasure from touching her!

Celine's half-closed eyes flew open.

It was for the pleasure of being with her, of touching her, that he pursued and isolated her. The sweet words—were because he felt what she felt.

"Celine?" His voice was different and he raised his face until she knew he was trying to study her. "What is it?"

There was a way. There was a way to beat Bertram Letchwith, to save her from a fate that would make her wish she were dead.

Bubbling with excitement, yet determined to let him see none of it, Celine twisted to face James. Composing her features into a serious mold, she rested her palms on his shirtfront and gazed up at him.

"What?" he asked, and she could see his frown.

"I believe far too many men and women marry for all the wrong reasons."

James's fingers, now laced behind her back, slackened and fell to her waist.

"Don't you consider it a tragedy that men and women considering spending the rest of their lives together don't sensibly make sure that they are completely compatible—*before* the ceremony?"

"Ah . . . well . . ."

"*Exactly!*" This would go extremely well. She could almost taste success, but she must be patient. Tonight would be but the beginning, and she must be prepared to suffer failure should it come her way. However, if she had judged the situation correctly, by persuading James that, while she desired his attention, she had no notion of drawing him into marriage, he might become the ally she needed.

"Exactly what, Celine?" James asked gruffly.

"It's absolutely imperative for parties considering marriage to get all the questions out of the way as soon as possible."

James dropped his hands, but Celine took firm hold of his coat.

"What sort of questions?"

"First, what do you think a woman should be able to expect from her husband ... in order to feel that they are matched, that is?"

He cleared his throat. "Probably ... the *deeper* elements that concern the wife?"

"*Exactly!* Oh, James, this is so exciting." Perhaps, eventually, she might even hope for something lasting between them. "Kindness and gentleness and a warm sense of being safe ... and total understanding, of course. Those are the things she should know he will give her. And *you* guessed immediately."

"Kindness and gentleness"—James voice was unusually faint—"and ... total understanding?"

"Oh, yes, yes."

"And what"—he sounded so thoughtful—"should this man expect from his wife?"

"Well ..." The obedience part really didn't appeal. "She should be understanding, too, of course. Whenever possible." Submissiveness was, in Celine's opinion, a word better forgotten.

"Go on," James invited.

"A husband should always regard his wife as his equal."

He coughed so forcefully that Celine contrived to thump a fist between his shoulders.

The cough stopped abruptly and she found herself trapped against him, her face barely an inch from his chest.

"And what else"—his voice cracked—"what else should the *husband* expect?"

This was going further than she had planned for the first step—not that she had actually planned the first step, or any step until a few minutes ago.

"Celine?"

"Oh, yes. I think the husband should expect to be

able to admire his wife above all others in the world—including himself."

This time he was silent for so long that she became uncomfortable in the steely crook of his arm.

"Was there anything else you thought might be useful ... for couples considering matrimony?" he asked at last.

"I'm sure I shall remember more, but for now there are just the absolutes. Perhaps I should mention those."

"The absolutes?"

"Exactly. It is absolutely essential that the husband understand those things his wife absolutely cannot tolerate. And then, naturally, there must be compromise."

The noise James made was probably a request for clarification.

"For instance, I absolutely could not bear having my husband read at the breakfast table."

"What should he do then?" How strange he sounded.

"Eat, of course. And talk to me. After all, there would be plenty of time to read while I was about my duties ... shopping and entertaining and, well, you know the type of thing."

"Are there other *absolutes*?"

"Yes. Certainly. I cannot bear to see a man march into a house in dirty boots. It's frightful. Clods of mud everywhere. I would expect boots removed. And there's the matter of imbibing. Drunkenness disgusts me. My husband would not drink."

"At all?"

"Not at all. And, since I have an unshakable fear of anything that creeps, he would be responsible for inspecting my bedchamber every night before I went to bed to ensure that no such horror was in residence."

"What about before *he* goes to bed?"

"What he does in his bedchamber would be of no interest to me."

He seemed to jerk.

"James? Are you all right?"

"Mm. Fine." If she didn't know otherwise she'd be convinced he was laughing. Or trying not to cough. Yes, he evidently had a cough. "Is there more?" he asked.

"Not now. I should go back to Lettie." Enough preparation had been laid for one night. Better retreat and see what developed.

"But . . ." His hands tightened about her once more and Celine strained to see his face. He stared over her head. "You're right. We should get back."

Celine tried to turn around. James held her fast.

"We cannot walk if you do not let me go, James."

"No. No, we can't." He held her even more firmly. Somewhere behind, she heard a swishing followed by the sound of cracking twigs. "James? What . . . ? Answer me!" He'd seen something. She knew he had. "James! Say something!"

"Time to go in," he said brightly. "My, but I'm tired."

The instant he began to release her, Celine spun around and searched in the darkness on the opposite side of the path.

"Let's go." James caught her elbow. "We must find our way back quickly and without being noticed."

"To save my honor," Celine said distractedly. "No need to worry about that."

"I beg your pardon?"

"There's someone hiding over there. I heard him and so did you." Catching James unawares, she darted from him. "Come out, you spy! Come out now! Show yourself, skulking coward!"

"Celine, please—"

"Fear not, James. I shall shame him out. Aha. I see

you!" The moon picked out a shiny garment and
Celine launched herself at the spy. "I've got you!"
She had, in fact, two handfuls of silky material, but
the wearer tugged fiercely and threatened to escape.

"Enough!" James roared. His arm shot around
Celine's waist and he hauled her feet from the
ground. "Liam! Do not move!"

Liam?

Celine stopped kicking and James let her slip
slowly down until her feet touched the pathway once
more. In front of her, with James's other hand
clamped on a fragile-looking shoulder, stood a tiny
young woman. Moonlight threw shadows over features so exotic that Celine caught her breath. This
was an utterly beautiful creature who could not be
any older than Celine, if as old. Her silvery, silken
garment was cut quite straight but did not disguise
her small, perfect woman's body. About her head
wound a profusion of blue-black braids that glistened with each haughty toss.

"You know this person?" Celine asked James.

"Does James know me?" The woman's voice lilted,
clipping each syllable in a faintly foreign manner that
Celine immediately wished she could imitate. "James
knows me very, very well. And I know him better
than any other. We have lived together for a long
time. Years."

"Oh!"

"Celine, Liam is of another culture." James continued to hold her arm and the other creature's shoulder as if they might fly away. "You would not
understand the relationship between us."

"No," Liam agreed. "You would not understand at
all."

Celine began to think that perhaps she understood
quite well. There had been mention of certain *unusual*
circumstances in James's household. A green girl she

might be, but she was not an utter fool. No doubt this beautiful girl—this poor, beautiful creature—was another who had fallen victim to James's undeniable talents in the area of *Passion* and had done so, evidently, when she was little more than a child.

Well, this would be one more challenge to be dealt with. "You are right, of course," she said, keeping her voice steady. "I certainly don't understand. But no matter. I will see myself back to the house. You should take Liam home now, James." She began to walk swiftly in the direction from which they had come.

"Celine!"

"Thank you, James." She began to run. Immediately a great, heavy lump formed in her throat. Her eyes filled with tears. No! She would not cry.

Footsteps pounded behind her. "Celine!" He caught her elbow.

"See," she said, grasping for breath. "The house is already in sight." It did not matter that another woman felt as she did with him. Her plan could still be made to work.

"I want you to understand about Liam."

"I do understand, James. And I really don't mind."

"You don't *mind*? What the hell . . . What do you mean by that?"

The girl was already beside him once more.

"It's perfectly all right that you keep a strange household."

"Damn and blast it. It's not the way you think it is, Celine. Liam is . . . She is my housekeeper."

She regarded them both unflinchingly. Housekeeper? She would have to ask David about that term. It didn't seem of quite the same kind as *abbess* or *nunnery*, but he had said there were a host of terms intended to divert one from reality.

Celine raised her chin. She was a woman with a

cause; to save herself and to save as many other helpless, misguided women as possible. Liam might prove difficult but, with David's help, a way would be found to set her on the path to worthier ideals.

"You invited me to ride in the park tomorrow, James?"

"What ... Yes, I did, but you said you'd be too tired after the rout."

"I've changed my mind. I'll be ready at four o'clock." She pulled away from his unresisting hand and started for the house. "I shall look forward to seeing you. We'll have a great deal to discuss."

He didn't respond, but she felt him watch her until she reached the steps to the terrace, climbed up, and crossed into the library.

As she approached the door to the rest of the house, she smiled grimly. How would he respond to the proposition she intended to present?

Once back in the melee beyond the library, she hurried in search of Lettie. Time to go home and rest—and consider her strategy for the morrow. Yes, one must choose words with great care when asking a man to ruin one's reputation.

Chapter 13

The girl would be his. On his terms.

James nodded at Miss Fisher and paced back and forth across the Godwins' dismal entrance hall.

"Are . . . are you enjoying your stay in London, Mr. Eagleton?"

"Yes." He must keep his frustration well hidden. "Yes, very much so."

"Good."

He nodded again and continued to pace.

Last night James had realized that the early victories with Celine had been due as much to the element of surprise being on his side as to his prowess. In the Arbuthnott garden, her reaction had been that of a young female suddenly very much aware of propriety.

And the talk of her expectations in marriage!

Good God, but females could be bloody infuriating. A husband should consider his wife superior even to himself? And he should not read at the breakfast table—or drink at all! And then she'd as good as commanded him to appear this afternoon as if he were no more than a lovesick cub whom she could lead about at her pleasure.

She would learn well the difference between a lovesick cub and a man of the world—and he would make certain she learned to be grateful for the revelation.

"I'm sure Celine will be down at any moment, Mr. Eagleton." Miss Fisher, having failed to persuade him to wait in the parlor, hovered between James and the foot of the stairs. "I can't think what can be keeping her. She came down once. Shortly before you arrived. But then she said she ... Well, anyway, she'll be down soon."

James stopped pacing. "I'm sure she will." He had startled the pugnacious Godwin butler by refusing to give up his hat, which he now held in one hand behind his back. Time was of the essence. Time was all. Even the moments required to retrieve a hat would be too many today. Not only must he race to secure his position with Celine before the Godwins arrived, but he must do so before some young buck could complicate things by pressing his attentions upon her. He hadn't failed to notice the male admiration sent her way at last night's rout.

"Do I recall that you told Celine you are a visitor to England? From foreign parts? China?"

"Not exactly China, Miss Fisher. Paipan—where my business dealings are centered—is a small island in the South China Sea."

"How interesting such a place must be. Mysterious, I shouldn't wonder."

"Interesting, yes. I suppose some might find it mysterious, but I have spent too long on the island not to find it commonplace." Not strictly true, but any suggestion of evidence he could present in opposition to the gossip circulating about him and his supposedly flamboyant household would be useful—particularly in these quarters.

Miss Lettie Fisher was a handsome woman in a quiet way. A little taller than average, with thick, lustrous brown hair worn in a simple chignon at her nape and clear dark eyes that held his with no suggestion of either temerity or guile, she could be no more than perhaps five and thirty. James decided he quite approved of her. In fact, she might become a valuable ally in his quest if he could cause her to approve of him, too.

One step at a time. First he must contrive to have her agree to wait in the carriage this afternoon while he and Celine took a walk together ... alone. That would be difficult enough. But today he intended to find a way to tempt Celine farther down the road to final seduction. Soon he must take her to the end of that road, an end from which she would never entirely return. He would do his best to spare her great grief, but there could be no compromising the promise he had made to his father.

"Do you intend to return to Paipan soon, Mr. Eagleton?"

He hid a smile. The lady's primary interest here was not in his plans but in how they might affect her charge. "I have no definite intentions in that direction, Miss Fisher." He smiled warmly. "I am, after all—first and always—an Englishman. England is my true home and I'm mightily pleased to be on English soil once more. My business can be as well run here as in Paipan. No, I don't think I shall leave again soon." At least, no sooner than the moment he'd accomplished what he came for.

"Ah, here she is." Miss Fisher's relief was visible. "Hurry, Celine. Mr. Eagleton has been waiting."

"It is of no matter," he murmured.

At that instant the waiting was definitely of no matter at all. Celine Godwin, descending the stairs with sure, unselfconscious steps, would have been worth a great deal more loitering in any hall, even one as graceless as this. Muscles in his jaw contracted—as did certain other parts of him. She was utterly desirable, from her beautiful, innocent face to every voluptuous inch of her body. James made a fist of the hand that held his gloves.

"Good afternoon," she said, smiling down upon him. "Please forgive me for keeping you waiting. I discovered my stockings were mismatched and needed to be changed. Oh, my, James, do be grateful you do not have to struggle with such female inconveniences as garters. What a fuss they are when one already as one's dress on and has to bundle it up—"

"Celine," Miss Fisher said ominously, bringing the girl to a halt. "I don't think Mr. Eagleton wishes to know of such things."

James thought to smile at Celine's naive chatter, but found himself capable only of looking at her. If she'd "borrowed" the carriage dress she wore, then its owner had singular taste and daring. But he rather thought that this creation was of Celine's own choosing.

A fine velvet pelisse in a shimmering shade of golden-orange fell from its high, tight waist to deep points tipped by tiny silver bells. The pelisse, cut into narrower points along its neckline, was fastened by a single chartreuse satin button below Celine's full breasts, and the dress visible beneath was of vivid chartreuse silk. Her bonnet was a close-fitting confection of the orange velvet and chartreuse silk, wound together and trimmed at one ear with a cluster of silver bells like those on the pelisse.

This house of miserly browns, this hall of dimness, faded in the girl's presence as it had on that first afternoon when he'd taken her into the rose gardens.

Frowning slightly, Celine continued down. "Is something wrong, Mr. . . . James?"

He realized he'd been staring. "Nothing, my dear. You are the most charming vision this man has seen in . . . has ever seen." And the devil was, he meant it.

"Come. The sun is more fickle than I'd been led to believe it might be. And I've no doubt Miss Fisher would prefer to enjoy the Park while we are still assured of a little warmth."

"I had thought I might remain at home this afternoon," Miss Fisher said. "If you wouldn't mind, Mr. Eagleton."

He looked at the woman sharply, then fashioned a smile of sorts. "Are you unwell, Miss Fisher?" This was a singular development, enticing in its implications for him, yet puzzling.

She produced a small handkerchief and touched it to her nose. "It's nothing. Nothing at all. And I could come, of course, if you insist. But I do admit to a slight indisposition and, in the absence of Celine's parents, it is my responsibility to decide what is appropriate and acceptable for her. I consider you a reliable man who will, I'm convinced, take every care with so tender a girl." She gave him a meaningful look which she was careful to shield from Celine. "I'm certain you will take such a trust most seriously."

"But of course." He managed to keep a somber, concerned note in his voice. A vague disquiet assailed him. Miss Fisher must have some mysterious purpose for such amazing disregard for propriety, but he was damned if he could guess what it was. "Perhaps you would prefer this outing to be postponed? We wouldn't want—"

"Not at all." If he didn't know better, he'd say Miss Fisher could scarcely wait to be rid of Celine. "Go. Enjoy yourselves."

Celine skipped down the final stairs amid the tinkle of little silver bells. An enchanting creature indeed, but he must not forget who she was and what she represented.

"Of course"—Miss Fisher coughed—"I could come

if you would feel more comfortable with that arrangement."

"We'll manage, Lettie," Celine said, her voice light and cheerful. "Shall we not, James?"

"Oh, definitely." They would manage *very* well. The decision to allow Celine to go unchaperoned in his company could simply be a flattering tribute to his apparently honorable demeanor. James frowned, growing increasingly disturbed by the turn of events.

"Don't worry about us." Hitching a ridiculously tiny reticule decorated with bells and feathers higher on her wrist, Celine slipped on chartreuse silk gloves. "Come, James. Lettie, what did I do with my parasol? I brought it downstairs earlier."

That lady quickly produced the required item and gave it to Celine, who, most surprisingly, kissed her companion's cheek and smiled affectionately before almost running to the door. "Do come along, James."

Yes, my golden girl, I shall come along and so shall you—very nicely.

Once through the door and into the sunshine, she laughed back at him, and a breeze whipped forward the curls around her face.

James paused at the top of the steps and watched her. She was like a wild young thing too long confined who had been unexpectedly freed.

Wild and so young. And upon that youth and inexperience he would prey.

In that moment he felt the weight of his cynicism and worldliness like a blackness of the soul. Perhaps he should catch this wild, colorful, tinkling butterfly of a woman and run with her, allow her to make him new again.

"Come, James!"

Too late for fanciful dreaming.

"I am coming."

By the time he gained the flagway, Celine was no

longer giggling and spinning. Instead she stood, utterly silent, before Won Tel.

This would not be simple to explain. "The landau pleases you?" James asked, hoping to slide by the questions she must be forming about his unlikely coachman.

Her face turned slightly toward him but her eyes remained raised toward Won Tel's. Her lips parted. Won Tel smiled so widely that his teeth appeared as a white slash from ear to ear between mustache and beard.

"I decided on the burgundy color because it has always been a favorite of mine," James said. In fact he didn't give a damn about the color. The carriage had been available for immediate purchase and that had been that. "And I thought the black relief particularly handsome. Do you agree, Celine?"

"Um . . ." Her face turned a little more, still without the remotest shift of her eyes. "Yes, the landau is splendid. I've never ridden in a carriage as splendid before. Our old town coach is a disgrace, but Mama and Papa don't care. They always take cabs when they're in town, or so I'm told. I really don't know anything about their life when they are here."

He almost laughed at her discomposure. "How often are your parents here?" Any clues he could use to his advantage would be welcome.

"Not often. Usually only when they've had one of their wild turns—a really wild turn—and then they disappear for days or sometimes weeks and it's said they come here, and . . . Oh! Why am I chattering so?"

James shrugged and made certain to show no particular sign of interest in her almost unconscious prattle. "This is Won Tel, Celine. He has been with my family for many years." There would be plenty of time to find out more about these "wild turns."

"Good afternoon, Mr. Won Tel," Celine said seriously. Her awe at the man's size and unusual mode of dress hung in each word. "Is driving a carriage in Paipan similar to driving a carriage in London?"

"Very similar," Won Tel said, without a pause, and without sending James the evil glare he must long to send. "I will drive you and your companion with great care." Entertaining Miss Fisher while James was alone with Celine was to have been Won Tel's mission.

The request for Won Tel's services as coachman had been received with ill grace. In light of the reasons given, James's old friend had eventually, if unwillingly, accepted his task.

"My companion will not be accompanying us," Celine said.

Won Tel paused in the act of opening the landau door. "She won't? What a misfortune. Perhaps I may have the honor of driving her on a future occasion." Relief at his reprieve relaxed his smile.

In his newfound cheerfulness, Won Tel seemed to forget that he should hand Celine up into the carriage. Instead, he slapped James on the back and went to check the horses.

James settled Celine and sat opposite in the open vehicle. He glanced at the sky, almost grinned at the dark clouds that had begun to scud across a paling sun and rapidly formulated a change of plan.

Won Tel had finally taken his place and they were about to pull away when the front door of the house opened once more, and Miss Fisher, her gray skirts flying behind, rushed down the steps. She did not, James noted, appear in the slightest indisposed.

"A moment!" she called, brandishing a basket that appeared too heavy for her slender arms.

Reining in the horses, Won Tel leaped down from the box.

"Oh." Miss Fisher's reaction to Won Tel was so similar to Celine's that James smothered a laugh. "Yes, well ..." Her dark eyes were huge. "This is a small refreshment in case ... I thought there might be an opportunity for ... Here you are."

Miss Fisher held the basket out to Won Tel, who didn't immediately take it. Instead, he regarded Celine's companion intently.

"Will you take it?" Miss Fisher asked quietly. She stared steadily up into Won Tel's face. "Are you from Paipan?"

"I am."

"I thought so. Is it mysterious?"

"Occasionally. Where are you from, madam?"

"It's miss. Miss Lettie Fisher. I'm from Dorset presently. I was born in Devon. On a farm. Then I went into service close by."

"My name is Won Tel." He took the weight of the basket without removing it from Miss Fisher's hands. "We shall be in Dorset shortly. At Blackburn Manor."

"Is that a fact?" Miss Fisher's serious face glowed with her smile. "Then perhaps we shall meet again, Mr. Won Tel. I'm in service very close to Blackburn Manor."

James narrowed his eyes in disbelief. Won Tel appeared to have forgotten the presence of his master and Celine. James glanced at Celine and found that his own amazement at their servants' exchange was mirrored in her face.

"Are you certain you wouldn't care to accompany—"

"I'll take great care of Celine," James interrupted Won Tel. "Good afternoon to you, Miss Fisher."

The companion turned and ran lightly up the steps and into the house while Won Tel placed the basket inside the carriage—beside the one Liam had provided—and resumed his position behind the horses.

James let a few minutes pass before making the first move toward his goal. "I do believe the weather may be changing."

"Yes." She didn't look at him.

"No matter. One of the beauties of the landau is that it may easily be enclosed."

"Yes."

So the chit was already becoming a little wary of being alone with him again. That could be bad, or it could be extremely good—if she responded to the promise of excitement as he thought she might.

No matter. He expected her to resist his advances. Last night's events had assured him that she thought all of life a great game, including his attentions. No doubt she would expect to enjoy his kisses and a little more of what she'd already shown a great appetite for, then simply return home feeling very pleased with herself.

"Perhaps the Park will be too dreary on such an afternoon."

Celine, her hands firmly clasped in her lap, her brows drawn together in a suggestion of deep concentration, didn't respond.

"We could drive out of Town a way. Toward Windsor, perhaps. Have you seen the castle?"

"No."

Wary indeed. "Well, then, we cannot go that far so late in the day, but we shall head in that direction and find a pleasant spot in the countryside for our refreshment. Won Tel! Windsor way, man!"

The carriage rumbled on past fashionable residences where ladies and gentlemen were, even now, departing for five o'clock driving in the Park. Won Tel had been told that the mention of Windsor would mean that they should travel in a generally northwesterly direction out of the city—toward Epping. He set the horses to a smart trot.

James could hardly believe his good fortune. He was, as he preferred, in command, and felt surprisingly confident. The business of London and the Season bored him more with each day. Dorset was where he wanted to be, Dorset, Knighthead, and the Sainsbury gems were his passionate preoccupation ... as was the rapid dispatch of Darius and Mary Godwin.

"Is the countryside far away?"

Celine's small voice, sounding quite unlike herself, surprised James.

"Not far at all." He settled back.

Celine watched the scenery.

James watched Celine.

"Not all of London is pleasant, is it?"

"No, Celine. Most of it is not, but then, most of the world is not."

Her generous mouth turned down. "We are fortunate."

James looked at the streets through which they passed. Already the grand buildings of Mayfair were left behind. The farther they traveled, the poorer became the quality of the dwellings and business establishments.

Quite suddenly, Celine laughed.

"What amuses you?" He leaned forward. When she laughed, she entranced him.

"That I sometimes don't see what is real. Look at the people. See their faces. Oh, some are resigned, sad even, but isn't that so of people in all stations of life? Most appear very cheerful. Particularly the children. If anything, they are happier than many a wealthy child."

He didn't have to look to know what she saw. Instead, he studied Celine afresh. "I do believe you have a clear mind and a dangerously tender heart, my dear." He flexed the muscles in his jaw. "Have a care that it is not too tender."

Tossing her head so that the bells on her hat jingled, she slanted him an assessing glance. "Do not be misled, James. I am merely observant. I assure you that I can be selfish and calculating."

"Hah!" Her brave attempts to appear sophisticated unsettled him far more than he'd care for her to guess. Far more than he himself was comfortable with.

Another half-hour took them deep into the countryside. As arranged, Won Tel slowed the pace as soon as he drove the landau into a prespecified wooded valley between gently swelling green hills. "Tell me when the view pleases you. I'll have Won Tel pull over."

Her face, so somber, became even more pinched. James stretched his arms along the back of the seat and looked down at her. Soon it would be time for Miss Godwin's next lesson in the pleasures of the flesh. There could be no question of his allowing the vulnerability he felt in her to make him change his course.

Absolutely no question.

"Here would be nice." She lowered her lashes and played with the chartreuse button that closed her pelisse. "If you think it nice, too." Her breasts rose and fell rapidly, deepening the shadowed vale made more enticing by the clever shielding little points at the neck of her pelisse.

James took a long moment to realize what she'd said. "Yes. Yes, of course. Very nice. Pull over, Won Tel!" Damn but his instincts as a man were at odds with those feelings he'd thought dead: the same feelings that had sent him to Liam's rescue in a Chinese marketplace. *Damn!* This was no place for outmoded chivalry and the urge to protect.

Won Tel drove from the road and brought the landau to a halt in a clearing surrounded by oaks thickly mantled with new leaves.

Immediately, Celine moved forward in her seat. "May we walk? I've only been away from Dorset a few weeks and already I'm stifled by ... I do chatter, don't I?"

James stood and bent over her while opening the door. "I find every word you say delightful." Crooking a finger beneath her chin, he tipped up her face and waited until she raised her golden eyes. "What you mean is that you miss your beloved Dorset and want to feel grass beneath your feet again, and smell tree sap and your precious wildflowers. Come. This can be arranged."

How easy it would be to press her down onto the seat, to take her lips, to dispense with velvet and silk and make of them a bed on which to take all of Celine.

He let out the breath he'd held, leaped to the ground, and helped her down beside him. "We have perhaps an hour before we should begin our return," he said, ensuring that he caught Won Tel's eye. In the absence of Miss Fisher certain other steps could be taken. "Perhaps we should walk a little and then take our refreshments in the carriage."

"If you have no objection, Mr. Eagleton, I will tend the horses and stretch my old war wound on that hillside." Won Tel nodded to a steep rise opposite the woods, a spot well-placed for a man to see a signal ... when another man decided he wished to send one.

"War wound?" Celine examined Won Tel's considerable length and bulk. "You have been wounded? Oh, dear. How did it happen?"

"Well, let me see." Won Tel squinted at the sky, a sky growing grayer by the second. "I wouldn't want to upset so gentle a lady, but, truth to tell, there are several wounds received in several battles."

James cleared his throat.

"Were you fighting that awful Mr. Napoleon's men?"

"Mm, well, certainly they were responsible for the puncture in my lung. But that doesn't cause me as much trouble as the thrust I took to the thigh—fierce that was—at sea against—"

"Won Tel is a man of great bravery," James said quickly. Napoleon? Battles at sea? "He also has considerable facility in the area of inventive ... or should I say vivid accounts of past events." There *had* been that time between the Chinese mainland and Paipan when their ship had been boarded by pirates. If memory served James well, more than one man had reached the end of that skirmish bearing wounds guaranteed to make them wish they'd never encountered Won Tel. And when the last intruder was suitably dispatched into the sea, the trusty liar himself had stood beside James and laughed—with not so much as a scratch on his person.

"I'll just stretch my legs a bit. *If* it's agreeable to you, that is, Mr. Eagleton." Won Tel executed a flourishing bow that might have shamed an accomplished fop paying obeisance in the presence of the Regent.

"Quite agreeable. Come, Celine."

Duly, she placed her gloved hand on his arm, and they strolled beneath the trees.

From afar came the very muted rumble of thunder. James pretended to hear nothing, and when Celine faltered and looked up at him, he merely smiled and transferred her hand into the crook of his elbow.

Won Tel would do his part, but not without sufficient time.

The air became still. James made no comment.

"How old were you when you left England?"

He would prefer not to discuss himself. "Ten. Almost eleven." How long had they been walking? The answer, he knew, was not nearly long enough.

"And you are happy on your island?"

This must be carefully handled. "I am becoming very happy in England." For his purposes it was necessary that Celine assume he intended at least an extended stay.

Breaking from the stand of trees, they came to a point where the meadowland fell steeply away. "The day has become so gray," Celine said. "I think, perhaps, there is going to be a storm."

James lifted his head and sniffed the air. "I think not," he lied. "Not soon, anyway." Should he press her now, or wait until they returned to the carriage?

"I like wild weather." She sounded almost dreamy. "Mama says that is because I am a wayward girl with an unpredictable nature."

James found he would rather not think of Mary Godwin now. "I think it's because you are a woman of powerful emotions," he said, turning toward her and holding her arms. "It's only necessary to look into your eyes—as I am now—to see that you feel very deeply about many things." Talking to her like this wasn't difficult. The words came naturally, simply because what he said was true.

"What do you feel deeply about, James?"

The question disquieted him. "I shall have to give that some consideration." There was a point when lying became distasteful and the truth impossible— except for one part of it. "I do believe I could come to feel deeply about you, golden girl."

She turned faintly pink and lowered her eyes. James noticed that the same brush of pink touched her neck and the smooth, white swell of her breasts where they peeped from beneath the pelisse. She drew in a long breath, and he longed just to touch that softness.

James locked his thighs and clenched the muscles in his belly. A man needed a clear head at such moments as these. Allowing a green girl to see how a man's body leaped at the thought of possessing her might frighten her off before he could get close enough to tempt her with the touches he knew would not fail him.

"James."

"Yes, my dear." He slipped an arm around her shoulders. She was stiff. "What is it, Celine? What troubles you?" Patience would be the key.

"Oh, I just *wish* I didn't keep thinking about David."

He flattened his lips over his teeth. "Your clerical friend?" Damn and blast it. Of all the ill-fated times for her to have high-flown thoughts about the guardian of her soul.

"I *know* he wouldn't approve."

James rubbed her shoulder lightly, just allowing his thumb to make contact with delicate skin above a velvet point. "What wouldn't he approve of?" He was afraid he knew the answer and that this conversation would only lead away from his purpose.

"Of what I intend to ask you."

He almost sighed with relief. "Ask anyway. Think of me as a dear friend, too. I'm certain Mr. Talbot wouldn't disapprove of your asking a question of a dear friend." It was bound to be some matter of silly, young female curiosity.

"Perhaps you're right." She bowed her head. The bells jingled very faintly. "I have . . . There is something . . . James, I want to offer you . . . Would you consider doing me a great service?"

"Name it."

A huge sigh raised her shoulders. "I must simply say it quickly and be done."

He waited.

"The sooner I do it, the better."

"Celine—"

"Would you please consider ruining my reputation?" Her breath whistled out loudly. "There. I've said it."

James shook his head. Surely he'd misheard. "I'm sorry, Celine?"

She wrenched away and stood with her back to him. "Forget what I said. I knew you would refuse. You're too much of a gentleman and now you will consider me quite beyond the pale."

What he considered was that she was losing her mind . . . or he was. No young female asked such a thing of a man . . . even a man who already intended to do exactly what she'd asked him to do. After all, a man wasn't supposed to be upstaged in his plans for seduction by a mere female!

"I felt a raindrop!" Her voice soared unnaturally.

"Celine," James said, deliberately keeping his voice level and soft. "Did you just ask me to compromise you?"

"Yes. But don't give it another thought. Forget it at once."

"Oh, but I couldn't possibly do that." Absolutely not. "Why do you ask me?"

"Because I absolutely *have* to be ruined," she wailed.

Carefully, he reached to stroke the side of her neck. Slowly, slowly, he stroked. "You didn't answer my question. Why me? Why not . . . your minister friend?"

She moaned and rocked her head. "Because David would refuse."

"How do you know?"

"Oh, this is hopeless. What a little cabbage head I am." Celine made no attempt to shift from his touch. "You must think me very foolish."

"I don't," he said quietly. He thought her marvelous, an answer to his prayers. But she wasn't supposed to play the part that was definitely a man's to play.

"We should return home. I'm certain I felt another raindrop."

James tried to calculate the time that had elapsed since they'd left Won Tel. Probably not quite enough. "Are you certain your David would turn you down?"

"Don't call him *my* David. He is my friend but he isn't *mine*." She leaned, ever so slightly, against his chafing fingers. "He'd probably insist upon offering for me."

James knew a moment's panic. "And you do not want that? Marriage?" He'd assumed that such an offer would be a necessity for the accomplishment of his ends.

"Not without love." She raised her head. "Marriage should not be a matter of duty."

The ground had definitely become shaky. "You do not think I could love you," he said.

"No." Her voice was firmer now. "No. I do not think you could come to love me."

This was becoming dashed touchy. "But you could love me? Perhaps you already do—just a little?"

She spun around, the color in her cheeks high now. "Such conceit! I have been warned about men like you. If what I felt for you was love, I should certainly know it."

"How would you know?"

"From the way you made me feel. It would be a warm feeling. I would sense your deep kindness, and that would make me feel warm—and safe. Very, very safe."

Kind? Safe? "And I don't inspire these feelings in you?"

"No!"

He laughed without mirth. "So vehement, little one. How exactly *do* I make you feel?"

"In danger." Her chin came up and her eyes flashed. "I think you are the most exciting, dangerous man in the world. A man who would accept a challenge because he couldn't bear to turn one down."

It was with difficulty that James stopped himself from grabbing her to him and showing her just how dangerous he could be. "Why have you chosen to issue this challenge to me?" This was a day and an hour he would surely never forget.

"Forget that I did. Obviously you find me forward and repulsive." She backed away. "Forget I asked you. I'm sorry."

The instant before she turned to run he saw tears well in her eyes. "Celine! Wait!"

"No!" She dashed on, picking up her skirts and stumbling in her haste.

James threw up his hands and started after her. "You little fool. Stop! Come here, I say."

As if in answer, lightning crackled and split the sky. Almost instantly a swirl of heavy wind whipped at the long grass and thunder roared across the heavens.

"Celine!" She was more fleet than he would have guessed.

And he was becoming angrier.

"Celine!" Won Tel would be sorry if he'd failed in his task. He would feel the lash of James's tongue.

James drew close enough to grab for Celine's arm, only to have her veer sharply to the left.

Lightning screeched once more and, with the next roll of thunder, huge raindrops began to fall.

"This is stupid." With a lunge, he caught her arm and swung her around. "I am *not* repulsed, you foolish girl. How could any man be repulsed by you?"

Her lips parted but she did not speak, only drew in great gulps of breath. The rain wet her face and the tendrils of hair not covered by her bonnet—and slashed her neck and collarbones. Beneath his hands she felt unexpectedly fragile.

"Please do not upset yourself." Releasing her, making to touch her face, he fought back the desire to take her right there, right then, deluged by the storm beneath a shrieking sky.

She grabbed the chance to run from him once more.

"Damn you," James said through gritted teeth.

Before he caught up again she gained the trees and dodged, in the failing light, between great trunks. One second he saw her. Then he didn't.

"Celine! You will stop this. Now!"

"I want to go home," she cried. "Take me home. Mr. Won Tel! Where are you, Mr. Won Tel!"

James smiled grimly and slackened his pace. Let her tire herself out. So much the easier for him.

He saw her break from the trees and into the clearing where they'd left the carriage. Within seconds he was at her side.

She bent forward, clearly short of wind. "Take me home, please."

James looked ahead and deliberately turned the corners of his mouth downward. "That may not be very easy."

"Do not toy with me, James. We will leave immediately and forget every word that has passed between us."

"Not possible."

"It is possible," she assured him vehemently. "You are a gentleman and you will behave like one."

"A gentleman I may be. A magician I'm not." He nodded ahead. "We have a problem."

Celine jerked around. "What do you mean? Oh, the hoods have been raised. Thank goodness Mr. Won Tel had the sense to enclose the carriage. We would have driven home in miserable conditions otherwise."

"Yes, indeed." He wiped moisture from his face and followed her as she hurried toward the landau. "But you do not appear to have noticed the most obvious development."

"What . . . Oh! Oh, no!" She whirled toward him, then back to stare at the carriage, then to search in all directions. "They're gone! James, the horses are gone!"

Chapter 14

As she whirled this way and that, the bells on her pelisse and hat tinkled incongruously in the graying gloom of the downpour.

"Mr. Won Tel!" Rushing forward once more, her skirts held high above her ankles, Celine started a circle of the coach. "Mr. Won Tel. Where are you?" Her voice faded into a despairing wail.

This was all he had hoped for and much more. There was no need for the little chit to suffer more discomfort. Ah, no, now was the hour for quite a different type of experience for his fledgling voluptuary.

Running surely and silently, he caught up. "Enough, Celine. You are soaked. Into the carriage with you."

"What good is a carriage without horses?"

For his purposes, more good than it was *with* horses. "They'll return."

"I'll wait here until they do." Her face was mutinous.

"Celine, you are a trial sometimes." With no more warning, he stooped, grasped her beneath the knees, and tossed her, face first, over his shoulder. "You are going into the coach, my sweet."

"I am *not* your sweet." She pummeled his back and wiggled, and James found that, despite the rain,

he quite liked the sensation. Her nicely rounded der-
riere, where he'd spread one broad hand to hold her
firm, squirmed in a most enticing manner. Yet again,
he found his breeches exquisitely uncomfortable.
That was an area he might have to attend to
elsewhere—with someone else—if the new direction
he'd started to formulate for his plans proved useful.

Reaching the coach, he yanked open the door,
dumped his bundle unceremoniously inside, and
climbed in beside her.

Celine promptly shifted to the seat opposite and
crossed her arms beneath her bosom in that manner
he found so marvelously arousing. One day he might
even tell her so.

"Well," he announced cheerfully. "Thank goodness
Won Tel thought to raise the hoods and windows. We
shall be warm and dry in here." And very, very intimate.

"Lettie will worry about me."

"I regret that. When we get back I will explain
these frightful circumstances." He might not like being an accomplished liar, but there were times when
the facility became useful. "Meanwhile—relax and
take off your clothes."

"What?" She folded her arms even more tightly,
hugged her ribs, and pushed her breasts so high that
they pressed against the pointed neck of the pelisse.
"I will certainly *not* take off as much as a stitch of my
clothing, sir."

"You're wet."

"So are you."

He unbuttoned his coat. "I'll take off my clothes,
too."

"You will *not!*" She turned her face away, and the
furious set of her lovely mouth, the way her nose
tilted very slightly up, and the charmingly skewed

angle of her rather bedraggled little hat beguiled him.

He would try another approach first. After quickly checking inside Miss Fisher's basket and finding lemonade and a substantial number of sandwiches, he reached for the basket Liam had prepared and flipped up the lid. He smiled appreciatively at the bottle of champagne that nestled there. He would praise Liam for her efforts.

After locating two crystal goblets carefully packed in linen napkins, he popped the cork and slanted Celine a smile when she gave a little squeal.

"This will warm us." He clamped the glasses between his knees and poured.

"That is champagne."

"Yes, it is."

"I do not approve of strong drink." He was presented with her profile once more. "What are we going to do?"

They were going to do a great deal. But not until he had loosened her tongue—and her luscious but rigid body. "If you would let me, I could put your mind at rest about this situation. It will not last too long, I assure you."

"How can you know?"

"It has happened before."

"It has?" She looked at him once more.

"Oh, yes. I have no doubt that Won Tel unhitched the horses to let them graze and, er, Anthony took off."

"Anthony?"

"Yes. The more dominant black. He can be unpredictable. And the other follows. But they'll only go so far. Won Tel will have watched the direction of their departure and be waiting to bring them back when they tire."

"How long will that take?"

He shrugged. "An hour. Maybe two."

"Two hours!"

"It could be worse. It could take all night."

"Precious little comfort if you ask me," she said, settling back. "The possibility of two hours spent—alone—with a man who despises one."

He set the champagne bottle on the floor and offered Celine a drink.

She shook her head. "I told you I don't approve of drink."

"This is not drink for the sake of drinking," he said persuasively. "It is for purely medicinal reasons so that a chill may be averted."

She peered at him suspiciously. "I do not ever intend to be drunk."

"One little glass of champagne will not make you drunk, my dear. Merely warm."

He pressed the glass upon her and she took it cautiously, raising it to her mouth and wrinkling her nose against the popping bubbles.

She took a sip.

James drank deeply, watching her over the rim of his glass.

Celine took a second, larger sip—and a third. "It's quite—nice?" She glanced up at him while tipping the glass up to cover her nose and finishing the rest of the contents.

"Very warming," James said matter-of-factly. He quickly refilled her glass. "Wonderful for warding off chills."

She giggled. "Who told you that? Your nanny?"

"I shouldn't wonder. Why do you think drinking is bad?" He waved a hand. "Real drinking, I mean. Not the medicinal kind."

Celine had taken another hefty swallow and was seriously regarding the pale bubbling drink she held. "Because it can cause wild turns—in some—and one would never know who might be sus-susceptible. Drinking makes me very afraid."

Miss Celine Godwin definitely had no head for any kind of intoxicating beverage, but then, he had no doubt that this was her first experience with it. "You refer to the kind of wild turns your parents have?"

"Mm."

"What exact form do these turns take?" His mind was cold and clear.

"I don't exactly see them."

James frowned but held his tongue.

"You see ..." She drank again and passed her tongue over her lips in a way that sent a burning surge into James's groin. "You see, when it starts to happen, they've always begun to drink first ... and they send the servants to their rooms. And Lettie and me. And we are locked in."

He pulled his bottom lip between his teeth. "Locked in? Not for long, I assume."

"Oh, yes." She sighed, and her eyes, when they met his, were huge and slightly unfocused—and sad. "Sometimes we aren't allowed out for a day, perhaps two. The longest was three. Most fearsome. Without my dear Lettie to hold and care for me, I believe I should no longer be alive."

Appalled, James struggled to concentrate on gathering facts. "But surely you have some idea why your parents prefer you to stay in your rooms. Perhaps they worry for your safety."

She shook her head and smiled a secretive smile. "Nooo. They don't want us to see them searching."

"Searching?" His heart leaped. "What makes you think they are searching?" This was more than he had dreamed of learning so quickly.

"Simple." She drank again. "Everything is moved. Furniture. Pictures. Ornaments. The kitchens turned out in the most frightful manner. Some things never get back. I don't even remember where they used to be anymore."

"I see. This must be very hard on you."

"I have learned to hide how I feel. They would enjoy watching my terror, so I never show it," she said with no sign of self-pity. "Do you suppose I could have a little more of this champagne—to ward off the chill?"

James poured again and then corked the bottle and returned it to the basket. He would not overdo things. For her sake as well as his. In the basket he noticed a small round dish firmly tied in a lacy napkin. At the top he could see that Liam had lined the lace with silvery paper and spread the knot to form a bow on top. Into the bow was inserted a single yellow rose, a Tillie's Charmer. He smiled. Yes, Liam would get his thanks tonight. He had misjudged her and he should not have. His little Chinese friend had always put his best interests before her own.

He lifted the prettily decked bowl and held it out to Celine—who was draining her glass yet again. He exchanged it for the bowl and saw her smile at the rose.

"Not as beautiful as you, I fear," he said. "Open it. There will be something very pleasing inside." Liam's delightful sweet confections would please anyone.

Celine held the bowl against her and turned her smile on him. "You are being so kind, yet I'm sure you're as upset as I am about this inconvenience."

"Don't worry yourself about me."

"I do. And I will." Her face was soft, her mouth relaxed and moist. If he kissed her she would taste of champagne—and she would taste inviting. "James, I'm sorry I embarrassed you with—"

"I've decided to accept your proposal."

"I will never again . . . You have?"

"Yes. But first you must explain exactly what you mean by wanting me to ruin your reputation and why you want such a thing."

"Well." She smelled the rose and he noticed how slowly, sleepily, her eyelids lowered. "You did hear that awful Percival Letchwith . . . You did see how he tried to make me do what he ordered at the Arbuthnott rout?"

"Yes."

"And you managed to get rid of him." She frowned. "How did you do that?"

He must be certain she didn't fall asleep too soon. Later such a state might be a blessing, but not yet. "Don't worry yourself about details. Tell me about Percival Letchwith. Why does the man threaten you?"

"He doesn't. Not really. It's his father, Bertram Letchwith. The rumors you've heard are true. My mama and papa have given him reason to hope that they would look favorably on his offer for my hand."

His stomach contracted. "And you would not be pleased?"

"He is despicable." She leaned forward and whispered loudly. "An old, fat man who smells of strong drink and pomade. He spits when he talks and presses close to me. Once"—she shuddered—"he squeezed my . . . He squeezed my . . . He said something strange. That he was testing the fruit."

Only by enormous strength of will did James stop himself from looking down at what the loathsome Letchwith had squeezed. The thought of such a creature touching this innocent girl sent heated blood pumping through his veins. The man would suffer. James would make certain he did.

"Don't think about him. Just explain the rest."

"Surely you already understand?"

He thought he might. "I need you to tell me."

"The only thing that might dissuade Mama and Papa from accepting Mr. Letchwith's offer would be a larger offer. And I assure you, that will not happen. So I am left with only one alternative."

"Which is?"

"To ruin myself so that Mr. Letchwith will no longer wish to marry me." She sat up straight. "There. Now you have it."

"Let me see if I fully understand. You want me to help you destroy your reputation. But you are not asking me to offer for you."

"Oh, no." She shook her head. "Absolutely not. I don't want you to give it further thought."

"You don't?"

"No. I know you are not interested in marrying me. Why should you be? You are much too daring and free-spirited a man to want to take an uninteresting female like me as a wife. Which is exactly why I discussed what I would require from a husband when we were together last night—to assure both of us that we would be entirely unsuited. Not that I would ever expect you to think of such a thing, anyway. But I do think you a good man and I do have something to offer you for your sacrifice."

He glanced heavenward. "And what would that be?" The chit confounded him far too often.

Celine's cheeks colored deeply. "I have made a discovery. And you will think me a silly goose for not knowing this before. But I do believe gentlemen feel . . . Well, they can experience sensations of Passion just as women do, can't they?"

He cleared his throat.

"Yes, well, in return for your helping me, I shall engage with you in activities that will bring you sensations of Passion. And, also, you will be assured of my undying gratitude and lifelong friendship. There." She nodded, but her mouth trembled.

"When ... How will you have me ... How long do I have to, er, *ruin* you?"

"Not long." Her tawny eyes became shadowed with worry. "It's really too bad Mama and Papa aren't in London already. We could simply get it over with on our return tonight."

"Get it over with?"

"I could go in, declare my ruination, and then you could tell them I forced you into it and that you have no intention of marrying me. Then it would be done and you could leave. But they aren't here and Lettie will insist that Mama and Papa hear your words with their own ears."

"Lettie is aware of what you are doing?"

"In a manner of speaking." She fidgeted with the bowl. "But not exactly. I didn't tell her I intended to be quite so bold."

"Understandable," he said with feeling. And the whole addlepated scheme was hopelessly askew. Compromise her he would, but slowly—as slowly as he had to in order to make the performance last long enough to gain his admittance to Knighthead and a place of trust with the Godwins.

"You think me a frightful romp, don't you?"

"I think you adorable," he said honestly. "And I will help you, I promise. But you must leave the timing and everything else to me."

"But—"

"No, Celine, not *but*. Leave it all to me."

She fiddled with the rose. "If you think so."

"I do. It would not work to move quite so fast."

"But I want it over." She pulled out the flower and smelled it. "I cannot bear that man near me. And I don't understand why he would want such an immature female as a wife."

James studied her and knew deep sickness. "Leave it to me," he ordered. How could any mother and father consign their child to such a fate? He knew the answer—for gain—but he still shunned the idea.

Celine set aside the rose and carefully undid the silver and lace knot atop the bowl. "I think perhaps I am a little hungry." Parting the wrapping, she looked inside . . . and screamed.

"What . . ." James reached for her as she flung herself against the back of her seat. "What in damnation?"

Celine screamed and screamed. "No! No! Stop it!" Throwing wide her arms, she became rigid, her face deathly white.

Then James saw it, and his teeth snapped together. That willful little baggage would pay for this.

Before he could stop it, a large, black spider with thick, hairy legs and an evil-looking wide back hooked itself over the edge of the basin and plopped onto Celine's lap.

Her eyes completely lost focus, and this time her scream made no sound.

Pushing open the door, James scooped up the creature and tossed it outside—and slammed the door again. He swept away the bowl into the basket and crammed the lid shut.

Liam would suffer for this—and for her damnable eavesdropping in places she didn't belong.

"I'm sorry," he told Celine. "It's all right now. It's gone."

Her lips worked before she made a choking sound, then she whispered, "How?"

"I don't know." Lying was becoming too much of a habit tonight. "But you're all right. You're safe. I'll keep you safe."

The flurry of gold and green and long tangled hair hit him without warning. Celine leaped from her seat and flung herself against his chest. Burrowing, she curled into his lap and wrapped her arms around his neck.

And shook. And shook.

Her bonnet hadn't just slipped. It lay on the floor in a crumpled blob. James smoothed the cascade of deep golden curls, damp around her face, that had shaken loose of its pins.

"Evidently I didn't do my job," he said, attempting lightness. "You told me you expected a man with whom you could feel safe to make certain no . . . horrors were in residence near you." And Liam had overheard that statement. A fact he could hardly wait to discuss.

"I said I would expect that of a husband," Celine said in a small voice. "Not a friend who has only agreed to help me because he's a gentleman."

"Don't—" He closed his mouth. He wished she wouldn't keep referring to him by that term—certainly not in this situation. "I'll do my best to protect you in the future. You're damp, Celine. I shall *not* be doing my duty if you arrive home ill."

"Just hold me."

He did hold her, firmly. And he stroked her thick, vibrant hair and her back and her slender waist. At the flare of her hip, he stopped.

She snuggled even closer, pressed her face into his neck.

James closed his eyes and inhaled the clean, floral scent of her. With difficulty, he ordered his concentration. "There's a blanket in the hamper beneath the seat," he told her. "Please. Take off your clothes and warm yourself. We'll spread your garments, and they'll be somewhat drier by the time we arrive back. You can put them on again then, and no one will be the wiser. At least you will not have worn them for so long."

"What of Mr. Won Tel?"

"He won't be back yet," he told her. Won Tel would not return until James was ready for him to return. "And when he does, he will not see inside. I'll attend to that." He set Celine gently down on the opposite seat again and closed the window shades. Only the vaguest suggestion of dusky light penetrated into the carriage.

But it was enough. Reaching beneath a seat, he found the hamper and pulled out the soft blanket he'd made sure was there.

Celine struggled with the button on her pelisse. He realized that, despite the champagne, her still-gloved fingers were chilled, and the satin button difficult to undo.

Swallowing, he stilled her hands. "Let me take off your gloves."

Obediently, she stretched out her arms, and James worked off the gloves. Immediately he began to chafe her cold fingers between his hands and she made small noises of pain as the life began to return.

"Shush," he said softly. "They'll be warm again soon enough. May I undo the button for you?"

When she nodded, James felt his insides fall away. A rushing, tingling heat rose to flood him. Sitting on the edge of his seat, he gripped the wet velvet and began pushing the button through its hole. With each small movement, his knuckles pressed into her breasts.

The button was freed.

He looked up and found her watching his face. "Thank you, James."

"It was my pleasure."

Still staring into her eyes, he pushed the outer garment from her shoulders and worked the sleeves down her arms.

She didn't move, didn't as much as blink or attempt to help him.

"Up a moment, sweeting." Sliding an arm around her waist, he lifted her and removed the quite sodden velvet. This he did his best to spread in a far corner.

He removed his own coat.

Celine gasped and he frowned at her. "What is it?"

"Nothing." She averted her eyes.

"No?" Dropping to one knee before her, he pulled her face toward him. "Have you hurt yourself?"

"No." Her glance dropped to his shirt, and she blushed violently and placed her hand over her heart.

James looked down at his fine linen shirt, plastered to his skin by moisture. A thought made him smile. "Does it disquiet you to see me without my coat?"

Celine frowned and studied him carefully. "No, but I think it ought to." Her words slurred together ever so slightly. "David said a female of sensitive nature might be quite overcome at the sight of a man not entirely dressed."

"Did he?" Smothering a groan, James was uncertain whether the saintly David Talbot deserved to be praised or cursed for his efforts. There was a certain excitement in the thought that a maid had not as much as seen a man without his coat ... to say nothing of the rest of his attire.

Celine continued to cast sidelong glances at his wet shirt, or—and he thought this more to the point—at the suggestion of his muscle and skin visible through the clinging fabric.

Her fingers, laid tentatively upon his chest—exactly where a flat nipple instantly stiffened at the touch—shortened his breath. What was he—a fool of a boy reacting to his first encounter with a female?

Hardly. It was the situation and the nature of this particular female that affected him so strongly.

"What are you thinking, Celine?"

"That I like the sight of a man not entirely clothed." She giggled, and James gripped his thighs convulsively.

Slowly, slowly. "You have never seen your friend David without a coat?"

She frowned. "Oh, no. At least, not since I was a small girl. I suppose I must have seen him without a coat then." Hunching her shoulders, she laughed, a silvery, joyous sound. "I had quite forgotten. I saw him in only his small clothes once—when he took me swimming in the river."

James narrowed his eyes. "How could you have forgotten?"

"Oh, because David told me to, I should imagine. He said it had to be our secret because our parents would disapprove." She covered her mouth, and her eyes widened. "And now I've told you! But I suppose it's all right, since you are my very special friend who is going to ruin my reputation."

He ignored the last. "What did you wear to swim in the river?" He tried not to grind his teeth at the probable answer.

Celine appeared surprised. "Why, my shift, of course. I would have taken it off, but he insisted I could not."

"Admirable of him. He must be a very chivalrous man."

"Exactly! Oh, yes. I *knew* you would share my admiration of David."

James grunted. He needed to concentrate on the matter at hand, but couldn't resist one more question. "How old were you when you tried this swimming with David Talbot?"

"Five. David was fifteen and said I was tiresome to insist upon going."

James smiled, and the weight of his irritation lifted. "Celine, you really do need to get out of your dress." The chartreuse silk stuck to her in smooth, transparent patches. There might be no saving it—not that such trivialities concerned him.

"Well . . ." pulling her shoulders up to her ears, with interesting results in other areas, Celine giggled again. "I will take off my dress if you take off your shirt. You really do need to get out of your shirt," she mimicked and fell back, chuckling helplessly at her own small joke.

"How right you are." He quickly undid the buttons on the front of his shirt, pulled it from his breeches, and let it hang.

Celine stopped laughing. Her mouth opened a little and he saw her swallow as she studied his naked chest.

"Your turn, I think," he said.

Awkwardly, she reached back, trying to accomplish the impossible task of loosening the tapes on her gown. Finally she stopped, raised her chin primly, and turned sideways on her seat. "I cannot do it. Will you help me?"

"Oh, yes," James murmured. "I will help you."

He crossed to sit behind her and deftly disposed of the wet knots that defeated her. Slipping his hands under the shoulders of the gown, he worked the wet silk down to her elbows.

Then he stopped. Gently, he smoothed the skin of her arms from elbow to shoulder and back, before wrapping his arms around her and holding her against him. The skill would lie in going as far as possible without going too far—or perhaps in making her think he had not gone too far. That must be judged in the minutes to follow.

A heavy pulse began in his groin. Keeping a clear head would doubtless become almost impossible, yet, if he lost it, he might lose all.

"You have hair on your chest," she said in a small voice.

"And you don't approve of that?" Moving slowly, he lifted aside her hair and pressed his lips to her shoulder. "You are very smooth, my lovely one. Like satin."

"I do approve of the hair. It makes you seem very large and fierce."

"Large and fierce," he said, shifting his mouth to the soft little hollow beneath her ear. "How does my seeming large and fierce make you feel?"

"Hot," she declared without hesitation. "Hot inside and as if I want to feel the hair."

His heart almost stopped. This untried creature had within her a natural passion which might very well be the end of him.

"Then you must feel it," he told her. As swiftly as he dared, he slipped the dress from her arms, lifted her once more, and took it all the way off. "Wait." He spread the dress, not caring how well it might dry.

When he turned, Celine sat looking up at him, her damp chemise no more than an erotically flimsy barrier between him and her skin.

He stood before her. "Part your knees, Celine. So that I may come closer." She did as he told her, and he urged her face against his naked belly. "Kiss me, my sweet one. Let me feel your mouth on me."

She made a noise, a keening sound, and he felt the moist pressure of her lips pressing his skin again and again, before she raised her face once more. "Like that, James?"

"Like that," he murmured. "We will enjoy this thing we've decided to do together. But you will leave the rest to me. Is that understood?"

She nodded.

He took her hands and spread her fingers on his chest. She smiled and stroked, gently, hesitantly. And his belly contracted. There had never been a woman like this for him.

He had no time or place in his life for emotion. Not foolish, romantic emotion.

To his amazement, she pulled him even closer between her spread thighs, reached up, and pushed the shirt from his shoulders. Down his arms she pulled the sleeves until they hung by the cuffs. Grateful he had remembered not to wear his knife, he tore them off and she leaned into him, kissed his body fiercely, again and again.

He felt his manhood leap at her touch. Dropping back his head, he willed his mind to be quiet. He must think, remain aloof.

"I feel that . . . that *sensation* again."

"Which sensation?"

What he felt was becoming unbearable.

"The . . . No, no."

"Celine." He dropped between her knees. "Tell me."

"The hot wetness." She turned aside her face, but not before the bright flush swept over her cheeks.

He laughed softly. "That is good, my golden girl. Very, very good."

The chemise molded to her nipples. Their centers were hard, shaded buds surrounded by enticing circles.

"Look at me, Celine."

She shook her head.

"Yes. Do it."

Slowly, she turned her head. Keeping his eyes on hers, James put a forefinger into his mouth, withdrew it slowly, and licked the tip. Then he touched it to a straining nipple and stroked.

"James!" she cried, involuntarily arching her back. Her breathing speeded. "Oh, James. It cannot be . . . Oh, I do not care."

"About what?" Stroking, stroking, he made circles over that hungry bud—and she closed her eyes, rocked her hips farther forward on the seat.

"I do not care if I shall fall," she gasped. "I want to."

Sometimes she was a puzzling baggage. At this moment he cared no more than she did.

Celine panted and rocked her head. "James, I want . . . I want . . ."

"What do you want?" He knew what he wanted.

Opening her eyes, she found his finger and pulled it into her own mouth. She sucked deeply, then placed it on her other nipple and began to rotate it as he had done. "That is what I want . . . I think. But I want . . . Oh, I don't know all that I want."

But he could show her, teach her.

Swiftly, he sat on the opposite seat, pulling her with him until she sat astride his thighs, her flimsy chemise bunched at the tops of her legs.

He smiled at her and fought to quiet his breathing. "I like you there, Celine. I like looking at you."

Smoothing shaky palms over his shoulders, up his neck, down over his chest, she smiled shyly back. "I like looking at you. And I'm glad I give you pleasure. That is what I promised you. It is part of the bargain, is it not?"

"Don't—" He bit back the denial. Of course it was part of a bargain and nothing more. She was the daughter of his parents' enemies. That was what he must keep in mind. "It is a fine bargain," he told her.

Where she sat, with her smooth, naked thighs revealed between the chemise and the tops of her lace stockings, she was totally vulnerable and open to him. James bent to kiss her throat and tried not to think of the warm, moist opening to her body, positioned so close to that part of him that he longed to sink into her.

"James—"

Fiercely, desperate to silence her trusting voice, he covered her lips with his own and plunged his tongue into her mouth again and again, until she clung to his shoulders, her nails cutting his skin.

With wild abandon, he rocked her face from side to side, punishing her mouth. He scarcely knew when she started returning his ardor, when she reared up and forced him against the seat to imitate the suggestive darting of the tongue. She could not know that this was only a substitute for what he needed to do, what he could barely contain himself from doing.

Gasping, she sank down to sit astride his legs once more. Her head fell back and her breasts were swelling globes he could no longer bear hidden from him, even by so flimsy a shield. With sure fingers, he tugged undone the fine cord that held the garment in place.

"James" was all she said before she dropped her arms and watched him bare her breasts.

Sweet, so achingly sweet and tender, they thrust at him. The smallest tug, and the chemise fell to her tiny waist. With reverent hands, he smoothed her narrow rib cage that only served to accentuate the ripe swell of her.

"When ... The other time you ..." She closed her eyes. "I liked what you did before."

"And you shall like it again." He closed his teeth over a puckered, tantalizingly rough peak, ran his tongue around the surrounding flesh, and heard her soft scream of pleasure.

"You were made for this," he said against her. Suckling, flicking with his tongue, nipping with his teeth, he pushed her breasts together. While his own need rose hard against her ready woman's center, he passed his mouth from one nipple to the other and back until she sobbed and clawed weakly at him.

Keeping his mouth fastened to her, James pulled her stockings down and stroked the satiny inner sides of her thighs. "Hold my shoulders," he ordered and, with a rapid move, tipped her onto her back along the seat. "Put your legs around my waist."

"Why?" Her voice was small, but heavy with longing.

"Because I want you to. And you will want to. You are rare, Celine. A woman meant for love more than for anything else."

In the dim light, he saw her glittering eyes—and her naked breasts—and the gleam of wetness in the hair at the juncture of her thighs. He clamped his teeth together and rent the chemise from her body in a single wrenching tear.

He must have some release.

Struggling, he opened his breeches and allowed his manhood to spring free. A look at Celine's face let him know that she knew nothing of what he was doing.

"Lie back," he instructed. "This is for me to accomplish. And you will not be disappointed. Trust me."

Trust him? His mind dulled beneath his desire—his need.

First he must make certain he bound her to him so tightly that she would never want to be free. "Sweeting," he murmured, bowing over her, kissing again her lips, each breast, her softly rounded belly. "Sweet, sweet, one."

Using his tongue, he ran a wet trail downward, and at the same time, he set his thumbs to work at the nubbin hidden in that glistening triangle of hair.

He smoothed, rubbed, listened to her mounting moans, until her hips rose, seeking.

"Wait," he said, and closed his mouth over her center.

Her shriek was mindless. She thrust against him, filled her fingers with his hair, and urged him closer.

"Mm." He sucked at her. "Yes. Oh, yes, my beautiful child-woman." Licking, nipping, opening his mouth wide to cover her, he drove his tongue hard and felt the final, violent spasm of her release.

"James!"

He smiled and darted his tongue, darted, darted, while her hips ground against his mouth and the ripple of her spasm spread.

James slipped his hands beneath her buttocks and cupped her while she fell, her body damp with sweat, onto the seat.

"Good, my lovely one?"

"Yes." She sighed. "Oh, yes. Do you feel good, too, James?"

"Almost," he said. Rising over her, he shoved his breeches farther down until he could push his cock between her slick thighs. "A little more and I shall feel as good as a man need ever feel." Better than most ever felt.

"Good," she said breathlessly. "Tell me what to do."

"Nothing," he rasped and began to move. She had no experience and would not know what he intended to accomplish, what he would accomplish.

"James?"

"Hush," he said, drawing his lips back from his teeth. "Press your legs together. Tightly."

She did as he asked—and became rigid. "What . . . James, what is that?"

"Do not concern yourself," he said with difficulty. "It is that part of a man that responds as certain parts of a woman respond. Hold it with your legs, Celine. Please, just hold it."

She held, forced her thighs together with more power than he would have thought possible, and he buried his face in her neck and pumped his shaft in and out between her thighs, felt the incredibly erotic sensation of her womanly hair scraping along the length of him.

He kept driving, kept drawing on the exquisite agony of swelling pressure within him—until he could draw out the ecstasy no longer. One final, fierce thrust and he felt himself explode. Almost sobbing, dragging air into his raw throat, he rocked against Celine and let the essence of his sex spurt between her unyielding legs.

"Aah!" Drained, he fell upon her, gathered her to him, and lay panting.

"James?" Her voice came to him, tentative and a little frightened. "Was that right?"

"Yes." He sighed, too exhausted to move.

"Have I hurt you?"

Laughing weakly, he shifted and managed to roll and pull her atop him. "No, my wonderful girl, you did *not* hurt me. You made me feel wonderful. Do you feel wonderful?"

"Oh, yes." She relaxed upon him and smoothed his shoulder gently. "I expect I am quite ruined now, aren't I?"

He squeezed his eyes shut. Not now. He didn't want to think about it all just yet. "Leave it all to me, Celine. There is nothing you have to think about. Such matters are not for you to think about."

"James!"

She caught at him with a slender hand, peered up into his face in the light reflected from street lamps.

"Hush, Celine," he told her, shifting her head from

his shoulder where she had slept since a few minutes after they'd begun the journey back into Town. "You will soon be home"

"Oh, dear." She hugged the blanket in which he'd wrapped her, tightly to her chin. In the flickering glow, her eyes were huge and her hair an unruly but glorious tangle.

"Yes," he said, laughing a little. "Oh, dear. I think we'd best prepare ourselves." Since she had slept so quickly after he'd sent his covert signal for Won Tel to return with the horses, there had been no time to do anything about her appearance.

His own shirt and breeches were in order. Deftly, he helped her straighten her stockings and chemise, stilling her hands when she tried to stop him.

"You don't have to feel embarrassed with me, my sweet," he said, not without a flash of satisfaction. "There is nothing I do not know of you, remember." Except for one thing, one very important thing—and that would be a prize worth the waiting.

"Please, don't say such things aloud," she said in a small voice.

"If you would prefer that I didn't—I won't." He kissed the end of her nose. "There. Think no more of it. But do not forget that we are partners in a certain matter. We are partners with a mission to accomplish, and you have appointed me your leader and guide."

"Yes." She raised her arms and began sweeping her hair into a bundle at her crown.

James found he could not resist dropping another kiss where her chemise gaped invitingly open.

Celine became still, and he looked up into her questioning eyes. "I am simply continuing with our agreement, my golden girl."

"I think we should not continue again quite so soon," she said, her voice soft. "We may find it hard to collect ourselves in time to go home at all."

She laughed and he laughed with her.

"You are a delight. A treasure." Gently, he covered her breasts and smoothed his fingertips over their tops, before securing the chemise and reaching for her gown.

He helped her dress and turned to replacing his coat and attempting to gather as much as possible of his composure.

"James? Oh, dear."

She sounded forlorn and he bent to see her bowed face. "What is it?"

"I fear my hat is beyond repair."

He took it from her. "I fear you are correct. Do not concern yourself. I will buy you . . ." He knew his mistake before the words were finished.

"You will buy me nothing!" Her lips pursed. "Ours is not an arrangement of . . . of *that* kind!"

"And what do you know of arrangements of *that* kind?"

"Oh . . ." She managed to pull on her gloves. "I know very little, except that David has mentioned certain things to me and explained their part in certain . . . certain *unsuitable* circumstances. Ours, James—your circumstances with me—are to be mutually beneficial and partly based on the very strong friendship I felt we could form with each other. I felt it from the moment we met. And my instincts have proven correct, have they not?"

He sighed. "They have indeed. When we arrive in Curzon Street—and we are already turning the corner—please allow me to deal with explanations to Lettie."

Anxiety flashed in her face before she subsided to wait on the edge of her seat, the hopeless wreck of a hat in her hands.

The carriage rolled to a halt and, in a trice, Won Tel was throwing open the door and pulling down the step. As had been the case when he came in response to James's signal, his face was expressionless.

James hopped down and handed Celine out. She was, he had to admit, too disheveled for there to be any hope of escaping considerable questioning.

"Mr. Eagleton?" Won Tel's tone held an inquiry. As always, he was at the ready to assist his master.

"Wait here."

James placed Celine's hand formally atop his arm and led her up the steps with what dignity was possible. The door opened as he went to ring the bell.

"There you are." Tense lines drew down the corners of Miss Fisher's mouth. She looked from James to Celine and back to James. "Come in."

"I cannot tell you how sorry I am, Miss Fisher," James began. "We have had a most unsettling adventure."

Backing toward the parlor, the woman didn't change her expression. "From Celine's appearance, I should imagine that *unsettling* is an understatement."

"The responsibility for this terrible debacle is entirely mine," James continued. He flexed his back, aware of a certain stiffness of the muscles that was hardly surprising. "We decided—I decided that since the day had turned somewhat grayer than expected, we would find a drive in the country more pleasurable."

"Did you?" She stared at the hat in Celine's hand. "I expect you'd like some brandy, Mr. Eagleton."

"No! That is, no thank you. I am anxious to return to my own home. And Celine must be completely exhausted from her adventure."

"Really?"

James was not at all certain he liked the way the woman raised her brows.

"Yes. We found a charming spot out of the city and decided to walk."

"I wanted to, Lettie," Celine said suddenly. "And it was lovely until a thunderstorm began."

"And rain," James added, shaking his head. "Torrential rain."

"We ran back to the carriage," Celine said. "But you'll never guess what had happened."

"I don't suppose I shall."

Celine turned up a hand. "The horses were gone. Mr. Won Tel had allowed them to graze and they ran away."

It was with deep relief that James saw some wavering in Miss Fisher's ominous stare. "They did?"

"Yes. And they didn't come back for *ages*."

"A shocking nuisance," James said.

Miss Fisher pushed open the parlor door and stood back. "You both look absolutely frozen. I insist you have brandy, Mr. Eagleton. I shall have Celine bathed and put to bed immediately."

"You are a wise woman," James said, bowing. He followed Celine as far as the threshold of the room. "I really cannot stay. But I will check on Celine's condition tomorrow."

"Well, if you insist."

Celine gave a sudden small scream.

"What is it?" He tried in vain to catch her arm.

"David! Oh, David!"

Slowly, James raised his eyes to meet those of a tall, exceedingly handsome, blond young man who moved from the shadows near the fireplace.

"Hello, Celine."

The girl ran at the man and flung herself into his arms. "David. Dear, dear, David. Why didn't you send word that you were coming?"

"There wasn't time," the man said, his voice deep and resonant.

"James." Celine looked at him over her shoulder, and her cheeks were flushed with pleasure. "This is my very dear friend, David Talbot. The Reverend David Talbot. For some reason he decided he should drop in and surprise me out of my wits." She sent a teasing glance in the direction of her old friend.

With eyes the color of translucent, green glass, David Talbot regarded James unflinchingly over Celine's head. There was no flush of pleasure on the clear-cut planes of his cheeks, no happy smile at the introduction. "Yes," he said, almost inaudibly. "And it appears that Celine is not the only one to be surprised."

Chapter 15

"**M**en can be very aggravating."

David took his time replacing his cup in its saucer and lowering the newspaper he'd held in front of his face ever since Celine had entered the breakfast parlor—what seemed like a very long time ago. "Did you say something, Celine?"

"Exactly! That is exactly the type of behavior I'm talking about. Deliberately aggravating nonsense that is peculiar to the male."

He rattled the paper. "If you are going to be difficult, perhaps we should wait until later to talk."

"I arose at ten when I'm not supposed to be up until at least noon, and I did so in order to spend a happy time chatting with you over breakfast."

"Noon?"

She averted her face. "This is London, David. And the Season. One adheres to certain accepted conventions." This was silly. With David there had never been any pretense or need for airs.

Folding the paper, he regarded her with an icy gleam in his green eyes. "Celine, that is poppycock. You have always loved the mornings. And you have always ignored convention. You, my dear little friend, are known for your waywardness, remember?"

"That is neither kind nor fair, David." And such meanness of spirit was unlike him. "I thought you were my champion."

"I am." He put the paper on the table and fiddled with a spoon. "You seem changed. You say you arose at ten as if it were a sacrifice when we both know that in Dorset you are often riding at eight." He stood abruptly and strode to the sideboard. "The eggs are cold. And the kidneys. The rolls appear still edible. What may I bring you?"

He was trying to smooth things between them. "A roll, please, David. And a little of the gooseberry jam." She could not contain herself. "I feel you have betrayed our friendship!"

David whirled around and barely caught the roll that would have slid from the plate he held. "Betrayed? Why?"

"Because . . . because . . ." She swallowed painfully. "Because Mama and Papa call me wayward, which you know very well is not true—not really true—and you've always said as much until now."

With his eyes on the plate, he walked to the table and spooned jam from a little silver compote.

Celine watched him with a mixture of lingering annoyance and sweet, poignant fondness. She knew David so well that she'd rarely studied him as a man. Sitting up straighter, she announced. "You are nine and twenty."

"What?" Once again he saved her roll from shooting to the floor.

"Nine and twenty. That's how old you are."

He stared at her blankly.

"And you are uncommonly handsome, David."

A red flush crept over his high cheekbones and he pulled at the knot on his austerely tied linen neckcloth.

"Tall, with a well-favored form." She began to enjoy his extreme discomfort. "No need for sawdust padding on those legs—or buckram stuffing on that chest or those shoulders. And—"

"Celine." The gruffness in his voice wasn't quite steady. "I cannot think why you would say such things."

"Because they are true," she said with a flourish. "Yes, indeed. You are a man guaranteed to cause any discriminating young female's heart to be lost in a trice. I'm hungry. May I please have my roll?"

"I . . ." He looked at Celine and back to the plate. "Yes." Seeming to regain some composure, he plopped it in front of her.

"This is important." She caught his hand when he would have retreated. "It is time you married and had children, David. I know you have much important work to accomplish, but the right wife would understand that and support you."

"You undo me, Celine," he said at last. "My matrimonial prospects and personal needs do not occupy my mind in the slightest."

"I thought as much." David's safe journey into a satisfactory family life must be added to her list of imperative accomplishments. "Tell me, is there no likely female for whom you've formed a fondness?"

"Celine—*enough.*"

She ignored his warning tone. "You have no family. But I am almost a sister to you, so I will appoint myself to help in this matter. I assure you that there is absolutely no reason for you not to succumb to natural desires for . . . for . . ." Oh, dear.

David set her hand carefully on the table but remained looming over her. "Natural desires for what, Celine?"

"Oh"—she drew up her shoulders and picked imaginary crumbs from the highly polished mahogany before her—"for companionship, of course. And for children. You are wonderful with children, David. I've seen how they all gather around you wherever you go in Little Puddle."

"I see." With ominously measured steps, he returned to his chair, sat down, and steepled his fingers. "I think we have much to discuss. First, I apologize for my thoughtless comment. I would not wish to show disrespect to your parents, but I do heartily disagree with their harsh assessment of you. Celine, you are a special girl with a kind heart, and we both know as much. Am I forgiven?"

She grinned at him. "You were never not forgiven. There is nothing you could do that would make me do other than love you. Without you—and dear Lettie, of course—I should never have survived."

David looked quickly away, and Celine fastened her gaze in her lap. By an old agreement, the subject of her parents' strict and often unfair treatment of her was never discussed.

"When are Mr. and Mrs. Godwin due to arrive in London?"

"We aren't sure, but we assume it will be soon."

"I have not seen them of late, but I was aware that they are still in residence at Knighthead."

Their eyes met and understanding passed between them. David knew of the incarcerations Celine had suffered. On more than one occasion, after not seeing her for longer than was usual, he had found a way to divert her parents and get food to her and to Lettie. He had steadfastly warned Celine that if there was ever to be physical violence, he would no longer be bound by his oath of silence on the matter.

"How is Ruby Rose?" Celine asked, determined to change the subject.

David slumped in his chair. "I think she does very well. Unfortunately Mrs. Strickland seems determined to spare no opportunity to inform both Ruby

Rose and me that the girl is the devil's own daughter." A faint smile turned up the corners of his finely formed mouth. "Fortunately, Ruby Rose is possessed of great spirit and good humor."

"And you, David?" Celine asked softly, smiling herself. "What of your spirit?"

He wrinkled his nose at her. "You are already aware that my own spirit is magnificent and I am never other than in fine humor."

"Hah!"

"Celine, there are certain matters I am bound to discuss with you."

David regarded himself as her self-appointed guardian and was using his "guardian" voice. "Must you?"

"Yes. But first I should tell you why I'm in London."

Celine pouted. "You didn't come only to see me?"

"Behave. The coquette is not a part you play well. I am expecting a difficult time while I am here. Lettie has been kind enough to insist I stay with you—which will be a boon to my finances. I hope I may complete my business and depart before your parents arrive." He appeared embarrassed. "Please forgive my bluntness."

"Fie." Celine shook her head. "There has never been pretense between us."

David drank from his cup and held it between his hands as he seemed to decide what to say next. "My business in London will not be simple. I may fail—at least on this first attempt—but if I do I shall return until I do succeed."

She was accustomed to his circuitous manner of conversation. "And your business, David?"

"Marigold. Another poor woman who has fallen from grace."

Celine contained the urge to press him.

"I gained word of her through an acquaintance of Ruby Rose's who came to visit."

At Celine's sharp glance, he leaned forward. "Don't worry. This was not one of those scoundrels I encountered when I first secured Ruby Rose's escape from the house of that woman Merryfield. An honest enough person came to inform us of Marigold's plight. And I am here to pay another visit to the spurious Mrs. Merryfield."

Celine frowned. "Mrs. Merryfield again? Is this Marigold at that woman's house?"

"She is indeed," David said gravely. "And I'm led to believe she is desperate to escape."

"So you will have to venture into that frightful dark area by the docks ... the one you spoke of. Where exactly did you say it was?"

David eyed her shrewdly and said, "I didn't say. I will go where I must go, and that is all you need to know."

She did so hate to be excluded from adventure. "Perhaps Mrs. Merryfield would respond more graciously to a female." Nonchalantly, Celine spread green gooseberry jam on a morsel of roll and popped it into her mouth.

"How so?" David asked.

"Well, given her occupation, she may have reason to distrust men. If that is so, dealing with a woman might be easier for her. Don't you think?"

"No, I don't. And you don't know what you're talking about. Which is exactly as it should be."

"But you've told me all about this," Celine protested. "Please, David, let me help. I could talk to Mrs. Merry—"

"*No!*" he thundered in a voice quite unlike any Celine had ever heard him use. "Do not ever mention such a monstrous notion to me again."

"But—"

"*No*, Celine. And that's an end to it."

"When will you go?"

He gave an exasperated sigh. "On Saturday evening. Now—"

"The night of the Casterbridge fete," Celine moaned. "Botheration!"

"I take it that means your social commitments will make it unnecessary for me to tie you up until I return. Good. Now to the other, more important matter at hand."

Celine did not like either his tone or his expression. "You did receive the last money I sent?" she asked quickly.

"Yes, I did. Thank you. I do not want you to worry so. The responsibility for providing the necessary support is mine."

"But you do need my help?" She thought guiltily that Lettie was right, there was a marvelously dangerous excitement in the plan she had devised for helping David.

"I am always grateful for any help," he said and smiled so warmly that Celine left her chair and rushed to hug him. He laughed. "Have a care, miss. A man has only so much strength and you are squeezing mine from me."

Celine released him. "In that case I shall desist. Your wife and children will need your strength."

He groaned. "Enough, I tell you, miss. There are matters we must discuss. No more clever little diversions, Celine. Who was that man?"

"Man?" Even as she said the word, she felt a blush climb her neck.

"Celine," David said warningly. "We will not play games. His name is James Eagleton. I know that much. But I don't know *who* he is, or what he means to you. I also don't have the faintest notion of what you were doing gadding about with him *unchaper-oned.*"

There had been no doubt in Celine's mind that this discussion would come, but she hadn't expected to feel quite so defensive. "Lettie can explain that."

"Lettie said *you* would explain it."

"You questioned Lettie?" Celine asked crossly.

He tapped her arm and waited until she reluctantly looked down into his face. "Make up your mind," he said. "You suggest that I ask Lettie for explanations, then you're angry when you learn that I already have."

"I really do not know why you are making such a fuss. James took me for a drive. Since the weather was somewhat uncertain, we chose to go into the country a way rather than to the dull old Park where there is nothing to see but other carriages." Surely David would not continue to press her.

"And you went without a chaperon."

Whatever she did, thoughts of James and yesterday must be kept at bay. Celine tried to concentrate very hard on wet leaves slapping a windowpane. "Oh, this is the veriest silliness!" If she really thought of James, David would surely see right inside her flustered mind. "Lettie was feeling not quite herself, and she trusts James, as I do. And, anyway, Mr. Won Tel drove the carriage." *There.*

"Mr. Won Tel?"

"Yes."

"An odd name."

"He is from the East."

"A coachman from the East was considered an adequate chaperon. I see."

If only she did not feel so . . . She could not tell David of the events she had set in motion. She *could* not. "Mr. Won Tel is not a coachman."

"But you just said—"

"Oh, David! You muddle me so and you are deliberate about it. Mr. Won Tel is James's, er, his very close confidant. I think."

"A close confidant who is a coachman and who is from the East. Celine, I believe it is my duty to discover exactly who this man Eagleton is and what his intentions are toward you."

Her heart slammed against her ribs in the most alarming fashion. "No one really understands James. He is . . . He is a very honorable man." The heat in her cheeks grew more intense. "Yes, extremely honorable."

"Why should you think I'm questioning Mr. Eagleton's honor?"

"Because you sound so gruff and suspicious. I know James and I know that he is above reproach as a gentleman, and that should be enough. He is proving a very special and trustworthy friend, and . . ." Oh, dear. Oh, dear. Now David would be hurt at the suggestion that someone else shared his position as her closest ally. "He is not my friend in the same way that you are. Not at all."

"No," David said thoughtfully. "No, I rather think that, at least, is correct."

Celine planted her hands on her hips and scowled down at David before stomping back to her seat. She lifted her cup and was mortified when her shaking fingers slopped coffee into the saucer. "I think people can be very narrow-minded," she said, carefully setting the cup down again. "All this *on dit* about James's household is purely the invention of shallow people who spend too much time sipping scandal broth and chattering meanly."

"Why don't you tell me what it is these mean people say about Mr. Eagleton's household over tea?"

"I will not! I do not approve of gossip. There are enough busy mouths—jealous mouths, if you ask me—prattling idly about exotic practices from the East and about Liam. I do not need to add to the unkindness."

David rested his elbows on the table. "What do you suppose they mean by exotic practices?"

"How should I know? Probably that ... well, I don't know. Perhaps there is a gong, or an incense burner. I haven't been to the house. And I know people do not believe that Liam is James's housekeeper. I did not believe as much myself,. at first, but now that I know him better, I—well—I certainly do believe it.". She did?

"Who is Liam?"

"The most beautiful Chinese girl I have ever seen." She thought a moment. "Not that I recall having seen one before. But had I done so, I just know I should regard Liam the most beautiful of all."

"How old would you say she is?"

"Oh ..." Tapping the end of her nose, Celine considered. "Perhaps my age. Nineteen or twenty."

"And she is Mr. Eagleton's housekeeper?"

"Yes." Certainly that did not sound particularly reasonable. "I think it possible that in the East people of the servant classes advance more quickly."

She could not tell what David might be thinking. He turned sideways in his chair and stared seriously at the faded paint on the plaster fireplace surround.

The silence became too much. "David, may I ask you some questions that have been concerning me deeply?"

He looked at her over his shoulder. "Always, Celine, you know that. There is nothing you cannot ask me." His face was deeply troubled.

She drew herself up and set her jaw firmly. "What exactly is it that happens to cause a woman to fall?"

Slowly, David settled himself to face her once more. "We have already discussed this."

"Yes, but not in enough detail."

"Why should you require more detail on a subject entirely unsuited to a gentle young female like yourself?"

"Pah! I am not a gentle young female. I am brave and determined. I am a setter of trends. Wait and see if I'm not. And now I require more information on this very important subject so that I may be of use in helping others who might fall prey to the deplorable condition."

She saw his throat jerk. "I forbid you to discuss the subject with anyone," he said sternly. "Do you understand?"

"No." In this she would not be turned aside. "You have explained that these fallen women have become enslaved by their need to recreate the intense physical manifestations of Passion."

"I did not exactly—"

"Yes, you did. What I want to know is: Who incites whom to these feelings?"

"Who?"

"Yes, David. Who? Is it in fact the man or the woman who starts the situation?"

He got to his feet and pulled his waistcoat down, held on to it with both hands. "Why are you asking such a thing?"

"Aha! As I thought. The situation is not as clear-cut as you at first led me to believe. I am asking because I want to know exactly where these feelings of Passion come from. Would you have me believe that—at first, at least—the woman simply dreams them up?"

He cleared his throat. "Probably."

"But how? What starts the dreaming? Is it always

there inside her, or is it somehow the result of something she sees?"

"Sees?" His voice cracked.

"Like a particularly ... well, like ... Could it be that the sight of a ... pleasant-looking man perhaps might incite these responses?"

"Celine, you are so ... Oh, I suppose it's likely." Agitation colored his face once more. "But that is not certain."

"Aha! Exactly! Could it not, in fact, be more the way a man *looks* at a woman? That by such a look he incites this tendency to certain dreamings and longings that lead to an inclination to pursue Passion?" She felt triumphant at the clarity of her analysis.

David approached her, a deep frown hardening his features. "What gave you such an idea?"

She would not be intimidated. "That is neither here nor there. Tell me, David, could the way a man touches a woman ... if he were to touch ... that is ..." A coldness formed in her stomach. "This is merely a conjecture on my part, but I believe it has merit." Her voice faltered. David did not look like a man who found merit in what she said. He looked coldly angry.

"I think, Celine, that I should pay a visit to Mr. Eagleton's exotic household."

James strode into the Grosvenor Square house with Won Tel at his heels. The covert witnessing of an early morning meeting of the Letchwiths' sporting club, followed by an exasperating interview with Uncle Augustus, had left James in a foul mood.

"The man gave his word to remain in Dorset." James's top boots clattered on the tesselated black and white stone tile in the hallway. "The man is an intolerable complication."

Won Tel followed him into the library. "You accomplished what was necessary, Mr. Eagleton. The marquess accepts that under no circumstances must either Miss Celine or the Godwins be aware of your true identity until you give him the nod. And he does agree to continue withholding the announcement of your father's death."

"God!" James drew off his leather riding gauntlets. "It is beyond understanding that my grandfather said nothing to his elder son about the reason for banishing the younger. Yet it is clear from my uncle's demeanor that he knew nothing."

"Your father told me that the old marquess was a very private man," Won Tel said quietly.

James rounded on him. "My father told you that?"

Despite the cold drizzle in which they had spent much of the past eight hours, Won Tel still wore no outer garment over his tunic. He planted his booted feet apart and tugged at his beard, staring into the distance as if preoccupied.

"When did my father speak to you of my grandfather?"

"On several occasions when he felt a—shall we say a grimness of spirit? Particularly when your mother was ill."

James closed his eyes against a rush of emotion. "Why have you never mentioned this to me?"

"You didn't ask. And your father wasn't really speaking to me. He merely knew that what he said in my presence was spoken as if he were alone."

Deep sorrow, the despair of irrevocable loss ... and hatred: James felt wrenched apart at the injustice that had taken his mother's life and, quite possibly, his father's. "Won Tel, I've always felt that if my father hadn't been preoccupied at losing my mother he might never have walked into the path of that wagon."

"But he might have, James."

"Why didn't he blame my grandfather for . . . Why didn't he blame him?"

"I don't know. It seems he accepted that his father had cause for the decisions he made and—as you have told me—he was convinced Darius and Mary Godwin provided that cause. Mr. Francis was a shrewd man, James. Trust him. And forgive your grandfather."

"And deal with the Godwins," James said, almost under his breath. "Pray God the present marquess keeps his word and draws no attention to our true connection until it is safe to do so."

"He will do as you have asked," Won Tel said. "Trust me. The marquess thinks of you as the son he does not have. He will do nothing to interfere with that."

James nodded. "I believe you." Too angry to be weary, he swept off his cloak and tossed it carelessly across a divan. "Damn, but I was not prepared for this morning's *entertainment*."

"Deplorable."

"The Letchwiths are vermin—father and son both." The debauched scene James had witnessed in near darkness from the shelter of a ruined church wall was still vivid in his mind. "I thought there was nothing left that could raise my bile. I was mistaken."

"The Letchwiths and their perversion are not your concern, unless they obstruct what must be done."

James felt his gut tighten, and the muscles in his jaw. "Regardless," he murmured. "They shall not touch Celine."

The faintest of shufflings caused him to look up—directly into Won Tel's dark eyes. James frowned. Had he caught a fleeting gleam in those eyes? "Is there some humor in this? I should certainly enjoy it if there were."

All expression slipped from Won Tel's face. "No humor at all, Mr. Eagleton. I'm certain your only interest in saving Miss Celine from falling victim to the perverted sexual practices of Mr. Bertram and Mr. Percival Letchwith is that you have certain uses for her yourself in the foreseeable future.

"No, there is certainly absolutely no humor in the situation. And I'm certain that, once your objective has been attained, you will have no further concern about Miss Celine falling into those gentlemen's—"

"*Won Tel.* I believe this discussion has served its purpose. Be so good as to call Liam."

Won Tel shifted from foot to foot.

"Well?" James brushed irritably at his mud-spattered buff breeches. "Call Liam."

"She is a headstrong female," Won Tel said woodenly.

"Indeed? I am grateful for this insight. Will you inform her I'm waiting, or shall I search her out myself?"

"I will go." Still Won Tel lingered. "You are the center of the child's world."

James opened his mouth and promptly snapped it shut again. He strode to the window and glowered out over the lawns turned a glistening gray-green under leaden skies that threatened more rain.

He had not slept since leaving the Godwin house the previous evening. Thoughts of Celine—conflicting thoughts about what he truly wanted from her, and for how long—had kept him awake and pacing until three when Won Tel had come with his urgent request for an unscheduled before-dawn outing.

Without turning, James answered Won Tel stiffly.

"Liam is no longer a child. And her malicious pranks can no longer be tolerated."

Use Celine and be done with her.

"Liam is a gentle enough little creature, James."

"Drivel."

Once in possession of the Sainsbury gems and with the Godwins safely ousted from Knighthead, there would be no reason not to banish Celine from his mind—for good. No reason.

"I'll call Liam, then, James."

"Do that." He didn't turn around. Gold and honey and softness and sweet, sweet trust. Gentle trust that allowed her to give to him as no woman ever had. Even without the final culmination, the final burying of himself within her, he had felt in those moments of spilling forth his seed between her satin thighs a sense of exultation and possession. She thought herself in control of her fragile little destiny. He was her honorable friend who would compromise her out of a union with the filth Letchwith. He laughed shortly. She would repay him with "sensations." God! The poor little baggage knew nothing—not even the true nature of being *compromised*!

His thighs tensed in remembrance. What a talented pupil in the subject of fleshly sensations was his little Celine. How soon could he trust himself to teach her again? And would he keep himself from taking what she was too innocent to withhold?

The softest of clicks let him know the door had closed.

"You wished to talk with me?"

He held his bottom lip between his teeth and turned to see Liam trailing her fingers along the back of a divan in a perfect imitation of a highborn English chit practicing her wiles on a desirable *parti*.

Only with difficulty did James contain a laugh. "You have caused me grave displeasure," he said.

Swinging her small hips in a manner that would have inflamed the fair Lady Anastasie's jealousy, Liam minced from behind the divan and settled herself on its cushions. Her crimson tunic, closed from high collar to hem with many-faceted jet buttons, shimmered against the dark green and gold.

"Explain your behavior."

"Master James, are your clothes wet?"

"Damn and blast you, girl. Do not seek to divert me."

She lowered her lashes to create dark shadows on the perfect olive skin over her high cheekbones. "You sound angry, Master James. I avoid discussions with angry people."

"You what?" He advanced to stand over her. Today her hair was drawn up from her face, loose and soft, into a braided chignon. From James's vantage point, he noted the blue-black shimmer of her tresses and the fragile curve of her young neck. Fixing his gaze on the leather-bound spines of books stretching across a wall, he steeled himself to ask, "What did you just say to me, Liam?"

She leaped up so suddenly that he stepped back.

"Liam—"

"Don't shout!"

"You try my patience, miss. How dare you interfere in my affairs."

She bowed her head.

"Do you understand what I'm saying to you?"

Liam crossed her arms, slipping her hands inside her sleeves. Today her precisely placed slippers were of the same black satin as her narrow trousers.

"Liam . . ." Perhaps Won Tel was right. Perhaps he should be very careful not to crush this brave little spirit. Who could possibly know what demons she fought daily in that active mind?

"The smallest of spiders." She used her smoothest, sweetest tone.

He narrowed his eyes. "I beg your pardon?"

"One very small spider. Hardly a spider at all by the standards of a girl of spirit."

"Liam, you have exhausted my patience. I have no alternative but to—"

"But to what?" Her face came up and she blazed an impudent smile upon him. "It was a test. I can only gather from your most upset countenance that the test was failed and that you were made to suffer greatly."

He could only shake his head.

"What did she do? Scream? Turn even more pallid than she already is? Good. Now you will see the mistake you are making."

"You put a spider into a bowl you knew Miss Godwin would open. Not a small spider, but a very large and grotesque spider, one certain to horrify any young lady."

Liam drew herself up. "Not me. Only a foolish, pettish, squeamish nothing who announced that she would expect a husband to be certain that no such 'horror' inhabited her bedchamber. Hah!"

"So you did overhear everything in the garden."

"Enough to know that you must be protected from such insipid nothings."

"I will not discuss Miss Godwin with you."

"Why? Because you fear I will show you the truth about her?"

This was not at all as he had planned this encounter. "You are not sorry about the spider?"

"No!" She raised her oval chin. "I am glad. Now you will see that this person is not suitable for you. You need a strong woman, not a pale little incompetent toad."

"Toast," James said, suddenly deeply weary. "And the word is not *incompetent*."

"I do not care." Liam's even white teeth snapped together.

A tap came at the door and James called, "Come!" without turning from Liam. "You will do as you are told, Liam. In the future you will honor my wishes and you will remember your place."

Pressing her palms together, she fell to her knees before him.

The girl was incorrigible. "Liam! I warn you. You will do as I require." She knew too well that he cared for her like a beloved sister and that she could usually charm him out of any ill humor.

Bending over, she touched her brow to his boots. "Whatever you demand, master. I am at your disposal.

"Mr. Eagleton."

At the sound of Won Tel's voice, James swung around. "Yes?" He blew out a slow breath. "Bloody hell! Isn't this a little early to come calling?"

David Talbot, with Celine at his side, stared fixedly at Liam's submissive pose.

Chapter 16

Bloody hell? Celine placed a tightly closed fist against her mouth and studied James's darkly angry face, then David's stony profile. *No one* cursed in front of David!

"Mr. Eagleton." Won Tel stepped forward, and Celine noted the unusually edgy set to the man's mouth. "The Reverend Mr. Talbot and Miss Celine—"

"I *know* who they are, dammit, man."

"James!" Celine could not continue to contain herself. "David is a—"

"I *know* what he is, dammit!"

"Oh."

James glared down at the girl huddled over his feet. "Liam," he said in the hardest of tones. "If you know what's good for you—"

"Desist, sir!" David drew himself up tall. "What manner of behavior is this? Humiliating and berating a fragile little female."

Liam only hunched lower over James's feet.

Celine suddenly realized that David was very tall, indeed. In fact, he had the look of a fierce and handsome stranger whom she might never have known.

"David—"

"You *will* be quiet, Celine," he said shortly. "This visit, sir, has nothing to do with my calling."

225

James pushed back his dark blue coat and rested his fists on his hips. "I am delighted to hear it, Mr. Talbot." Mud spattered his light-colored breeches and caked his top boots. How splendidly his breeches smoothed those strongly muscled thighs, and . . . Celine glanced up and found herself staring into gray eyes turned almost black by the force of whatever violent emotion raged within the man.

He was magnificent.

"Does what you see distress you, Celine?" The corners of his mouth turned up—in challenge, not in humor. "I know how you disdain mud . . . particularly on boots."

She would not blush.

"See here, Eagleton." David covered the distance between himself and James with sure steps. "Frightening the weaker sex may be your idea of sport. It is not mine."

James's next breath expanded his chest. Celine could not help but remember how it had felt to be trapped beneath this man's powerful body. She closed her eyes. If she was fallen, then she hoped she never got up again.

"Are you feeling unwell, Celine?"

At James's inquiry, she opened her eyes. "Not at all. Merely overwhelmed."

"Overwhelmed?"

Could he not *feel* what she was feeling, *think* what she was thinking? Surely, when two people were almost of one mind—and they definitely were—there was no need for words in moments such as this.

"Should I order refreshments, Mr. Eagleton?"

James turned to Won Tel. "I intend to have a large whisky. If our guests would care to join me, you may pour. Otherwise, please take Liam away."

Standing in the middle of this lush room with its dark woods and black lacquer, its brilliant silks and satins, its strange gilded dogs and jewel-eyed jade dragons, James was a mysterious, powerful presence in surroundings that were a perfect complement. Celine met his eyes once more and curled her fingers into her palms. A mysterious, powerful, enigmatic presence. She could scarcely believe she had known him so intimately ... scarcely wait to know him as such again. His gaze never wavered, even as a lazy smile curved his lips.

Won Tel cleared his throat.

Finally James turned his attention to David. "Speak up, Mr. Talbot. Whisky? Or perhaps strong drink is too earthly for a man of God?"

"Your behavior is insufferable, sir," David said. "Which is as I had expected it to be. Neither Miss Godwin nor I care for any refreshment in this house."

This was going so badly. Celine attempted a cheerful smile. "I do hope you'll forgive us for intruding, James. David will not be in London too long and I wanted him to have a chance to meet you."

"Why?"

Celine's skin felt tight and hot. She had never seen James quite like this and had no idea how to respond.

David moved restlessly. "This visit was my idea, Eagleton. I have a few questions I intend to ask you."

"Really?" Muscles flickered in James's lean cheeks. "Won Tel, remove Liam."

The little figure in red raised up just enough to wrap her arms around James's legs and rest her cheek against his boot tops.

"This is insupportable," David muttered. "The poor creature's spirit is broken."

If only David had not insisted upon coming. Celine struggled to open her green velvet reticule with its trim of white feathers that matched the banditti on her pleated bonnet. "Here you are, David." She offered him a minuscule vial Lettie insisted she carry. "Hartshorn. Perhaps it will help Liam." He did not take the vial.

"God!" James looked heavenward.

"James, I cannot think what has caused this . . . this fit of temperament." Celine raised her chin. "It is not at all like you to be so inhospitable. If I had known you would treat us like this, I should certainly not have come."

"Fit of temperament? Inhospitable?"

"Indeed, sir," David put in.

"I had thought to have my . . . my very good friends meet each other. And . . ." Something in James's granite stare stopped Celine. He was not as he had been—not ever in her experience. Surely he had not already changed his mind about assisting her. "James, if you would prefer it, we will leave at once." Her voice broke annoyingly.

"Not until I have done what I came to do," David said.

"Shall we soon learn what that was?" James asked, all heavy sarcasm. He glanced down at Liam once more. "Kindly get up, miss."

"Insupportable," David said through gritted teeth. With a challenging glare at James, he bent over Liam and touched her shoulder awkwardly. "There, there, little one. I shall ensure that you are not hurt."

"Good, God!" James looked to Won Tel, who shrugged and bowed his way from the room. "How perfectly bloody marvelous. Besieged and abandoned in my own home."

Celine pursed her lips. "You will have to look to your language, James. Particularly in the company of one as young and innocent as Liam."

His laugh amazed her. "For shame, James," she said.

"For shame, James," he mimicked. "I feel I am a wanderer into some very bad theatrical production."

"What did you mean by making off into the country with Celine yesterday?" David asked while he settled his long, fine hands on Liam's slender arms.

James looked over David's head and directly into Celine's eyes. She shook her head slightly and sent him a silent plea for caution. He set his mouth in a hard line, but she thought she saw a slight softening of his expression.

Murmuring softly, David attempted to ease Liam to her feet. She had yet to show her face, and she merely clung the tighter to James's leg.

"Come, my dear. Let me help you." David gently pried Liam's fingers free and raised the girl to her full, if diminutive, height. He turned her toward him and she looked up. "Let me . . . Let me . . ." His lips remained parted and he stared down into Liam's beautiful upturned face.

Seconds passed. Many seconds.

Celine saw the slight widening of David's very green eyes and the drawing together of his fine brows.

Liam, her hands in his, continued to regard him steadily.

James crossed his arms. "What were you quizzing me about, Talbot? My attempt to kidnap Celine yesterday?"

"James!" Celine took a step toward him, but James shook his head slightly.

"She was unchaperoned," David said vaguely.

"Indeed," James agreed. "Quite unchaperoned. For hours."

Celine pressed a hand over her heart. This was not at all what she had planned. In her rehearsals, James told her parents that she was ruined and they simply took her back to Dorset and never mentioned the subject—or the hated name of Letchwith—again. David should never be involved.

"In the absence of Mr. and Mrs. Godwin and with no other responsible male to speak for her part, it is my duty to ensure that Celine is protected."

"Admirable," James said. He smiled at Celine, touched his fingers to his lips, and blew a kiss past the unsuspecting David and Liam.

Celine shivered inside her green pelisse and carriage dress. A heavy ripple passed through regions she refused to identify.

"Are you all right, my dear?" David asked Liam, bending to look into her face—as if he weren't already close enough.

She nodded quickly, and the braid wound at her crown slipped to unravel down her back. "I became somewhat confused, sir," she said in a light, clear voice. "I had displeased Master James and he was—most appropriately—admonishing me."

David held his bottom lip in his teeth. He stood, fully a foot taller than the girl. Broad and lithe, his well-favored frame made her appear even more fragile, even more beautiful ... even more an object to steal the vulnerable heart of a gentle man.

Celine shifted her weight and puffed out a loud little breath. What a moon-minded goose she was. David was reacting sympathetically to someone he judged needy of his help, just as he always did.

"No one should ever admonish you," he said to Liam, very quietly. "Oh, no."

A slight movement returned Celine's attention to James. He regarded David and Liam with an air of complete concentration.

"From now until Celine's parents arrive, Mr. Eagleton," David said, plainly distracted, "you will consult me before approaching Celine."

"Or kidnapping her again?" James smiled wickedly at Celine.

"Most certainly." David transferred both of Liam's hands to one of his and touched her cheek. "Is there anything you wish to tell me, Liam? Anything I should do for you—arrange for you—now?"

Liam inclined her head. "Perhaps ... No, thank you." Her hair completely escaped the remnants of the braid and swung around her face and shoulders like a black satin waterfall that fell below her elbows.

"Um, David," Celine said uncertainly. "Do you think we should consider going home?"

"Are you certain, Liam? Nothing? Nothing at all?"

What Celine was witnessing was not the invention of a moon-minded goose. The Reverend David Talbot of Little Puddle, conservative Dorsetshire village, was gazing with stunned admiration at Liam, James's housekeeper, a Chinese girl from Paipan in the South China Sea.

He was lost to this foreign female.

Celine found her hands were shaking. What had she done? What potential disaster had she unwittingly engineered?

"I am very happy with Master James," Liam said, her voice almost too soft to hear. "What you witnessed was simply a silliness of my own making." She turned to her employer. "I can be most trying, can I not?"

James failed to mask his surprise in time. "Ah—"

"You see," Liam said, "sometimes it is necessary for me to be reprimanded—"

"Never," David broke in with fervor, and to James he said, "Treat this young lady with less than the greatest care and you shall answer to me, sir. Do I make myself plain?"

Celine let out a little gasp. "Have a care, David."

"Fear not," James said. "I'm sure our man of God

will not resort to violence in the defense of the object of his affections."

David was already lost in Liam once more. "Are you here of your own free will, my dear?"

"Oh, yes." Fathomless dark eyes shifted from David to James and back again—and Celine noted that when they rested on David, loyal adoration became something quite different. Liam's half-lowered lashes, her heightened color, became the marks of a smitten girl.

Quite abruptly, David straightened and seemed to realize how intimately he held Liam's hands, how near to her he stood. He stepped back and released her. "We must leave."

Liam, her head bowed, passed between them, leading the way to the hall. David followed, his face drawn into tense lines. When Celine would have followed, James caught her arm.

"You played a dangerous game today, James," she said sharply. "If David were to get wind of my plans he would doubtless do his best to stop them."

He pulled her around to face him. "He didn't even hear what I said."

"That was not your doing."

Watching her mouth, he bent nearer. "No, my golden girl, it was fate." As the sound of soft voices came from the hall, he brushed his lips back and forth across Celine's, slipped his tongue just inside her mouth to tease the tender skin within.

She sighed and allowed her eyes to drift shut. "I have discovered more interesting details about all this." Experimenting, she copied what he did with his tongue, and his deep moan excited her.

His hands came down on her shoulders, and he raised his head. "What details? Details about what?"

"About how these sensations come to be." She leaned against him, settled her fingers in the lean

hollows at his hips. "About looks and touches . . .
and what causes what . . . and how." How easy it
was to spread her hands so that her thumbs, capable
thumbs she'd been told, could rub circles over his
rigid stomach.

James groaned again—and grabbed her hands
quite fiercely. "You may yet drive me completely
mad," he whispered close to her ear. "And yet you
do not even know what you do."

"Oh, but I do," she protested. "I know all about
these things now."

Smiling slightly, he rested a finger on her lips. "Let
us follow your protector and my *housekeeper*, before
they wonder where we are."

"Of course." Feeling heavy, almost slumberous,
Celine swayed away from him. She did not want to
be anywhere but with James.

"You will be at the fete on Saturday. We shall meet
there."

A small, panicky fluttering assaulted Celine. "I
cannot be certain that my parents will have arrived."

His eyes questioned. "Of what concern is that?"

"Well"—she fussed with her bonnet strings—"I
thought perhaps it was time to . . . to . . . for us to
deal with what we agreed upon."

James shook his head and held her arm. "We are
already agreed, Celine, that I shall be the one to decide upon that matter." He guided her to the door.
"More time is needed. I will inform you when I decide the perfect moment has arrived."

In the hall they halted, side by side, and Celine felt
James's hand tighten.

"Thank you, Liam," David was saying. "You will
not forget?"

"I will not forget." The girl bowed. "I will never
forget."

David raised a hand, and Celine felt as if her heart

had stopped. Very carefully, her old friend—her old friend with no time for matters of the heart—passed his fingers over Liam's hair. Celine saw him falter before lifting a lock slowly to his lips. His eyes closed for an instant, then he let the hair fall.

Beside Celine, James muttered something under his breath.

"What did you say, James?"

"I said *bloody hell!*" he whispered vehemently.

Chapter 17

"**O**h, Lettie, I think I should like to go back to Curzon Street."

"No such thing, Celine. People are looking at you. There would be talk if you tried to slip away."

Celine stood amid the frightful squeeze in the vast entrance hall to Casterbridge House and felt she might faint away from the heat—and from the sheer splendor of her surroundings.

"So many people," Celine whispered into Lettie's ear, and when Lettie shook her head, uncomprehending, Celine shouted, "How would anyone know who was or was not here? And the noise!"

Lettie nodded and pointed to where a string quartet on a raised velvet-draped platform bent industriously over their instruments and produced nothing more audible than the occasional note.

"There is no point to this," Celine said. The crush swept along by the pressure of new arrivals, flowed like a shimmering multicolored river toward a central staircase.

"We can't get out now, Celine," Lettie said, frowning.

Celine was pleased with her companion's appearance tonight. A russet brown dress, too severe in cut for Celine, had been a prize bought from a friend of

235

Isabel's who had gladly parted with the gown—as yet unworn—for a pittance since she did not care for the color. On Lettie it became a rich complement to her dark hair and eyes. Celine herself wore Isabel's marvelous pink satin, adorned with the deeply scalloped Belgian lace flounce and a ruffle at the neck from a piece she had managed to match. One asset presented by so large a crowd was that no one was likely to remark on recognizing the gown.

Carried onward by the press of the crowd, they reached the foot of the stairs and Celine looked up at flights that rose and bifurcated to reach opposite sides of a circular gallery. "How grand it is."

"Indeed," Lettie said. "The pale green walls are so pretty, and the white plasterwork. All so delicate."

Celine caught Lettie's hand and squeezed. "And we don't know a soul. Surely there will be no way to see a friendly face in such a press."

"Then we shall just enjoy the experience of it all," Lettie said, her eyes bright. "And talk about it when we are safely back in Dorset."

Lettie's smile faded. For a moment Celine felt the chatter and the laughter and the wafting strains of music fade. She and Lettie regarded each other, and Celine knew that they both longed for Dorset and home—and for those blissful days or even weeks of peace between the wild turns. But most of all they longed never to hear the name Letchwith again.

Then there was David, and the unpleasant journey he would take this night. Celine had offered to plead a headache to get out of attending the ball and go with him. David had merely shaken his head, but he had seemed touched at her concern.

"I do hope David will be safe tonight," she said, forgetting that Lettie knew nothing of David's business. "I mean that I hope he won't be too bored sitting alone in Curzon Street," she added hurriedly.

"Miss Fisher?"

A man's deep voice said Lettie's name very clearly, and both women turned to look behind them on the stairs. Mr. Won Tel was not hard to find, even in this crowd. Somehow, in the melee, his odd costume appeared at once more suitable, yet more outrageous than in less rich surroundings.

Lettie smiled and tried to extend her hand, only to have it swept back against her body by a boisterous rakehell already half in his cups, who bellowed with laughter while he dragged a shrieking woman up the stairs in his wake. Dressed in bead-encrusted scarlet, the female was well into her middle years and so rouged as to appear apoplectic. Openmouthed, Celine watched the pair's progress and heard outraged pronouncements of "Foolish chub" and "Rattlepate" and "What an argle bargle" on all sides. Mr. Won Tel was now nowhere to be seen.

Then, miraculously, there was a space before Lettie and Celine, caused by a parting of guests somewhere behind. Celine glanced over her shoulder and barely stopped herself from gawking. "Mr. Won Tel!"

"Please proceed upward, Miss Godwin, Miss Fisher."

Lettie and Celine looked at each other again and giggled—and did as instructed. Mr. Won Tel climbed majestically behind them, his arms outstretched, forcing others to find a way around him and the charges he chose to protect.

At the top of the stairs, he contrived to form a vacant area where they could stand. "Where do you wish to go?" he asked formally.

"Well . . ." Celine felt breathless. "I should like to go home, but—"

"But that is not an option," Mr. Won Tel finished for her, even as Lettie opened her mouth to give her opinion. "You would disappoint certain people were you to fail to grace the occasion."

"What people?" Celine asked, knowing well who he meant, but wanting to hear him say James's name.

Mr. Won Tel's eyes crinkled, or she thought they did, before he turned to Lettie and bowed again. "Are you enjoying London, Miss Fisher?"

"Lettie."

"Lettie." There was no mistaking his smile this time. "I thought you missed the country."

"I do," Lettie said, and she looked into his face for rather a long time before adding, "Celine should pay her respects to her host."

"Oh, no!"

"Oh, yes," Lettie said. She leaned closer. "Celine, the more eligible people you meet, the better your chances of, well, you know."

"Yes." If only she felt she could take Lettie more completely into her confidence over the arrangement she had made with James. Unfortunately, Lettie might not agree with the lengths to which Celine had *already* taken the plan.

Lettie gave her a little push. "We should find the marquess."

"But I have never actually *met* a marquess. He may be terrifying."

"He is not . . ." Mr. Won Tel cleared his throat. "That is to say, I have observed the Marquess of Casterbridge and he appears an affable person. When I last saw him he was in the grand ballroom. Allow me to lead the way."

"You know this house," Celine remarked, following.

"I was in the ballroom a short while ago," Mr. Won Tel said. Walking before them, he provided as effective a pathway as he had at their heels.

"Oh!" Celine paused at the entrance to a large

room. "Look, Lettie. Have you ever . . . No, you haven't. A moment, please, Mr. Won Tel." She pushed to the doorway to survey supper tables too fantastic to seem real. "Colored fountains on every table. And, look! Parrots on golden perches—and palm trees. Oh, Lettie! There is a pool in the middle of the room."

"Did you want to move closer, Miss Godwin?"

She did, but she also wanted to see James. Why didn't Won Tel give her some message from James? "Just a little closer perhaps."

He escorted them past tables laden with many-tiered silver dishes from which exotic fruits cascaded, and golden platters of delicacies, many of which Celine did not recognize. Guests jostled, exclaiming over the food which they devoured in indecent quantities.

"There," Celine announced with satisfaction as they reached the pool. Shaped like a huge seashell, it was nestled on a bed of white sand, and from its blue surface rose a fragrant, warm steam. "Oh, look! A mermaid!" Celine pressed her hands to her cheeks in wonder.

"A pretend mermaid," Lettie said, sounding disapproving. "Hardly a stitch on and lying on an artificial rock. Very unsuitable, I should say."

Lettie turned away and Celine was forced to follow, but not before she took a very careful look at the rather plump female on the bright green rock, whose long, blond wig flowed over her breasts without covering quite all of their considerable extent.

Celine decided she loved it all, including the mermaid's silver tail. "I'm glad I'm here now," she said, breathless from hurrying to keep up. "Lettie! There are jewels tossed on the tables! Rivers of them. Oh, I should have been most upset to miss the only real fete to which I'm likely to be invited."

A few minutes later she felt disposed to change her mind again. The supper room paled before the lavish and intimidating splendor that was the grand ballroom at Casterbridge House.

At the top of a wide, curving staircase, a noble-looking manservant in white wig, gold satin livery, white satin pantaloons, and white silk stockings bent his head to Celine and listened to her name. She thought he elevated his long nose a trifle higher before he announced her.

"How silly," she told Lettie, descending the staircase with as much confidence as she could summon. "Who could hear anyway?"

Instantly, a small, colorless man in nondescript evening dress stepped before her. "Good evening, Miss Godwin. I will show you to the marquess."

Nonplussed, Celine turned to where Won Tel had stood. "Gone again," she said crossly. "He does have an unnerving way of popping in and out of places."

"This way, Miss Godwin," the little man said. "And you, Miss Fisher."

There seemed no choice but to follow. The man slipped swiftly between clusters of gloriously garbed guests surrounding the dance floor where smiling couples moved expertly through the sets of a cotillion.

Overhead, rows of candlelighted chandeliers hung from the frescoed panels of a high, many-arched ceiling. Gold silk glowed on walls lined with white statuary dramatically displayed in alcoves painted in deepest purple.

When Celine faltered, Lettie urged her gently on until they reached the outer edges of a most splendid circle of people.

"Casterbridge remembers how to put on a memorable fete," Celine heard a man say to the woman at her side.

Leaning toward him, diamond-studded turquoise plumes swaying, the woman replied from behind her fan, "Not simply memorable, my dear. *The* event of the Season. What one wonders is *why* he chooses to do such a thing when he hasn't been in town for a season since who knows when."

With a firm yet unobtrusive hand, the man who was their guide made a way through the crowd, and then Celine stood before a tall, distinguished-looking, ruddy-faced man. She didn't fail to note the impressive cut of his evening clothes, or the dazzling gold decoration he wore on the blue and gold sash that crossed his chest beneath his jacket. She also took note of the exceedingly beautiful brunette whose hand he seemed happy to keep tucked in the crook of his elbow.

"Lettie—" Celine glanced back and was horrified to discover herself apparently alone. Then she caught sight of the lustrous brown dress, and its wearer, and its wearer's face upturned toward Mr. Won Tel, who had reappeared she knew not when. While Celine tried to send desperate signals to her companion, that lady nodded up at Mr. Won Tel, who seemed to address her seriously before leading her out of Celine's sight.

Alone.

Abandoned.

No familiar face in sight.

"Good evening, er . . ." The distinguished gentleman's voice reached Celine seconds before she realized he addressed her.

"I . . ."

A hand came to rest lightly at her waist. "Good evening, my lord. Allow me to present Miss Celine Godwin."

James's voice carried with such absolute confidence that a hush fell on the group.

"Miss Godwin"—he urged her forward a step—"Augustus, Third Marquess of Casterbridge."

Gathering her wits, Celine sank into a curtsy and was surprised when the white-haired marquess promptly reached for her hand and urged her to stand once more. "Godwin, hey?" Although he smiled, there was something cool in his blue eyes that made Celine swallow and run her tongue over the suddenly dry roof of her mouth.

"Miss Godwin is making her first Season," James said smoothly, and she wished she dared look at him. Instead, she smiled and lowered her eyelashes in the manner described in the book she and Lettie had studied on the subject of female manners.

"Pretty piece," she heard a male voice say close by and with no effort at subtlety.

James's hand moved to hold her waist. "Miss Godwin is from Dorset, my lord. I understand her family is known to you. The Godwins of Knighthead?"

Intensely conscious of the pressure of James's strong fingers on her side, Celine barely heard the marquess's succinct "Certainly. Welcome, Miss Godwin. I hope you are enjoying my little party."

Titters came from all sides, and mutters of "Little party, indeed."

"Where are you in residence, Miss Godwin?"

Celine was surprised that the marquess would bother to spend more time on her. "In Curzon Street, my lord." Increased pressure at her side stopped her attempt at another curtsy.

"And your people—your parents. They are in London with you, of course?"

"They are expected shortly." With deep discomfort, Celine felt interested gazes settle upon her. "Mama has been indisposed and had to postpone the trip."

"My sympathies." The marquess cleared his throat.

"Well, my ... my old friend's son clearly has good taste in the company he chooses."

Uncomprehending, Celine looked politely back at the marquess.

"James Eagleton here is the son of my oldest and dearest friend Algernon Eagleton—departed now, unfortunately." He appeared genuinely saddened.

"I'm sorry," Celine murmured.

The lady at the marquess's side tapped him with her fan. "I'm sure you meant Alfonse Eagleton, didn't you, my lord?"

"Er, yes, of course. That's what I said. Alfonse. My dear," he said to Celine, "this is Sibyl, Countess Lafoget, a true light and blessing in an old man's life, even in the tiny moments she can spare from her many admirers."

The lady smiled delightfully and tapped his arm once more.

"Anyway," Casterbridge continued, "James is descended from the Cumberland Eagletons. Fine family."

"I believe that was the Northumberland Eagletons," Countess Lafoget corrected.

A spark of irritation tightened the marquess's mouth. "As I said, the Northumberland Eagletons."

"I say, sir," a familiar voice broke in. "You probably don't know that you're addressing a young lady who has started *the* trend of the season."

Roland, Viscount Yeatbury, who had been obscured by a taller man standing before him, moved to the front of the group with Beatrice Arbuthnott on his arm. Beatrice smiled delightedly at Celine.

She felt the pressure of James's fingers increase even more.

"It's all such fun," Beatrice said, while Celine noted with amazement the familiar green dress the girl wore. "You are such a clever thing. Why, I doubt if there's anyone who *is* anyone who'd be caught dead in a oncer." To the marquess, she said, "Celine has persuaded us all to become more aware of the plight of the less fortunate, my lord. By encouraging us to purchase gowns already worn once, she has invented a quite marvelous system of producing sums of money for charity." She turned to Celine. "Do you have a particular charity picked out for our patronage, Celine?"

Celine observed that an increasing number of enthusiastic girls with attendant beaux were pressing in. She began to feel flustered. "Oh, yes," she said. "I will ensure that you are contacted with the details."

"So clever," another female voice announced. "Quite the thing now, Celine's little cause."

Lady Daphne DeClair's red hair clashed somewhat with the striking crimson trim on the white dress Isabel Prentergast had worn at the Arbuthnotts' rout. Celine had wondered why the gown had not been offered to her for purchase. No doubt Isabel had shrewdly calculated that Lady Daphne would be a less accomplished bargainer.

The marquess guffawed loudly and slapped James's shoulder. "Quite the little lady of enterprise, hey, James? Just like your father, you are, m'boy. He always looked for the unexpected in his friends."

Celine felt her color rise. How could it be that she was the center of attention in so august a gathering? She searched once more for Lettie, of whom there was no sign.

"Celine." A voice close to her ear startled her and raised the tiny hairs on her spine at the same time. Surely it could not be. Not here. Not at this moment. She turned her face slowly and looked directly into Bertram Letchwith's round blue eyes. "How are you, dear little girl?"

"Well, thank you, sir."

She felt a stir within the circle, yet could not look away from Letchwith's fat, shiny cheeks; the thin, colorless hair waxed into preposterous curls about his face; his bulbous, red little mouth.

"You certainly look well, sweeting. Very, very well." His expressionless eyes passed over her, and he wet his lips with his tongue.

Celine heard a woman's husky voice pronounce, "There you are, James! How naughty of you to arrive so late when you knew I would be waiting for you."

"Perhaps we should take a turn on the terrace," Letchwith said, bringing his face so near that Celine saw the web of tiny red veins on his cheeks and nose. "Percival mentioned the, er, *incident*, of the other evening. Most unwise. Particularly for a young girl in your position."

Glancing back, Celine saw the gorgeous, auburn-haired female who had spoken to James and who now peeked adoringly at him over a fan of pure white lace that matched the bodice of her dress—what bodice there was.

"Did you hear me, Celine?" Letchwith rasped, his breath a wheezing whisper.

"Yes," Celine said, careful to keep her voice low. "What position do you refer to, Mr. Letchwith?"

He smiled. The pupils of his eyes swelled to all but obscure the irises. "I think you know. There is an understanding which, I'm certain, your admirable father has conveyed to you." Spittle gathered at the corners of his mouth.

Desperate, Celine turned within James's still-firm grasp and looked up at him. He smiled, somewhat strangely, she thought, at the green-eyed creature who chattered to him alone.

"Celine." Letchwith's pudgy hand settled on her wrist. "Your participation in these events is designed purely to rid you of any foolish female longings for

something considered missed—*after* we are, ahem . . .
at a later date."

James seemed a solid, unmoving presence at her
side. She wished she could close her eyes and trans-
port herself—and James—to some distant place
where there were no auburn-haired temptresses or
Bertram Letchwiths.

"You will soon come to appreciate your good fortune in having caught the eye of a, shall we say, more
mature man, my dear." Letchwith pursed his lips,
then added very softly, "Let us move away. Your reputation will not be enhanced by the company of this
fast young blood. I hear that every romp and opera
dancer in Town trembles over him. Surely you
wouldn't be counted among such empty-headed
swooners?"

Celine felt not empty-headed but decidedly light-
headed. "Your words seem harsh," she told Letchwith. No, where James was concerned she didn't
want to be counted among any group—but she did
want him—to herself.

The marquess was speaking again, "James, Lady
Anastasie has been pestering me for hours. She as-
sures me you will be lost without her company at my
tedious fete."

"That is *not* exactly what I said, James," the lady
said, dimpling and swaying, and flipping her fan
open and shut. "All I did was to remind Lord
Casterbridge that you and I had an agreement to
guide each other happily through this delightful evening." Below the wisp of a lace bodice, her white
muslin skirts were all but transparent.

Thank goodness, Celine thought, that she had decided on the delicately modest effect of adding lace
to the low, square neck of her own gown.

"We shall dance," Letchwith announced, driving

the tips of his fingers into the soft underside of her wrist.

Celine became cold, then extremely overheated.

"Aren't you going to ask me to dance?" Lady Anastasie said to James, curtsying and offering him her hand.

"Ah, but I should certainly enjoy doing so," James said. He turned to Celine and, as if Bertram Letchwith were invisible, said, "However, Miss Godwin has already agreed to accept me as her partner for the next dance, and I do believe I hear the first strains of a waltz."

Celine managed to smile up at him.

"Shall we, my dear Miss Godwin?"

"Oh, yes."

Letchwith's hand still gripped her wrist. James settled his gaze upon the man, a gaze that had turned from warm invitation to steel threat.

Letchwith dropped her arm. Celine spared an instant to see Letchwith's shiny, red face set in masklike fury—and Lady Anastasie's bright flush behind the rapid flutter of her fan—before James walked her to the dance floor.

She faced him, and he swept her into the dance—and she began to giggle.

James raised one dark, finely arched brow. "You find my dancing amusing."

"No-no," she sputtered. "I find it wonderful, but I have never waltzed before, and I cannot believe that I am here and doing so now."

"You must have waltzed. You move beautifully." He whirled her about, bending her to the music.

How could she not move well with a partner who danced with such lithe, confident grace? There could be such moments of bubbling bliss, even when the potential for disaster clung to the very air she breathed. And she could laugh!

"You look absolutely beautiful," James said, turning her, his steps so fleet and sure that her own feet scarcely touched the floor. He regarded her seriously, his brows drawn together in a faint frown. "A fine, perfect jewel of a girl among so many tawdry imitations."

Despite his somber countenance, her own mirth only increased. "That is a fib, sir. Poetical, but still a fib, and you know it. There are hordes of lovely and charming women present tonight."

"None to compete with you," he said, sounding so sincere that she wished she could believe him.

Celine tried unsuccessfully to swallow her chuckles. "Did you . . . ? Oh, dear."

"Did I see Letchwith's face? Was that what you were going to ask?"

She nodded. "Exactly." The ballroom had become a spinning kaleidoscope made of the blending of pastel muslins and brilliant silks and satins beneath the spearing glow of a thousand candles.

"The man's heart may not survive his foul temper too much longer," James remarked. He moved with the agile elegance of a champion swordsman, or a lean pugilist. "It could also be that the fair Lady Anastasie's heart is, as we speak, in danger of exploding from rage."

She didn't want to think about the lady . . . or Letchwith. He had been so bold, so certain of her. If James refused to fulfill what he had already promised, she would be lost.

"Suddenly so serious," He swept her around, around, around. "No more laughter? Tell me what you're thinking."

Could she tell him?

"Celine?"

The music did not sound as sweet. "That man . . ." She hesitated. "He . . ."

James held her arm more firmly. "You have no reason to fear Letchwith." He guided her ever more swiftly through smiling, gliding couples.

"He said there was an understanding." They were far from the marquess's group now and drawing steadily closer to the tiers of stairs at the entrance to the ballroom. "James, that man expects to . . . to . . ."

Another revolution, and James propelled her from the floor and into the milling groups engaged in conversation. "Come with me, Celine."

Holding her hand, he took the stairs two at a time. Celine bunched her satin skirts high enough from her ankles to allow her to run and keep up.

"James!" They reached the balcony above the entrance hall. "Where are we going?"

"We are going . . ." he said, shepherding her around the circular walls until he thrust open and door and passed into a darkened room. "We are going to a place where we will not be interrupted.

"James!" She tried to hang back.

He smiled down upon her, swept her up into his arms, and strode through the gloom like a creature of the night approaching his bliss. At the far side of the room, a panel slid open beneath his fingers and, when they were inside, he closed the aperture once more.

Before them, illuminated by a blue-white glow from above, wound a narrow stone staircase. This James proceeded to climb, carrying Celine as if she weighed nothing.

She clung to his neck. "Please, James. You frighten me. Where are we going?"

The blue-tinged light cast his eyes in glittering black and turned his cheekbones into high, sweeping blades. Shadows clung to every angle and plane of his face.

"James?"

"We are going to forget that Bertram Letchwith exists."

Chapter 18

The tower room.

James held Celine in his arms and made a slow circle. "We will not be found here," he told her and felt a slight shiver run through her warm, supple body. Moonlight sliced through high windows to slide over the dusty surfaces of gilt-framed mirrors that lined the walls. "No one comes here anymore."

"Why?" she asked against his throat.

"Because—" *Caution.* It would not do to tell her that he'd come here as a boy of ten, brought by his father on what neither of them had known would be their last visit to this house together. "As you heard the marquess remark, my father was a close friend of the Casterbridge family. My father found this room many years ago and told me how to open the panel." *Not so far from the truth.*

Celine slipped her hands around his neck. Her fingers threaded into his hair. Her brow rested against his jaw. James closed his eyes an instant and took a deep breath. There were decisions to be made—as calmly and with as little emotion as possible.

He kissed her hair, inhaled the soft, fresh fragrance of flowers. This rushing desire to protect was foreign. This was not the urge to care for a defenseless child, such as he'd felt and, to some extent, continued to

251

feel for Liam. This was an entirely male drive to defend, and possess ... and it held as much potential for danger, for failure, as for a powerful and intoxicating victory that beckoned him in the form of the woman he held.

"How can you be sure no one else will come here?"

He smiled against her brow. "Does that mean you want to be certain we will remain alone?"

She buried her face in his shoulder, and he laughed a little. "Come, my golden girl. Show that spirit I already know you possess and tell me what you're thinking."

"You press me too hard, James." Her voice was muffled. "I simply want to know the answer to my question."

Very well. He must be more subtle in his quest to find out her true feelings. "Because only I know how to open the door. My father found it when ... when he was visiting." When he was visiting, as he had every year until James's tenth year. "He said no one else knew about it. My father never made idle statements." Not about a house where he'd spent many happy visits to Town and where his mother, James's grandmother, had been the one to share this room with him. "Their secret," as she had called it. She had loved her son Francis deeply. For her, as well as for his father, James must ensure that her legacy of jewels passed into the hands she had chosen.

And that was why whatever happened here tonight, and whatever followed as a result, must not be allowed to dim his purpose.

Slowly, James set Celine down to stand up on the flagstones, but she stayed close as she surveyed the odd room. "Whatever can this have been?"

He laughed shortly. "A lady's secret sanctuary."

His grandmother had invented strange, sad stories to entertain her son.

"A room filled only with mirrors?"

"Once there were cushions upon which she reclined." James's father had passed the legends on to James and done so convincingly enough to make them appear real.

Celine moved scant inches from him and surveyed the moonlit room. "I suppose it would be nice to have such a peaceful retreat. But the mirrors, James. Why?"

"Because she felt a need to see herself." His only thought had been to find the one place where he knew they could be alone. He should have expected her curiosity. "The lady had suffered a great loss."

"A loss that made her want to look at herself?" Celine wandered from him, passing through the moonbeams like some perfect creature formed of shadow and light, her pink satin gown turned to a shimmering fall of rose-tinted ice.

James felt his body tense. "She needed to reassure herself."

Celine moved from mirror to mirror. James went to lean a shoulder against the wall and waited until she approached and turned to frown at her own reflection. "What made her need so much reassurance?"

"She gave herself to a man," he said quietly and reached to touch Celine's cheek. "He had declared his love for her and promised to ask for her hand."

Celine stared straight into her own eyes in the mirror. "What then?"

It was so easy to trail the backs of his fingers down her smooth neck and along her shoulder to the demure lace fichu affair that did more to arouse desire than to create the modest effect she had no doubt sought.

"What happened, James?" Celine raised her jaw.

This girl was so ready to be everything a man could want ... the right man.

James shrugged away from the wall and stood behind her. Their eyes met in the mirror. "I did not bring you here to tell old stories." He must wait to touch her, prolong the ecstasy of watching and waiting—and imagining.

"I should like ..." Her lips remained parted and her bosom rose as she must have felt, as he did, a heaviness in the air, a seething. "I should like to know the story."

"And you shall," he promised. "But it can wait. We have our own business to attend."

Her eyes closed and he studied her face, the passing of intense emotion over her features. "You are very young, Celine." Young and unconsciously voluptuous. "Perhaps too young to deal with some decisions you may soon be forced to make."

"Decisions?" Her lashes lifted slowly, almost slumberously, and she stared at him in the mirror.

Glancing up, he realized that all she could see of him was the dark mass of his body looming behind her and the glint of his eyes and teeth, the suggestion of features in shadow. Yet she looked at him with trust ... and desire.

Very gently, James crossed his arms around her shoulders and eased her back against his chest. "You are being forced toward decisions, Celine." He used a thumb to smooth her neck and tilt up her chin. "You are expected to make a decision about how you will spend the rest of your life."

Her breasts rose against his arm. "They want me to marry him," she said, her voice tight.

"A young girl should take her time to make up her mind about such matters."

Sighing, she let her head fall back on his shoulder. "I could only decide to marry for love."

James spread wide his fingers, slipping beneath the gathered lace to stroke the swell of satiny skin that was at once familiar, yet sweetly, freshly intoxicating. He tightened his belly against the leap of his shaft, but was helpless to stop the pulsing pressure.

"For love?" he managed to say. "Can you come to love Letchwith?" Even the name jarred his teeth together.

"Never!" She covered his hand and trapped it against her breast. "I would die before I would go to him!"

"Do not say such wild things." His craving mounted, his need for this female he had been determined never to need as more than a weapon for his cause.

"You brought me here because you are kind," she said, her voice low and intense. "You would like to help me, but you cannot."

"Why do you say that?"

She relaxed against him, folded her hands over his on her breast. "Do not think me so childish that I don't know I have given you some ... pleasurable sensations. In the carriage." Her eyes closed tightly once more. "It embarrasses me to speak of it, but I saw how great your pleasure was. Perhaps as great as mine. But it was not enough. It *is* not enough. Other than such moments, I have nothing to offer in exchange for the very great favor I asked of you. Please, do not feel sorry for me. I understand. It is enough that we have shared ... so much. And that I have come to know that there are men possessed of deep kindness and concern for others."

Her words brought him as close to self-disgust as any ever had. "I said I would help you. Just now. In the ballroom. I told you there would be no further need to fear Letchwith."

She sighed. "No. I cannot allow you to help me

anymore. Why should you? You have already done enough."

I have taken a great deal from you, little one. "What you have to offer is enough incentive, Celine, I assure you."

"I will not allow you to suffer insult and outrage in my name. No, James. I thank you, but please make my selfish request a thing of the past."

Like hell. "Celine," he said, bending to place a lingering kiss beneath her ear. "I decline to put your request in the past."

He felt her shudder.

"Whatever happens between us could never bring me insult," he murmured. "Look at yourself in the mirror."

Slowly, she did as he asked.

"Do not look away," he told her when she tried to avert her eyes. "I want you to watch and to learn—to learn about yourself and about me."

Her eyes raised to meet his in the mirror and widened. When she would have turned, he held her in place before him. "Do you have any idea how you appear when you respond to me?"

She shook her head, and he knew that, if there were more than the moon's light, he would see a deep blush.

"Then watch, dear one. See the woman you are. The woman you are meant to be."

He felt her breathing quicken, and the steady trembling that passed in waves beneath his fingers. "Hush," he instructed, as gently as his hardened body and raging need would allow. This would be the greatest test of his will—greater even than that previous, vividly remembered occasion—if that were possible. Greater because here he had no doubt that, should he choose, he could take his time, and whatever else pleased him . . .

"James!"

Leaning over her shoulder, he turned her face up to his and settled his mouth at the corner of hers. She breathed out softly, and her lips parted to admit his tongue. "Look into the mirror," he ordered, dropping a kiss on her shoulder.

Slipping his hands down her back and beneath her arms, he covered her breasts and smiled at her small cry—and at the stiffening of her nipples through the satin bodice. He flattened his palms to make circles and could not contain the thrust of his hips as she strained into him.

"That's it, darling one. That's the way you are to be, the way you are meant to be." He spared a look at her mirrored reflection and caught his breath. Her face shone, creamy porcelain-pale, and her lips glistened. She arched her back and forced her hands between them to drive her fingertips into the rock-hard muscles of his thighs.

"James," she said, gasping his name. "James?"

"Yes, my sweet? Tell me what you want."

She stuck her small, white teeth into her bottom lip and squeezed her eyes tightly shut. "I cannot help what I feel. If it is wrong, I would not change it."

He drew back his own lips in a rigid attempt at control. The lace at her neck was an enticing veil that crumpled beneath his fingers. Pulling it aside, he exposed the lush fullness of flesh to his gaze and sucked in another burning breath.

Heat clawed at his groin.

Swiftly, he loosened the tapes at the back of her bodice and forced himself to pause, to gather his wits. "Watch," he said huskily. "Watch carefully."

Again he eased back the lace, hooking his fingers into the neck of her gown and pulling it down, taking with it the small puffed sleeves.

"No!" She plucked ineffectually at his arms.

James waited until she moaned and slackened her grip. He smiled, a small smile of victory, and captured her hands. Molding them to her own flesh, holding them firmly beneath his own, he stroked the final barrier of satin and lace from her full, rounded breasts and, with her mindless help, urged up rosy, turgid peaks ready for his pleasure.

"This cannot be . . ." She panted and, when he flipped his thumbs over her nipples, moaned afresh and tried to turn her head aside.

James stopped, barely keeping contact with the puckered skin that drove her to wildness. "Look, Celine. Do not stop looking."

Slowly, she did as he asked. And he looked at her also. Her hair had slipped its carefully contrived chignon and ringlets to fall in a glorious tangle about her shoulders.

"Good." He smiled at her, held her eyes while he gradually bent to capture a nipple in his teeth. Kneading her other breast, he suckled until she gave a strangled scream and struggled to hold him.

Laughing, he evaded her hands and contrived to anchor her before him once more. "There will be more, my dearest, much more. I may have to teach you patience." He worked her gown swiftly from her body and let it fall. "Patience is of the essence in truly great lovemaking. And you will learn to make such great love." Lifting her, he swept the gown aside, leaving her in only a flimsy chemise that hung open to her waist.

"James, I cannot bear it," she said, and her naked breasts rose and fell rapidly.

He laughed again and dodged to repeat the sweet, agonizing attention to her other nipple. Standing behind her once more, he ran his fingers over both wet and glistening tips. "Just when you think you cannot bear it, you will bear more, Celine, and more." And he would bear more and more and pray he would not break with the effort.

Before she could guess his intent, he delved between her legs, cupping her mound through the thin lawn of the chemise.

His eyes were on hers when her mouth made a shocked "Oh" and she writhed, reaching back blindly for him. "James, I want to touch you."

He dipped his fingertips into her, felt the heavy, hot moisture well and the helpless drive of her hips against the tempest of need that was his shaft, then onto his fingers.

Too much. He could bear the pressure no more. With deft haste, he opened his breeches, and scarcely contained his gasp of relief as his manhood sprang free.

Bracing his feet apart, he pulled the filmy shred of fabric she wore above her hips and rested himself against her small, firm bottom . . . and fought to control the urge to do what could be so easily accomplished.

"James! What are you doing?" Her voice was light and breathless now.

With great effort, he contrived to smile into the mirror at her wide, darkened eyes, and while he smiled, wrapped his arms around her once more and ripped the chemise open until he could see the glistening, golden hair between her legs.

"You are beautiful," he said against her ear. "There will never be a moment when I do not want you exactly as you are now."

She began to return his smile, but gritted her teeth. James curled his fingers into the heated, creamy folds shielded by that golden hair and rhythmically stroked, fended off her flailing hands, and played her harder and harder.

"James! Please!"

"Yes, my dear one. Yes."

"Yes!" she echoed, and her climax broke, rippled over her body in wave after wave.

At last Celine sagged against him, her face turned sideways on his chest. James held her gently but firmly. He allowed a last greedy spear of near pain to surge from his shaft, where it probed her soft, female flesh, then willed his mind to draw free of his body's appetites.

A small noise penetrated the darkness in his brain. He bowed over Celine. "What is it, my love?"

Soft, steady shudders racked her and James eased her far enough from him to straighten his breeches.

She was crying.

"Don't, my love." He went to his knees and pulled her down until he could cradle her across his thighs. "There is no need to cry. Everything is exactly as it should be."

"No," she said brokenly. "No, it's not. But I wish it were." Struggling to kneel before him in her tattered undergarment, she contrived to glare. "I think that these sensations are wonderful. And I want to feel them again and again, with you. I refuse ever to lie about that to you, James!"

He bit back a smile. "I'm glad."

"Whatever happens, I shall remember this night and know I have experienced the best there can be between a man and a woman."

Not quite. "Celine, I want to ask you something." Why should he not have both the girl and his revenge?

"First you will tell me about the lady and the mirrors."

He shrugged. Sometimes females, no matter how brave and enticing, must simply be humored. "She was . . . She was a myth. A legend. Supposedly a relative of an earlier Casterbridge. After she fell in love and expected to be married, her lover cried off. Her reputation was ruined and no one ever asked for her hand again. She supposedly created this room and came here to study herself in solitude."

"But why?"

"To find proof that her beauty was not waning."

"Oh." Celine sat on her heels. "How horrible. It must have waned eventually."

"No. She died quite young," James improvised. "Of a fever and quite peacefully, I believe."

"Poor, dear soul." Celine looked as if she might cry again.

"Poor, dear myth. Don't give her another thought. How do you think your mama and papa would view a new request for your hand?"

"Mm?"

"Another suit. If some man other than Letchwith wanted to marry you, what do you think your parents would say?"

He saw her swallow and glance down at her virtual nakedness. She attempted to gather the shreds of lawn about her.

"Allow me." Lifting her to her feet, James stripped the garment away and reached for her dress. This he slipped over her head and fastened before bringing her to face him once more. "What do you think they would say?"

"Papa can be so difficult," she said, awkwardly rearranging the lace at her neck. "It's hard to explain, but a man, a terrible man took away his dreams. He stole what should have been Papa's and now there are the wild turns and the unpredictable responses to almost any new occurrence."

James made himself smooth Celine's hair and help her gather it back into some semblance of order. "What was stolen?"

"I don't know. All I know is that Papa often says

he wishes he could kill the man and his family. I always hope they are far away so that no such dreadful thing can occur. Will I be able to return downstairs and go home without raising a stir?"

"Fear not. Tell me more of this man. The one who wronged your father."

"I know nothing," Celine said. He thought her eyes glittered with unshed tears. "But surely no one could be as evil as . . . Surely not."

"Who is he? What is his name?"

Celine continued to dress her hair. "I don't know. At least, I know nothing except that his first name is Francis."

James barely restrained himself from springing away. "Francis?"

"Yes. But that is all I know."

So. It was true that Godwin considered himself deprived of some great treasure by a man named Francis. James had no need to ask more questions. He knew that his father's suspicions had been correct. And he knew what must be done.

He would have his revenge, and he would have Celine. The one factor that had changed was his feeling for the girl. He no longer regarded her as expendable. No. He would have her and he would have her respect. Perhaps, through her, he would even gain some measure of hope and joy in his life. And perhaps he was dreaming the dreams of a silly moonling.

Regardless, he would wreak his revenge.

"Let us return you to Curzon Street, my love," he said, praying Celine could not hear the fury in his voice. "I will make sure Lettie is brought home immediately afterward. She will believe my story that you became indisposed."

"I see," Celine said in a small voice. "Very well."

"Look at me," James ordered, and when she did

so, he smiled down before placing a kiss on her brow. "Now. What I am about to tell you will become fact very shortly."

She raised her shoulders and waited.

"Within a few days I will have offered for you, and my offer will be accepted."

Chapter 19

"Don't you *ever* sleep?" James stalked past Won Tel and mounted the staircase.

"Welcome home, James."

"Have a care, sir. My mood is precarious." He started up.

"It is four in the morning."

"How long I choose to spend at my club is my affair. Sleep, man."

"James."

Too furious to be more than vaguely aware of weariness, James paused, but did not look back at Won Tel.

"You missed your un— I mean, you missed the Marquess of Casterbridge."

James frowned and turned slowly. "He came here?"

"Yes. Not more than an hour since."

"But he knew I was leaving his damnable fete and going to Boodle's."

Won Tel avoided looking James in the eye. "Perhaps he forgot." There was an unusual agitation in the man's movements.

"I told him as I made my farewells," James said slowly. "Did he leave a message?"

Won Tel cleared his throat. "Merely that he hopes

you will consider well any major decisions you make."

"That was all?"

"Yes . . . except that he suggested you pay heed to your reactions to . . . He said you might soon be disposed to view certain things in a different light."

"Riddles! Was there more?"

"No."

"I bid you good night, then."

"Good night, James."

"Good night." Damn his uncle's coded messages. "James!"

He looked over his shoulder into Won Tel's upturned and troubled face. "Yes. What is it, man?"

"Nothing. Good night."

Cursing, James gained the balcony at the top of the first flight and marched onto the second that led to the large suite of rooms converted for his sole comfort.

The hours at Boodle's, and the large quantities of hock he'd consumed, had solved nothing. In fact, they had added a thunderous headache to his existing foul humor.

The matter that bedeviled him would be discharged—immediately. In the morning, or whenever he could gather his dissipated wits, he would set out to take the next and essential step toward his goal.

He threw open the door to the small study that led to his bedchamber and strode through, dropping top hat, garrick, and scarf as he went. "Damn!" He tossed aside his gloves, and they slid from the desk to the floor. "Won Tel makes an abominable manservant." The fact that Won Tel was not a manservant and that he was unaccustomed to relieving visitors and household members of their outer clothes at the front door did not make James feel more kindly disposed.

"God!" His head pounded. At least the fire in his bedchamber had been lighted. He saw reflected flames leaping over deep green silk-covered walls and entered, already pulling loose his neckcloth.

"Hello, James."

He started, then stood absolutely still on the threshold. "What in hell's name . . . ?" Lady Anastasie sat, or rather curled, in a leather wing chair before the fire.

"Now tell me how pleased you are to see me," she said, her husky voice slow, possibly as a result of the half-empty bottle of champagne that stood on a Chinese bronze table near her hand.

Eyeing her—and there was considerable cause to eye the lady—James pulled off his neckcloth and removed his jacket. These he dropped on a chair that matched the one Lady Anastasie sat in. "What are you doing here, my lady?"

She giggled. "I was *delivered!*" Throwing wide her arms, splattering champagne from the glass she held onto James's priceless Chinese silk rug, Lady Anastasie tipped up her chin and laughed. Her hair hung loose about her shoulders. She was completely naked.

Slowly, allowing his gaze to slip leisurely over her, James removed his coat and his waistcoat and began unbuttoning his shirt.

Lady Anastasie wriggled and lowered her lashes seductively. "Darling Augustus seems very, very fond of you, James," she said, in the closest thing to a human purr he had ever heard. "He told that strange person in your employ—"

"What strange person?" The shirt joined the coat and waistcoat, and James sat to pull off his boots.

"*You* know. The one with the funny tunic and cap who is big and really rather frightening. Only he doesn't frighten me, of course."

James shoved aside the boots and sat back in the chair. He stretched out his legs.

"We're going to have fun," Lady Anastasie said. She trailed her fingertips up one thigh, through the triangle of red hair at the apex of her legs, and across her rounded belly. "Finish undressing. I'm Augustus's little gift to you."

"Mm." His headache had not improved, yet his wits were sharp once more. "I see you are still grieving for your lost fiancé. That must be a great trial, my lady."

She licked her lips slowly and pouted. "It has been a great trial, but a girl needs to live again, to forget." The glass wobbled, but she brought it to her mouth and sipped loudly. "On lonely nights a girl needs a man to keep her mind off such unpleasantness. A man such as you, James. Someone big and strong, and *real*. And *ready*." She studied his crotch, and he had no doubt that she saw the natural effect she had upon that part of him.

He let his head rest and watched her from beneath lowered lids. *Succulent.* Augustus had timed his test well. This was a test. The old man was far from pleased by the thought of James's involvement with the Godwins, to say nothing of his declaration that he intended to take the daughter as his bride. Lady Anastasie's presence was a deliberate attempt to make James decide that as a man soon to be declared an earl and one who would eventually become a marquess, he needed a more worldly and brilliant female at his side.

Augustus had undoubtedly sensed frustration in his nephew and judged it, correctly, to be at least in part due to a need for sexual release.

James looked at Lady Anastasie's breasts. Bared, they were somewhat too large for his taste, but not too large to entertain a man most adequately for as long as he chose to play.

"You like what you see?" she asked. Taking a distended nipple between finger and thumb, she pinched, and James heard the quick outrush of her breath as she began to arouse herself. "Why don't you do this for me, James?"

He said nothing, but saw her note the spring of his shaft against too-tight breeches and smile knowingly.

Everything this woman did, she had done before, or had experienced at some man's hands—before. She was using her body as she had learned to use it, for her own pleasure and to get what she wanted.

"Come, James. I see how ready you are." Raising a knee, she revealed womanly folds already engorged and shining. "I'm ready, too. Come, James."

Still he watched her. He was no more to this woman than a means to fulfill her pleasure, pleasure readily aroused in the manner of a practiced cyprian.

She was used, well used.

Her knee lolled and she sought her own nubbin of desire.

James shifted.

"Take off your breeches," she said, her voice almost humming the words. "Let me show you what a clever mouth I have, James."

He made his mind still and brought before him the image of Celine as she had looked kneeling before him and declaring, in her barely quickened womanhood, that she refused to regret the pleasure she found in him.

Lady Anastasie's breathing became louder and faster—keeping time with her fingers as they slid back and forth. "I am almost there, James," she panted. "Almost. Come. Take me, now."

I think that these sensations are wonderful. And I want

*to feel them again and again, with you. I refuse ever to lie
about that to you, James!*

"James!" The woman sounded petulant now, de-
manding.

He closed his eyes and relaxed.

"James?"

Allowing his jaw to slacken, he managed the suggestion of a snore.

"Oh!" The sound he heard was her skin squeaking
over leather. "Never! Never has a man fallen asleep
at such a time. I will *not* tolerate this!"

His next snore was louder and made his nose itch.

"I have *never* been so insulted. Oooh!" she
squealed, and James heard her bare feet pound
across the bedchamber and into his study.

Cautiously, he opened his eyes and listened. He
had stood the test and now he had proved not only
to his uncle, but to himself, that no woman would
tempt him as Celine Godwin tempted him.

"Ooh! The marquess shall hear of this!"

"I sincerely hope so," James murmured under his
breath.

A giggle from Lady Anastasie made James frown.
Surely she would not try her wiles on him again.

The giggle became a laugh, a loud and raucous
laugh.

Unwillingly, he levered himself from the chair and
walked softly to the doorway. The lady stood on the
far side of the study, where she had evidently left her
clothing atop a chest.

"Oh!" she laughed, clutching her shift and rolling
helplessly against the wall. "Oh, I cannot stop laughing. Oh!"

James frowned and moved farther into the room.

Gradually, the laughter subsided and Lady
Anastasie glared at him between outbreaks of chuckling. She grabbed her white gown and struggled into

it, managing to fasten the ties and hoist her bosom high above the tight constraint.

"You shall regret this," she said, and laughed—and frowned.

James crossed his arms and narrowed his eyes.

Sinking to the edge of the chest, the lady hauled on a stocking, making certain James got yet another view of what she had offered him. She pushed back her hair and her eyes widened—and widened.

James watched, deeply interested.

Progressively, her face became pinched and she began to sneeze; one huge sneeze after another. With great difficulty, she contrived to pull on the second stocking and stand up—and sneeze, and sneeze.

Tears squeezed from the corners of her eyes and her cheeks grew bright red.

"Something—" She sneezed. "Something is—" She sneezed again.

James covered his mouth.

Gasping for breath, Lady Anastasie grabbed a white satin slipper and pushed in her foot—and screamed yet again—an instant after a series of loud pops issued from the region of her toes.

She sought wildly about. "What is it? There is a gunman present. We are under attack!"

"Do you think so?" James asked calmly and declined to add that she, not he, was under attack and that he might be persuaded to deal very leniently with her opponent.

"Help! *Do* something!" Hopping like an ungainly and disheveled white bird, she struggled into the second slipper and immediately leaped about amid loud bangs and an issue of colored smoke that rose from her feet to waft about her head, producing a fresh onslaught of sneezing.

"Amazing," James remarked.

Wild-eyed, her arms waving, Lady Anastasie

rushed past him and threw open the door to the hall. "A carriage," she screeched. "A carriage at once!"

There was another, even louder bang before the thunderous pounding of her feet sounded from the stairs.

James sauntered to the landing and looked over the banisters to the flights below. Won Tel's dark head and blue tunic appeared as Lady Anastasie gained the entrance hall, and James saw his trusty companion take a firm hold on one pale, flailing arm and heard the murmur of soothing words.

"Liam," James said without turning around. "Come here."

Soft footfalls approached. "I am here, James."

Straightening, he faced his small woman-warrior, dressed in this early morning in some floor-length sleeping garment of many layers of heavily embroidered pink muslin. With her hair loose and swinging past her waist like a shining, black cape, she was, he had to admit, a beautiful sight—despite the smug line of her mouth and the defiant tilt of her chin.

"You have interfered in my affairs once more, Liam."

"Indeed, Master James."

"*Master*. I am always *master* when you are pretending respect. You tampered with Lady Anastasie's clothing. I thought I had told you to leave your witch's tricks in Paipan."

Her gaze didn't waver, or her pleased smile.

"Would you care to explain yourself, miss?"

Liam bowed low. "If you wish."

"I do wish."

"Well, then, the answer is simple." Still bowing, she continued: "Exotic practices are to be expected of people from the East."

Chapter 20

S he must concentrate. "You did speak to Mrs. Merryfield?"

"I have already told you as much." David checked his watch.

"And she refused to release Marigold?"

"Again, I have told you as much."

Celine frowned at the parlor rug. "And you were unable to speak to Marigold?"

David sighed. "As I said, I approached her and she withdrew before I could finish what I wished to say. She appeared . . . frightened, I assume. Although, for a moment, there seemed some element of anger in her."

"Are you certain this was the right woman?"

"Naturally." Impatience weighted David's voice. "The description I was given matched her perfectly. And even if there could be two women in that exact location with hair the color of a rouged carrot, they would not both answer to the name of Marigold."

"You cannot give up."

"Celine, I have word from my parish. I am needed there."

"Now?"

"Mrs. Strickland informs me that Ruby Rose is beyond redemption."

"Mrs. Strickland is an unreasonable—" Celine saw David hide a smile. "You are deliberately trying to befuddle me!"

"No, my dear. I simply anticipate your reactions with great accuracy." He lowered himself to the edge of the couch. "The unfortunate truth is that I must return to Dorset, not to assist Mrs. Strickland, but to protect Ruby Rose from that lady."

Celine rubbed her temples. *James, James.* He was all she could think of clearly, visualize clearly—*feel* clearly. Last evening, after what had sounded like a true marriage proposal, he'd become so silent. She closed her eyes. He probably already regretted his words—words spoken too close to moments of incredible Pleasure that had, no doubt, temporarily weakened his thinking. Even hoping otherwise would be foolishness. At least she felt some certainty that he would help her evade Letchwith. James was so dear and good—

"Are you ill, Celine?"

"No! No, I am perfectly well. But what of Marigold, David? The poor thing cannot be abandoned when she has expressed a desire to be rescued."

"I agree," David said. "But first I must attend to the young woman who is already in my charge. I will return to Town as soon as all is once more calm. How long has Liam been with Mr. Eagleton?"

"Perhaps Marigold . . . I beg your pardon?"

"How—"

"Liam?" David was usually so clear in his thoughts and speech. "James? What has this to do with Marigold and Mrs. Merryfield?"

David spread his hands on his knees. "I asked you a simple question."

"And I do not know the answer," Celine responded, with some asperity.

"Such a gentle creature should not be in a household that appears to consist entirely of males."

She stared at him.

David looked away.

"I assure you that Mr. James Eagleton is above reproach." A blush began its ascent of her neck. "He is completely responsible and is undoubtedly more concerned for Liam's welfare than you are, David." What would David say—do—if he knew of the times Celine had spent with James?

"I merely asked—"

Whatever he intended to ask was cut off by the sound of great commotion in the hall. Raised voices and clattering footsteps made a speedy path to the parlor, and the door was thrown open.

David shot to his feet. "Good afternoon, Mr. and Mrs. Godwin."

"Mama," Celine said weakly. "Papa."

"Mama. Papa," her mother mimicked, ignoring David and rushing to the center of the room. "Is that all you have to say? No delighted greeting for your parents whom you have brought to a sorry pass? A sorry pass, indeed."

Celine wound her hands together and looked to Lettie, who had also entered the room. "I cannot guess what you mean, Mama."

Mama's youthful, bright green carriage dress and high-crowned bonnet with an organza-lined brim did not especially complement her full figure, or her blond hair and somewhat florid complexion. Overset, as she clearly was, she looked even more red in the face than usual, and her light blue eyes had the hard appearance Celine had come to dread.

"Celine is a good and dutiful daughter," Lettie said in a strong voice and moved protectively closer to Celine.

Papa turned on Celine's companion. "You will

hold your tongue, Lettie. My wife and I will judge how good and dutiful our daughter is."

"We can count ourselves fortunate"—Mama shook her head and heaved a great breath—"fortunate that Bertram Letchwith is a reasonable man."

"What has Mr. Letchwith—" Celine saw her father's ominous expression and pressed her lips together. How angry he could look. Anger always made him seem even taller and more stoop-shouldered and bony. Today, dressed in an obviously expensive claret-colored jacket and yellow trousers, rather than the invariably rumpled, country-squire garb he favored in Dorset, he appeared somehow different. Celine reminded herself that this was the first time she had seen her father in London. Here he probably chose to wear clothes he considered fashionable. They did not appeal to her at all, particularly not the turquoise waistcoat embroidered with red-eyed black peacocks.

Papa raised his thin-bridged nose and took several stalking steps toward Celine. "As your mother has said, miss, you are fortunate that Bertram is a reasonable man. And *we* are fortunate that he rode out to meet us early this morning, rather than simply deciding to withdraw his interest in you."

Celine's knees weakened. A movement caught her attention: Lettie giving a discreet signal of some kind.

"Ah, excuse me, Mr. and Mrs. Godwin," David said immediately. "I have some business to attend."

Papa's angry gaze shifted to David. "What are you doing here, Talbot?" His hooded eyes slid back to Celine. "Didn't think Town was your sort of thing."

"David brought me news from the village," Lettie said, sounding completely calm. "And we insisted he stay here while he dealt with his business matters in London. I'm sure you would have wanted as much. Would you like me to call a cab for you, David?"

"That would be very agreeable."

David left with Lettie. Celine watched the door close and stared at it miserably. Within seconds the front door thumped shut. Now she must face the anger and accusations alone.

"Never mind David Talbot," Mama said. "What have you to say for yourself, Celine?"

Letchwith would have spoken also of her money-saving notion. How dreadful it would be if she could not continue her wonderful scheme. "I did not know you were coming," she said distantly. At least there was no question of David's role being revealed.

"Evidently you thought we might never come." Her father flipped aside his coattails and sat in a beechwood armchair that creaked on its frail legs. "Or rather, you *hoped* we wouldn't. You assumed you could continue your fast games at will. I'm grateful we decided to send word to Bertram. He knew where we planned to pass the night and was able to intercept us before we left. It was only with difficulty that I managed to dissuade him from accompanying us here this afternoon."

Submissiveness could become so tiresome. "I'm surprised you bothered. Fast games indeed! Why not allow him to come and tell his stories in front of me?"

"That will do from you, my girl. How could you be such a little fool? Becoming involved with a brood of hoity-toity misses far above your station."

Celine stared at her father and waited for the rest of his questions. Would he make this an excuse to lock her away? She trembled at the thought, but made certain no hint of her anxiety showed. At an early age she had learned how any sign of fear excited her father and made him appear to relish punishing her the more.

Mama twitched her skirts. "Setting trends. The idea."

So they did know what she'd been doing.

"I'm glad you have the sense not to deny that you've allowed yourself to be drawn into a circle that has tempted you in the way of spendthrift habits." Papa jabbed a long, thin finger in Celine's direction. "Please God we're in time to ensure that you haven't spent every penny of the allowance you so craftily insisted you would *manage*."

Relief made Celine weak. They didn't know. "Oh, I assure you I have not, Papa." The ridiculous Letchwith had misinterpreted events. Celine chose to thank rather than beseech God. "I am well within my budget."

Mama came forward, her skirts rustling mightily. "And you think that will dispose us to think of you more kindly? The question of who has mistakenly befriended you and what silly notions you may have entertained about decking yourself like a princess are of no consequence. That you gave Mr. Letchwith the cut direct certainly *is* of consequence."

"I—"

"Silence!" Papa's voice rose like a roar. "Sit down and be silent while your mother and I determine what course will be best."

Best for whom? This was impossible, unfair, infuriating. Celine braced herself for the sentence of banishment to her room—and the sound of a key grinding in the lock.

"We shall have to find a way to appease Bertram," Mama said.

"I did not give Mr. Letchwith the cut direct." Celine raised her chin defiantly. "He was rude and—"

"Enough!" Her father stood once more. "Sit!"

Celine retreated to a chair in a distant corner and did as she was told.

"Darius," Mama said. "I think we should get this marriage under way as soon as possible."

"The first thing to be dealt with is the settlement," Papa said. "I'd hoped to up the price substantially, but the girl may have ruined any chances of that."

Celine listened and her parents talked, and talked—as if she failed to exist, as if she had no importance and certainly no mind or will of her own. Half an hour passed—an hour—and Celine's back ached with the tension of waiting.

That poor creature Marigold was not really so unlike Celine. Neither of them had any control over her own life. Celine tried not to hear the continuing rise and fall of her parent's arguing voices: "He'll pay." "He suggested she was soiled." "Soiled goods, indeed. He's trying to find a means to attain a cheaper piece of innocence." It was really not to be borne, yet what choice did she have?

If she could continue with James, even exactly as they were, she would. There could be no question of an interest in Pleasure with any other man, Pleasure for its own sake.

That was the difference.

No, she was not like the poor, fallen ones. They were caught by their bodies' desire to experience the sensations, but Celine . . . There could *be* no Pleasure for Celine without James.

The revelation brought great sadness—and a measure of warmth. Her sadness was for what lay ahead if she was to live forever without him. The warmth came from the knowledge that she wanted James, his touch, his presence, for reasons much deeper than Pleasure or the hope that he would help her be rid of Letchwith. She loved him, love him desperately.

"We will have him to dinner at once!" Mama's agitated tone cut into Celine's reverie. "I'll speak to Cook about it. And Celine must attempt to make amends."

"It is not necessary for her to do anything," Papa said. "She need not even be present."

As far as they were concerned, she was something to dispose of at a profit. And there was little she could do to alter the situation. But Marigold ... Perhaps she *could* help Marigold.

A discreet knock on the door brought no more than an impatient "Go away" from Mama.

The door opened to admit Baity. "A visitor," he said perfunctorily and with no sign of disquiet at his employers' ill humor. He offered the silver tray holding a calling card.

Papa snatched it irritably. "Eagleton? I know no Eagleton. Send him away."

Celine half-rose, but plopped down again, willing her heart to be steady and her head to clear.

"He says he has a matter to discuss which will prove advantageous to you, Mr. Godwin."

"Mm." Papa sniffed. "Let him come in, but don't be too far distant in case he proves undesirable."

In the moments that followed, Celine's disobedient heart fluttered like a hummingbird's wings. Then James strode into the room, and her heart completely forgot to beat.

Only for an instant did his eyes meet hers, but that was long enough for her to see that today their gray was the color of steel. The wind that rattled windows behind her had ruffled his black hair, but Celine doubted the wind's responsibility for the faint color along his harsh cheekbones.

James's broad chest expanded visibly beneath the perfection of his unquestionably bespoke black coat. Although tall, Papa appeared much smaller, much more fragile of build in the presence of this brutally beautiful man.

Brutally beautiful.

In the beat of an instant, Celine made a study of James, from unruly hair to wide shoulders, to slender hips and powerful legs.

He had yet to speak. She glanced at his face and drew a short, sharp breath. Surely she did not see hate in his clear eyes, trained upon her father now?

"Eagleton, is it?" Papa looked from the card he held to his visitor. Disdain, as well as annoyance, shaded the question.

"James Eagleton." The intense concentration James leveled on her father made Celine's stomach clench. "I'll not bore you with details today. You may visit my solicitor and certain other references I shall give, to verify that I speak the truth."

"The truth, sir?"

Mama produced a yellow and green fan and fluttered it extravagantly. "What is it, Darius? What does he want?"

"Please, Mrs. Godwin, do not overset yourself."

"He knows us?" Mama said faintly.

James's smile was not a sight to induce comfort. "Certainly, Mrs. Godwin." His white teeth barely showed in the feral parting of his lips. "Rather, I know *of* you."

"Don't toy with us, man," Papa said.

"Never, sir. I shall be brief and then remove myself—for today. I am the sole owner of an island in the South China Sea, where my considerable shipping and trading interests are centered. In addition, I hold a handsome property here in London and another in Dorset . . . not far from your own, I understand."

Mama's fan stilled.

Papa only frowned more deeply.

"Those are but my most obvious holdings. I am, Mr. Godwin, an extremely wealthy man."

"What is this to me, sir?" Papa watched James with wary interest.

"To you, Mr. Godwin? I am certain it will be of the greatest interest to you in the near future.

"I intend to marry your daughter."

Chapter 21

"**W**hy?" Mary Godwin flung away from the boudoir window.

Apparently absorbed in the scrutiny of his fingernails, Darius lounged on her treasured pink satin chaise. "Why what, my dear?" he asked without interest.

"Why would a man like that want her?"

"A man like that?"

As always, in her presence Darius would choose to be obtuse. "James Eagleton could have his pick of women." She visualized him and felt a deep, erotic thrill. "What would he want with an insipid little nothing like Celine?"

"His reasons are of no interest to me. His money is. Mr. Eagleton may be the answer to our prayers. You heard the extent of the settlement he suggested."

Eagleton was older than would normally be her preference in a man, but there was a dark promise of heat in him, a heat that would burn slow, and deep . . . and long.

"Mary?"

"Bertram has already offered for her."

"And we have not accepted his offer. It is not sufficient."

"If we anger Bertram, dealing with him might be

282

far from amusing." She had heard how Bertram Letchwith dealt with his enemies. "He could make our lives insupportable in Polite Society."

"We have nothing to fear from him. Trust me in this."

The curl of Darius's lip gave her a measure of confidence. Perhaps the nature of what her husband shared with the Letchwiths was even more titillating than she suspected.

"It's possible there are certain other elements that may soon become bothersome," she told him. This issue had been skirted long enough. "Would Augustus go against the old marquess's wishes and put us out of Knighthead? After all, the house is his."

Darius continued to observe his fingernails.

"Did you hear me?" She had suffered too much, she thought, too long. "Darius! Answer me." The sight of her hated husband in the boudoir she considered entirely her own sanctuary—hers and whomever she chose to favor—brought her close to tears of fury.

"Celine was invited to a fete at Casterbridge's house," Darius said finally. "He has ignored us for so many years. We are bound to wonder if he is reassessing the situation with the estate."

"What could inviting Celine possibly have to do with anything?"

Darius draped an arm over the back of the chaise. "Idle curiosity, probably. He knows nothing of his father's reasons for banishing Francis, of that we can be certain. At the moment it is Eagleton who interests me more."

Mary walked back and forth, tossing the train of her beautiful new silk robe behind her. The deep rose color became her well. Even that foolish Freda had been forced to agree as much when she'd helped Mary change out of her traveling clothes.

She tweaked the gold bow that settled so pleasingly between her breasts. Still beautiful, enticing breasts ... ah, yes, that marvelous, blond groom she had bedded for the first time before leaving for Town had been gratifyingly excited and more than eager to worship her body. The clenching between her legs reminded her of how the boy—even in his inexperienced fumbling—had brought her satisfaction. Yes, Colin was indeed a pleasant reason to anticipate returning to Knighthead.

"If we give her to Eagleton, our money worries will be over," Darius said without looking at Mary. Not that he ever looked at her. "I'll appease Bertram. He'll be more than willing to share in one or two little entertainments I have in mind."

Fool. All the man thought about was sex with his doxies. "There never was anything in writing about Knighthead. The old marquess said we were to live there as long as we wished. That's all."

Darius laughed. "And as we both know, the Casterbridges abide by their word—even if it costs them a son." He tipped back his head and guffawed. "Gad, but it still pleases my gut to think of how we duped the old fool into disinheriting Francis. Fear not, m'dear, Augustus is cut from the same thin cloth. He'll carry out his father's wishes. We're safe at Knighthead for as long as we want to be ... until we get our hands on the gems."

Mary threw up her hands. "Until? Twenty years, Darius. For twenty years we've searched and we've found nothing."

"We will. I can feel it. This marriage could be exactly what we need. With fresh blunt in the coffers, we'll not have a thing to worry about."

"Still we have no *key*. All those years ago you heard Francis's mother tell him to guard the key. I *know* that without it we will never find the Sainsbury fortune."

"Damn you, madam." Darius bared his teeth. "And damn the day I chose to tell you exactly what I heard. She said: 'This is the key. Guard it well.' And then she said, 'Discover the power of the eye.' When will you accept that there is not and never was a physical key? *The eye is the key*, madam. It is the *eye* for which we search. *And we shall find it.*"

"If only you had had the courage to wait long enough to hear the location of that precious eye of yours."

Darius averted his face. "How many times must I tell you that my hiding place was about to be discovered? I could not risk being seen. I had to make my escape. Anyway, it is probable that I heard everything that was said."

"No." She shook her head. "No. You did not. And for that I have been forced to suffer and waste the best years of my life."

"Hah!" He looked at her with that detestable, knowing leer that made her long to see him dead. "The *best* years of your life, madam? Would you have me believe that you have exhausted the supply of unlicked cubs ready to rut with you?"

Blood rushed to her head. "Don't—"

"Don't what, madam? Don't remind you that you have no stomach for *real* men? Don't remind you that you are excited only by children who cannot measure you against *real* women?" His mouth turned down. "What do you imagine they say of you after you have opened your legs for them and sucked them dry? How do you imagine they laugh at a vain old fool of a woman who drools at the thought of taking them to her breast as she never took a son of her own? You, madam, could never bear me a son!"

She covered her ears and squeezed her eyes shut.

"You are jealous," she whispered. "Jealous because I am able to find pleasure, true pleasure, while all you find is perversion."

Silence lasted until she opened her eyes and saw Darius's impassive features. Whatever happened, she must not lose control, must not give him the chance to deprive her of what was hers—the cursed Sainsbury gems. They *would* find them.

"Sometimes I worry," Mary said, almost to herself. "Francis could return."

"He won't."

"But what if he did?"

Darius settled deeper into the chaise and crossed his arms. "We have discussed this issue too many times. Francis cannot know more today than he did twenty years ago. He drew the conclusions we planned for him to draw—the fool. He accepted what he thought his father was accusing him of then. And now the old man is dead, who will tell dear Francis otherwise?"

"No one." Darius was right.

"I'm glad you agree. Francis believed his father had learned of his visit to a brothel. He believed that the lost ring his father offered him, and which he took, was the sign and seal of that event. And he knew that the marquess had unshakable religious beliefs—and that his parents loved Francis's wife as the daughter they never had."

"Yes," Mary agreed, savoring the memory. "That little paragon, Sophie. Her union with dear Francis was never to be defiled by the mundane events that are part of every normal man's life. Her husband could not take his pleasure with a cyprian, lest Sophie's tender sensibilities be harmed. And for doing so, Francis believed his father would banish him from England. How perfect."

"Perfect indeed," Darius agreed softly. "And it

soothed the wound of your hate, did it not? Your hate for Sophie because Francis chose her, rather than you?"

She flung back the train on her robe and turned aside. "I never wanted him. It was he who wanted me. He only married her because he could not have me."

"No matter." What Darius truly believed was heavy in his words. "You and I struck a bargain and we have lived by it. Each for himself. Francis was disposed of and the old marquess gave the price we asked for our silence in the matter of his son's supposed debauchery: Knighthead. What good fortune that he never knew about the gems his wife's family had passed from daughter to daughter for generations—until there was no daughter, only poor fool Francis. And he played into our hands."

They laughed together, and Mary's heart softened a little toward her husband. The night stretched ahead, long and boring, and she did so hate boredom.

"Darius."

"Yes."

"Are you at home this evening?"

He looked at her and frowned slightly. "I had not thought to go anywhere until the morning."

"Perhaps that's good." Mary slowly undid the golden bow on her robe, parted the garment, and let it fall. "It has been too long since we took a measure of pleasure in each other. Shall we see if we can amuse ourselves?" Swaying her hips with each step, she approached the chaise and stood, smoothing the transparent gauze of her nightrail over her breasts.

Darius regarded her, then crooked a finger, and she sank to her knees beside him.

She leaned forward. "I have been curious about what it is that fascinates you so with your, er, *diver-*

sions. Teach me, Darius. Perhaps there is still time for us to learn to please each other—when it suits us both."

"Curious?" He grasped the neck of her nightrail and, with one sharp jerk, tore it open. "Is this what the boys enjoy?"

Mary felt the rush of heat to her face. "Yes," she whispered. The sudden violence in Darius thrilled her.

"Interesting." With nostrils flaring, he reached to take a nipple in his teeth.

"Darius! You're hurting me." She could not pull away.

He didn't reply, only filled his hands with her breasts and squeezed hard while he gentled the biting and sucked strongly instead.

The force of his mouth and hands shocked and weakened her—and excited her. Deep in her belly a sexual ache became a gnawing desire for release. "Yes," she murmured. "Yes, yes."

As abruptly as he'd seized her, Darius took his hands from her breasts and opened his trousers. "Just a small lesson tonight, my dear. This is the first thing you can do to please me."

She stared as he pulled out his cock—his limp and shriveled cock.

"Show me how much a *real* woman you can be," he demanded.

A moment's hesitation was all she needed to quell revulsion. Smiling into his pale eyes, she bent and drew him into her mouth. She drew him in and released him, and nipped the flaccid skin until it grew tight, and ran her tongue over the smooth end of his rod until he began to make his own essence.

"You learn quickly," he said, his voice thick. The hand that found her breast again was shaky, but the fingers closed in spasms until she cried out, but

Darius only smiled and pinched her nipples rhythmically as he might a cow ready for milking.

"Very good," he murmured, his thin hips thrusting up from the chaise. "Do not stop, *bitch*."

Mary's hate boiled and with it the fervor of her ministration over him. His shaft soon leaped, full and throbbing and ready. She started to take her lips from him but he clamped her head in place—and spurted into her mouth.

She heard him laugh and laugh, and finally he allowed her to lift her head. She wiped her mouth with the back of her hand and made to mount him. Her own body wept for its climax.

"Stay," Darius said, narrowing his eyes. "Let us take this new experience slowly, my dear." Pushing her aside, he sat up and closed his trousers.

Bemused, her nightrail hanging in shreds about her waist, Mary watched him. "I want—"

"I know what you want," Darius said. Disgust etched every line in his face. "What I wanted has been accomplished. Find yourself a new stableboy, madam. You'll be well ready for him."

She fell back from the chaise. "You can't."

"I have. Now there is business to attend. I shall go to Eagleton and accept his offer."

Chapter 22

The fog that rolled in from the river burned Celine's nose and eyes, and seared her throat. She'd thought to pull on boots over her slippers, but the heelless bottoms slipped alarmingly on moisture-slick cobbles.

Cupping her mouth, she called, "Wait!" *Wait, wait,* her voice echoed back, but the woman darting ahead through a narrow alley never faltered. "Marigold! Wait!"

The woman flitted through the feeble shaft of yellowed light cast by a street lamp at the far end of the alley. For an instant her hair glowed orange-crimson amid the misty gilded swirl.

"Marigold! Let me help you!" For David. She wanted to do this for David. Perhaps, if she could show him how useful she could be, he'd let her continue to help him even after . . . She would not think of James now, of his brave but stiffly hostile offer. She would not think of his curt bow in her direction before he'd left; the bow of a stranger who was displeased with what he saw.

"Marigold!"

Celine rushed ahead as fast as she dared, and halted. Slowly, the woman she knew must be Marigold turned and stepped back into the light.

"Whatcha want?" The voice of a young woman, high and clear.

"To help you." Celine decided not to move closer for fear the other girl would run again.

" 'Elp me do what?"

This was something she should have rehearsed. "Change your life."

Marigold made no move to run, but neither did she reply.

Even in the shadow of her hood, ribbons of dampness swathed Celine's face. From nearby came the eerie, tinny sound of a hurdy-gurdy winding out the notes of "Oh, Susannah!"

"What's wrong wiv me life, then?" The girl's chin went up, a sharp silhouette against the darkness outside the light's beam. "Who are you to come 'ere askin' me ter change it?"

Celine gathered her woolen mantle into clenched fingers and searched about. Persuading Baity to find the cab David had used to come here on the night of the fete had seemed such an excellent idea. Now, alone in the warren of squalid streets near this section of the river, she felt that her decision to come after Marigold had taken on a sinister and altogether unpleasant cast.

"A friend of yours brought a message from you. She said you wanted to get away from Mrs. Merryfield, and—"

"Like 'ell." The figure moved from the light. "You're another one o' them do-gooders. Like that gent what come."

"Marigold." Celine started forward again. "I know you're just afraid of what Mrs. Merryfield might do. Don't be. We'll help you get away from London and learn how to make an honest living among decent people."

Now Celine ran, stopping only to swallow a

scream at the roaring trundle of approaching wheels. "Eels," a croaking voice called dispiritedly. "Eels. Beautiful eels. Get 'em cheap while they last." She flattened herself against a wall and a cart rolled by, pulled by a wheezing nag and urged on by a shambling figure swathed in black rags. The rotting-fish stench that overcame even the sulphur-laden fog turned Celine's stomach.

In the distance, Marigold's hair passed through another struggling beam of light. Casting aside caution, Celine darted on, passing other human wraiths as she went.

Her feet made a muffled, rasping noise on the cobbles, a different noise from the footsteps behind ... Celine stopped once more and looked back.

Nothing.

Turning to follow Marigold once more, she saw the girl open the front door of a house and pass inside.

"I will not be afraid," Celine said aloud and walked on, more slowly this time—as slowly as the footsteps behind her.

In front of the door Marigold had entered, Celine paused to peer through the fog—and jumped. The figure of a small, well-dressed man emerged, marching determinedly along. He drew level with her and tipped the brim of his top hat. "Good evening, miss."

"Good evening," Celine said faintly.

"May I help you find your way home?" His voice was familiar. He inclined his head. "Newgate is hardly a safe place for a young lady."

Celine gathered her mantle even tighter. "Thank you, sir." If she wavered now there might never be another chance to prove her worth to David. "Thank you, but I am home now."

"Are you certain?"

"Quite certain."

He stared directly at her, nodded, then passed on to be enveloped by the fog almost immediately.

Celine raised a hand to knock on the door. She had seen that man somewhere before ... a small man with gray eyes ...

The door swung open. "Whatcha want?" a throaty female voice demanded from the shadows beyond.

Celine jumped. "I—"

"In 'ere." A hand descended on her shoulder with a thump that almost sent her sprawling into a hallway that reeked of heavy perfume. "Get up. Whatcha got ter say for yourself?"

The door creaked shut behind Celine, and she scrambled to her feet. "I'm here to talk to Marigold," she said in a rush to the huge woman who faced her. That this was Mrs. Merryfield, Celine had no doubt.

In the pinkish light that illuminated a hallway lined with gilt-edged mirrors, the woman was a towering figure dressed in layers of flounced, plum-colored satin. "I don't know no Marigold." Garishly applied rouge glared from a heavy layer of white powder on a fleshy face.

Celine stood very straight and was, for once, grateful for her more than average height. "Marigold came into this house only minutes ago. I saw her." Poor girl. Trapped in this dreadful, so-called *nunnery*.

"Did you now?" The woman's smile was not a pretty sight.

This was a situation where extreme diplomacy was of the essence. "Are you Mrs. Merryfield?"

Dull black curls bobbled. "Who wants ter know?"

Celine managed to laugh gaily. "I knew you must be she. David ... I mean Marigold described you perfectly—and most complimentarily. I did try to catch up with her in the street but ..." She let the rest of the sentence die.

"Yes. But?"

Celine hid her trembling hands. "But she didn't see me," she said, keeping the smile in place. "If you could just let me know where she is, I would be so appreciative. We have so much to talk about."

Movement in the darker regions of the hallway distracted Mrs. Merryfield. A female wearing . . . wearing very little at all approached. She eyed Celine curiously. "Ready, Mrs. M. Wot number did yer say?"

"Number—" Mrs. Merryfield fashioned another unpleasant smile. "You wait a minute, Belle, I'm seein' ter the young lady, 'ere." To Celine, she said, "You go on up the stairs, me dear. The party in number nine will tell you what you want to know."

"Oh, thank you. Thank you very much." On tiptoe, Celine walked past Mrs. Merryfield and Belle and climbed stairs so narrow that walls on either side almost touched Celine's shoulders. Most men, and certainly Mrs. Merryfield, would have to turn sideways.

A corridor lighted by sputtering candle sconces stretched from the top of the stairs. Celine, still on tiptoe, crept forward, peering at numbers on doors as she went. The grisly floral perfume didn't quite cover an unrecognizable musty smell.

Number nine was the last door on the right. Timidly, she tapped a panel and waited.

Rustling from inside the room was the only response.

Celine tapped again. "Hello! Are you there?"

A muffled voice, speaking words she could not hear, sounded encouraging.

She turned the doorknob and entered the room slowly. "Hello?" A collection of guttering candles flickered atop a heavy wooden chest against the opposite wall. Overhead, a row of colored paper lanterns jiggled in the current of air from the corridor. "Where are you?" Celine said, her voice cracking.

"I'm here, my love."

The voice was still slightly muffled.

Celine peered behind the door and stifled a shriek.

"Are you close now, my love?"

She drew in a breath and held it.

"Come to me. Don't hesitate. I am your servant."

Amazed, Celine ventured closer to the bed from which the instructions were being issued. Stretched on top of a yellow silk cover was a man of average dimensions with a fringe of dark hair skirting his shiny bald head, an overlarge nose, and a thin, very red mouth.

"Are you . . . do you feel quite well?" Celine kept an eye on the door and tried to gauge how quickly she could depart.

"Oh, I shall be, my love—once you've had me do your bidding."

Round-eyed, Celine studied him from head to foot. No, she had not been mistaken. The man on the bed wore a pink satin mask, dusty hessians . . . and a thin lawn nightrail that didn't cover his bony knees.

"A red-headed prostitute?" James roared, not for the first time since he and Won Tel had set out from Grosvenor Square. "Bloody hell!"

"Be calm, James," Won Tel said, although there was a suspicion of concern in his deep voice. "My informer rushed to us directly after seeing Miss Celine."

"Gad!" James pounded on the peephole behind the coachman and waited for the wooden trap to slide open. "Make time, man! Faster!"

An affirmative shout did nothing to mollify James.

"We will soon be there," Won Tel said. "It is assuredly not more than three-quarters of an hour since my informer saw Celine enter that house."

"That bloody brothel, you mean? What in God's name can the little fool be thinking of?"

"My informer—"

"Damn your informer. He should have dragged her away regardless of what she told him." He peered through the windows of the coach at the dismal streets through which they passed. Unsavory-looking characters lurked in the entrances to alleyways, their drunken banter audible even over the clattering grind of the carriage's wheels.

"We're stopping." Won Tel moved forward on his seat and grasped James's arm as he would have leaped from the carriage. "A moment, please, James. It might be most unwise to do anything precipitate."

Grudgingly, he nodded. "Very well, but we must act quickly."

Won Tel's grip on his sleeve tightened. "We will not have to," he said distantly. "There she is."

Craning to follow the direction of Won Tel's stare, James narrowed his eyes to see through thinning fog. "Mad," he muttered. "Completely addlepated." With that he threw off Won Tel's hand and jumped from the coach.

Celine, vaguely bedraggled in a brown woolen mantle with hood trailing, walked directly into his chest. "Oh! I'm so sorry!" She brought her startled amber eyes to his and her lips parted. "What are you doing here?"

If he wasn't very careful he'd find himself turning her over his knee for the sound spanking she deserved. Instead, James swept Celine into his arms and bundled her into the carriage. As he got in, Won Tel got out, and the vehicle sagged as he climbed up beside the coachman.

As she huddled in the corner where James thrust her, Celine's countenance was mutinous. "I asked you what you are doing here? And what, pray, do you mean by tossing me around like a sack of vegetables?"

Fighting to remain calm—and sane—James slid open the peephole once more and called, "Drive. Drive to some clean air, dammit, and do so *now*." He thumped down opposite Celine and glared.

She tried, completely without success, to smooth her hair, then wriggled and twitched the mantle into place. "I see you are angry," she said without looking at him.

"How very perceptive of you."

"I cannot imagine why."

"Kindly be quiet." He needed time to try to gain some control over his fury.

"It is very nice of you to come and escort me home."

"Be quiet."

"How did you know where to find me?"

"Be quiet!"

"Oh."

The carriage rocked and swayed. James remained silent and would not allow himself to look at Celine. Outside, the scenery gradually changed from huddled gray buildings to wider streets and graceful houses. The sky was clearer, and soon, as they rolled on toward the outskirts of Town, an ice-white moon cast an ethereal wash over a straggle of small dwellings with rambling gardens. A strong wind, the wind that brushed pale clumps of cloud from the moon's face, buffeted the carriage. How long must he wait to smell the wild sea once again, to walk the open countryside his soul thirsted for?

James felt a little calmer and dared to glance at the girl in the opposite corner. She sat stiffly, her hands folded in her lap, a worried frown on her brow. What in hell's name had possessed her to venture into such danger?

She met his eyes once more and caught her bottom lip between her teeth.

James shook his head. "Why? Why did you go there? What, in God's name, did you *do* there?"

"I'm very sorry if I've made you angry."

If she didn't answer his questions he'd become a great deal more angry. "Why?"

Celine's shoulders rose beneath the mantle. "There are many women less fortunate than I."

He frowned. "Yes. What has that to do with this debacle?"

"Someone has to help them. I heard of a certain young woman who wished to better herself from her dreadful plight." She gave a small cough. "So I went to try and help her accomplish that. Surely you understand that I was right to do so."

A dark wave of emotion shook James. Foolish as the words sounded, he believed her. Celine actually thought she could venture into one of the most dangerous districts of London and "save" people. Before him sat a perfect innocent, an innocent with an unspoiled and completely generous heart. *Little idiot.*

"James, you look so very cross."

"I feared for you," he said gruffly.

"That was kind, but unnecessary." Her mouth jerked down. "I'm afraid I failed to rescue Marigold."

"Marigold."

"It's very probable that it is too late for her. I believe she may wish to continue just as she is."

He would not pursue this subject much further. "Promise me you will never venture back there again."

Her face came up sharply. "But I might—"

Before she could finish, James swept Celine from her place and plopped her on his knees. "You will not ever go there again! Do you understand?" He shook her once. "Do you?"

"I . . . yes." Tears shone in her eyes. "You were concerned for me?"

You terrified me, my golden girl. Gently, he pulled her into his arms, rested her head on his shoulder. "As I have already said, I feared for you, Celine. Where you have been is no place for a gentle, pure girl."

"Hardly pure."

"What?"

She held his lapel and said in a small voice, "I am no longer pure, James. We both know as much and I shall never regret the fact."

Incredible. Amid a society where virtual depravity reigned, this creature was untouched. She did not know that what they had shared, delightful and erotic as it had been, had fallen far short of the total satisfaction he craved. His body stirred at the thought.

"Please don't think I am not grateful that you came for me. I was really quite frightened."

He closed his eyes and ran his hand over her smooth cheek and satiny hair. "You will not be frightened again. It is now my responsibility to ensure your safety."

A shudder passed through her. "Don't worry about me, please. I am *not* your responsibility."

James caught Celine by the shoulders and righted her. "You *are* my responsibility."

She appeared bemused.

"You are my fiancee." The words, so foreign on his lips, filled him with a fierce, overwhelming emotion he wasn't ready to examine. Celine stared up at him, her face open and questioning. Her heart was in her eyes, and she offered that heart to him. For the first time in his life he knew the potential joy of a gift of trust from an unspoiled soul.

He wanted this tender, beautiful girl as he had never wanted anyone or anything before. Gently, he shook her. "My *fiancee*, Celine. Do you understand what that means?"

Her mouth trembled and she touched his jaw lightly. "No, James. Thank you, but no. I shall not hold you to your kind gesture. There must be other ways to rid myself of . . . James, I do thank you for all—"

"Hush." Before she could finish, he wrapped her tightly in his arms once more. He had no experience with women who did not regard themselves as prizes worthy of any man.

"May I tell you something?"

He rocked her gently. "Anything."

Her fingers stole to find his face once more. Her touch was like a butterfly's wing brushing over his skin, hovering shyly on his mouth. "You are like no other man."

His breath caught. "I . . . You jest."

"I do not jest. I have realized that I . . . I . . ."

"You?" Carefully, he tilted up her chin. "You what, my sweet?"

In the pause that followed, Celine studied him, her eyes luminous in the dimly lighted coach.

"Tell me, Celine."

"I can see you wherever I go. Whatever I do. When Freda brushes my hair, I drift and imagine it is you who touches me. And if I close my eyes . . ." She hesitated, lips parted.

"If you close your eyes?" His throat constricted.

"Then I see your face," she whispered, and the shimmer of tears turned amber to soft gold and clung to thick lashes. "You are beautiful, James. As beautiful inside as you are out. You touch my spirit."

James looked at the lovely, trusting woman in his arms and pressed her face to his shoulder once more. There were no words—none that he dared speak for fear of revealing how she had taken *his* spirit into the palms of her slender hands.

Could he have her? Could he be for her what she

already thought him to be? Was there any hope that when he crushed the foul people who, unbelievably, were her parents, she could ... Would he keep her then?

Despair bit through his flesh to the bone, to the nerve—to what this precious creature called the spirit. Whatever happened, he could not turn back from that which he had promised his father—and himself.

Celine would come to know he had used her— what then?

"You think I am foolish," she whispered.

"I think it would be wise for us to marry very soon," he said, scarcely trusting his voice to remain steady. "Toward that end, I shall urge your parents to return with you to Dorset immediately."

"You will?"

"I will."

"Where will you be?"

He smiled over her head. "I shall also be in Dorset. I can hardly marry you if we are not together."

"You really intend to marry me?"

"I am going to marry you, Celine. I want to."

"Oh."

"You say that frequently."

She snuggled and his smile became a grin. Somehow he would bind her to him. He contrived to rap the peephole, giving the signal to return home.

"James."

"Mm?"

"The money is uncomfortable. I should like to remove it."

He jerked away, and Celine fumbled beneath her mantle. Concentrating fiercely, she struggled, evidently with her bodice, until she produced a leather pouch containing something that clinked.

Setting the pouch on the seat beside him, she

wrapped the mantle close again. "I'd like to go back and tell that Mrs. Merryfield exactly what I think of her. She calls herself an abbess, you know. And she refers to her dreadful house as a nunnery."

James became very still. "What happened while you were there?" By God, if she'd been touched . . .

"That woman told me that if I went upstairs to a certain room, someone there would tell me how to contact Marigold—not that I could understand why I wasn't simply sent to her directly."

"Did you go to the room?"

"Yes."

He clenched his teeth. "And there was someone there?"

"Oh, yes. A man. A very odd person."

A blanket of black wrath enveloped James. "In what manner was he odd?"

"His dress was quite singular. As were the things he asked me to do."

Controlling his voice took supreme effort. "Tell me about the things."

"I did them." Her hand settled on his throat above his neckcloth. "And I took the money. Quite a lot of money, I should think. But he didn't know where Marigold was."

"To hell with Marigold!" James's head pounded with the strength of his fury. "You took money from the blackguard?"

"Certainly. Money is a very precious commodity to people who don't have any. If we were all more careful with it, there wouldn't be so much need. I'll make certain this money goes to a good cause and—"

"Silence." He stopped her from pulling away. Looking upon her face would be unbearable. "Never mind your damnable causes. Tell me this instant: *What* happened in that room?"

A sigh shifted her body. "I told you. I did what he

asked. I bound him to the bed and gagged him in order to be ready for what he wished done next."

James held still and waited. When she said nothing more, he asked, "What did he want you to do next?" He would return and find the filth.

"I do believe I'm growing quite sleepy. This has been an extraordinary night."

"Celine, explain what the man had you do next."

"Nothing," she said faintly. "Since he was gagged, and wished to remain so, he could not tell me his further instructions."

Chapter 23

"**M**y head is still spinning." Celine laughed up at James. "I cannot believe I am already back at Knighthead and you are here with me." She could scarcely believe that all of her life had not suddenly become a dream from which she might, unhappily, awaken.

The one slight detraction from her joy was that James appeared withdrawn. Why, he had said barely a few words since he arrived almost an hour previously. This was the first time she had seen him in the week since he rescued her from that horrible place in Town, and she had *so* much she wished to speak to him about.

"James?" She touched his arm tentatively. "Have I displeased you?"

He turned slowly from his contemplation of Knighthead's deep lawns and the banks of rhododendrons matured to tree height and laden with pink and purple blossoms. "What did you say, Celine?" His skin was so tanned against his snowy, austerely tied neckcloth.

"You are unhappy."

"No." He shook his head. "No, how could I be when I am walking in the most beautiful gardens in

304

... that I have ever seen with the woman who will soon become my wife?"

Wife. Celine slowly twirled the pale turquoise parasol that matched her batiste walking dress. "You are still resigned to that course then, James?"

"Resigned?" With the warm early afternoon sun at his back, his face was shaded, his dark eyes impossible to read. He circled her waist so suddenly that she fell against him.

Celine glanced toward the house where her mother hovered, supposedly tending roses that bordered the terrace. "James. We shouldn't, not with Mama—"

"Hush. Your mother is merely going through the expected rituals of propriety. We will be married soon. Then your conduct will be my affair—entirely my affair." The expression in his eyes might be shuttered from her, but the harsh lines of his face, the sharply pulled down corners of his sensual mouth, the flare of his nostrils—these Celine could see all too well. She didn't understand the reason, but that James's mood was volatile she had no doubt.

In his dark blue coat, clinging buff doeskin pantaloons, and top boots, there could be no more imposing figure of a man than James Eagleton. When Celine had seen him arriving, sweeping up the drive astride a massive black hunter, she'd felt his power to command, to exert his will. Beside James, others paled. Yet he insisted he was pleased to marry *her*. Disquiet speeded the beat of Celine's heart. *Why?* He could have his pick of brides.

"I thought you wouldn't come." The words tumbled out before she could stop them.

James spanned her waist, rubbed his thumbs slowly back and forth. He regarded her with such intense concentration that she finally bowed her head.

A gentle shake forced her to look at him once more. "Celine, with me you will learn your true worth. That I promise you." He laughed. "Ah, yes, you have much to learn, about yourself and about me."

For what seemed a very long time he continued to observe her. When his gaze slipped to her lips, she felt the warmth and longing only he could inspire.

Then she remembered Mama on the terrace. "I should like to show you the house," she told James hurriedly. "It is really quite lovely, although there are parts that are ... they need refurbishing. Why wouldn't you come in when you arrived?"

"You shall show me the house soon enough." His jaw came up. With the breeze ruffling his hair, Celine *knew* he was the most handsome, most appealing man in the world. "I wanted to see the grounds. I ... I have heard so much about them."

"We have not had an opportunity to discuss matters, James. I had wanted to ask you why you chose to offer for me so precipitously."

"Talbot," James responded shortly.

"David? What of him?"

"Miss Fisher sent him to me. He explained what was occurring with your parents." He studied Celine afresh, all the way to her turquoise satin slippers embroidered with clusters of ornamental knots. "Is Talbot at all to blame for your dangerous preoccupation with what you call causes?"

She would not speak of this to James, not yet. "How kind of David to try to help me. My parents were really ... They were displeased with me."

James toyed with a soft curl that blew across her cheek. "They will not be displeased with you again. And I think Mr. Talbot had more than one motive for coming to my house." He seemed to become lost in thought. "I wonder how long he remained there after I left."

"Why would David remain?" As soon as the question was asked, she knew the answer. "I expect he wanted to speak with Liam. He is always most concerned for those he considers in need of guidance."

James gave a sharp and not altogether pleasing bark of laughter.

"I fail to see any humor in what I've said."

"None at all." But the corners of his mouth twitched.

Celine eyed him suspiciously, but decided to abandon the topic. The smell of freshly cut grass rose gently on the breeze. Buttercups and daisies nodded their cheerful heads. She wanted to celebrate with the flowers, but could not dismiss the disquieting notion that, for some strange reason, James seemed more angry than pleased.

"Let us walk on," he said abruptly and tucked her hand between his elbow and his hard body. "I should like to see the lake . . . and the copse of oaks on Miller's Hill."

Puzzled by this unsettling sensation she could not identify, Celine allowed him to guide her downhill toward the willows that surrounded the lake. Holding aside sweeping branches to let her pass, James became immobile, staring straight ahead as if he saw something Celine could not see.

She stood still, watched him, and pressed her hands together. Here he seemed so different from the man she had met—and fallen in love with—in London.

Passing Celine, James went to the edge of the water and looked down into depths that had become murky with the years and overgrown with rushes at the edges.

She approached him cautiously.

"There were swans," he said in a voice quite unlike his own.

Celine frowned. "Swans? Oh, no. I assure you there were never swans."

"There were *swans*, I tell—" He spun toward her, and his features moved as if with some deep and disturbing emotion. Then his face cleared and he drew an audible breath. "Forgive me. I am rambling. The journey was grueling. I did not rest on the way."

"Why?" His comment surprised her. "Why did you not—"

"Because I could not wait to be with you." He smiled and tilted up her chin. "And all the way I thought of your hair like honey and your eyes like gold . . . and your lips so soft and waiting to be kissed." As if to prove his words, he bent to smooth his cheek on her hair, to study her eyes, and finally, to kiss her lips. Settling his hands loosely around her neck, James kissed Celine very gently, almost chastely, and when he drew back, she thought that he appeared sad.

"James—"

"I want you to promise me something," he said, his voice low and urgent. "Will you?"

She nodded. "Of course." Foreboding welled in her heart.

"Promise me you will never draw away from me—"

"I will not!"

James gripped her shoulders so tightly she winced. "Not ever, Celine. No matter what happens, you will trust in me to look after you and to be a good husband to you."

"Yes," she said faintly, shaken by his vehemence. "Please, James, you are troubled. It is because of me, isn't it? Because you feel you must do this thing to help me when you would rather not."

For a moment she thought he would not answer.

Just as she prepared to speak again, she saw James look past her and frown.

"Talbot," he said. "Good day to you."

Celine turned in time to see David approach, a hand beneath Liam's elbow. "Good day, Eagleton." David's green eyes were speculative when they settled upon James, but at least the dislike of former meetings had disappeared. "I called to see you at Blackburn Manor. Liam was kind enough to tell me where you were and show me the way." David coughed, then went on quickly. "Mr. Won Tel also accompanied us. He is taking refreshment at the house with Lettie."

"Show you the way?" Celine remarked, bemused, and saw a faint flush rise in David's cheeks. She decided against reminding him that he had been a frequent visitor to Knighthead since he was a child. "Welcome, Liam. What do you think of the manor? Are you comfortable there?"

The brilliance of Liam's smile, the first she had ever bestowed upon Celine, was stunning. "It is a most overwhelming house." Tucked into the girl's lustrous crown of braids, purple rhododendron flowers became exotic blooms that echoed the lilies embroidered on her lavender-colored silk tunic.

"Squire Loder used to live there." Celine giggled. "He was a hermit. When I was a little girl I believed he might be some sort of demon."

"You may have been correct." Liam wrinkled her small, perfect nose and cast a sidelong glance at David—who watched her with rapt attention. "I have already engaged a number of women from the village of Little Puddle. Is that not a strange name for a place? I believe they will put things in order quite quickly. The furnishings are not in James's taste but he will correct that quickly, I am certain."

"You will manage beautifully, my dear," David

said. His solid frame accentuated Liam's fragility, but Celine noted that the tiny female was very much a woman.

"With the help of David's wonderful housekeeper and her assistant, I feel confident we shall do very well."

James stirred restlessly, but Liam's comment riveted Celine. "Mrs. Strickland has volunteered to help you?"

"Oh, yes. She is most resourceful. It was she, not I, who actually spoke with the village women and told them exactly what should be done. Mrs. Strickland and Ruby Rose are obviously a congenial team. I envy David." Her glowing smile blazed upon him. "Of course, it is natural that those he employs should be happy and wish to serve him—and others—well."

For once Celine found she could not think of a thing to say. Mrs. Strickland and Ruby Rose? *A congenial team?*

"Was there some particular reason why you wanted to see me, Talbot?" James spoke sharply. "Liam, your slippers are wet."

Celine looked from the slippers in question to James's disapproving face, and back to Liam. The latter's smile didn't waver.

"If you remember, Eagleton," David said, stiffly formal now, "you asked me if I could assist you in a certain matter. What you requested has been accomplished. I was able to arrange for the banns to be called on the very day of my return to Dorset. They were announced for a second time yesterday. Next Sunday will be the final reading. And this is in order." He produced a folded document. "The license."

"Good!" James strode forward to administer a resounding slap to David's back. "Admirable, Talbot. Admirable!"

David winced. "I reiterate what I told you in Lon-

don, sir. This appears to be in Celine's best interests.
If I should ever discover otherwise . . ." He raised his
brows significantly.

Celine found she was adrift. "What interests? What
are you two talking about?"

James turned and offered her his hand. When she
placed her fingers in his, he pulled her to his side.
"We are talking about a wedding, Celine. Ours; yours
and mine. We will be married one week from today,
on Monday next."

Sunlight through the stained-glass windows of
Knighthead's salon dappled the room with rich col-
ors. James felt the house settling about him like a beloved and perfectly tailored coat. Familiar sights and
scents awakened memories that were almost unbearably poignant even as they fanned the banked embers of his thirst for vengeance to licking flames. The
week ahead would cost him dearly. No trace of his
true feelings must be allowed to show at any moment, unless he was alone, and there would be precious few such moments.

"I'm sure Celine knows how very fortunate she is,"
Mary Godwin was saying. "Providence only knows
why so successful and accomplished a man as yourself has chosen to overlook her headstrong, wayward
nature. However, we are delighted that you have
done so."

James looked upon Celine's pale, unhappy features
and fumed behind the impassive facade he'd assumed.

"I'm sure I don't have to tell you that a firm hand
is never wasted on girls of weak spirit, Mr. Eagleton," Mary Godwin said.

"Quite so," Godwin said with a suggestive leer
that sent James's right hand to his left sleeve and the
sleek, hard outline of his stiletto. Just as quickly, he

let his hand drop. He must wait, and he must remember that death would be too merciful a punishment.

Seated on a beautiful Grecian chaise lounge, the very chaise lounge that had been James's mother's favorite, the Godwin woman smirked obsequiously. "A week from today. I must say it all seems a little precipitate." Her cunning eyes slid to Celine and lingered. "One could not blame those less generous than ourselves for wondering at such unseemly haste." She gave James a suggestive smile and smoothed the folds of her too-girlish pea-green satin gown.

James settled an elbow on a ledge of the handsomely carved Elizabethan fireplace and maintained a cool demeanor. All would be settled to his satisfaction—and soon.

"We men understand these things," Godwin babbled. "No time like the present for sampling ripe fruit, eh, me boy?"

James stared.

"Yes, well, anyway ... Er, you and I still have some matters of business to discuss and, no doubt, Mrs. Godwin will want to arrange the necessary, er, necessary arrangements with all due haste."

"There will be an engagement supper at Blackburn Manor on Sunday evening next, the eve of our wedding." James smiled reassuringly at Celine and was pleased to see an answering tilt of her lips.

"See here," Godwin said. "Surely it's my place—"

"I think not," James said shortly. "In the matter of my marriage everything is quite definitely *my* place."

Mary Godwin rose to her feet, her bosom heaving impressively. "To whom should we give our guest list? There is little time for our friends who are in London to—"

"This will be a very small party." He took grim

pleasure in the ugly rush of blood to the woman's face. No doubt she had once been handsome enough, but he felt some deep malevolence in her, some evil that might surpass even his expectations.

Her too-blond ringlets bounced with the sharp toss of her head. "You will not wish to raise any more gossip than this sudden union will already cause. I do expect my closest—"

"No." James said, but in a pleasant tone that clearly confused both Godwins. "Time will prove there is no question of unseemly haste in our marriage. It is my wish to make everything about the wedding a pleasure for Celine. The engagement celebration is a part of my gift to her. I'm sure you would want no less for your only daughter."

He then turned to Godwin. "You and I will speak further within the next few days, sir. For now, I know Celine is anxious to show me . . . her home." Soon it would be her home, and his, and no one else's.

Celine rose and almost ran to the door, remembering herself just in time to wait for James to open it for her. In the entrance hall with its high windows and worn flagstones, she made as if to hurry ahead. James caught her hand and pulled her into a quick embrace. "All is well, my sweet one. Hush. I can feel your heart like a frightened bird. You are safe now. Please believe me."

"I do." But her lower lip trembled. "Thank you, James."

A movement caught his eye, and he turned to see Miss Fisher slipping rapidly toward them from the small parlor that had once been his mother's.

She pressed a finger to her lips and beckoned them into the corridor leading to the back of the house. "I was waiting," she whispered, drawing them into the shadows. Her soft brown eyes glowed. "Perhaps I shall not have a better chance to speak with you both before . . . before the marriage."

Celine took one of her companion's hands in both of hers. "Dear Lettie, what is it?"

"Nothing . . . *Everything*." The woman appeared flustered. "I am so happy. This is . . . Oh, forgive my forwardness, Mr. Eagleton, but I am so happy for Celine. And for you. God will bless you both, I know He will." She appeared close to shedding tears of happiness.

"Thank you, Miss Fisher," James said gravely.

"Please call me Lettie." Her free hand flew to her face. "Forgive me. You must think me presumptuous. But I am happy. *Happy* that at last my little lamb has found a man who will love and care for her—and keep her safe." She bent to press a cheek against Celine's fingers.

James frowned. He had heard how loyal companions could be, indeed, he knew as much from his own experience, but surely this was excessive emotion from a paid servant.

"Thank you, Lettie," Celine said softly and drew the other woman into an embrace. "I am very happy, but you shall always be a part of my happiness. Isn't that so, James?"

He watched thoughtfully. "As you wish, of course."

Lettie made a muffled noise and spun away. "I have things to do," she said. "I must return to my duties."

"Your companion loves you," James said when they were alone again. He drew Celine back into his arms and rested his chin atop her hair. "I understand why."

Time slipped by while they stood, swaying slighting, lost in the sweet, intimate warmth of the moment.

The sound of a throat being cleared nearby alerted James to the fact that he and Celine were not alone. Won Tel had arrived exactly as planned.

"Mr. Eagleton." Won Tel bowed. "Please excuse me, but Liam is most anxious to have what she terms, um, an important discussion with Miss Celine."

James hid a smile at Won Tel's deferential manner. "An important discussion?"

"Yes, sir. On the matter—she says—of Miss Celine's hair."

Celine's hand went to her head.

James clasped his hands behind his back. "I cannot imagine what Liam means."

"My fault, sir." Won Tel bowed again. "I believe I was supposed to say that Liam is an expert in such matters and would like to confer with Miss Celine on the subject of how her hair should be dressed for her wedding. She is in the garden with Mr. Talbot."

James noted with satisfaction that a pleased smile had transformed Celine's worried face. "I can scarcely believe that this is happening," she said, looking up at him. "I should very much like to speak to Liam on this subject. Her own hair always looks so beautiful."

"Mm." And Liam was spending altogether too much time with the good cleric, a matter he must address when he had more time.

"You do not approve?" Celine promptly spread her hands to Won Tel. "I am to show James our home. Please tell Liam—"

"Nonsense," James said quickly. "Run along. There are things I need to discuss with your parents. Now will do nicely. I'll join you all later."

The moment Won Tel and Celine passed from sight, James headed back in the direction from which he'd come. At the salon door he paused long enough to hear the murmur of the Godwins' voices before heading with swift, silent steps along a corridor he remembered very well.

James might have been only ten when he was last in this house, but he knew exactly how to reach the library by the shortest route.

"Dammit to hell," James muttered through gritted teeth.

He checked his fob watch and slipped it back into his waistcoat pocket. He dared not spend much longer in the wreck that had been Francis St. Giles's splendid library.

Silvered beams spanned lofty ceilings in the handsomely proportioned room. The walls were lined with bookshelves—bookshelves emptied of books that lay scattered in broken heaps upon the stone floor.

Sidestepping the fine Thomas Moore carpet Sophie St. Giles had been so excited to acquire for her husband, and which was now carelessly rolled and pushed to one side, James studied again the jade dragons flanking the fireplace. Their eyes were smooth, with nothing to suggest a relationship in the deep-cut insignia in Francis St. Giles's ring. Once more, James pulled the soft leather pouch from his pocket and removed the heavy ring. Three offset pyramid-shaped sections had been carved from a massive crown that should have borne a family crest for use as a seal. With this, and with the delicate locket that would become Celine's on the eve of their wedding, he would finally take possession of his grandmother's legacy.

A scraping sound came from the passage outside the library. James stuffed the ring back into its pouch and returned it to his pocket before continuing around the room with measured steps while he studied the molded cornice between bookcases and ceiling. If discovered, he would simply say he'd been wandering through the rooms while awaiting Celine's return.

Leaves and berries formed the cornice—with no hint of a pattern to match the ring.

He must leave.

Backing toward the door, he took a last inventory of skewed furnishings, of ornaments and clocks, of pictures removed and stacked against the walls.

The scraping noise approached the room, and James straightened his waistcoat before throwing wide the door ... and almost falling over a cat that immediately squalled and shot away.

He pushed back his hair and retraced his steps. The Godwins had not found what they wanted, of that he was certain. But they had searched; oh, yes, they had searched. He smiled grimly. At least he was assured that they did not know for certain what he knew: the Sainsbury fortune would indeed be found in the room he had just left.

Perhaps separating the Godwins from any opportunity to continue their quest would be enough. Even as he toyed with the idea, James knew his need for justice would never be satisfied until he could dangle the gemstones before his enemies and watch their impotent rage and frustration.

Would that be enough?

He thought not, but for now he must remove himself from this house where the Godwins' presence was a violation he could scarcely bear for another instant.

The fresh air beyond the thick front doors was a blessed relief. James circled the house and set off across the lawns. The sound of feminine laughter soon reached him, and he smiled despite a bitter and urgent thirst to end this quest.

Above the sunken garden where his mother had taken such pride in a collection of small, white statuary, he paused and kept out of sight.

Won Tel was not to be seen, or Miss Fisher, but David Talbot leaned against a pillar to watch Liam working over Celine.

"I shall need practice." Liam's voice rose clearly. "We will start again." With that, and the deft removal of a few pins, she let Celine's hair fall about her shoulders.

"No!" The Reverend Talbot slapped his thigh and looked at the sky. "Not again!"

"Yes, again," Liam said with her customary lack of concern. "It shall be perfect. Such beautiful hair. See how it plays with the sun."

James leaned to get a clearer view. Celine's heavy, golden hair slipped through Liam's uplifted fingers.

"Yes," he murmured to himself. "See how it plays with the sun." Molten strands sprayed softly free and settled slowly, gently into warm honey waves.

In a few days he would bury his face in that satin hair where it spread over the pillow of his marriage bed. He would bury his face in her hair and his body in her body.

The violence of his quickening smote a seething blow. He wanted it all: Knighthead, the Sainsbury gems ... and Celine.

Only death could foil him.

Chapter 24

Celine breathed in the night air and faced Black-burn Manor. Tomorrow she would marry James.

"Really, Celine, I *do* wish Lettie had followed my instructions. That dress is unsuitable for a girl's engagement celebration. I just *know* it is."

"Don't fret, Mama. And don't blame Lettie—for anything. This was the dress I chose. It feels exactly *suitable*." The russet silk, touched at the neck with narrow, ivory-colored lace, was simple in cut but Celine knew that it was a perfect foil for her coloring . . . it was also not a "oncer," a thought that brought her almost unholy glee.

"Lot of fuss about nothing, if you ask me," Papa said. "The business is settled. Can't think why Eagleton don't collect his piece, pay his vowels, and be done with it."

Celine gathered her rich, deep green velvet cloak about her and walked ahead of her parents toward the lights that blazed from the manor's open front doors.

The engagement celebration is a part of my gift to Celine, James had said. How could there be so much happiness in the world?

She heard strains of music from some mystical instrument, the like of which she had never heard before.

"Stuff and nonsense," Papa muttered behind her. "Never thought I'd see the day we'd be dancing to some upstart's tune in old Loder's place. Slum, I daresay. Eagleton's an eccentric."

"He may well be," Mama agreed. "His taste definitely bears question."

"His money's good. That's all that counts."

Celine pressed her lips together. She would not allow anything to spoil her anticipation.

Colin, the new groom Mama had unaccountably elevated to the position of coachman, hovered uncertainly. He'd been instructed in his duties, told he should approach Blackburn Manor and knock for admittance—but the open door clearly confused him.

"Open to any common gawker," Papa said, not at all quietly. "What would you expect from a savage? No idea of the done thing. Fits in with the stories they're telling in the village. Odd practices. Odd goings-on."

They arrived at the top of very solid stone steps and stood in a cluster.

"Er, Mrs. Godwin?"

Mama waved the novice coachman away, but smiled a smile that was not at all like Mama. "The idea," she said, patting the tight blond curls arranged to frame her face beneath a magenta turban. "No butler. What are we supposed to do—"

"Good evening, Miss Celine." Won Tel's appearance had its usual silencing effect. "Good evening, Mr. and Mrs. Godwin. Mr. Eagleton expects you."

"I do indeed."

Time stopped.

Celine heard the magical strings that sang of places she had never been, felt the light of a thousand candles in glittering crystal chandeliers, and smelled the sweet, subtle fragrance from hundreds of yellow roses heaped and threaded and clustered throughout the warmly paneled reception hall and up the beautifully carved staircase.

She saw only James.

He came, a tall, broad-shouldered, satanically handsome man who eclipsed all before him. Celine felt the air grow thin as if it fled in his wake. Shadow cast his face in echo, dark, as dark as his eyes, centered only on her, and stark, classically pale where lean flesh covered autocratic bone.

"Come to me, Celine," he said, offering a long, strong hand that closed about hers. "Here. I broke off the thorns." He gave her a single, utterly perfect yellow rose.

She took the flower to her face and closed her eyes. "Tillie's Charmer," she said, remembering that first afternoon. "Can we only have known each other so short a time?"

James drew her near and said, for her ears only, "You remember, too, my golden girl."

"Yes. I remember every moment we've spent together."

"So do I. After tomorrow there will be no more times apart, my sweet." In a perfectly cut black evening coat and elegantly simple white linen, he felt as strong as a great tree, rooted like the foundation and wide like the branches. He offered shelter and succor, protection . . . and Passion; Passion leashed by rigid control and made the more drugging through the dangerous force of its ultimate release.

James smiled at last. "Let me take your cloak." While he did so, Celine became aware of Liam kneeling on a silver cushion, a strange instrument across her thighs. From this, from the long strings beneath the girl's delicate fingers, issued the haunting notes that stroked the air.

"Hello, Celine." It was David who greeted her from a shady corner behind Liam. "You look beautiful."

"Doesn't she?" James said.

Celine couldn't speak, could only go to David and kiss his cheek, and return Liam's softly mischievous smile.

Mama and Papa had already given up their outer garments and passed by; Celine did not know when. Staring silently around, they followed Won Tel through double doors.

James offered his arm. "Shall we?" He led Celine into a small but finely proportioned dining room where crystal and gold sparkled and scintillated in subdued candlelight. He seated her on his left.

When all were at table, David included, Mama raised her nose and said in ringing tones, "Six!" whilst disapprovingly regarding the intimate number of table covers. She produced a painted fan in shades of magenta with a bronzed overlay and flapped dispiritedly, causing the curls about her overpink face to flap similarly. "Not what a proud mother would hope for her only daughter at such a time."

Celine regarded her parent, trying valiantly to suppress the hostility she felt. "How have you achieved such a fairy tale in one week, James? It's all so beautiful."

"I—"

"He ordered and demanded, of course, Celine," Liam announced from behind James's back. Tonight she was almost demure in light blue. "Just as he always does. And just as he always does, he got his way." She clapped her hands sharply and turned her small mouth down.

Celine grinned, ignoring James's narrowed eyes and the sardonic rise of one arched black brow.

"It is as well that this dinner is not being held in

Grosvenor Square. Since much that was there is now here, you would be dining on the floor!"

Another clap of Liam's hands cut through the guffaws of James and David—and Mama's tutting—and servants entered by a door near the rococo-faced fireplace.

Won Tel had taken up a position beside a shimmering sideboard of some black wood and supported on brass feet shaped like bearded fish. At a subtle signal from James, he came forward and bent over his master. A moment later, Won Tel withdrew from the room.

While an under butler and two maids dealt with finger bowls, a formidably tall butler began ladling soup from a beautiful Wedgwood tureen of black basalt.

Celine found her hand drawn into James's beneath the tablecloth. He set her fingers atop his hard thigh and stroked them rhythmically.

"Would yer like a little lemonade, Celine?" a voice said close to her ear. "Yer looks fair loverly, but wored out."

Startled, Celine looked up—directly into Ruby Rose's bright blue eyes. "Ruby—" From the top of her pristine, frilly white cap, to the toes of the sensible, highly polished black shoes that peeped from beneath her black skirts, Ruby Rose was the perfectly turned-out housemaid. "Thank you, Ruby Rose, I'd love some lemonade."

Celine tried not to stare at the extraordinary transformation that had occurred in the young woman who had arrived from London a few months earlier decked out in gaudy frippery. The next face that caught her eye was even more amazing. Mrs. Strickland, her dress appropriate to senior servant status, observed Ruby Rose's efficient efforts with barely concealed satisfaction resembling that of a proud parent. Feeling herself watched, Celine caught David's smug grin and smiled in return.

The seat to James's right remained empty—which seemed to concern him not at all. Celine glanced at it from time to time. Perhaps Won Tel could eventually ... No, of course not.

She barely tasted the soup, or the fish course that preceded game pies and elaborate puddings, preserves, and a lemon syllabub. Dishes were served and removed while Mama and Papa ate stolidly and David with gusto, as did James. Celine managed to swallow small bites and smile—and feel James's presence to her very soul. Only James mattered.

Pressure on her hand brought her attention to his face. He leaned toward her and whispered, "Do not be startled, my sweet, but there is to be a small surprise."

Before she could try to question him, Won Tel reappeared and cleared his throat. "Your last guest, Mr. Eagleton. Augustus St. Giles, Third Marquess of Casterbridge."

James immediately rose to his feet, as did David.

Surprise indeed. But Celine's joy was full enough to include and accept anyone who wished to join this wonderful celebration. Why had Papa not risen? And why did Mama appear stricken?

The marquess entered, looking richly sleek and fit. He smiled in all directions. "Evenin' all. Auspicious occasion. Very auspicious. Understand congratulations are in order." He slapped James's shoulder and took Celine's hand to his lips, murmuring, "Not difficult to see why the cub's infatuated with you, m'dear."

Waving aside Won Tel's effort to seat him, the marquess summoned the butler. "Fill the champagne glasses, my man. Keep filling 'em. This is an auspicious occasion. Ah, yes. A great deal of ground to be covered tonight." He looked toward Mama and Papa. "Darius and Mary Godwin, no less. And lookin' passable, very passable. Auspicious occasion for us all."

There was no draft, yet an icy chill passed over Celine's skin. Mama's dislike of being judged "passable" showed in the sharp flare of her nostrils. Papa gripped the edge of the table so tightly his knuckles had turned white.

The marquess motioned for James and David to sit. "I wanted to say what I'm about to say some months ago. James persuaded me to wait."

With no apparent concern for propriety, James settled a warm hand on Celine's nape and smiled reassuringly into her eyes.

"Darius and you, Mary, will remember Francis and Sophie St. Giles very well." He raised the glass of champagne he'd been handed and waited for the rest of the company to follow suit. "Let us drink to a wonderful couple: to my strong, honorable brother, Francis, and his beautiful, gentle wife, Sophie."

Amid utter silence, glasses were raised to lips—all but those of the Godwins. Celine thought Mama's pallor had taken on a gray tinge, and Papa appeared to have forgotten to close his mouth. Celine drank, but her heart pounded. She understood nothing of this.

"What you do not know, Darius and Mary, is . . ." The marquess paused, settling his gaze solely on Mama and Papa. "What you do not know and what will undoubtedly bring you the greatest satisfaction and joy, is that the man who sits beside your daughter, the man who will become her husband tomorrow—and your son-in-law—is not who he says he is."

In the stinging pause that followed, Celine looked from face to face, past David's bemused frown, to her parents' utterly frozen countenances, and on to James. Sadness. What she saw in him now was deep, deep sadness. What she felt herself was the edge of desperate fear. There was nothing of this that made sense.

"Darius!" Mama's voice approached a thin shriek. "What is he saying? What is happening?"

"Aha!" Grinning, the marquess raised his glass. "We are all delighted by this singular event, are we not, Mary?"

James's fingers tightened on the back of Celine's neck, and he studied her face before leaning to touch his lips to her cheek and whisper, "All is well, love. Trust me."

"*So*," Lord Casterbridge thundered. "It is my extreme pleasure. My honor. My delighted duty, to congratulate James on the occasion of his engagement—on the eve of his marriage to Celine—and to announce that the name Eagleton is one that he agreed to take until the time came when we could announce what pleases me most to announce."

Liam had taken up a position behind David. Her hand stole to his shoulder and he covered it with his own.

"May I present"—raising his glass high, Lord Casterbridge sent a fierce stare in all directions—"James St. Giles, Earl of Eagleton, my nephew and sole heir."

The marquess drank, as did David. Celine managed to take her glass to her lips in a shaky hand. Mama and Papa appeared cast in stone. Why? Celine herself had every reason to be distressed. The man she was supposed to marry on the morrow had failed to tell her his true identity and, if the event were still to take place, she was to become not Mrs. Eagleton, but *Lady* Eagleton. It was all too much.

•

"Why?" Mama's voice, still unnaturally high, cracked, and she pointed a finger at James.

"Simple," James said quickly. "I wished to be certain Celine would want me for myself, rather than out of some misplaced sense of duty."

"Duty?" Celine frowned.

"Our fathers were close friends, my sweet. I did not want you to agree to marry me simply because you felt you owed it to that friendship. And I'm sure you agree with that course, Mr. and Mrs. Godwin." He turned to her parents in appeal. "I almost expected you to remember me. But, after all, I was merely a boy when we last met—before my father decided to pursue his fortune overseas—and I am considerably changed, no doubt."

"Considerably," Papa said slowly. At last he drank champagne and Mama followed suit. "I have been saddened to lose touch with your parents. Did Francis, er ... Why did he ... He never communicated after he left."

"I know." James shrugged slightly. "My father was consumed with his business interests, I fear. He and my mother seemed to separate themselves from England once they were established in Paipan."

Mama appeared agitated but somewhat restored from her evident shock. "And dear, er, Sophie. Is she ... No doubt she and your father are about to arrive even as we speak. I cannot imagine that she would miss her son's nuptials."

Taking his hand from Celine's neck, James indicated that he wanted his glass filled. While the butler complied, he regarded his uncle, who nodded as if there were no need for words between the two.

"My parents," James said, looking into his champagne, "are both dead. Apparently you have forgotten my saying that I inherited my business from my father. He died more than a year since. My mother passed away some months before that."

Celine stifled a small cry of sympathy and wound her fingers together in her lap.

"Oh." Mama, Celine thought uncomfortably, showed more sign of satisfaction than distress. "Oh, dear. Poor Sophie. And poor Francis, of course. They spoke of our ... close friendship, you say?"

"They did, indeed," James said. "My father particularly mourned the loss of what he shared with Mr. Godwin."

"The loss?" Papa said sharply.

"It was inevitable that distance should curtail the closeness you once enjoyed."

After emptying his third glass of champagne, Papa said, "Quite so. Damn shame. Expect you'd as soon call it an evening, my boy. Draining. Very draining for all of us. You'll want to talk with his lordship and prepare for tomorrow." He ducked his head in Lord Casterbridge's direction. "Never have spoken much about the other matter. Glad to do so—"

"No need," the marquess said loudly. "No need at all. What we all have to do is adjust to the new order, as they say. Damn glad to do so, I can tell you. About time I could look forward to some new stock in the Casterbridge nurseries."

His meaning dawned slowly on Celine and she blushed wildly. James found her hand once more and squeezed.

"I have a gift I should like to give to Celine, and this seems the perfect moment." From his pocket he produced a worn black leather box. He opened it to show her the contents. "This belonged to my mother. It was given to her on the eve of her wedding by my father's mother. Now it's yours, Celine."

Nestled on old velvet lay a gold locket of singular design. The intricate chain was formed of leaf-shaped links bound together by their stems. Hinged on each side of an oblong frame, the center of the locket was fashioned into a heavy, flower-encrusted cross.

Tears rushed to Celine's eyes. "It's so lovely. So old."

James stood. "My mother would have wanted to put this on you." He moved behind her.

"I shall do it for poor Sophie." Mama's voice, strong again, rang out. Dabbing at her eyes with a lace handkerchief, she rose from her chair and fluttered, arms outstretched, to James. "Poor, dear Sophie. In her stead I shall put the locket on Celine. How she would have loved this night. To see her only son about to be joined with the only daughter of her husband's dearest friend." Two huge tears squeezed from her eyes.

Mama took the locket from James and fastened it carefully about Celine's neck. "Perfect," she said, her voice breaking. "Oh, there is the loveliest diamond in the clasp . . . mm . . . well, I'm glad I could do this for our departed friends."

"Now, Godwin," Lord Casterbridge said. "Know this isn't quite the done thing, but I'd appreciate some time with this young beauty me nephew's managed to bag. Get to know her a bit before she starts expectin' me to dandle new Casterbridges on me knee."

Celine bowed her head to hide her face and heard James chuckle.

"Anyway," his lordship continued, "I'm sure you'll trust me to escort your chick home later. I'll make sure she's abed in plenty of time to be ready for the rigors of the morrow, eh?"

Male laughter gusted around the table and Celine continued to regard her lap.

"Very well," Papa said. "Come along, Mary. We, too, will need our rest if we're to be at our best for tomorrow's festivities. We'll look forward to seeing you all then."

Her parents' departure, aided by Won Tel and Liam, was speedily accomplished. David, after receiving a nod of approval from James, wrapped Celine in a bear hug and kissed the top of her head. "I'm happy for you, my lady," he said, smiling gently. "James—Lord Eagleton is a very lucky man."

"James to you, David," James said almost brusquely. "I'm grateful for the friendship and guidance I know you've given Celine."

David departed, leaving Celine alone with James and his uncle. The servants and Won Tel and Liam had slipped away unnoticed.

"Shall we go into my study?" James suggested. "It's far from complete, but comfortable."

Lord Casterbridge shook his head and replaced his glass on the table. "If it's all the same to you, I'll retire. I understand a room's been prepared for me for the night?"

Celine saw the men exchange a glance. "Indeed," James said. "I look forward to showing Celine around Morsham Hall in the near future." To Celine, he added, "Morsham Hall is some two hours north. It is my family's estate."

"And your future home when—"

"No need to speak of that now," James interrupted hurriedly.

"If you say so." Lord Casterbridge regarded his nephew fondly. "This is a happy day for me, m'boy. I'll bid you good night."

Left alone, Celine found that she and James seemed incapable of doing other than stare at each other.

"The old bounder has a good heart," James said finally. "I didn't ask him to do that—to leave us alone. I'm damn glad he did."

"Me, too." But Celine's legs trembled, and her stomach. She felt confused and expectant at the same time. "I'm not certain I can become accustomed to you as an earl, my lord."

"I can very easily become accustomed to you as my lady," James responded softly. "Oh, yes, indeed. My lady."

Seconds passed. He took the single step that brought him close and slipped a hand along her jaw. His fingers stroked her hair and played with the curl that teased her cheekbone—and he waited until she closed her eyes and rested her face in his palm.

She felt him move close, but he did not take her in his arms. When his lips brushed hers, smooth and firm—and infinitely gentle—she drew back with a small gasp, but did not open her eyes. And in an instant, James found her mouth again and kissed her with such exquisitely tantalizing restraint that she parted her lips and sought to deepen the contact.

"No, sweeting." His tongue made a fleeting dip into the corner of her mouth. "If I do not return you home now, I know I shall not be able to stop myself from taking all of you and keeping all of you this very moment. That must wait until tomorrow, when we are man and wife."

Throbbing with her need for him, Celine kept her eyes downcast while James brought her cloak and wrapped it around her shoulders. "I will summon a carriage," he told her.

"No!" Celine caught his arm. "Could we ride, James? I have never ridden with you."

He searched her face and glanced at her unsuitable clothing, but nodded before pulling the bellrope beside the fireplace. Won Tel appeared almost immediately, and James dispatched him for suitable horses.

Within minutes, the sound of clattering hooves could be heard, and James, after sweeping a dark gray, many-caped cloak around his own shoulders, ushered Celine from the house.

"Oh, what a pretty little chestnut." The mare James settled her upon gleamed beneath the moon.

"She is yours," James said while he arranged her skirts and pulled her cloak forward. "Not that you will want to replace your gelding—Cleopatra was it?—completely. Damn these sidesaddles. Foolish nonsense." He held her ankle and guided her foot into the stirrup.

Celine looked down at his dark curls and smiled. Hesitantly, she rested her hand atop his thick hair and felt him grow still. "Thank you, James."

He raised his face slowly, his hand remaining on her ankle. "For what?"

"For being who you are. For rescuing me even though I may not be what you had hoped for in a wife. I'll do my best for you, James."

"When will you believe that you are all I will ever want? More than I could have hoped or dreamed of."

Emotion clogged her throat. She smoothed her fingers through his hair, and he turned his face to kiss her wrist.

"James—"

"Come," he said briskly, stepping away and swinging astride his own mount. "You tempt me beyond reason, my lady."

"I am not your lady yet."

The black moved restlessly and James reined it in, wheeling toward Celine. "In my mind you are already my lady. In my mind I see you as my lady in every sense. My body can hardly bear that there are still so many hours before I can make the pictures in my mind a reality. Let us get you home."

Knighthead lay a scant three miles from Blackburn Manor. The distance was covered too quickly for Celine. Riding in the wake of James and his massive hunter, she longed to be free of the sidesaddle and cantering as she did in the secret hours of early morning when there was no one to see and criticize her conduct.

The hunter hit the gravel drive leading to the house, sending clumps of rocks flying in its wake. Celine's little chestnut flew valiantly along but arrived before the front doors at least a full minute behind its stronger companion.

The black blew noisily and reared, still anxious to run. Bareheaded, with moonlight etching his sharply masculine features, James leaned into the horse's neck to quiet the beast.

"He is magnificent," Celine called, drawing level. She did not add what she thought: that in raw, flamboyant power, the animal matched its rider.

James came near. "I will count the minutes until tomorrow."

"I, too," Celine said, and her heart took up the wild beat that was becoming so familiar. "It makes me happy that David will marry us."

"Mm." He raised his head to look skyward, then swung to the ground and lifted Celine down beside him. "You must go in now." His voice was gruff and he grasped her hand abruptly.

As she ran to keep pace with him, Celine's heart beat even faster by the time they stood at the foot of the front steps. James faced her and lowered his head slowly. She closed her eyes, feeling his breath, sweet and warm upon her lips.

"No!" he said sharply.

Celine's eyes flew open.

"No, precious girl. I must be strong now so that I'll suffer less this night." His laugh was hard and mirthless. Stepping back, he raised his right hand, extending the palm toward her.

For a moment Celine didn't understand, then she

caught her bottom lip in her teeth and lifted her own right hand, pressed her palm against his and felt his fingers slip between hers.

"Forever," he said, and the blue-ice moonlight painted his face once more, lingered on the sensual curves of his firm lips, sending that weighted fire shooting deep into Celine's most sensitive places.

"Forever," she agreed, feeling their palms fuse, skin to skin, fire to fire . . . life to life.

He released her, and Celine darted to open the door. As she closed it behind her she could still see him, silhouetted in the darkness. Many more seconds passed before she heard the pelt of hooves on the driveway.

Tomorrow.

There was no justice.

That insipid little nothing should not be bound for the bed of a man like . . . like James St. Giles, Earl of Eagleton. Mary pressed closer to the window in the small upstairs storage room that overlooked the front driveway. For a moment she'd looked down on his tall, virile form, then he'd passed from sight into the shadow of the doorway—with her.

Kissing her. Fondling her breasts. Using his beautiful mouth and tongue . . . Mary pressed her hand between her legs. Through her nightrail she felt her own damp heat. Colin would welcome her visit as soon as it was safe to go to him.

The door slammed and she grew still, listening for footfalls on the stairs. They came and went as Celine passed on her way to her room.

Tomorrow Celine would go to his house, to his room. To his bed . . .

Eagleton was already in the saddle and riding away, leading the horse Celine had used. So much for Casterbridge's word to bring the chit home. Damn the name of

Casterbridge. Damn the name St. Giles. Francis had . . .
She would not think of Francis except to shout her glee
that he was dead, he and the holy bitch he had chosen
when he should have been Mary's.

She made to turn from the window. Something had
moved, slipped swiftly through shadows thrown across the
driveway by ancient yew trees.

Someone approached the house. Pressing stealthily into
dark, concealing places, a man—and she knew it to be a
man—drew steadily closer to her house. Her house and
only hers!

Mary brought her face to the glass once more and
peered.

And the figure broke from darkness into the moon's re-
vealing wash.

James Eagleton. Lord Eagleton, as his cursed uncle had
so proudly pronounced him to be. He must be returning to
steal secretly into Celine's chamber. Mary shuddered. He
meant to have her tonight—in this house.

As she watched, Eagleton hesitated, searching in every
direction, before creeping rapidly on—not toward the front
door and the staircase leading to the family's rooms, but
around the building toward the back.

Pure, cold panic attacked her. He was Francis's son. It
was only to be expected that father would tell son what he
knew about the gems.

Mary hesitated in the seething little room with its
moisture-clouded window. Darius had always been so cer-
tain that Francis had known nothing more than Darius
himself had overheard the old Lady Casterbridge say.

Stumbling over traveling trunks and shrouded, uniden-
tifiable heaps, Mary gained the door and eased it open.
Stepping carefully, quietly, she approached the stairs and
started down.

Chapter 25

$\sim\!\!\!\sim\!\!\!\infty\!\!\!\sim$

The last time he'd sneaked in through the dairy window he'd been considerably smaller.

Rubbing at what felt like a bruise in the making on his shoulder, he climbed from the iron draining board beside one of several deep sinks and crept through the cold room with its smell of curdled milk.

Once into passageways that threaded between scullery and game larder, fish and meat larder, back house, and lamp room, he moved swiftly, with the sureness of a man who remembered every inch of the quarters beneath the stairs. In those distant days of his childhood he'd spent many hours in the fond company of Cook, formidable to her staff but a coddling haven to James.

Only minutes passed before he reached steps leading to the passageway he sought, the passageway that brought him to his destination.

Before entering the library he paused, listening to the silence of the old house settle about him. Somewhere above stairs his beloved Celine would, even now, lie in her bed. He'd wager her tawny eyes were wide open yet and staring, as his would doubtless be until the morning. He smiled at the thought and let himself into the library.

He must be quick and he must not make a sound.

If his uncle hadn't made his surprise suggestion that Celine remain after her parents' departure that evening, James would not have thought to further his search even before gaining the unlimited access to Knighthead his marriage would bring. As he'd ridden away, he had found he could not resist the temptation to try the experiment he had planned in the days since his last, too brief visit.

Working swiftly, he lighted a single candle and grimaced at the meager glow it cast over the ruined room. Nevertheless, he could not risk a brighter light. Straining to remember their rightful situations, he positioned pieces of furniture as they had been in his childhood. The effort of lifting some items brought sweat to his brow, and he gritted his teeth against the strain.

The desk was the most difficult. Tilting it onto one leg, he swung the solid Jacobean mahogany piece and eased it down. His hand slipped. "Damn," he whispered through his teeth, grappling to regain purchase.

The scraping thud that ensued was muffled, but James blew out the candle and waited until the black cloak of night had pressed in upon him long enough to bring relief. He lighted his single candle once more.

Soon all ornaments, vases, urns, and figurines were back in place and most of the books pushed into heaps closer to the bookcases. No doubt the vicious Godwins would scurry about asking questions when they found the changes. No one would give them answers.

James smiled again.

The candle flame flickered and dipped.

A current of air. Jerking around, he looked to the window and saw the fringed draperies sway. Letting out the breath he'd held, he approached the stacked paintings. The casement in here had never been tight. A flaw his father had intended to correct—before he was summarily ousted from his home.

Replacing the paintings was a simple matter. Faded areas on the walls led the way and, one by one, the landscapes, hunting scenes, and portraits resumed their rightful places.

James stood back, feeling an unexpected and unwelcome pang of longing. The last time he'd stood in this room, surrounded by these paintings, his father had been seated at the Jacobean desk he'd so prized.

All that remained was the rolled carpet.

He began to kick it into place. *Sophie, my love, you spoil me.* James heard his father's voice so clearly that he closed his eyes. *Not as much as you spoil me.* And his mother had laughed, her charming, musical laugh.

Damn them. Damn the Godwins.

He opened his eyes and bent to speed his progress—and stopped. Sitting back on his heels, James frowned. On the flagstone closest to his left knee a small, round light glowed.

He peered closer, touched, and gasped. A circle, cut almost invisibly into the stone, lay within the light. Inside that circle were three points that pressed against his fingers. His heart began a heavy, droning beat that thudded in his ears. Looking up, he followed a thin shaft of light that shot like a pale, pointing finger to the spot on the stone floor.

James got slowly to his feet and glanced at the window. Of course, the Godwins were more practiced in the art of clandestine searching than he; they would have closed the draperies to shut out prying eyes—just as he should have. And if he had, the moon would not have found that other eye.

Discover the power of the eye.

And he had.

On this night, the night he'd been destined to come to this place at this time, a high, white moon struck a painting on the wall beside a bookcase. The moon struck and brought to life a prism of green light in the eye of a man long dead.

James approached the painting and brought his face close to the other, that of a somber, green-eyed ancestor whose name he had never known.

"My God," he murmured. "A jewel to find jewels." Set into the painted eye, so cleverly placed that in any other light it would appear no more than an adroitly executed brushstroke, was a small emerald. "The power," he said to himself and retraced the beam to the circle on the floor.

With fingers that trembled slightly, James found the leather pouch in the specially made pocket inside his jacket and extracted the ring. He knew before he lowered its crown to the stone that it would fit into the frosted green spot like a key ... Wiping sweat from his brow, he pressed the three indentations in the ring over the tiny, matching stone pyramids that awaited them, and turned. The ring became a key that softly released some hidden mechanism.

Before his straining eyes, the flagstone slid noiselessly down and back. James stared down into a formless void from which no air rose, only deep, deep, deathly cold.

The ring was the key.

Raising the candle aloft, he tried, without success, to see below.

To possess the treasure without holding the locket in your hand would mean death. Francis St. Giles had repeated his mother's warning to his son.

Still holding the candle high, James tried to decide what to do. He could not leave the ring where it was. And he could not retrieve the locket from Celine's neck.

A soft swishing sound came and, while James lifted the candle even higher, the stone slid back into place. He frowned. The stone had moved of its own volition.

Shaking his head, he retrieved the ring, studied it briefly, and returned it to its pouch and pocket. No matter. Soon he would bring Celine here and they would retrieve the jewels together. He could already anticipate her eager excitement.

The door slammed and James jumped. In an instant, the stiletto was free of the sheath on his wrist and he strode swiftly toward the passage. Bringing his breathing under control, he pushed the door open and braced himself, knife poised to strike.

No one. Another current of air through some unsealed crack had done its work. But it was time he was gone for now.

The unlit passage was empty and still. Spending the instant it took to extinguish the candle and set it aside, he retraced his steps. This time he let himself out by the scullery door and prayed no servant girl would be chastised for leaving it unlocked.

Once remounted on the black he'd left at the end of the driveway, he rode away, ducking his head beneath trees that overhung the lanes, urging the hunter to fly and the little chestnut somehow to keep pace.

Celine would be his. The treasure would be his. *Revenge* would be his. Tomorrow.

He laughed at the moon.

Chapter 26

Hands had him by the throat.

Darius awoke and struggled to sit. "Stop it! Stop! Aagh!" He flailed, grabbing at air. Nails scratched and probing fingers clawed at his neck.

A woman's fingers.

He reached for the sobbing, white-clad figure that leaned over him and filled his hands with thin lawn and soft flesh. The grip slackened, but not the sobs. Darius smiled and hauled the lush, female body across the bed until he could pin her beneath him.

"Champagne made you want me, did it, Mary?" He smiled into her hazy face and remembered how he'd thwarted her last such offer. Tonight he'd suffered a desperate shock, shock enough to arouse him. Tonight he needed one such as Summer Peach to rut over and help sweat out his brush with fear. Mary would have to do.

"Your fault." She panted and struggled.

"Spread your legs for me, *wife*. Give me some of what you lavish on pretty Colin."

The scream that issued from her throat seared every nerve, jarred every bone. She screamed and screamed and struck at his face.

"Stop it!" Her hands eluded him. "Stop ... Damn you, bitch! You've blinded me." He'd felt her gouge the thin skin over his eye. Warm, sticky blood trickled to blur his vision.

"You!" Mary screamed again, and drove upward, kicking, clawing. "You wasted our years."

At last he caught one of her hands, then the other. Binding them together in one of his own, he contrived to shift aside and light the lamp next to his bed. Huddled beside him, her face a mask of hate, her hair a tangled dull blond fright, she appeared mad.

Mad?

Darius tried to draw back, yet could not risk releasing her. "Be calm," he said, and heard his own voice shake. "You are overset. This has been a difficult evening."

"Difficult?" Her bosom rose and fell mightily beneath her disheveled nightrail and robe. She tried in vain to shake free of him. "This night has been hell!"

"Yes, yes." He must rid himself of her, and soon.

"It's there." Tears had made channels in the heavy rouge on her cheeks. "There, I tell you. There all the time!"

"Yes, yes. Be calm, my dear."

With a mighty heave she managed to throw him off. "Calm?" Before he could catch her, she leaped from the bed and retreated to a far corner. Crouching, she pointed at him. "Be calm? Can't you hear me? The jewels are there! The eye is there! Do you hear me?"

Darius swallowed and frowned. "What are you saying?"

"In the library. One of the flagstones moves. It reveals a secret place below. What do you suppose is in that place? What, Darius?" She came slowly toward him, her eyes wide and glittering. "Tell me."

He licked his lips. "Are you sure? How do you know?"

"I saw it. That's how sure I am."

"But—"

"Him. *Eagleton*. Francis's son. I saw him come to this house in the darkness and I waited until he entered belowstairs. Then I followed and watched. He had not closed the door. But then it slammed and I had to hide in that old chest in the corridor lest he find me."

A slow, heavy pounding attacked Darius's temples. "He knew where the eye was?" he asked, more to hear the words himself than in hopes of gaining an answer. "All the time he knew and he was planning to gain our trust through his supposed *love* of Celine. Hah!" He spat his venom at the thought of the betrayal. "Where is he? Is he with the jewels now?"

"No. He closed the stone and left."

Darius stared. The woman's eyes continued to bore into him. A thin line of spittle formed along her lip.

"Tomorrow he is to marry Celine," he said, strangling on the words. "What can he be planning?"

"To use his chances to be in this house for however long it takes to remove what is ours. I believe we were right in guessing the bounty to be huge."

"He did go below?"

"No. He opened the stone, looked, and closed it again. He needs more time, I tell you. That is the only reason for this marriage. I knew he could not want her."

His mouth dried. "We must stop the wedding."

"We must *not* stop the wedding." The fevered light in her eyes faded to a vicious gleam. "Through the wedding we will remove Celine from this house. Then we shall keep vigil. He will find his newfound *family* less than welcoming ... until we have done what must be done."

"What must be done?" His tongue felt swollen and his head smaller, tighter. "Make sense, woman. What do you intend to . . ." A sick dawning came to him. "No. No, that is finished, woman. It must never be spoken of again."

Mary approached until she stood over him. "It? It, Darius?" Drawing closer and closer until he smelled the scent of her sweat mixed with heavy perfume, she spread a hand on his chest. "No doubt you mean the *other* story? The real story we told the old marquess? Fear not, husband, that is one tale I never intend to repeat . . . unless . . ."

"Unless?" He shrank back.

"Unless it becomes the only way to get what we *will* have. I would retell our little *shame* if it were the only means to feel those gems in my hands."

"You cannot—"

"I *will*, damn you!" Throwing up her hands, she made fists at the heavens. "Damn you, you fool. You had it in your palm. You *had* it!" Straining wide her eyes, she parted her lips and screamed afresh, sent up a gurgling, flesh-rending shriek that froze Darius.

Dragging breath past his raw throat, he crept slowly, carefully, until he could sit on the edge of the bed. "Please, Mary, be calm. We must make plans."

"We?" She began to laugh and cry and gasp. "We? *I* shall make plans. *You* will do as I tell you."

"Yes, sweeting. Whatever you say." If only he could keep her quiet, he might be able to accomplish her removal before she ruined everything for him.

"Look at me, Darius."

He did so.

"Is there not a question that you need to ask?" She rocked back and forth, plucking at the ribbons on her crumpled robe. "Don't you want me to tell you how Eagleton opened the stone, husband?"

"How did he?" He managed to swallow.

So swiftly he had no time to retreat, she clutched a handful of his nightshirt and twisted. "You *had* what he did it with." Her voice fell. "You gave it away. You, the man determined to make his old *friend* pay for having been born wealthy when you were no more than the son of an impoverished squire. *You*, who resented the very kindness that friend and his family showed you until your resentment turned to poison. *You* designed a plan that would bring us both the justice we deserved and *you* gave away the *key* to that justice."

His limbs quaked. Sweat slid between his shoulder blades. "The key?"

"The key! You chose to use Francis's ring to incriminate him. When he took it back from his father, he banished himself from this house and from this country. But he carried with him the only means to gaining the treasure. He took the *ring*, husband, and he gave it to his son.

"That ring is the key!"

Chapter 27

Dawn breaking over Dorset's hills.

From the top of Blackburn Manor's front steps, James gazed skyward, followed a flight of swifts piercing a path through yellow-streaked indigo. The birds rose like a spearhead and dropped again on a current of air. A wind, fresh from stroking moors he could not see, brought scents of heather and gorse.

His wedding day.

Closing his eyes, James bowed his head and willed his mind to be still.

Celine.

A surge, warm, searing, driving through him with unfamiliar sweetness, filled all the empty spaces. Soon enough would come the time for the other—time for retribution and final confrontation with evils of the past. Today there was only Celine.

"Mr. Eagleton!"

He started and searched around.

"Down here."

"Who's there?" He walked to lean over the balusters and looked into Miss Fisher's upturned face. His heart made a mighty leap. "What is it? Celine?" Taking the steps two at a time, he dashed down to confront the woman.

"Oh, Mr. Eagleton . . . I mean, my lord. I—"

"What's happened?" He advanced and she cowered in the shadow of the steps. "Tell me."

"I'm afraid."

He stopped. "Of what?"

She looked all around. "There are things you do not know."

"Where is Celine?"

"At Knighthead."

"Does she prepare for our wedding?"

Miss Fisher covered her mouth and nodded. Dark smudges beneath her eyes, together with unkempt hair, suggested she had not slept.

"Then what is it, madam?"

She shook her head. Her eyes grew huge.

James calmed himself. "Is Celine in some sort of trouble?"

"No. It's . . . She has not had an easy life. I should have been able to stop them . . . I should have found a way to take her away." Her slender fingers wound together. "I was not . . . I made poor decisions."

"Are you talking about what Celine calls her parents' wild turns?"

"Yes, yes. She suffered, Mr. . . . my lord. Evil does terrible things to people, and there has been great evil in that house, evil that drives them to wickedness."

"Indeed," James said patiently. "But that is over now."

"No! No!" She caught his hand. "Please. It is not over. It can never be over until . . . You don't know the danger. You don't know how far they are capable of going."

The poor creature had no means of knowing the Godwins would soon be banished from Knighthead and from her life—from all of their lives. He smiled.

"Go home to Celine. Take care of her this morning, Lettie—until I can take care of her myself."

"I need to tell you—"

"No, you don't. Please return home. Everything will be well now."

"Celine told me what happened last night. She told me who your are."

"Yes, yes." He patted her hand. "I'll have Won Tel take you back."

"There is danger, my lord. You must be cautious."

As so often happened, Won Tel appeared as if he had heard his name before James spoke it. "You need me, James?" He came down the steps but gave his attention not to James but to Miss Fisher. "Good morning, Lettie."

"Good morning." Miss Fisher's troubled gaze settled on Won Tel with what appeared to be hope. "He will not listen to me."

"Miss Fisher is needlessly upset," James said. "The excitement has disturbed her. Kindly return her to Knighthead."

"But . . . You must listen to me."

"I *know* what it is that you want to tell me," James told her with great kindness. "Do not concern yourself further. I shall look forward to seeing you at my wedding."

He left them then and returned to his chamber. The time had come to make his own preparations.

The rapidly lightening sky beyond the windows drew him to look outside. From there he could see Knighthead.

Miss Fisher had been deeply troubled . . . more deeply troubled than should be reasonable.

He shrugged and stripped off his shirt. This was no time to be pondering the peculiarities of servants.

* * *

"I do." The deep, possessive fire in James's eyes was echoed in his voice.

David was speaking again, in clear, ringing tones. Celine didn't hear a word. She watched James's face and saw him nod and smile at her.

She smiled in return, folding her fingers tightly into his. A sniff made her glance aside—at Lettie, who held a handkerchief to her nose and smiled through glistening tears.

"Celine?"

She started and looked at David. "Yes?"

A gust of laughter passed over the congregation in Little Puddle's tiny church, a congregation swelled by the number of villagers who had pressed in to see the spectacle of a noble wedding.

"Celine," David repeated, frowning at her. "*Will* you?"

"Oh, yes. Absolutely. That's *exactly* what I'll do."

The laughter became louder, and Celine bit her lip. "Did I say something wrong, James?"

"No, beloved. What you said was *exactly* right!"

"Good," she whispered. "I'm very nervous."

"I know." James took her hand in his. "This will be a sign that you are mine and I am yours." With that he slid a ring onto her finger, a band of emeralds that blazed green fire from every perfect stone.

Celine looked from the ring to James. "I never thought I'd own an emerald. Now I do." And she had him, that was the most wonderful, the most amazing truth.

David cleared his throat. "You are man and wife."

"We are?"

"We are," James said, gathering her into his arms. "We have been for at least a minute, my golden girl. My *lady*." Amid the rustle and whisper of the congregation, he kissed her lips, holding her so tightly she could scarcely breathe.

The organ struck up a rousing march, and James turned her to face the world for the first time as Lady Eagleton. "They're cheering," she murmured, and caught Mama's eye. Rather than cheering, Mama had pressed her lips together fiercely. She stared back at Celine before turning her head abruptly away.

They shall not spoil this day. Celine rested her hand atop James's arm, and they began their walk down the aisle. From James's right, where he'd stood to act as groomsman, Won Tel moved to fall in beside Liam. A vision in sapphire brocade with turquoise silk pants peeping from beneath the hem, Liam had been ecstatic with her role as Celine's bridesmaid—despite Mama's ranting about the unsuitability of "elevating" savages above their stations.

Liam touched Celine's arm and returned the bouquet of yellow roses she'd held for her during the ceremony.

The congregation became a smiling, whispering blur that Celine saw through a film of happy tears. James covered her hand atop his arm and swept her firmly from the church to the flower-decked silver-gray landau that awaited them.

"I wish I need not sit beside you," James said when they were settled.

Celine glanced at him in puzzlement.

His face serious, he studied her. "I want to be where I can look at you. Celine, I will never grow tired of looking at you."

"Or I, you," she said without embarrassment. "Every female on earth must envy me today—as they will every day for the rest of my life."

James raised a brow. His dark gray cutaway coat drew a sharp contrast to a deeply ruffled white shirt and waistcoat. Flouting the expected, he had chosen trousers of a paler gray and black hessians rather than pantaloons and silk stockings.

His sudden smile dazzled. "Am I to assume you truly like what you see, my lady?"

"Exactly!" Celine tossed her head and ventured to trace his long, tanned fingers where they rested on a hard-muscled thigh. "There is at this moment a veritable army of small winged beasts on the loose in my stomach—and elsewhere. There is nothing about you that doesn't thrill me, James. I suppose that is an inappropriate remark from a young female, but since I am a married lady I consider myself free to speak as I please."

James laughed aloud, but managed to wave and pluck flowers from the coach garlands to throw to onlookers. "You, my girl, are soon to learn exactly how I intend to set those winged beasts free." He inclined his head to a couple who waved. Then he found a coin to throw into the outstretched hands of a small boy. "Let me see, the return to Blackburn Manor will take perhaps half an hour, or a little longer allowing for brief stops."

"Mm," Celine said as the coach rolled slowly forward. A cheerful bellow brought her attention to Lord Casterbridge's tall figure. With a flourishing bow he saluted her while the small, gorgeous Countess Lafoget, resplendent in rose-pink satin, held his arm and dropped into a deep curtsy. "This day is . . . It is too much, James. And I do not want to wait half an hour to be alone with you. I don't want to wait a minute."

"Wait you must, my passionate lady." Continuing to acknowledge well-wishers, he dropped a hand to her leg and grinned when she jumped. "Half an hour and we are at the manor. Hours more for the wedding *déjeuner* and who knows what other foolish ritual. But fear not, I shall entertain you for the drive at least."

"Entertain me?" she said through a smile. "How so? Shall you sing, perhaps?"

"You mock me, madam. And you show a remarkable lack of confidence in my ability as an entertainer. I am going to tell you a story—more an account—of what is to occur."

"You mean our going away?"

"No. I mean what will happen before our going away."

"You have not told me where we are going."

"I shall tell you soon enough. In the meantime, let me explain how I intend to undress you."

"What?" A throbbing, fluid burning flooded her body. "James! Not here."

"Yes, here. Who will hear, but you?"

"The coachman?"

"Hardly." His sultry gaze traveled her length. "I shall not begin with that fetching lace whatnot that floats so beguilingly from your hair."

"You won't?" Her face grew hot.

"No. I have other plans for that. First, the dress."

"Oh. Not my gloves? My slippers?"

"Definitely not. You shall turn your back to me . . . Ah, we have an audience—do wave at that old Ruby Rose."

Celine pulled a rose from her bouquet and dropped it into Ruby Rose's hands, then selected another for Mrs. Strickland, who stood beside her.

"When your back is to me, I shall undo the tapes of your gown," he whispered. "Have I told you that when I saw you walk toward me in the church, I decided that on you, white lawn and silver lace becomes a diabolical design intended to cost a man his mind?"

"You have not told me." She could scarcely breathe.

"I decided that the only way I may save my mind

is to ensure that I touch you everywhere that clever confection covers you."

"James, please." She fidgeted on her seat, shocked by the heavy heat in her belly.

"Please?" He played with a curl by her ear. "You do not have to beg. I will do these things gladly. The silver lace is particularly provocative. What witch would have devised those clever points beneath your breasts—the points that end where your succulent nipples begin? Undoubtedly the design is to ensure that I know exactly where to dip beneath the bodice and find that flesh. That pink, thrusting flesh is stiff now, is it not, Celine? Stiff and yearning for my touch."

She parted her lips on a gasp, and turned her flaming face toward him. "You are the very devil, my lord. You know what you do to me, don't you?"

"Oh, yes. I do, thank God. Those other silver points." His eyes traveled downward to where the lace overskirt on her dress finished at her hips. "They are also markers, my love. Beneath those you already grow moist and aching, do you not?"

"You destroy my composure, my lord."

"Indeed, I hope I do. The gown will slip easily from your shoulders and I shall lay it aside. Then, very slowly, so very slowly, my hands shall learn you. Your face and throat, your shoulders and back—to that tiny waist—and your beautiful breasts. Ah, yes, I intend to test and trace them with great care—to prepare them, Celine."

"I do not—"

"Yes, you do understand. I will make them ready for my lips, sweeting, for my tongue and teeth."

She closed her eyes and drew air into her lungs. The sway of the carriage sent her against James's unyielding arm. In steadying her, he contrived to make the most fleeting contact with a straining nipple, and a small cry escaped her lips.

He groaned and she looked into his face. In the rigid tautness of his desire, tanned skin stretched over sharply defined bone. "I knew you . . . When we were together before, I knew it brought you pleasure," she told him. "I long to bring you that pleasure again."

"That pleasure and more," he said, his voice thick. "More than you can yet know."

He shifted, straightening his back sharply. Celine glanced down and pressed her stomach. What she had felt on those previous occasions was now clearly visible beneath the skin-hugging contours of his trousers. "You are . . . You are very large, my lord."

Grimacing, he followed her stare. "I pray I do not frighten you."

"Why should you?"

He groaned and took his lower lip in his teeth. "My innocent little one. You drive me *mad*."

"You are in pain? Oh, James, how can I help you? Let me do something to ease you now."

"Silence." Crossing his legs, he turned his finely sculpted mouth down. "*I* am entertaining you. Next, I will remove your chemise."

She did gasp aloud at that. "While I stand, my lord? And in the light?"

"Most definitely. And now you will be facing me."

"But my gloves," she said in a small voice. "My stockings."

"Mm. What a picture I see. Your perfect, full breasts. Your rosy nipples begging for my attention. Your softly rounded belly and hips and the golden hair that shields the place where you are totally a woman and totally mine."

Surely the coachman, even over the grinding

wheels and horses' hooves—and the shouts from passersby—must hear *something* of what James said.

"Then it will be time to use that delightful wisp of lace from your hair. When I remove it, the time will have come to let down your beautiful hair, beloved, to take out the roses and the pearls that so become Liam's braided masterpiece. The roses will feel marvelous as I trail them over your skin—all of your skin. And the lace will make a most provocative veil when I drape it about you. A veil that will only make more unbearable our joint desire to revel in each other. I will kiss you through the lace, Celine. My mouth will dampen the lace, the lace that will graze—and craze you."

"There are the gates of the manor," Celine said, her hands at her throat. "We are almost there."

"Almost there indeed." James bent to kiss her neck. "At the very last, I shall remove your gloves, finger by finger, and your stockings. Ah, yes, your stockings shall receive extra attention. They will probably require exceedingly slow attention. In fact, I believe it will be necessary for me to kneel before you to do justice to the task. And to improve my concentration, I may find it appropriate to test that part of you that was so responsive to my attentions when last I checked."

Celine gave a small shriek and covered her mouth.

"You do not think you will enjoy this?"

Aware that she must be scarlet, she nodded.

"Good." James sounded immensely gratified. "In that case, we must hope this polite social nonsense will not take *too* long."

"James?"

"Yes?"

"Shall I tell you how I intend to undress you?"

For an instant he showed surprise. Then he caught her hand and brought it to his smiling lips. "You are an impudent little romp in lady's clothing. We shall see who does what when the time comes. Now. Prepare yourself to appear demure and overwhelmed by the appropriate sensibilities."

She scarcely heard the happy clapping of James's household servants, but she held her husband's arm and managed to turn up her mouth and murmur thanks as she mounted the steps.

In moments she was once again seated at the table in the small but perfect dining room. A further transformation had been accomplished since the previous evening. Twisted white satin ribbons were looped from the chandelier to the walls, forming a softly shimmering canopy. In the center of the table stood a tiered bride's cake that sparkled in its crystallized white-sugar coating.

Maids came and went, placing and removing dishes, listening to the murmured instructions of the formidable butler. Celine ate not a bite until James placed a perfect sugar swan upon her plate and broke off a tiny piece. This he raised to her lips and, watching her mouth with hooded eyes, waited until she allowed him to place the morsel upon her tongue.

The company sighed and Celine lowered her gaze to her lap.

For what felt like an interminable length of time, the meal continued. Mama and Papa drank an inordinate quantity of the wine and spirits that flowed ceaselessly. The little Countess Lafoget giggled and administered frequent and sharp raps of her fan to the marquess, who showed obvious pleasure in indulging her. David and Liam whispered together. Lettie sat stiffly beside Won Tel and seemed unable to relax.

"I believe it is time to allow our moonlings to retire." Lord Casterbridge's sudden announcement produced instant silence. "We are selfish in keeping them."

James found Celine's hand. A muscle in his cheek flexed. "If you insist, Uncle."

"I do, my boy. But first there is the matter of a certain decision I have made. I believe it will meet with everyone's approval. You will remember Windham, James?"

James nodded. "Indeed. The family retreat a small distance from Weymouth—on the coast."

"The very place. It was a favorite of your father's. In the old King's time your grandparents used to take Francis and me there during the little season when King George chose to bathe in the sea there."

Celine felt James's restlessness. "I believe I remember the stories, Uncle," he said.

"When the royal bathing machine—had a crown on the top, y'know—when it rolled into the waters, a second such vehicle rolled beside it from which a band played 'God Save the King' repeatedly throughout the whole process. Odd, if you ask me."

"Yes." James's grip on her hand tightened, and Celine chewed her lip to suppress a smile at his impatience.

"Yes, anyway." Lord Casterbridge straightened his shoulders. "Windham is yours, James. Yours and Celine's for when you feel like going for a few days of complete privacy—as young people ought to do—frequently."

"Thank you, Uncle."

"Thank you," Celine echoed, overwhelmed.

"Of course, Morsham Hall will be yours in time—"

"I don't want to—"

"Talk about it," the marquess finished for James. "Thank you for that. Our estates are considerable. I won't waste time listing our homes in Yorkshire and Wales. For now the important issue is your present home." He held up a hand. "No, James, let me finish. We have missed too many years. I want you to stay nearby. This is a pleasant enough little place, but you belong in something that *means* something. Knighthead will do nicely for some time."

Celine saw James frown and followed his sharp glance toward her parents. They continued to smile fixedly at the marquess. She was surprised that they would be happy with the prospect of having not only their daughter, but her husband in residence.

"You, Darius and Mary, have not been forgotten. As Celine's parents you are my responsibility. I shall not shirk that duty. The fortuitous discovery of a delightful cottage in Sussex has pleased me, just as I know it will please you. I will arrange for you to move there directly. You should be well installed within the fortnight."

Celine's breath caught in her throat. Surely she misunderstood the marquess; he could not intend to put Mama and Papa out of their home.

Mama and Papa's fixed smiles turned slowly to horrified stares. Papa made a strange noise and choked. Coughing against his brocade sleeve, he sputtered until his face turned purple.

"Think nothing of it, old chap," Lord Casterbridge said expansively. "No need to be overwhelmed. Least I could do for me nephew's new in-laws. I'll make sure Knighthead is put in perfect order by the time the bride and groom return from their going away.

What would happen? Celine passed her fingers to her cheeks. Nothing would happen. After today there would be no more fearsome hours of imprisonment.

Mama rose from the table so abruptly that her chair overbalanced and, followed by Papa, she rushed from the room.

The marquess flapped a hand at Celine. "Don't

worry about them, m'dear. Difficult handing over the only daughter, don't y'know. They'll get over the loss, and no doubt the new quarters will keep them busy soon enough.

"Now, James. Take your bride to bed, boy!"

The steadiness of his hands pleased James. Now, for Celine as well as for himself, he must be in total command. This first time would doubtless be difficult for her.

Standing in the gloom of his dressing room, he removed his coat. His jaw clenched, with passion and concern. At last he would possess her. For that he praised the fates. His rod sprang full within his trousers, but he could scarcely bear the thought of causing her pain.

Even now she was in her chamber, separated from his by this room. She would be waiting for him, simply waiting, expecting him to guide her into the fulfillment of her passion.

This he would do. And later, when their bodies joined again, she would be ready for the total ecstasy he knew could be hers—and his with her.

With a single snap, he tore free his neckcloth and cast it aside. His arousal drove him. He must let Celine see his adoration of her, his longing for her—but he must do all in his power to save her from the fear that could come in that last moment.

Now. Now it was time. He approached the door to her chamber.

"Wait, James."

He spun around, disoriented. "What?"

"I told you to wait." The door to his quarters opened wider to reveal Mary Godwin. "Come here, James."

Rage flooded his veins. He made fists at his sides, afraid that if he did not control his hands he might take this woman by the throat. "Get out," he told her and heard the hiss of his voice. "Leave me at once."

"I cannot." She shook her head. "You would not want me to do so. Come closer and let me see you."

Disbelieving the moment, he approached until he towered over her. "What do you want?"

Before he guessed her intent, she stroked her fingers over his mouth.

James caught her wrist and thrust her hand from him.

Mary Godwin's lips twisted. "So like Francis. Why didn't I see it? You have his eyes. Those gray eyes, like rapier steel by moonlight. Hard. Francis was a hard man."

He tried to push her away, but she clawed a handful of his shirt and hung on. "You must listen to me, James. Listen well. Leave this house immediately. Do you understand?"

"Leave?" Incredulous, he laughed. "*Leave?* I am about to join my bride, madam. It is you who will leave immediately."

Prying loose her hand, he tore away. "Go!"

Again she sprang at him, but missed her mark. Panting, she fell to her knees. "It is you who will go, *my lord.*"

James turned aside and made to approach Celine's room.

"No!" the woman shrieked.

He swung around, loomed over her. "Silence! Do you understand? Silence, before you frighten my gentle wife."

"Gentle *wife*?" Still kneeling, she spread wide her arms. "Don't you know? Can't you guess? She cannot be your *gentle wife*. Not now. Not ever."

"Madam—"

"I should have stopped this last night. But I was so ashamed—"

"You shall not hinder me—"

"Your father raped me, my lord."

"No!"

"He raped me although he was already married to your mother and although he knew I did not want him."

James shook his head. "No! Go! My father was the most honorable of men."

"Hah!" She drew her lips back from her teeth. "Why do you think your grandfather banished him from his sight—from England even? The old marquess learned what his son did to me."

His head thundered. He could no longer see other than blackness shot through with red, red fire. "You lie."

"There was a proof that I offered. Your grandfather offered that same proof to your father, and when he took it, he admitted his crime against me and against his family."

"I do not believe you."

"Believe what you like." Her voice fell to a whisper. "But hear this one thing, son of Francis St. Giles. You cannot go to the woman you call your bride."

"No, no." He shook his head and moaned at the crashing pain behind his eyes. "This has nothing to do with me."

"It has everything to do with you," Mary Godwin said. "You father violated me, and the result of the violation was a child. Celine is that child."

"Stop!"

"You, my lord, have married your *sister!*"

Chapter 28

A t last she would hold the Sainsbury gems in her hands. Sending Darius back alone had been a brilliant stroke. The poor coxcomb had been entirely in his altitudes by the time she'd given him into Colin's care for the homeward drive. By now her dear husband would be abed and unconscious.

She waited until the coach she'd borrowed from Blackburn Manor left, then flew through Knighthead's front doorway and along the corridor toward the back of the house. By the time Darius faced the dawn and finished casting up his accounts she, Mary Godwin, would be far from here and a rich woman.

Hurrying, holding the little leather pouch that contained her future against her breast, she remembered Eagleton's anguished face, the way he'd thrown her aside and dashed from his chamber—without a jacket. The ease with which she'd gained possession of the pouch and its contents had been an unexpected boon. She held back a laugh. At this moment Francis St. Giles's beloved son was wandering the countryside alone with his torment. And Celine . . . ? Who cared what frightened meanderings her mind must be taking as she waited in vain for her arrogant, irresistible prize of a husband?

When she reached the library, Mary threw open the door . . . and smothered a scream.

Darius stood, swaying, in the center of the room. "Hello, Mary." He rubbed the back of a hand over bloodshot eyes. "They said you'd come straight here. Said you were *cunning* . . . Yes, that's what they said. You'd find a way to get it. That's what they told me, and they were right!" He hiccupped loudly.

"*They?*" Mary said carefully. She dropped her hands and edged them behind her back. "Are you hearing voices, Darius?"

"They," he said, sounding petulant, looking past her.

Mary's skin grew tight and cold, and the tiny hairs on her spine prickled. She rotated slowly around . . . and came face to face with Bertram and Percival Letchwith.

"Mary." Bertram made an exaggerated bow while his court card of a son grinned, showing yellowed teeth. "Such a clever woman," Bertram continued. "We thought we would have difficult work ahead of us, but you have made the way simple—for all of us."

She spun back to Darius. "What is he saying? What does he mean? Answer me."

" 'S nothing, m'dear. Had to do something to make up to Bertram and Percival for the loss of Celine. There'll be plenty enough for all of us down there." He nodded to the flagstones. "We'll split the bounty in half. Half for Bertram and Percival and half for me. Couldn't be fairer. Give me the ring."

"Half for you?" She heard her voice soar out of control. He intended that she receive nothing of what she'd spent her life to obtain. "Half for *them?* Never! Do you hear me? Never!'

"Give me the ring."

A hand closed on her wrist behind her back. "Here

it is, Darius." The pouch was wrenched from her helpless fingers. "Mary was keeping it safe for us, weren't you, Mary?"

She opened her mouth to shriek, only to find herself yanked against Percival Letchwith's bony body. His hand, clamped to her face, shut off all but her muffled moans.

"Quiet, Mary," Darius said, straining his eyes open and placing a finger on his lips. "Shh. We don't want to awaken the servants. You just sit over there and wait while Bertram and I go below and see what we can find."

Letchwith was already on his knees, scrabbling about, running his fingers over the dusty stones.

"I'm coming with you," Percival announced. "I can come, can't I, Papa? To, er, help watch over our interests."

"Got to stay with her," Darius said, slurring his words together. "Can't trust the bitch."

Mary managed to part her teeth. She bit down hard on one of Percival's fingers and promptly found herself tossed to the floor.

"She bit me!" Percival capered about, shaking his hand. "It hurts!"

"Here it is." Red-faced and puffing, Bertram grinned up at Darius. He produced the ring and pressed it into the place for which it had been made. "Darius, bring the candle. Of course you shall come, Percival."

"And so shall I," Mary announced. Be damned if they would ever be alone with what belonged to her.

"You'll stay here," Darius declared. "You watch her, Percival."

"It's opening!" Bertram struggled upright and peered down into the widening hole at his feet. "It's true, by God. Come, Percival."

Ignoring Darius, Bertram sat on the edge of the

opening and dangled his scrawny legs until Mary heard his feet hit something hard. A step. There were steps leading to her treasure and, thanks to Darius, this thief was about to use them.

"Wait for me," Darius said, tottering after Bertram's disappearing form.

"And me." Percival followed. As his head sank from sight he called, "Remain there, madam. We shall return."

She remained—until the hollow sound of footfalls stopped. Then she counted to five. "Twenty years," she said aloud. "Twenty years I have waited for the triumph of this night. You shall not wrest it from me."

Bundling her skirts, she stepped into the hole.

Chapter 29

"**B**ring some brandy," Lettie said, and Celine watched disinterestedly as Won Tel left the bedchamber. "Liam, how long ago did James leave?"

"I cannot tell. Celine was wandering in the corridors. That is all I can say." Liam's soft voice shook, that much Celine knew, but she could not seem to think.

Won Tel returned quickly bearing a glass and a decanter upon a tray. He poured brandy and gave it to Lettie. "This will help revive her."

Lettie held the glass to Celine's lips. "Sip, little one. Take a sip for Lettie."

She shook her head. "Where is James? I want James."

"Hush," Lettie said, stroking Celine's hair. "We shall find James for you. Drink a little, *please*, Celine."

She parted her lips, took a small swallow, and coughed. The spirit burned her throat. "Why has he left me? How have I offended him?" When they'd come upstairs from the wedding breakfast, he had been so loving, so anxious to be with her forever. "He came to me . . . There was such anger in him. Then he left . . . he just left."

"Won Tel," Lettie said. "Surely you saw him."

"I did not, more's the pity."

"When *I* see him I shall use his wicked little knife to chop off his toes!" Liam, her hair wriggling free of its braids to snake down her back, marched back and forth across the chamber. She pounded her small fists against her hips. "It is in order for a girl to fear her wedding night and to wish to flee. It is *not* in order for a *man* to do so. Oooh, I am exceedingly vexed, and he shall rue that he has made me so."

"Liam," Won Tel said sternly. "There is something here of which we know nothing. You will not speak so of James."

"I will speak as I please! I do not accept the will of men unless it pleases me to do so."

"Please," Lettie said imploringly. "Can't we spend our energies finding his lordship and discovering the meaning of this?"

He had left her because, after all, he found her displeasing.

Loud voices sounded from the hall below. Celine recognized David's raised tones and shifted to sit on the edge of the blue Egyptian couch on which Lettie had made her recline. "David. I want to see David."

Before anyone could react, Liam darted from the room to return in a matter of seconds, clinging to David's arm. "James has run away," she told him, glaring around. "He has fled his own wedding night like a blushing female, and—"

"Be calm, Liam," David said, patting her hands. "I came straight here from seeing James. I hoped someone could explain what has happened."

Celine leaped to her feet. "You have seen him? Where is he?"

David's green eyes darkened with concern. "You are not yourself, Celine. Sit, I beg you."

"Tell me where James is!"

"Tell us," Lettie echoed. "Something terrible has happened and we must right it immediately."

"James rode past me on that black hunter of his. He appeared, er, removed from the world."

Dizziness assailed Celine and she closed her eyes.

"I had scarcely returned to the rectory from the wedding breakfast when I remembered I had left some books I needed at the church. I was on my way there when James passed."

"Where is he?" Blackness drifted behind Celine's eyelids.

"At Windham, I believe," David responded simply.

"Windham?" The collected company repeated the word.

"Yes. As luck would have it, I had not yet stabled my horse. I rode after him. He said . . ." David frowned in concentration. "He said he was getting away, that he wasn't going back. Never. That's what he said. He ranted about evil fate—and a mistake—and when he turned his mount into a gallop I heard him say Windham. At least, I believe that's what he said."

"Then it's to Windham that we shall go. How far distant is this place?"

"Not far," David told Lettie. "Less than two hours' ride to the south. I will go with you."

"Celine and I will go alone. I'll trouble you to explain the way to me, David."

At the grating anger in Lettie's voice, Celine opened her eyes.

Already her dear friend had left her side to rummage through the clothes that had been moved from Knighthead to Blackburn Manor the previous day. She brought forth one of Celine's heaviest cloaks and draped it around her shoulders. "Come," she said, smiling, but with determination in her eyes. "We shall find your husband and hear together his reason for this cruel outrage."

* * *

The night mirrored his brain, his very soul: black and storm-shattered.

Celine was his *sister*, his father's daughter by Mary Godwin.

God! Surely not. Yet how could he not believe the woman? Celine had been born a few months after Francis St. Giles fled England with his wife and son. Why? When James insisted to Mary Godwin that his father had not known exactly the reason for the old marquess's deep displeasure, she had been quick to point out that a father was unlikely to tell his son that he'd raped a woman and left her expecting his child.

Your grandfather insisted that his illegitimate grand-daughter be brought up in the comfort of one of her libertine father's family residences. The old marquess was a deeply religious man, deeply honorable. I threw myself on his mercy. I feared that Darius would cast me aside. The marquess said that he would give Francis a chance to defend himself against my accusation.

With Windham's whitewashed walls and slate roof at his back, James turned the black hunter toward the sea and urged the animal downhill to the edge of the cliffs. Lightning rent the sky, ripped downward, and bled wide like rupturing veins of blinding light, satisfied only when their paths clawed into the shifting ocean.

To give your father his due, he did not deny his crime. And so, in exchange for keeping his bestiality a secret from your gentle mother, Francis left England. The marquess persuaded Darius to take Celine as his own—which he has done with admirable kindness—and to shield my shame. You do see that I could not allow this travesty of a marriage to continue?

James had seen. It was more than he could suffer. And at the end of his life, the man who had sired Celine had still yearned to reclaim Knighthead and the Sainsbury gems. Despite his own guilt, despite the just settlement that caused the forfeit, he had urged his son to take it back. Francis could never have guessed that James and Celine might fall in love.

"Damn you!"

The wind took his voice and sucked it into a barreling roar of thunder.

"Damn." His throat burned. "Damn you, Father!" The heavens opened and rain sliced earthward. Pressing the hunter forward, James stared downward over the sheer drop of limestone. Roiling spume bit at bundled needles of rock jutting from the narrow beach.

No man could survive a plunge into those screaming jaws.

The horse tossed up its head and the whites of its eyes glowed. The beast pawed the rough ground and made to rear away; its flesh quivered beneath James's thighs.

"Hold," James ordered. "Hold, I say."

But the animal wheeled and skittered, and James searched for what might have unnerved it, besides the storm. The reason was immediately evident. Two horses picked a path toward him, the rider of the first leading the second. Two women, the first upright, the second bowed forward over her mount's neck.

James waited. Two women riding alone, in the dark of a storm? They drew closer.

"James? Lord Eagleton? Is that you?"

He drew in a great breath and that breath froze within his breast. "No. No! Go back!"

They continued downhill until the first woman, Lettie Fisher, peered at him from beneath the hood of her cloak. "We will *not* go back, my lord. I have brought you your wife."

"Oh, God!" He turned up his face and closed his eyes. "Why must I be tormented further? Go. Go, I beg you. Take her. Make her forget she ever saw me."

Rather than follow his directions, Lettie spurred her horse on until she drew level with him. Leaning to grasp at his own mount's bridle, she fastened her eyes on James's. "I will not take her away. And she will never forget you. Any more than you will forget her. You are suffering, my lord. Please, in the name of the God you plead to, tell me what has happened."

He wiped the sheeting rain from his eyes and made himself look at Celine. She all but lay upon her horse's neck, and even in the darkness he could make out that her cloak was soaked.

His heart pummeled his chest and pounded in his ears. "She will become ill," he said, scarcely above a whisper. "Take her home to her bed, I beg you."

"Her bed is your bed, James. She is your—"

"No! Do not say that word again."

"Celine is your wife."

"Stop it!" Celine lifted her head and her hands slid from the reins to brace her weight against the saddle. "I do not care, Lettie. He doesn't want me. We will leave now."

"James," Lettie said, plucking her sodden garments away from her body. "We will not leave this place—not until you explain yourself."

"She will become gravely sick, I tell you," he said. Celine's face was a pale shadow beneath her hood. "Please—"

"Tell us."

"Tell you?" He laughed and averted his face. "All right. I'll tell you. Celine's charming mother paid me a visit and explained the circumstances of her daughter's birth."

When Lettie didn't respond he looked at her. "It would have been better had you not forced this issue, madam. But, since you insist, it appears that Celine's mother and my father had a . . . a shared incident. The result of that incident was . . ." Now Celine would suffer the horror that had been his these past hours, and he would have spared her that had there been a way. "The result was Celine. My 'wife' and I had the same *father*, madam. Does that information satisfy you?"

Lightning struck again, casting the faces of Lettie and Celine as stark, frozen masks. In that instant James saw Celine's eyes, at first dull, gradually widen in numb horror.

"I was wrong." Lettie grabbed his sleeve. "I should never have allowed it."

He covered her hand. "You knew?"

She shook her head. "You don't understand." Lettie turned in her saddle and shortened the leading rein, drawing Celine nearer. "This is all my fault. I was young—seventeen—and I was alone in a great house far from my home. He was so powerful and yet so gentle—and I was so lonely."

"What has this to do with what has happened tonight?"

"The Godwins visited my master and mistress—I was a maid—and Mrs. Godwin spoke to me on the day I was to be sent away."

"This is irrelevant." He could not bear to look upon Celine's face, yet he could not make himself look away.

"The man was a guest, a foreigner. From France. He convinced me that he wished to bring me comfort and . . . and . . ."

"And?"

"And Celine was the product of the *comfort* he brought me. I did not know what he was about until it was too late. He spoke to me sweetly and drew me with him . . . and then he left forever. When I came to you this morning, it was to warn you that the Godwins would stop at nothing to get what they want."

Very slowly, James turned to Lettie. "Celine was . . . ?" He frowned, trying to understand.

"Yes," Lettie said softly. "Celine is *my* daughter. The Godwins had been unable to have a child. They persuaded me to allow them to take her as their own. In exchange they would make sure we were both cared for and they agreed to my one demand, that I be allowed to remain close to Celine."

Blood seeped back into James's veins. "You let those people use Celine? You let them abuse her and lock her away and arrange to marry her to that filthy, perverted Letchwith?"

Lettie's chin came up. "I cared for her always. I would not have allowed anything terrible to happen to her. And I would have managed to take her away rather than see her married to that man. But I had no choice when I was little more than a child myself and expecting a babe. I could never have given her anything."

"You could have given her *love*."

"I gave her love," Lettie said, very low. "Love doesn't fill the stomach or put clothes on the back. I did what I thought was best, and then it was too late—for both of us."

"Did you know the foul trick the Godwins played on my father?"

Lettie bowed her head and whispered, "Yes. God help me, yes. It was that wickedness that I tried to tell you this morning. Several times when Mrs. Godwin was, er, in her cups, she boasted of how she had tricked the old marquess by foisting another man's bastard upon him. She told me she did so to make things right for her and Mr. Godwin. He'd had so much less than your father, and she never got over the fact that your father didn't want her. They plotted to get rid of him and lay their hands on what was his—his home.

"Mrs. Godwin managed to obtain the ring that your father always wore—a gift from his mother—and she told the marquess that your father gave it to her out of guilt after he—after he had been with her."

James ground his hands together and willed himself to remain silent and listen.

"She told the marquess that he should offer the ring to Francis," Lettie continued. "If he took it without question, he would appear to confirm her story. Francis did take it. Mrs. Godwin said he did so because he believed the ring had been returned by a . . . a woman of ill repute in whose company he had awakened after being drugged. He remembered nothing of the event, but assumed he had sought the female's services. The marquess would not suffer debauchery."

"The Godwin woman *told* you all this? And she didn't fear you might reveal her secret?"

"She spoke of it when she had been drinking—which was often. And she was certain I would never jeopardize Celine's position. Mrs. Godwin reminded me often that Celine would hate me if she discovered I had given her away." Lettie made to touch Celine, but withdrew her hand again. "When I discovered the truth I should have said something to the marquess, but by then the lies were told and your parents had left. And they were still rich, even if they did have to leave England."

Finally he knew it all. "England, the country they loved. The East killed my mother. Did Mrs. Godwin ever tell you what they were searching for at Knighthead?"

"No. Not exactly. But I am certain they believed something valuable was hidden there."

"And I know what it is," James said, almost to himself, and immediately swore under his breath and vaulted from his horse. Celine, silent throughout, slid sideways in the saddle and began to fall.

He caught her as she would have hit the muddy ground and cradled her in his arms. "She's fainted. I must make her warm. Quickly. Bring the horses."

"I tried to tell you." Lettie's voice held agony. "You would not listen."

"And that I regret."

Leaving Lettie, he strode uphill to the little lodge and booted open the door. Praise fortune that the place smelled clean and aired. No doubt his uncle had made certain of that.

Struggling, he managed to locate and light a lantern. Still holding Celine against him, James crouched before the wide, rough stone fireplace and lighted the fire that had been left prepared.

"She must be put into dry clothing." Lettie had entered behind him and came to kneel anxiously at his side. She pointed. "Will I find anything in there?" A door opened from the main room, revealing a bedchamber beyond.

"Yes, I'm sure. As I recall, there were always things kept here in case someone paid an unexpected visit." Flames leaped up the chimney, sending a blessed glow over the walls and the simple but comfortable furnishings. "Hold Celine here by the fire. I'll see what can be found."

Within minutes he returned with an armload of female garments. "Help me take off her cloak," he instructed Lettie.

Beneath the rain-soaked wool, Celine still wore her wedding dress. James swallowed. "What have we all done to her? Please, let her be all right. Somehow we can recover from this and carry on. We must get her to bed."

A slender hand, descending on his wrist, pushing him away, startled James. He glanced up and met Celine's wide-open eyes.

"There, there," Lettie said. "Everything's going to be all right. We're going—"

"James," Celine said. "You sought me out at the theater that first night because you intended to use me, didn't you?"

He parted his lips, but could not form a reply.

Lettie started to move away. Celine caught at her cloak and made fists in the fabric. "You are my mother?"

"Yes." Tears stood in Lettie's dark eyes. "I did what I thought was best. If I'd gone on alone I might never have given birth to a healthy child, and I couldn't bear the thought of losing you. It seemed for the best at the time. I had no notion of their true reasons for wanting you."

"Celine," James said gently. "You need to be warm and get some rest."

She trained her remarkable golden eyes upon him. "Lettie will take care of me," she said clearly. "She is my mother who has spent her life trying to do the best for me."

"Of course." He smiled, deeply touched by her generous, forgiving heart. "We will both take care of you from now on."

Shrinking from him, using Lettie's strength to help her to her feet, Celine confronted James. "You want whatever is hidden at Knighthead. Just as my . . . just as those people want it. And you pretended affection for me in order to get close to the prize you sought. Then you decided a marriage would be the final touch to your plan. By marrying me you could use your uncle's influence to remove them and install yourself. You used me to gain revenge and some sort of fortune. Didn't you already have enough money, James?"

"You don't understand. The Godwins tricked my father, and when he was dying, he asked me to come and recover what should have been mine by right. I had a sacred trust to fulfill his wishes."

"Of course. Well, now you will have what you want. I will trouble you no further with this charade."

"No." James tried to put his arm around her, but she shrugged away. "I do want you, Celine. More than my life."

"Lettie . . ." Celine turned to smile at the other woman. "I'm glad you're my mother. You were always the most important person in my life."

"You forgive me?" Lettie asked.

"I forgive you. I understand. Providing for a bastard would have been almost impossible."

"Let me get you to bed," James said. Celine's withdrawn manner undid him.

"No, thank you. If you don't mind, I'd prefer to be alone with . . . with my mother, who has suffered as I have suffered. She will care for me."

"But, Celine—"

"No, James. I will thank you to leave us." She turned from him. "Tomorrow Lettie and I will make plans. Your lodge will not be harmed."

"I am your husband."

"You became my husband to punish the people you believed were my father and mother. You never wanted me . . . and now I will try very hard not to want you."

Celine slid carefully from the soft bed into which Lettie had tucked her. The house was silent, but she knew James had insisted he would wait by the fire until she awakened. Won Tel had arrived some time earlier and taken Lettie back to Blackburn Manor to retrieve more warm clothes for Celine, who had not had energy enough to protest.

Now energy was seeping back into her chilled limbs. She would not stay.

Slowly pushing open the low casement, Celine gave thanks that the wide windowsill was but inches above the ground. She gave a thought to the need for a cloak, but the only one she had here was soaked and in the room with James.

Once her bare feet touched slippery earth, she shivered violently, but stood upright and made directly for the horses she could see tethered to a tree: James's black and her own dear Cleopatra.

She led the horse some distance, softly encouraging him, before using a tree stump to help her scramble onto the animal's bare back.

Clinging to Cleopatra's mane, Celine spurred the horse into a gallop. Rain still fell and before many moments passed, the thin lawn nightrail she wore was flattened to her body. The beach, she must get to the beach where she could watch the sea and smell the precious scents that had been her friends since childhood.

Hugging the path along the cliffs, Celine thanked God for the white gravel that showed her the way. She reached the track to a secluded beach she knew very well and started down . . . and heard the thunder of other hooves closing on her.

"Go. Go, Cleopatra!" Always a game horse, the gelding slithered on loose rock, but plunged downward.

James voice came clearly on the wind: "Celine! Celine, wait!"

She would not wait.

Surf boiled onto the beach. Celine clucked and drove Cleopatra toward the shimmering white foam.

But even as she rode, calling for the animal to give more and more, Celine knew she could not outdistance James.

"Stop at once, you little idiot."

He drew level and Celine yanked Cleopatra's mane, forcing him into the sea.

James caught her as the water rose about their horses' hocks. "What in hell's name do you think you're doing?"

"Let me go."

"Never. You are mine."

She tried to pull away, but James had Cleopatra firmly by the mane and was hitching a bridle over his head. When he held the rein in his hands, he sat tall and stared at her. The full-sleeved white shirt he wore clung to his magnificent body. An iridescence from the surf showed the hard muscle of his torso and arms through the fabric.

"Let me go," she whispered, unable to tear her gaze from him, from his powerful form, from his unbearably handsome face and wildly wind-tousled hair. "You have what you want. Let that be an end to it."

James did not reply. He was looking at her with the dark intensity of passion, looking at her face, the tangle of damp hair that tumbled about her shoulders and hung to her waist. Celine glanced down and felt heat invade her veins. She might as well be naked. The thin, wet nightrail adhered to every dip and swell, clung to her breasts like a lover's hands, plainly revealing skin and hugging pink, budding nipples.

Before she guessed his intent, James took her chin in his fingers and pressed his thumb to her bottom lip. "What I want, Celine, is you. What I want *most* is you."

She shook her head. "You used me."

He smiled, and her heart turned over. "Yes, my golden girl," he said gently. "I did use you—at first. But all that changed. I admit I still wanted to regain my father's inheritance, but somewhere, somehow, I knew that it would mean nothing without you at my side. And perhaps we should not forget that you also set out to use me, my dear one. I was to be your means to avoid marriage to Letchwith."

"I—"

"Hush." James shifted in his saddle and plucked Celine from Cleopatra's back. "I will not listen to further arguments. We have both made mistakes, but, thank God, we have not lost each other." He settled her before him on the hunter and pulled her against the solid wall of his chest.

"You are an earl." She must think clearly. "I am . . . I am a bastard and completely unsuitable as a wife for you."

James chuckled. A most disconcerting sound. "You are completely suitable for me, and I for you. There will be no more argument." As if to seal his claim, the hand he passed around her settled on her breast.

A searing ache burst from the taut nipple beneath his brushing thumb to become buried in the sensitive places between her thighs. "What of Mama and . . . How can we deal with them?"

"We can't tonight," James said as they began to ride toward the path up the cliff. "Tomorrow morning will be soon enough for a confrontation. Tonight I have very different matters in mind."

Chapter 30

James poured heated water into two china basins and carried them to the bedroom. In the doorway he stopped. Swathed in a blanket, Celine stood before the fire he'd lighted.

Very quietly, he edged farther into the room and set the basins on the marble-topped washstand. "Celine."

She looked at him over her shoulder. "Yes?" Her tangled hair tumbled across her back. Beneath the blanket he saw that she still wore the tattered and mudstained nightrail. Her slender feet showed signs of the abuse they had received.

His heart made a great leap. "Come. Sit down and let me tend your feet."

She didn't move.

James smiled into her wide eyes and willed his face to hide some measure of the desire that beat in his veins. Doubt veiled those golden eyes—despite her innocent assumption that she had already tasted the ultimate intimacy.

He settled his hands on her arms and felt her tremble. "You are cold," he said, pretending dispassion. Pulling a wing chair closer to the fire, he guided her to sit. "That nightrail is wet. It should be removed."

"It has dried. You shirt is still wet. You should take it off."

"So it is. And so I should." Promptly, he unbuttoned the shirt, pulled it free of his breeches, and stripped it away. Tossing it aside, he planted his fists on his hips, braced his booted feet apart, and smiled at her. "There. Observe how obedient I am, my lady?"

Her gaze slipped rapidly from his face, over his body and all the way to his feet before she quickly returned her attention to the fire.

James's smile broadened a little. His young wife was far from unaffected by the sight of him. He brought a bowl of water and a cloth and knelt before her. She tried to draw her feet beneath the blanket.

"Celine, I want to do this for you." Gently, he found a finely boned ankle and lingered, learning the shape of it, smoothing the soft skin of her calf to the back of her knee. She shuddered. "You and I shall learn together about being a husband and wife, my dear one," he told her. "Whenever you need, I will fill that need. And I know you will be my faithful helper throughout our lives."

Her lips parted. She looked down on him and her eyes filled with tears. "You are . . . James, I am a little afraid. I want to be everything you need. But I do not know all there is to know about the business of being a wife, do I? About what truly happens between a husband and wife?"

"You have nothing to fear. Do you trust me?"

She nodded yes.

"Then believe that I will teach you tenderly—with passion, for I am a passionate man with a passionate wife—but always with tenderness." Dampening a cloth, he ran its moist warmth over her foot and watched her toes curl at his touch . . . and he smiled anew. "Your feet are sensitive."

He washed her other foot. Already self-control was costing him dearly. Raising a knee, he settled her foot there and dried it. With the backs of his fingers, he stroked the high arch, bent to place a kiss—and groaned at the jolt in his groin when she gave a small cry.

Moving cautiously, James edged up the nightrail and followed his fingers with his lips, all the while stroking the sweet curves of her leg.

He heard her breath quicken and glanced up to see her lips part and draw back. She was indeed afraid. Somehow he must hold back, move slowly. He could not bear the thought of bringing her pain—and he knew there might be no way to do otherwise this first time.

"May I brush your hair?"

She nodded again. Her face was pale. "There is a brush on the chest by the window."

He already knew as much. While Celine had slept—before her flight to the beach—Won Tel had brought Lettie back with supplies Liam had gathered.

"Kneel in front of me," he told Celine, offering her his hand. She placed her fingers in his and let him help her to the fur rug before the fire. Obediently, she sat on her heels with him behind her and waited, head bowed.

Already the honey-colored waves had begun to dry. Carefully parting heavy handfuls of locks, James patiently worked out tangles until the hair spread in a shimmering curtain about her.

Celine sighed and her head fell farther forward. The blanket slipped down around her hips but she showed no sign of having noticed.

James paused a moment to let his eyes wander down her straight, slim spine to her tiny waist and the flare of her hips revealed through the ruined nightrail. He gritted his teeth against a fresh surge within his breeches.

"Are you finished?" she murmured.

"Not quite." Using slow, rhythmic strokes, he passed the brush from her crown to the curling tips of her hair. With each lift of the brush, a mass of fine strands sprayed upward to catch the leaping glimmer of firelight. "I may never be finished. I didn't know how soft a woman's hair could be—or how touching it could make me feel." By God, he had never known or even guessed.

Drawing the hair back into one hand, he bent to place his lips on the side of her neck where the chain of his mother's locket shone against white skin. He had left the ring at Blackburn, and it didn't seem to matter. There would be time enough to use it. Celine arched her head against his shoulder, and James closed his eyes. "You smell of rain and wind—and your wild Dorset grass." He parted his lips on her skin. "And you taste of the sea . . . and this nightrail isn't dry, Celine."

She said nothing, only waited quietly while he left her to bring the second bowl of water.

He dropped to the floor at her back once more, spread his knees, and positioned himself to accommodate her hips between his thighs. A flash of exquisite pain seared his loins. Cradled against his body she seemed small, a small but voluptuously perfect woman waiting to be made his.

With palms flattened, James haltingly rubbed her shoulders and spread his fingers over the delicate bones above her breasts. The slightest tug released the tape that held the nightrail in place and, with palms still flat, he inched the frail garment down until it settled at her elbows.

She gasped and rested her weight against him,

arched her back, thrusting her breasts so that he looked down upon their full splendor.

Calling upon reserves he'd never known he possessed, James took a new cloth and soaked it in the clean water. First he smoothed her neck and shoulders. "This will soothe you," he said, hearing raw desire in his voice. "Your skin will warm from the touch."

"You warm me, James. With your touch. With no more than a look. My husband, you make me throb. Is that normal?"

"Throb? Where?" He looked down at her again and winced at his self-inflicted suffering.

"In—odd places. Here." She pressed a hand into her lap.

The motion all but undid James. She shifted and managed to grind his rod the harder against her soft woman's bottom. "Low in your belly?" he asked, barely trusting himself not to throw her down and mount her now. "In the place between your legs?"

"Exactly." For once the response was subdued, embarrassed, and he could not suppress a smile.

He must touch her. Dipping the cloth into the water once more, James slowly washed a breast, watched the nipple spring tight. His breath came in labored gasps. He repeated his ministrations on her other breast and saw her hips rise. Helplessly, Celine reached up to throw a hand over his shoulder.

"Yes, my love," he encouraged her. "Yes. Show me what you want. Tell me."

Her answer was to raise her other arm, thrusting out her breasts, rubbing her back against his chest.

He felt he might die if he couldn't release himself from the pressure of the breeches, yet he must wait, must hold back until he had done everything it might take to make this treasure he'd miraculously gained entirely ready for him.

"Not enough," she murmured.

"No, sweeting. Not enough." James supported the weight of her silken breasts and grazed his thumbs back and forth over the rigid satin of her nipples, pinched and rubbed them gently in his fingers. He passed his tongue over his lips, anticipating the taste and texture of those ripe buds between his teeth.

Celine writhed and twisted toward him—and James felt pounding at his temples. The longer he made her wait for what he knew she wanted, the more intense the eventual ecstasy would be.

"James." Her eyes flew open wide. "James?"

"Yes, sweet?" With one fingertip, he traced the valley between her breasts, trailing a curving line around each one.

"I want . . ."

"You want?" Using two knuckles, he brushed back and forth along the soft, heavy undersides. "What do you want?"

"I want . . . Oh, James. Oh, James."

"Mm." Bending, he covered her mouth, parted her lips with his own, and sipped deeply of her. Tracing the contours of her mouth with his tongue, he slanted his face over hers, rocked her head from side to side. When her breasts heaved against him and he could barely contain his growing lust for her, he darted his tongue past her lips, teased her, drove her until she chased him with stabbing forays of her own.

As abruptly as he'd possessed her mouth, he raised his head and watched frustration pass over her features. Layering her body on his, she flattened her breasts to his chest, found his hand, and forced it between them, rubbed it back and forth while she keened out her need.

His control broke. Pressing her over his arm, James drew a nipple into his teeth, opened wide his mouth to fill himself with her. And when he sucked, she moaned aloud and clutched handfuls of his hair.

Flicking from one breast to the other, he tugged and wet them, buried his face between them, and closed his eyes. She made the sounds of a drugged woman, drugged with desire, and he would use her abandon to ease the way.

Gathering her tightly to him, holding her face against his neck, he learned again every line of her body until he ventured into the springy hair between her legs. The moist heat that met his fingertips dried his mouth and brought sweat to his brow.

Celine cried out and tried to pull away.

"Hush," James murmured. "Let me bring you the pleasure again, Celine."

She panted. "I want to bring you pleasure, James."

"You will." Oh, yes, she would indeed. His dipping finger met hot, wet flesh—ready flesh. He pushed deeper and withdrew.

"James?" Her voice rose in a thin, mindless wail.

"Yes, sweet, yes." This time he inserted two fingers and worked her tight, slick passage. When she panted, he closed his eyes and flipped his thumb over the sensitive little woman's nub that brought her undulating toward him.

"I can't," she gasped. "James, I . . ."

"Yes, Celine. Yes, you can." Taking away his hand, he eased her to lie on the soft fur. Fastening his eyes on hers, he hooked her legs over his shoulders.

Celine tossed her head aside. "No!"

"Yes," he told her firmly. "You will enjoy everything that we do, my love. That I promise you."

Parting her folds and bringing his face to her, he found the swollen center of her desire with his tongue . . . and she screamed. Reaching to hold her shoulders, he pinned her and continued a rough probing of the part of her that even now was tearing reason from her brain.

Celine flailed, her hips jerking, and drove her fingers into his shoulders. He grimaced with glad pain and felt a violent shudder ripple through her in shock waves that rolled on and on while she babbled meaningless words. Throwing her hands above her head, Celine gave herself up to the molten tide that brought the rain of her release, heated and primal-tasting, to his tongue.

"James!" His name escaped on a gasp and she fell limp. "James, teach me."

"Teach you what?" Rising over her, he kissed her lips. "Taste your own sweetness, my love. The sweetness we shall share again and again."

She kissed him deeply and he felt the heaviness of her afterglow. "I want to taste you," she said, her voice husky.

James barely stopped himself from grasping for his rod. "You shall," he told her through his teeth. "But first, it is time to make you wholly my wife."

Edging away, he worked off his breeches and returned to her. "You know nothing of this, do you? Not really?"

She shook her head and watched his eyes.

"At first there may be pain. But it will pass each time we love each other, it will be better."

"Do it. Do it now."

He dropped his face to her neck and laughed. "My dear one. My life will never again be an empty place—or a dull one."

Rather than comment, Celine tossed her hips from side to side beneath him. "Show me, James. I ache . . . there. I need something. Show me."

He could not speak again. Spreading her legs once more, he took her hand and closed it around his shaft. She sucked in a breath.

"This will enter you, Celine. It will be by that entering that we become one."

"Oh." She wet her lips. "It is . . . You are very large."

"And that frightens you?"

She frowned. "This will be something that pleases you?"

"You answer a question with a question. Yes, sweeting, it will please me more than anything in the world."

Her frown deepened. "Then do it."

James sighed. "You *are* afraid. We should wait."

Celine's answer was to tighten her hold on his manhood and guide his tip to the entrance of her body. "I will not wait. Only I don't see how . . . Will it fit?"

He could hold back no longer. Touching a finger to her kiss-reddened lips, he pressed slowly into her tight channel and saw the widening of her eyes. He encountered the barrier of her maidenhood. "Should I stop?" He was a hair's breadth away from bursting within her.

"Don't stop." Raising her chin, she clamped her mouth shut, and he knew he had hurt her.

"My darling—"

"No." A smile gradually curved her lips. "Already it fades. Push, James. Please push."

He pushed—sucked in a shallow breath and pushed, burying himself in his wife until there could be no deeper joining. Air jarred into his throat and the rhythm became a primitive beat no longer of his own making.

He drove and heard Celine gasp. Their bodies beat together. In the dark beauty of their hunger, they rolled until Celine sat astride his hips. She rose from him just once, pounded down upon him just once, and the essence of his maleness exploded. Still he moved, moved until he felt her convulse around him.

"I love you!" Celine arched up, only to fall onto his chest and bury her face in his neck. "I love you, my lord."

In the flicker of firelight, James kissed his wife's hair and closed his eyes. "And I love you, my lady—my love."

The weight was gone.

Celine opened her eyes and saw glowing embers in the bottom of the fireplace. Her body was stiff and sore, but a deep, pleasurable contentment spread through every muscle and nerve.

Turning, she lay on her back and pushed the blanket away from her chin.

She'd been ... "James!" He was gone. Throwing aside the blanket, Celine sat up—and looked directly at him. He was slouched in the wing chair with his eyes closed.

For a moment she studied his face. Flickering slightly against his cheeks, his lashes were thick and black. In sleep, his face was more boyish, although there could be no softening of the flamboyantly carved lines of his nose and jaw, his high cheekbones, or his firm lips.

Celine got fluidly to her feet and tiptoed to stand looking down at him. Across his lean hips he had draped a blanket, a blanket that had already slid low, very low. The dark hair that spread wide on his chest and narrowed to a line down his belly, flared again where ... She bit her lip. Undoubtedly she was the stuff fallen women were made of, for, yet again, hot need stabbed into her center. His body was hard, ridged and banded with gleaming sinew and muscle, a beautiful body, so strong and so different from her own soft form.

Did wives ...? What would James think if she ...?

With a finger and thumb, she took hold of the edge of the blanket and tugged it from him. Drawing in a sharp breath, her lips remained parted. Even in sleep, his ... He appeared somewhat ... James would seem to be prepared for more of what they had already enjoyed.

When a strong hand shot out to close on her arm, she shrieked.

He looked up at her, a wicked smile on his lips. "Do you like what you see, *my lady*?"

"Um, y-yes."

"I'm glad." He pulled her closer.

"I thought you were asleep."

"I know. I tricked you. Until you began to awake I sat and watched you."

"You did?"

"I did. A beautiful sight." He shamelessly indicated that part of him under discussion. "And you can see the result."

"Mm. Yes."

"What do you think we should do about this condition?"

"Well." Celine swallowed. Gathering her courage, she leaned to bring her breasts to his face and heard a sound, part sob, part groan, tear from his throat. James covered and supported the weight of her breasts and proceeded to lave her nipples. Instantly, threads of white-hot fire seared down to bury themselves in the place where she longed to feel James again.

"Wait," she told him. Slipping between his thighs, she held his distended shaft reverently in her hands. "So powerful," she said.

With growing awe, Celine traced velvet skin covering iron arousal, followed pulsing veins with a finger.

Then she showed him with her mouth how she cherished every part of him and—finally and with a sense of wonder—she tasted him.

"Celine!" His voice broke and he pulled her up. Breathing rapidly, James captured her hands. "And now, my lady, I believe we should press on."

"That decision should be yours, my lord."

"Exactly!" He laughed, somewhat shakily she thought, and showed his strong white teeth. "And it is time for me to teach you something new."

With that, he lifted her to sit atop his thighs. "James?"

Grasping her hips, James raised Celine, spread her legs wide, and brought her down, buried his shaft in her. "Cry my name, my lady," he said, clamping his fingers into her bottom. "Cry my name." And with a thumb he began the unbearable exquisite torture of that small part of which she had known nothing until he entered her life. "Cry it!" he implored.

"James!" The tide began to break. "James!"

He dropped back his head and shouted, "I love you!"

Chapter 31

❦❦❦

"There is no need for you to be present," James told Celine. "Please, sweeting, let me have Won Tel take you to Blackburn. Wait for me there."

"No." She shook her head firmly and threaded her arm through his to mount Knighthead's front steps. "Where you go, I shall also go. From now on, my only place is with you."

He checked his stride. "Indeed it is." Her face, so dear to him, had the power to shatter his composure. Forcing a laugh, he continued up the steps. "After last night you may find yourself hard pressed to be rid of me for a moment."

Celine laughed softly and pink washed her cheeks. "Do hush, James. I should die if I thought we were overheard." She glanced back toward the carriage that had brought them from Blackburn. Won Tel, the afternoon sun dappling his blue tunic, was in conversation with the coachman.

"Summer at Knighthead," James said, his gaze sweeping the lawns and moving on to the gently swelling hills beyond woods bordering the estate. "Do you think you'll enjoy helping me make the gardens as beautiful as they once were?"

"Oh, yes. There is nothing I should not enjoy doing with you."

Ignoring the creak of the front door opening, James looped his hands around his wife's slim neck and brushed his lips slowly, sensuously over her soft mouth. Predictably, another part of him leaped and he flexed his thighs. "You undo me, my lady. I think perhaps I shall carry you back to Blackburn this very moment and have my way with you."

Her laugh was silvery. "I am yours to command—as long as you are mine to command."

He groaned. "What have I created?"

"A woman doing what she was born to do," she responded innocently. "I have been planning to make a more thorough examination of you, James. I must definitely leave no portion unsampled . . . or unused."

"You are a witch." He grinned, but what was presenting itself inside his trousers would soon be no grinning matter, and they had business to attend. "Now. Allow me to concentrate, if you please. And remember my instruction that you are to allow me to deal with the Godwins on my own terms."

Won Tel joined them and indicated that they were being observed.

"Lettie!" Celine broke from James and flew to the top step where, abruptly, she halted. "I mean . . . I do not know how to call you."

"Give it time," Lettie responded, but tears brimmed in her eyes. "We have the friendship of your lifetime to build upon, Celine. Perhaps the rest will follow naturally."

James wished that he might leave them alone, but there would be time enough for that later. "Good afternoon, Lettie. We are come to see Mr. and Mrs. Godwin."

Lettie smoothed the skirts of her gray morning dress. "I returned early this morning," she told them. "I assumed Mr. and Mrs. Godwin were asleep, but their beds have not been slept in and none of the servants has seen them since last night."

"They did return?" With Won Tel at his elbow, James entered the house behind Lettie and Celine.

"Cook tells me that Mr. Godwin arrived first and sent Miller—the butler—to the kitchen for refreshments. Miller said he required three bottles of hock for Mr. Godwin and his guests. That was before ten."

Frowning, James strode past Lettie and threw open the door to the salon. The room stood empty. Dust motes swam lazily in a shaft of sunlight from a window, the same sunlight that settled on used goblets atop a cruelly marred tulipwood table.

He swung around. "Guests? What guests?"

Lettie pressed her hands to her cheeks. "Mr. Bertram Letchwith and his son," she said. "I am afraid all is not well here. This is something I feel, my lord."

"James," he said abstractedly. "We are related now, Lettie."

"Yes . . . James." She indicated the goblets. "The Letchwiths drank here while awaiting Mr. Godwin's return from Blackburn Manor after the wedding. Afterward, according to Miller, the three of them left this room and went we do not know where. The visitors' horses are still in the stables and neither the Godwins' coach, nor any of the horses, have been removed."

"What of Mrs. Godwin?" Bile rose in James's throat at the remembered picture of that desperate and despicable female.

"Evidently she had sent Mr. Godwin on alone. We do not know why, but one of the coachmen at Blackburn Manor reports returning her here at a later hour. Perhaps eleven."

"And they have no means of knowing that you came to Windham and spoke to me?"

"None."

"We shall search the house," James declared. "If we are fortunate, they have packed their bags and left rather than face me. It would be in keeping with their infamy and cowardice."

"Very well," Lettie agreed. "But there is no point. I can find no sign of them and, as far as I am able to ascertain, nothing has been removed. Freda helped me check the trunks and their possessions."

"Nevertheless, please do as I ask and help me search again."

An hour later, having helped search every inch of the bedchambers and attics, James set about covering the ground floor. Cook and Miller assured him that there was no sign of any unusual activity belowstairs.

Celine, her slippers thudding softly, followed James. It was not without a twist of his heart that he noted how her face had turned pale. It might be well not to rush back into residence at Knighthead where, unlike James's, her memories were not of idyllic childhood days.

He knew he had saved the library for last.

"There is no sign of them, James," Won Tel called, striding silently along the corridor to join James and Celine. Lettie's quick footsteps weren't far behind.

James opened the library door and entered.

Utter stillness.

Celine, barely a step from his side, shivered and rubbed her arms. "This room is always so cold. I do not like it here."

"Then you shall not remain, my love. Obviously we are too late to trap our quarry."

"James." Fingering a jade statue, Won Tel stood beside the desk. "Look at this."

James did look. He saw three used goblets and an open decanter of spirits. "They were here." Instantly his attention switched to the flagstones. "Celine, please go with Lettie. Return to Blackburn at once and wait for me there."

"James?"

"Please, my love. Go quickly." He placed a restraining hand on Won Tel's arm. "Remain with me."

Celine caught James's sleeve. "My place is with you, James." Fear shone in her eyes.

"I will return to you soon. You have . . ." The chain around her neck glinted. "You have my word. Please leave your locket with me for good luck."

She opened her mouth to argue, but closed it again and reached back to undo the clasp. Dropping the trinket into his palm, she rushed from the room with Lettie.

James waited until their footsteps faded before turning to Won Tel. "Prepare yourself, my friend. This may not be pleasant." He removed his watch from the pocket of his waistcoat. Three o'clock in the afternoon. Many hours had passed since Mary Godwin had left Blackburn Manor after revealing her "truth."

"The time has come for me to reveal to you the rest of my father's story."

Won Tel's impressive brows drew down. "The rest? There is more?"

"Much more." James crossed the room and knelt beside a shiny object embedded in the stone floor.

The ring.

"What is that?" Won Tel bent over James. "Is it . . . Surely that is your father's ring, the one he always wore."

"Indeed. And this is the purpose for which it was made." James settled the crown more firmly over the tiny stone points made to fit so perfectly, and twisted. "It is a key, Won Tel, a key that fits only this lock. Bring me a candle." As he spoke, the flagstone slipped silently down and back to reveal a black hole in the earth. James looked at the locket in his left palm, took the candle Won Tel gave him, held it aloft, and listened.

"Explain, James. How do you know of this?"

"My father told me. I hear nothing, do you?"

"No, nothing."

James leaned to peer downward and whispered, "The Godwins were here. Of that I'm sure. Perhaps . . . if they decided to go below, they may be lying in wait. Remain here. This locket . . ." He showed how the center of the trinket revolved on central hinges to form yet another small, unique key. "This releases the stone from the other side, I believe. But if I do not return quickly, use the ring again."

"I shall block open the stone," Won Tel said as the space began to close again. "You will not go down there alone."

"I must. Don't forget the knife you taught me to use so well. We have nothing to fear."

With that, he opened the trap again and stepped down into the hole. Before James reached a second step, Won Tel was already jamming the tall statue of a marble dog into the aperture to foil the mechanism.

James found another step and stopped. His candle sent wavering fingers of yellow light over bone-dry stone that surrounded him in a vertical shaft.

His nostrils flared and revulsion shot into the pit of his stomach. A powerful stench rose to close his throat and cramp the muscles in his jaws.

He knew that stench well. Men faced with certain death produced just such a fetor. He peered around, moving the candle. Marks streaked the stones—dark red marks. *Blood!* Smears of blood dashed this way and that as if painted by mad fingers.

Closing his eyes and marshaling his roiling insides, he descended yet another step and drew back. His booted foot crushed on something that shifted. "Dear God." His breath slid from his lungs in a rush.

He had reached the bottom of the shaft.

Slowly, cupping the candle flame with a hand, James looked down . . . into the dead and staring eyes of Mary Godwin. His foot rested on her hand, a hand already crushed and covered with congealed blood—its nails torn off from flesh gouged to purple pulp.

And from those fingers trailed ropes of gems: emeralds like green fire and diamonds that glittered like starlight on virgin snow.

Fighting the urge to rush back the way he'd come, he moved his foot. The thundering in his head kept time with his hammering heart. A passage opened to the right, a passage so narrow a man would have to turn sideways to enter. It was in front of this that Mary Godwin's body, hung about with the tatters of her gown, lay. Beneath her, and tangled in a grotesque parody of intimacy, Darius Godwin and the Letchwiths were piled one upon the other as they must have fought to tear open their grave and escape before falling down to die. Over and around them were strewn riches of jewels so numerous as to stun even James's jaded eye.

He turned away and climbed slowly upward until Won Tel's strong hands slid beneath his arms and all but hauled him into the library. "James! My God, you are ill. Let me get—"

"No, no." He waved a hand. "I am sick. That is all. Made sick by the depth of evil I have encountered this day. They are down there. Dead."

Won Tel glanced toward the opening. "How so?"

"The ladies of my family hid their treasure well. The space is deceptively small and airtight. At the bottom of the shaft is a narrow passageway. The Godwins and the Letchwiths entered it and found jewels that have been in my family for generations. They must have been right there, exactly where their greedy hands could grab." He shuddered, visualizing Mary Godwin's destroyed hands. "The trap closed them in and they had no way to open it again."

"Because they didn't have the locket," Won Tel said.

"Yes." James shook his head wearily. "They clawed the stones trying to get out. Won Tel, they found what they spent twenty years searching for, and it killed them."

Epilogue

At the foot of the hill lay Little Puddle, its thatched-roofed buildings clustered about the Norman church.

"Lie with me, Celine."

She turned and smiled down at James. Booted ankles crossed, hands stacked beneath his head, he lay stretched out on the blanket they'd used for their picnic. A stalk of grass jutted from his teeth. "A tempting offer," she said at last. "But I can see the whole world from here."

"Mm." He squinted up at her. "Tell me of this whole world you see. Entertain me." He had discarded his jacket, displaying his broad chest and strong arms to advantage in a full-sleeved white shirt.

"Very well." She would prefer simply to watch him. "Well, immediately below—to the north—we have the delightful village of Little Puddle with its now famous church."

"How so? The church being famous, I mean."

"Simple, sir. It was in that church, a mere month since, that the Earl of Eagleton married Celine Godwin."

"Ah. Then it is indeed famous. What else?"

"Due west lies Blackburn Manor, the current home

of the earl and his countess, and to the south there is an excellent view of the English Channel. Today it appears as a slim band of gray beneath an English summer sky in shades of blue and violet—brushed with wisps of cloud, of course."

"Of course."

"To the east one spies that lovely old Jacobean house—Knighthead, where the Eagletons will soon take up residence." She buried her teeth in her lip and touched the locket at her throat. Still she could scarcely believe that the Godwins, together with the Letchwiths, had died beneath that house. "So much has happened in the months since spring, James. Since spring and our meeting."

"It was not until spring that my life began, Celine."

She closed her eyes and breathed deeply the fragrance of sun-dried grass and clumps of full-blown dog roses. Faintly came the drone of bees searching out their honeyed treasure and the contented scuffling and munching of Cleopatra and the black hunter.

"For wealth, James. For the chance to possess the Sainsbury gems, they died. Mama . . . She actually held this locket and put it around my neck. With it, she could have unlocked the trap from below, as you did. Their hands were so torn from tearing at stone. Until there was no more air . . ." She hadn't seen the gruesome heap of bodies that greeted James, yet her mind made the picture.

"Try to forget," he told her. "If you remember at all, let it be because it was their greed that brought us together. For my part, I must say that there was never a woman more suited to wearing those jewels. Can I hope that you *will* wear them for me one day, Celine?"

"Perhaps." She had avoided as much as touching

the fabulous pieces since the day James presented them to her. "Don't let us think of that now."

There was a question that needed to be asked. Already it had waited too long. "What of Paipan, James?" There, she had said it.

"What of it?"

"When will you feel you have to return?"

"I have no plans to do so."

Celine blinked. A breeze lifted curls at her temples and nape. "But I thought—"

"No. I have other plans for Paipan—without my presence. I shall visit again one day. And when I do I hope you will accompany me, although we must be certain you are not ... I could not approve of your traveling in a delicate condition."

She pressed her abdomen and smiled. "No. Nor could I. And I hope that will soon be the case." Joy swelled her heart. He did not intend to make a permanent home in that foreign land again. "What time is it, James?"

"Don't know." He rested the back of a hand over his eyes.

Impatient, Celine leaned across his body to pull the watch from his waistcoat. Promptly she found herself dumped on his chest, her legs splayed in the most unladylike fashion. "James!" She struggled to no avail, but managed to see the watch. "Noddycock! You were to watch the time."

"Why?" He settled a long, strong hand behind her neck and unerringly guided her lips to settle upon his. James kissed Celine thoroughly before allowing her to gasp for breath. "What does the time matter?"

"You oaf!" She tried to pummel him. "I promised Liam that she should have our undivided attention at three o'clock. There is some important matter she wishes to discuss with us, and it is already almost three. James, release me!"

"No." He smiled and pecked the tip of her nose.

"James, I warn you."

He collapsed and spread wide his arms, leaving her sprawled on top of him. "Really, I do apologize to you for my wife's behavior. She simply can't seem to get enough of me."

"What?" Resting her weight on her elbows, Celine peered suspiciously into his dark eyes. "What are you talking about?"

"I was apologizing, my dear. To David and Liam."

For a moment she remained still, then, slowly, she leaned away and looked behind her—at the sturdy legs of a gray horse—David's gray. Her eyes traveled up until they met that gentleman's laughing green eyes. He managed to sweep off his hat and bow—not a simple accomplishment when he held Liam before him in the saddle.

Scrambling, Celine righted herself and sat brushing dried grass from her skirts, picking it from her hair. "How nice of you to bring Liam, David. Somehow the time got away from us and we should have been late to meet her."

"Them," James said. "Late to meet them."

Celine ignored him. "Please dismount and join us. There's wine left and some little cakes Ruby Rose made. Is all still well between Ruby Rose and Mrs. Strickland?"

"Very well indeed," David said, swinging down and lifting Liam to the ground beside him, where she continued to cling to his arm and gaze up into his face. "I don't believe we are late, James."

Celine frowned from one face to the other. "James asked you to come here today? But I thought—"

"How do you imagine they knew exactly where to find us?" James said offhandedly. "I told David that I thought this would be a very suitable place to speak of important matters."

"Yes," Liam said. In a tunic of simple, flower-sprigged yellow cotton and with buttercups in her hair, she glowed. "David says the sky is God's roof and the whole world His church. Isn't that a delightfully poetic thing to say?"

Celine dared not look at James. "Yes, indeed."

"So, under the roof of David's God, we are come to ask James a most important question." For once Liam's young face lost its impish confidence, and she lowered her eyes. "I hope it will not displease you."

David cleared his throat, and Celine saw a muscle jerk in his cheek when he looked at Liam. "I love her," he said simply and rested the fingertips of one hand on her mouth. "We both know it will not be easy, but we should like to marry."

Celine clasped her hands together and felt tears spring into her eyes. "Then you must," she announced and choked.

"Liam and I have spoken of this at length," David continued, "and we know such a liaison would be difficult in England. If you agree, James, we should like to return to Paipan. Liam seems to think there would be plenty of work for me to do there."

Celine looked to James and narrowed her eyes. He smiled like a smug parent confronted with the perfect groom for his favorite daughter.

"Plenty of work indeed," he said. "You will marry here and return to Paipan shortly afterward. My house there needs tending. Liam will do that admirably. It will be our wedding gift to you. And you, David, can keep an eye on certain business aspects for me—in addition to saving souls, that is. Will that be agreeable?"

"You expected this," Celine accused him.

"In matters of the heart I am an expert," he told her.

"In all matters of the heart?" Liam asked in a tone

that caused Celine to regard her closely. "I think not. After all, you are merely a man."

Celine covered her mouth, but Liam smiled widely and leaned against David. The latter exchanged a look of mock exasperation with James.

"Here they come," Liam announced.

"Who?" Celine searched in all directions before catching sight of a movement. Gradually, another horse came into view, and another—Won Tel rode the first, Lettie the second.

"I shall have words to say to you later," Celine informed James in a low voice. "You arranged this. We should have brought more food."

"Join us," James called.

Won Tel and Lettie did so. "A fine day for a ride," Won Tel said, appearing anything but comfortable. "Most generous of you to invite us to come."

"Invite them to come?" Celine muttered. "Secretive behavior. I'll have an explanation for this, my lord."

Lettie pulled a pannier from her horse's neck and set it down. From this she removed a bottle of champagne and six glasses carefully wrapped in white linen. "I thought this might be appropriate."

Celine slapped crossly at her skirts. "There is some conspiracy here. I will not have it. I will not be excluded."

James took the champagne bottle and deftly dispensed with its cork. "Sometimes it is necessary to avoid telling a woman everything. So much the better way to ensure discretion."

"James St. Giles!"

"Ah, ah." He caught her raised wrist. "You will spill this excellent champagne. Hold the glasses instead. I do believe Won Tel and Lettie have something to tell us."

Celine lowered her arm slowly and regarded her mother and Won Tel with disbelief. "You do?"

"We do," Lettie said promptly. "Horace and I have decided to become betrothed."

"Horace?" Celine repeated and her voice cracked. She glanced around. "Who is Horace?"

"Celine," Lettie said sharply. "Kindly mind your manners. Won Tel is Horace and he needs to become proud of his name. He has certainly hidden it quite long enough."

"Horace?" James's amazement clearly matched Celine's. "What in God's name do you mean?"

"You should not take the Lord's name in vain," Liam announced.

James glared at her. "That will do from you, young lady. Explain—*Horace.*"

"To you I am Won Tel," that gentleman said with hauteur. "Only Lettie shall call me otherwise."

Lettie nudged him. "Tell him the story."

Won Tel shifted his weight and gave his beard a ferocious tug. "Mr. St. Giles—your father—discovered me hiding in one of his warehouses in Paipan."

"Sneaking from the hold of one of his ships was the story I heard."

Won Tel shrugged. "Just so. I was sixteen and had stowed away to escape . . . I had been accused of killing my father and had to flee."

"Is that a fact?" James leaned forward. "And did you?"

"The man who had abused me since I was a small boy was not my father. He merely appropriated me from the streets and used me."

"So you escaped," James said, and Celine felt the sealing of an agreement never again to mention what had happened to the man from whom Won Tel had fled. "That doesn't explain the name."

A most interesting change came over what could be seen of Won Tel's face above his beard. He blushed a deep, glowing red. "I am a Scot," he announced."

After moments of stunned silence there was a chorus of: "Scot?"

"Yes. Or should I say aye?"

"*Aye!*" Lettie said excitedly. "Horace ran away from Scotland. Then, when he got to that place—China—he knew he had to make sure no one ever discovered who he was or where he'd come from, you see."

Celine nodded.

James shook his head. "No, I fear I don't see."

"Please allow me," Won Tel told Lettie when she prepared to continue. "I needed a disguise. I determined to say nothing until I had listened to others speak for long enough to be able to copy their accents."

"Yes," Lettie said quickly. "And with his lovely dark coloring and hair, it was perfect to pretend to be from some eastern place that was never exactly mentioned."

James bent to see Celine's face and they shook their heads. "But your *name,* man," he said. "Explain."

"Simple," Won Tel said. "Your father said that either I give him my name or he would turn me over to the authorities. Being a little hard-headed in those days, I resisted."

"Yes?" they said in unison.

"Mr. St. Giles persisted." Won Tel surveyed the sky.

"And that's how it happened," Lettie sang out and clapped her hands. "Being a Scot who had yet to lose his brogue, Horace said, 'I won' tell.' "

James lounged on the bed. "Can you believe that all these years I didn't know his name was Horace?"

"Yes." Celine's voice came from the dressing room.

He pushed the pillows up behind his head and unbuttoned his shirt. "No, you can't."

"Certainly I can. Men are obtuse."

"Hah!" Shifting, he pulled the shirt off and let it fall to the floor. "How much longer are you going to be?"

"No longer." Swathed in a voluminous white silk robe, she trailed into the room, unpinning her hair until it fell about her shoulders. "I have been thinking and I believe it is time for me to delve deeper into my considerable talent for . . . Pleasure."

James let his eyelids lower while he studied his wife's glowing face, her pouting lips, the provocative pressure of her nipples against the silk robe. "I cannot tell you how much it pleases me to hear you say this. Things have become really quite dull of late."

"Dull?" She planted her hands on her hips and glared. "*Dull?*"

"Well." He could not stop his smile. "Does this mean that *I* shall be allowed to accompany you in this *delving*?"

"Possibly." As she approached the bed, a softness stole over her features and a glittering light entered her amber eyes. "Do you remember how I abhor wasteful use of money?"

"Yes," he said uncertainly.

"How I do not believe in the purchase of excessive numbers of new gowns and so on? Especially when the careful selection of items that are of outstanding value can result in their remaining in excellent condition through many, many a wearing?"

"Indeed," he said, unable not to allow his attention to wander to her hips, swaying in the most tantalizing manner with each step she took. "Ah, yes, I do remember, Celine."

"Good." She smiled sweetly and began to undo the robe's sash. "Very good, because I have settled on an item of such unequaled value that it will suffice all on its own whenever I choose to wear it."

Celine dropped the robe, and James drew in a sharp breath.

"Do you like it?"

"Yes," he whispered, making fists at his sides.

"Then I shall come to you like this whenever it pleases you."

Celine advanced to stand beside the bed, took one of his hands in both of hers, and brought it to the shadowed place between her breasts, the place where the largest diamond in the fabulous Sainsbury emerald and diamond collar nestled.

"Beautiful," James whispered, reaching for her. "And I don't mean the jewels."

"Perhaps not," Celine said, climbing smoothly to sit astride his hips. "But you will agree that I have finally settled upon the ultimate economy in dress."